Introduction

...But life for me was at its end—without my pumping blood, or beating heart, and with lungs now stopped. Like so many others, I sadly had not made it past the Gate. So with my final bit of energy, I frowned and laid myself upon the ground, looking up, and let the snow create my grave, and bury me entirely. I would be the latest skeleton upon the Mountaintop....

I felt it needed to be said.

If you read it, and it changes you, then pass it on, and put a pic on facebook.

Thanks to the following who critiqued and or edited this work; your efforts were a great help: Cory, Keleny, and Lance.

Summary: Adult Fiction: Experience the psychological, mind-bender, adventure that sends Tiz on a mysterious, motivational journey—but also into a mental institution. Their band, FLYTHEBLUE, has reached the top, number one songs on the radio around the world. But Tiz claims a great quest is leading him on a distant adventure to places never seen, to attain things not known, and experience things never thought …. The world wants to hear his music, and all he has to do is admit the journey was make-believe … but he swears he has proof it wasn't only in his mind. Is it real, or an illusion? His story, plus eighteen songs he wrote, bring you: Journeys to Elgobon.

Genres: Psychological, Motivational, Adventure-Mystery

Available formats: ebook, paper book, audio book

Music soundtrack previews of all eighteen songs and CD available at:
http://www.journeystoelgobon.com/

ISBN-13: 978-0692289891

Journeys to Elgobon

Table of Contents

Journeys to Elgobon
—The Mountain—

The Journal of an Insane Man's Journey

By Perry Crompton

McKellen-Caffey Publishing

In Search of the Rule of:

The Dry Lake
Clear Skies
The Mirror
The River Running Free
The River Rocks
The Next Tree
The Stars
The Fire
Pavlov's Dog
The Mountaintop

To Evade: The Beast

To Attain: The Secret Maps of Ages

To Pass: Gate One

— Part One —

Chapter 1

Pre-Journey: The Old Man's Message

As I lay on the dead, dry lake, my mind withered and body decayed until all was just a foggy blur. For a couple days, I lay, still and morbid in my death-like state, until finally a couple vultures started pecking at my clothes and then found flesh and took a couple chunks from off my arms. In my mind's fog, I thought perhaps I felt something—and wondered why I allowed it all to come to this.

My name is Tiz (yes, my first). To think I endured that dry lake's agony voluntarily, and almost died intentionally, I know must make my saneness appear unclear. But please don't judge me too harshly for my insanity—for the course I chose was challenging, and the same might have happened to you! And just because others heard me talking to people they couldn't see, or had to listen to me talk about my "other world," it doesn't necessarily mean I'm crazy. You need to know the story.

Anyway, I thank you ladies and gentlemen for asking me to speak to you this beautiful spring morning at this prestigious institution and filling every seat in this great auditorium. When I was walking in, a person outside yelled, "We want to know if you made it past the Gate!" And I wondered how she knew to ask, for I haven't told anyone about the Gate. So all the throngs of people outside, and the confusion, and the television cameras filming me and asking for an interview have me mystified. What is going on? Why my sudden world-renowned celebrity? There are newscasters from all around the world! I also asked this to the crowd outside when I was walking in, and someone shouted, "Because you are us, Tiz!" And the whole crowd yelled, "YEAH!"

My exit from the mental hospital was a few hours ago, to give this speech, so I'll tell my story, and in it you'll find out why I was admitted. And then I'm told I must return.

[Standing at the side of the auditorium, Tiz saw the mental hospital director and the school superintendent from the school district where he taught, and he knew why they were there. Tiz had been told his sanity wasn't proven yet to be released, and his teaching job would be permanently revoked if he was deemed psychologically impaired. But teaching, and his students, were his greatest loves, so he couldn't let that happen. So his extended release from the mental hospital was based on this speech. He had to make them believe. *This* was his trial—and *he* the only witness. He looked at the director and superintendent, then at all the others and continued. "It will be up to each of you, at the end, to decide for yourself if my story is true—or if I'm still deranged—telling fantastical stories. But I have a prayer: that I can describe my ordeal in such a way to convince you I am *not* crazy!" (But Tiz hid the fact that he had to convince himself as well!)

Then some teen agers in the audience yelled over to the director, "Let him out! He's fine! We want to hear him play his songs! FlyTheBlue has concerts to play this summer—a world tour is scheduled." And many agreed, starting to shout.

But others countered, "Get real. He's deranged. Listen to his story."

Tiz held up his hand to calm the audience, but the shouting heightened. "You don't know what you're talking about," some yelled at others.

"Let him out! You have no right." others yelled to the director.

Tiz spoke to calm them, "It's okay, let it be." But it didn't help. Many kept yelling at others. Some now were standing—the confrontation louder. "Please," Tiz said, but the yelling kept growing—more now standing yelling back. Then music was heard over the speakers—music to calm the soul. Tiz was holding his smart phone to the microphone. The confrontation broke, and Tiz spoke over the music, "This is the last song we recorded before I was admitted. I wrote it for a friend who lost someone dear:"] (Called Heaven, track 1)

Like a seed, that's in the Spring
fell to earth, grew, then, started blooming
and changed our lives, for all of time

Pedals bright, and fragrance nice
reaching towards, that Heaven, we all, knew before
towards open arms, and softer nights

Chorus:
Towards a world, we all knew before, called Heaven
Towards a kinder, gentler place of peace, we lived in
da da da da da da da, where all is right, and love does thrive
Towards a world, there's so many we've known, to embrace us
Towards the place, where we'll meet again, called Heaven

Verse:
Like the light, from fireflies
brightened our world, then fluttered, away, to another place
to brighten theirs, and soothe their cares

Specs of white, up in the night
twinkle and shine, so we'll know, they're fine, living up with him
where they went up to, the world we knew

Chorus Repeated

Smooth sun rays, on cloudy days
shining right through, a hole, to our world, so we will know
they're thinkin of us, and the love we shared

Sprinkling down, to wash away our frowns
every rainy day, is just a time, when they do play
in the sprinklers there, on those beautiful days

Chorus Repeated

Now, let me continue my story. I'm a regular guy, blond hair, six-feet-three, American of German and Danish descent, love my sports, my fishing, my hiking. I was only twenty-three when it all began, but I sort of felt like something was missing—some grand adventure I yearned for, and felt that might be out there. Or maybe it was a girl to meet who would turn out to be "the special one" for me, or maybe enlightenment and seeing the grand purpose of the universe unfold for me. Which of these, I did not know, or maybe all of them, or something different, but this I knew: I had a strange feeling … something very different was coming.

It was while contemplating this at a park at the end of spring, sitting in a lounge chair, amongst some trees, and overlooking a lake, that I was distracted by someone preaching or instructing. I looked down by the lake, and there by a tree, a man spoke out loud to the world. He looked old and weak—maybe in his eighties. He spoke in a low, hoarse voice, and was perhaps of South American origin, with shoulder-length white-gray hair and goatee. He wore brown, pointy leather shoes with buckles, and his clothes were worn and tattered, but fancy: corduroy pants of royal blue, a yellow shirt with thin vertical black lines, and puffy, long sleeves, and a vest of green with large, gold buttons. While speaking, he waved his arms around wildly, and sometimes broke into singing. Everyone ignored him, and steered wide of him when walking by.

His animation, though, interested—and amused me, so I watched. Then ... even though I was twenty yards away and sitting mostly concealed in my shaded grove of trees, the man stopped ... pointed directly at *me* with a straight arm, and spoke for a few moments in a garbled voice—or perhaps some foreign language. His hand remained there pointing for several seconds after he finished, then it fell to his side and his shoulders slouched, and he slumped to the ground sitting and leaning back against the tree.

I was a little aghast and looked to either side of myself, beyond the trees, to see if anyone had seen. There was no one. I didn't know what he had said. Garbled nonsense? Or profound prophecy? Ninety percent to ten. But what if? I am a curious sort, so I found myself getting up and walking there.

I sat in front of him (*This should be interesting,* I thought), and when he looked up and saw it was me, excitement filled his eyes. He again pointed at me and he spoke in that low, hoarse voice: "It was you who brought me here. For what you search, there are many paths—both here, and in the other world. For everyone, the paths are different—but they all intersect at the Gates. Follow the paths, here, and on a distant journey—beginning in a dream—but expanding for those who journey outside of it. Pick up all the Pebbles you find along the way. With those, you'll find the Rules that you desire—the secrets of life. There's no one here that you can follow. Your destiny is Elgobon, but that should never be your goal! Get the Guidance from the Elder. Find the Mountain. Find the Grotto. Find the Island. But remember that looking is far more important than finding; and finding is not easy, for the Rules are hidden in living.

"Keep a little book and write down what you lack, and what you learn … and note the Pebbles, the ten Rules, the Secret, the Truth, and what opens up Gate One—for these are what will cure you from your demons, but also perfect you. When you have found them all, success for you is assured. Put them together and the puzzles are complete. They make up the Maps of Ages that lead to a treasure of ultimate success: gold and riches if you like, or fancy cars and mansions, or island retreats in faraway places— or perhaps the ultimate for you is peace of mind. The Maps are secret and cherished, written over thousands of years by those who took the journeys before you, and very few do see them. But they're only found upon the Mountaintop. And when you've opened up Gate One, something you could never imagine, you will see—and you'll be changed forever!

"… A word of caution though. It will not be easy, and forces of evil will conspire against you. So don't take the journey unless you are sure you want to! And when at the Mountain's base of which you seek, concentrate with focused mind—for if you don't, the pain you will endure will kill you even before the lack of blood from being torn apart." (And I will tell you, that advice from the old man was true—my whole left side a bloody mess.)

He stopped and just looked at me—like he was done.

"What mountain?" I asked. "Where is it?"

"For everyone, it is somewhere different."

"How do I get there?"

"It depends what path you choose. Many lead there."

"What is Elgobon?"

"I can't explain it. Like salt, you would have to taste it."

I looked at him and him at me—for quite a while. I almost laughed and sarcastically thought, *Not much to go on. Not many clues to find a treasure hidden somewhere in a whole world!*

"Two last things," he said, "Come back every so often, for if you stay too long in the other world you'll never get out. And … practice how to breathe and see."

Then I really did laugh out loud. "I think I know how to breathe and see."

"Maybe that's why you really fully don't," he responded.

I studied him, and finally asked, "Anything else?"

"Nothing else can be said. But return here for the final Pebble. And until that time, summon me when you will."

I stood and turned around and raised my eyebrows and mouthed the words, "Craaazy" to myself while walking with slow methodic footsteps back to my chair. Although I didn't see, the man's mouth forged a wry and sly smile as if to say, "He's fallen in my trap." Then he suddenly didn't look so crazy! While I walked, I squinted and thought, *That was strange, and yet intriguing, but mostly bizarre*, and I had to chuckle. "I'm the one that brought him here?" I mumbled to myself. "What does that mean? But how did he know about my demons? And I already have my own 'other world,' and am already looking for Rules, so how did he know?"

When back in my chair, I looked at him again. When I did, I saw a finch fly down and land on his hand. She had one discolored feather in her right wing—white, not brown. He lifted her up near his face and pet the bird with his other hand and seemed to be talking to her. Then the man looked around before holding the finch to his ear. He listened for quite some time as the finch seemed to be communicating ... something! Then tears began to flow—and roll, off the old man's cheeks. I watched for a while and then looked down at the ground pondering for a minute. When I looked up, he was gone! ... And I found no trace left of him, and no one at the park who saw him.

I never saw him at the park again, and part of me wondered if I really ever had—or if my imagination had created him. Had I been talking to a ghost from my mind? Had I drifted off to sleep and dreamed it all? I decided yes—the most realistic dream I've ever had ... so realistic it scared me, and I tried to put the incident behind me and forget about it. Weeks went by ... but his memory wouldn't leave me. Then one day while sitting at the park, that finch with the discolored feather, flew down and landed on my knee—and stared at me, not blinking. Then she started chirping, and continued for ten seconds before finally flying off.

That shook me. Was it a sign? Maybe the old man *was* real. Was there a message the bird was conveying? That night, while dressed in my pajamas I thought of the bird, and the old man's words. I contemplated in my bed, *What have I become? What could I be?* Then in my dreams, in vivid detail, I saw myself walking in a distant land in search of something. But it was like I was really there, for in most dreams you can't hear, but I could in this one—and I also felt and saw and smelled.

In the morning when I awoke, I was in the same clothes as in my dream and my shoes were on—with mud upon! But no mud was tracked in on the floor around me. The hair on the back of my neck stood up. And on my windowsill outside I saw that finch looking in at me—staring. That scared me … and I knew I couldn't wait and must investigate, and started the process post-haste to prepare to leave to the "other world."

Chapter 2

Pre-Journey: Nurturing Insanity

The old man's message was not what first sent me to the other world—it was what others called my growing insanity, that showed up periodically for a couple years prior to meeting him! But the perilous journey to open the Gate heightened that insanity—which some years later earned me a private bed at the local mental hospital (and a fresh new set of clean white clothes). Or maybe insanity is too harsh a word—it's what others used. I just called it mental anguish from life's normal daily routine that many of us encounter—that many call headaches, stress, or anxiety.

My journey was amazing, but I don't wish it on any of you in this auditorium or to those that might someday read my journal—for there are difficult clues that you must find, immense landscapes you must traverse, deathly drapes that you must open, Beasts you must defeat, and incapacitating confusion! But if you also choose to go, my description of it might help you make it back—with your sanity intact.

Let me explain how my great journey began and my steps to this insinuated insanity. It is said if you put a toad in cold water and then in tiny increments, over time, increase the heat to boiling, he won't jump out . . . . I'm a toad, for the demons snuck up on me slowly (like jaguars hidden in shadows stalking their prey), so I didn't notice they were there—and by the time I did, it was too late. They sprung and took me down.

I had just graduated from college a year before and was starting my second year of teaching ninth grade history and music in high school in a small town in the United States. I have to laugh, for although my teachers taught me very thoroughly, nothing could have prepared me for my students and their shenanigans.

Mr. Tiz, they called me, and they would comment on everything about me, saying things like, "Mr. Tiz, your snoring last night set off our car alarm three houses down—how 'bout you put a sock in it?" And, "Mr. Tiz, I like your hair today—its wave is big enough to surf on!" And, "Mr. Tiz, there's an odor coming from your way. It's either your smelly socks or ... something else you've done. So please keep it to yourself—I can't concentrate!"

This was my plight each day, so I laughed and dished it back when possible. But it was thirty against one, so it was hard to get the upper hand.

They were great, though—and enlivened me. I respected them, and our bantering was epic! They were my extended family. They were full of love for life, and life was still full of possibilities. If my lessons were interesting, they were filled with wonder at what they had not heard before, and what I taught them were their endless capabilities. I ate my lunch with them and coached their sports and watched their plays, and in a few short months, we were very close and many confided in me of their life's difficulties. One boy's sister had almost passed away, and mine had almost too. I felt what they were going through, and at these times I tried to listen more than speak. I loved my job, for I knew it made a difference in this world.

Life was busy, for besides my work, my friends and I enjoyed sports, barbeques, computer games, band gigs, and fixing the problems of the world. We discovered how to end all poverty, and how to live in peace in a pollution-free environment, and we patted ourselves on the backs for doing it.

We tried to beat each other at everything we did, but we were pretty evenly matched, which made it good, for we traded winning with each other. But we always consoled each other when we lost: "Oh, I'm so sorry I beat you! I'll let you win next time."

Watching sports, one told me, "My team is going to crush yours."

I laughed. "After my team wins, let's get some dessert. I'll get cake, and you can have some humble pie!"

My friends and I were all musicians and formed a band that played on the weekends wherever someone would let us play— bars, parties, grand-opening events. I wrote songs, played guitar, and sang. We called ourselves, *FlyTheBlue*, for it's what we wanted to, up in the sky, not in a plane, just arms as wings that took us there, up in the air—gliding through clouds of white— sky of blue.

Before we sang, I started asking our audience some questions which I called *The Anthem of the People*, and people who heard us before would answer back:

I yelled:
Who are you?
I held out my arms for them to answer:
Who are we?
And we'd all yell together:
We are the children of the world—we sing!

Then we would start our songs.

Besides my family, my friends were my support group, and I theirs, and we helped each other with our fears.

I had other hobbies as well—had just finished a model of the Santa Maria ship that my hero Columbus sailed, and I always made time to go out fishing. I would tie the artificial flies during the week and test them out on Saturdays. Often my dad accompanied me, and we ate sack lunches under pine trees with views of slow, winding rivers in meadows and the distant mountains beyond. When leisurely casting a fly like this in the cool of early mornings on water with a slight mist rising, you can't help but contemplate what life is really all about.

My mom was a great one to talk to on this subject, and after finishing college and becoming a teacher, I would always make a point of driving through the pine trees to the next town over, where they lived, for Sunday dinners. Their house was beautiful—old, but well kept up. Been in the family more than a century. Sitting on the porch, we would look at the park across the street, watch the setting sun, and talk about my students and their antics, our life concerns, and what the future held. From these times, I began to try to look beyond what I could see—and this prepared me for my future journey.

Those were the great times that slowed the water's rising temperature, and they should have been enough, and for most they are, but other things occurred that started the water boiling, and summoned up the demons. Like many people, I let things get to me too much.

I had this new boss (a principal just transferred to my school), who loved authority and to feel his power rumble and strengthen through ever-increasing temper tantrums. And me being the newest teacher made me the dartboard, and the humbler I was, the more darts were thrown. He would yell, "Your students should score a perfect grade on the state exam. What's wrong with you? You're making me look bad! I thought your degree was in teaching!" He was a sour one for sure, and he didn't like my music, and hammered me about my band, "And quit that silly band. You're a teacher now. Your music is annoying! On weekends you should be at school, grading papers, preparing for the next week, not playing at the local pub." But I wouldn't quit. My friends and I had too much fun at it, and this enraged my principal even more—that I would defy him!

And I was a magnet for each newly invented government tax, or fee, or fine, or mandatory-voluntary donation. So when the wolves were gone, there was just barely enough meat left on my bones to feed my vulture landlady (okay, that's mean; I actually liked her, but she also had to pay *her* wolves). Anyway, you know how it goes—then BAM the big one hits: "That's $400 to fix your radiator." I was counting every penny and wondering each month if I would be able to pay my bills. And I worried about a friend I had with an illness, and meeting Ms. Right.

And it's all the little things that stuck inside my head: the friends that moved away, the ticket for a rolling stop, the little sister I worried about, the sorrow for others on the nightly news. I'd contemplate my weaknesses, my nothingness, my lowly, worthless state—or so the demons taught. And although I had a great support group, which I tapped, I tried not to trouble them with my problems, and kept many of these things inside. (But later on, more than these concerns determined my fate—the worst of all in the other world.)

Anyway, I started calling these different stresses my "demons," for they started taking hold of me—squeezing me inside my head, pulling me toward a cliff. For it was like a tug of war between the good and bad—myself the rope! And soon the bad would pull me over the edge.

Chapter 3

Pre-Journey: The Portal / My Fateful Decision

So I started going to a park on Saturdays when the demons were circling me. Grand Park was its official name.

I got the idea from a television program I had recently seen about a man named Nikita Volkov in an insane asylum in Russia. He was perhaps in his late-twenties, and claimed he was taking trips to a different world. He said he got there by sitting in a park, relaxing his mind, and envisioning he was there. I laughed at first, but then felt sorry for him. They showed him in a straitjacket being interviewed and he looked so nice and so sincere—believed his statement fully. He seemed intelligent, yet down to earth and very humble. "Come with me," he even said. "I'll tell you how to get there. Where I've been is incredible. There is a village there, by a jungle. It appears and disappears! I know there's many who struggle, but I can help with what I've learned." He would not relinquish his belief in other worlds and so they kept him there.

Poor guy, I thought, and my heart went out to him. But even though he was insane, I liked his idea of mentally relaxing at a park. That would prevent *me* from becoming like *him*.

I sat in my lounge chair in the shade amongst a little grove of eucalyptus trees overlooking a lake, enjoying the fresh, clean scents, breathing the crisp, pure air, eating my lunch, and watching the many people enjoy their various activities. It was my escape whenever life was just too much, and caving in. It was beautiful, and sitting there, I ingested peace!

It was so nice that after a while I wanted more ... and most would say *that* was my mistake! I started drifting away, and the people I saw, and voices heard, started becoming blurred—for I was envisioning myself at a different place—my perfect world with no one else at all around: no mean boss berating me, no tax man following, no police officer ticketing, no dumb wars, evil dictators, or political disagreements to read about. It was just me and peace—eyes closed imagining. I envisioned myself sitting under pine trees overlooking a quiet, green meadow, with a stream, and birds, and squirrels, and beautiful, clear sky—to get away entirely. For there, no demons existed. (Or so I thought back then—for as I found out later, there was a type of evil spirit even worse! But by that time, I was well into my journey in the other world and I wouldn't quit, for I was getting closer to the treasure, and it was something I would risk my life for.)

Then when it was time to return to my park, I found it was getting harder. My imagination was becoming my other world— where I was living a second life. Then one day, I refused to go back—the peace and beauty was too much. But I was conflicted—for part of me wanted to stay, and part wanted to go back. "Let's go," I was told by myself. "This other world is insanity." But *I* then surprised *MYSELF,* by yelling back, "I WON'T!" My adventurous side and cautious side were at odds. *I* loved that new place, and wanted to explore it. So there I stayed, for all that night, sleeping in my chair in the world from where I started—"World One"—but awake in my new world that I began referring to as "World Two." (Maybe I should have accepted the advice of *MYSELF*, for later on, in my journey in World Two, I became aware of someone following me—tracking me, and trying to kill me. Three times it happened, and three times I narrowly escaped. But each trap was becoming more elaborate, and I worried the fourth might be my last.)

[The audience groaned at his admission of having a split-personality, and the director and superintendent looked at each other and raised their eyebrows. Tiz continued.]

I know what you're thinking, but let me explain.

Had I gone crazy, arguing with myself and refusing to return to World One, and insisting I stay in World Two—experiencing the wonder of what I saw there? Was I lost to the "real" world from where I came—a victim of insanity? I forced my hazy mind to try and think. My breathing quickened, wondering. Was it a dream as *MYSELF* insisted? Maybe so, for he was the grounded side of me. He looked at things calmly—I saw them impatiently.

He was the one always saying, "It's okay." "Don't worry about it." Like when I broke my arm, *I* thought they would amputate, but *MYSELF* laughed, "No! You're going overboard. Relax. It's not so bad."

I loved that side of myself—he always had a smile on his face. I went to him when I was stressed. He cared about everyone—always had something good to say, "Have you lost weight?"

But I was not the same—overreacted often—always in a race. "Let's get out and do!" *I* was the adventurer, the fisherman—the energetic one that started the band. *MYSELF* enjoyed the conversations with my mom. *I* was always on the go, "How bout that mountain peak today?" He would suggest we contemplate, "Here's some lyrics to that song." *I* thought nights were a burden—going to sleep. But for *MYSELF*, night was a wonderful, relaxing, carefree time—a time to dream! We were so different.

So was World Two a dream? Or had I found a portal to somewhere others hadn't gone, aided by this place in the park I sat, or the way I thought. For in my dream, beyond the meadow, the world looked so real—so detailed, all the sounds I heard, the coolness of the air, the smell of the trees. Dreams aren't that realistic—right? That is what I hoped and felt. Maybe it was somewhere like eternity. I knew that others would tell me it's just inside my mind—but others are often wrong I've found. Others told Columbus off the edge *he'd* fall—and we all know how that turned out (like me, he also found a New World ... mine was just bigger). (But later I prayed World Two really was a real world, for there was someone there that I had met, when my head lay upon her lap and I looked into her eyes, and I had to find her once again. For I wondered if she had touched my soul—unlike any others had before ... and I would only know if we met again.)

In the morning, I felt a tap on my shoulder and heard the words, "Sir, you can't sleep here overnight. The park closes at nine." It was a police officer.

"Oh yes, yes. Sorry. I fell asleep. From now on, by nine," I said.

Then I wondered, *Should I cancel my meditative trips to World Two?* For it was becoming too hard to make it back, and *MYSELF,* was cautiously insisting we not go. But I didn't like my cautious side, and it really upset me that he often lectured my adventurous side on what he should do. And my distaste for his fearful spirit started growing like mildew in my heart, until *I* started hating *MYSELF* and felt him becoming my enemy for all our differences. So both sides of me were tearing apart.

I thought for quite some time amidst a heartbeat steadily quickening, and breaths shorter and more often than before ... and then I made a fateful decision: I would not cancel my trips to my new world—I would live in both! I would *split* my personality—the cautious, *MYSELF,* would stay, and continue living his normal life in World One, and while he did, the adventurous, *I,* would go ... to World Two—in the back of *MYSELF's* mind. So at the same time, we would both be living separate lives—him, our normal life teaching school—and me, the great adventurer, exploring. One of us here. One there.

[As Tiz said this there was another loud disappointed groan from the audience as they knew how much this hurt his chance to prove his sanity. The director sighed and looked at his feet. But Tiz rebutted, "As I said earlier, wait for the whole story to judge."]

MYSELF hated this decision, "It's just a fantasy!"

"No, it's not fantasy," I countered. "I don't care what *you* want. *I* want it!" (For *I* had a selfish streak.)

I said out loud, "I will chronicle the furthest reaches of my mind and what I encounter in its dreamy depths—nightmare, fantasy, or something else (But *I* didn't really think it *was* in my mind)! Oh my gosh!" I realized. "I'm just like Nikita Volkov . . . but . . . *I'm* not truly crazy—*I'm* not in an insane asylum!"

Then I fantasized with pride: *Maybe events in this new world fulfill a mission in my life not tapped. Perhaps there are great and powerful insights to be learned—mystical truths that <u>rule</u> the world—or just ourselves: "Rules," I called them, not fully understood before—that will make me great and help me change the world . . . and I will be known as "Tiz, the Great Discoverer," the one who first discovered them!* I smiled and stood up straighter—chest out a bit, thinking of my newfound fame and inspiration I would be to others (for *I* had a proud streak).

That was the fateful day when I first saw the old man by the lake, and *MYSELF* advised, "The old man wasn't real! He's just part of your insanity—your own mental creation."

"No!" I countered. "I spoke directly to him. I saw the wrinkles on his face."

MYSELF added, "If real, how do you know you can trust him? He was just a stranger—perhaps the evil one! Maybe what he really wants is our demise—us pulled apart—all the way to insanity. He saw the seed of insanity you planted and now is watering it. There is no treasure—it's really a mental dungeon he's going to lock you in."

"Well you're the cautious side of me, so of course you would think that," and *I* refused to listen. "No, he's not evil—he's no demon." I liked the old guy.

Then I met the bird and had the dream—mud upon my shoes, and that convinced me, *No, this is not just in my mind.* That is when I knew, without a doubt, my journey in World Two was about to begin. The old man's explanation was lacking, but I thought that maybe Pebbles were the little lessons you learn that lead to bigger, major insights called Rules which lead a person to the cherished Maps of Ages, and to the treasure, and to see what's beyond the Gate. For how does a baby learn to talk? One sound, one word at a time. A child rides a bike, but first he crawls, then walks. *But ooh*, I thought. *That treasure does sound good and I want it!* (For *I* had a greedy streak).

Now, after years on my life-changing journey I stand before you. What I learned, I'll share. There are many struggling just like I was, so like Nikita, I am standing tall—admitting what I've done, so I can help. So this is the truth and the story. This experience will be told in the voice and perspective of *I*, for it comes from his adventure, and from his journal, and from experiences conveyed to *MYSELF*. But he's still there, and I don't even know if he's still alive.

I traveled through landscapes never seen and years of time— beginning at my peaceful meadow in my mind. For I thought of what the old man said, and pondered what he meant, and then I practiced it: how to breathe and see. I'd breathe in deep through my nose, then exhale in a long, slow stream through pursed lips, trying to relax. And as I totally relaxed, I focused my thoughts to see *beyond* that peaceful meadow—every tree, bird, grass, and leaf. And because of that, I was able to venture into the world beyond.

And I met the Elder, and lady with the spear, and I prayed to evade the Beasts. I met the Scholar, and the Disciple, and felt the travesties in the abandoned villages and then I cried. I met the sun and the river running free through the grassy meadow, then in the cave, the ancient family long since dead, and after that, the Prophet. Sometime later, I opened my arms and I breathed deep—with fear ... for the agony I knew was soon to come!

Chapter 4

Journeys and Death in the Other World

Rule #1: OF THE DRY LAKE

[Liz paused—and breathed deep, thinking of what he was about to tell the audience, knowing the perception of absurdity of everything he was about to say. Then he smiled and continued.]

I left my mind's peaceful meadow with my backpack of essentials and journeyed into that other world of mine, World Two, my goal to find, as the old man said, the Rules and treasure map, and to open up Gate One. And I prayed the old man and his advice had not just been my mind's creation.

I was amazed by all the differences in this world—many dangerous ... to the degree of death, that would soon come down upon me! There were no countries or cities or fences, but occasionally I passed ancient ruins. Mainly, though, I walked through open land and forests, and only a few people here and there I spied, with whom I talked. This world seemed older maybe, for it had all the same vegetation but also more and varied, like it had more time to evolve over many more years. Animals I saw that weren't in ours, like a camel once with a slender trunk to get her water with; bird tracks bigger than I'd ever seen, and tracks I found of giant reptiles thought to be extinct. *Dinosaurs*? I wondered. I shivered, but also filled with curiosity. Most of the trees were towering sequoias and redwoods, so I felt so small walking underneath, but also different types of trees and flowers I saw that I had never seen before: some trees with only one huge leaf on top, some not straight but growing curved, and others with canopy halfway up and then another on its top; some flowers popped or spit when touched, some were taller than a tree, or larger than my head. Game trails I walked upon, over the land and through the brush, to make the going easier. The skies weren't blue—but a light green, and the night was black and as I camped, a fire warmed me. When full, three moons shone of different sizes and lit my way—one mainly during the daytime, though. And those skies were of a pristine clarity not seen in World One—so clear in fact that besides the moons, large asteroids were seen as well, many close, as well as far away, so some looked like little moons at different distances. Many birds this world enjoyed, but the most I saw were ravens; thousands were often in the sky—flying by in giant flocks in elevated altitudes. They were keeping their eyes on me ... and it convinced my eyes to widen and my throat to swallow extra times! But at that time they did not attack, so why mainly above *me*? For the rest of the sky was largely vacant.

Mile after mile I traversed, and I listened to the songs of the forests' different birds and their rivers' rocks chatting to each other with the water running over. My mind in its weary, delirious state imagined the water over rocks was whispering something to me. How long I walked, I cannot say; all I know is many months I went, as my beard was evidence (and I wished my better walking shoes I'd brought—and would the next time there)!

Elevation decreased till I reached a tropical environment— monkeys in the trees throwing banana peels and figs at me—until scared away by a gorilla swinging in, screeching at them, and accompanying me—then many of his friends also joining us, so a little army then I had. I experienced many things, and although I recognized them not as such, they were the Pebbles that I sought; like when the sun arose in all its majesty and I took its light, and warmth, and beauty with me. It made me want to also share what I could give. Or like the squirrel-house in a hole in a tree I saw, versus the bird nest on a limb. It taught the importance of lasting versus temporary things.

As I walked, I reflected on *MYSELF's* opinion, and had to wonder if this was all a dream, and I decided on another question to ask my audience and add to *The Anthem of the People*:

How do our minds create the things we dream?

Then one day on top of a mountain, looking out over a rainforest valley, in the far-away distance to the east I saw a beam of light shining intensely to the sky. I wanted to go, for it seemed some sort of magnificent beacon. I hadn't even found a Rule so doubted it was the treasure—but something great—something needed, I was sure.

But I also saw a vast lake below me—an island in the middle. The lake was inviting, living, glistening—something special. Its blue pulled me to it, for I could practically taste what looked to be enchanted waters. I couldn't resist. I wanted it—and down I went.

When I got to the lake's edge, I found that death I referenced awaiting me, for the lake was pretending. It had fooled me, for it was dead—dry—as a bone—was mud, now dried and cracked! Its living water was a mirage. I was amazed! And I couldn't believe it, given the rainforest it was within—it rained there almost every day! I had been in the jungle's heat and humidity walking so long and was so tired, with not enough to eat, in delirium, I hopefully thought, *Maybe, instead, its dryness is truly the mirage—a disguise of sorts!* So I slowly knelt in weariness and scooped some with my hands. I was so fatigued, so hot, and wished it was water so much, I looked at the substance in my hands and saw its liquefied enjoyment . . . so I drank a mouthful

... but no, it was not water—it was dirt (or the driest, dirtiest water in the world, my mouth informed before I spit it out)!

I stood at the edge of the rainforest and the dry lake—clear skies, angry sun, and I searched the bareness of the dry lake's baked and arid surface. See-through heat waves stealthily escaped. I considered walking across to make the other side, for the jungle I was in was thick—hard to walk through, but the dry lake was so large—seemed miles across, and I was so tired, the sun looking even hotter out on the dirt, so I feared I would perish on the way; and if I didn't make it across, those ravens would have their dinner for the night.

I could see the island far away at the lake's center. Light seemed brighter there. *Maybe I can get there and rest.* A bird flew by, and although I couldn't feel any, it must have hit some wind, for it carried the bird, against its will, as it fought against the wind, until the bird landed on the island.

I walked ten feet out to test the dirt, but decided against and turned around to walk back to the jungle. But while upon the dry lake, I felt an energy from its inner core like it was a magnet pulling me to its center, and I was a helpless paper clip. My feet were suddenly heavy, like my shoes were made of lead and each step away from the center was heavier—till I couldn't walk. I turned back around toward the center, and my steps were light—shoes now made of feathers—like I was being pulled. After considering my options, I felt I had no choice—and with humble obedience I started to follow my feet across the dry lake's arid flatness.

From behind some trees I was secretly being watched and I heard something step on a dry branch that snapped. I spun around in a flash and looked, sensing a foreign presence observing me, but nothing was seen, as whatever it was had hid in time. But my breathing had stopped, the hairs on my arms on end, as it left me with the chilling feeling I was being followed—or maybe stalked.

I turned back around to the dry lake and decided then for sure I'd go that way. But I dreaded what I then would do. I took a breath and let the power take me. I walked and walked to get across—was very large—my tiring feet! My steps became so labored, small, and slow—a snail's pace. After hours in the heat, red and sweating, I approached the center island—under a glaring sun that increased its rays and warmth—didn't want me to succeed—didn't want me to make it across! Wobbling, staggering, finally I fell on my knees at the dry lake's core when I was just too tired.

I gasped, though, for the island wasn't made of dirt ... it was made of skeletons—animal, bird, and people's bones! Hundreds stacked on top of each other. "Oh my! Where have I come? What have I done?"

I was going to rest and then get up, but after sitting, and drinking, and eating some, at this place, I was even more fatigued. Even after sleeping, I was worse and couldn't get up. I looked up at the sun—the dry lake's only friend. I neared to death after days lying in its heat—all moisture sweated out of me—my consciousness and mind delirious, until I couldn't tell if I was among the living or the dead. My stomach ached. The earth was still. I saw vultures approach and circle overhead, underneath the ravens. When they did, many ravens flew down and landed all around me. I figured, to protect their claim to the ample meat. But neither they nor the vultures made a sound. All was perfectly quiet, as if afraid of death, and my heart's beating was twice as slow as usual. Then a great jolt—the earth shook mightily. But I was too far gone to notice much. I knew I had not much time left, and I closed my eyes to die. My body tingled slightly—an out of body feeling. With my last thought I realized, *The old man sent me to a place where all I did was die. Had I been duped? MYSELF correct—the old man wanting my demise?*

In that state of death that I endured (if indeed I really was), the more I felt. Suddenly the water of the lake I started feeling on my skin, seeping up from somewhere underneath that baked and broken mud, and my cells I felt replenishing—sucking up moisture like a dried-up sponge. As they did, my eyes opened in the slightest slits to see the water on the dirt. Then far away on the dry lake's edge—people I saw, and huts of dead woven plants. The water, more—as the lake kept quickly filling until covering me, then deeper and deeper still. I Treaded water then, but with weakened body, I struggled to keep my head above. Finally, not able, I slowly sank beneath with only my hand raised out. Then a shadow, and the bottom of a canoe I saw and someone grabbed my hand and pulled me in. I was groggy and questions asked of me, and busy conversation in a different tongue I heard between two fishermen. They gave me some green juice from a plant I had never tasted, and the haze vanished and I was new (although I might have also liked a little sandwich offered).

I talked in mine, and they in theirs, but the hands talked alike. The fisherman in front of me looked young and strong—maybe in his mid-thirties. He spoke in a low, hoarse voice, and was perhaps of South American origin, with medium-length black hair and goatee. We paddled toward the distant shore and I was lost to all of this. The lake had been dry, I'm sure—and now was filled, sparkling, and beautiful! We paddled toward a village on the shore that I had not seen before while lying on the dry lake's dirt. I was confused. Where was I? Was I just dreaming this—like maybe I was doing while sitting by the lake in World One? Was I inside a dream, inside another dream? But like World Two, this felt so real. I reached down and felt the water with my hand. I could feel its coolness—wetness.

The village was under palm trees, and banana plants, and carved out of green jungle foliage. When arriving there, the village people stared—like they were amazed to see me. I wondered who these people were. They looked of every nationality—women, men, and children. I looked around at the place and felt a sense of Déjà vu somewhere deep inside.

The people came and greeted me, and I noticed the man with the black goatee some ways off talking to an older man. As they spoke, they were both studying me with serious faces and I felt uneasy. Then the older man, perhaps in his seventies, came, and the people backed away. He gave me another type of juice to drink—this one red, and I felt a surge of energy inside my head. My mind was suddenly awake like never before, like when sniffing smelling salts. Then in the spoken words around me, I could suddenly hear common repeated vowels and syllables, and the words themselves, and how they were arranged in sentences—how each word interacted with the others. Then I could decipher the meaning of the words and I could understand the people talking near me, and I was so amazed! I looked at them then back again. The older man smiled and he moved his hand a certain way like a fish swimming, then stopping it, and with his palm lifted toward me, suddenly my throat went dry as desert sand—and working its way up through my whole head. I started coughing—my head hurt, and I looked into his eyes. His smile stayed as he also stared at *me*, seemingly okay with my predicament and studying its effects. I couldn't get a breath, I choked and gasped but he just watched. Was he the cause of my misery—myself his lab experiment? If so, I guess he wished a slow and painful death. Finally when I was near my end, he reached to a nearby table and gave me a cup of another type of juice to drink—this one yellow. I drank, coughing some more, and a warmth enveloped my throat and rose to my head—and mind—my mind now even more alert than before with the drink. I told him, "Loggi oh," and I was surprised at the foreign words— for I knew they meant, "Thank you." Then as I listened more to others, all the words I spoke were of that other tongue!

The people told me they were travelers, like me, just in a different sense—going somewhere different. And when I questioned them, they said I'd find out what they meant—but time and experience would have to be the teacher. They were simply clothed, with sandals made of dried-up, woven plants, and shirts and shorts or skirts, all made from coarse cotton fabric— but comfortable looking. All the adults wore exquisite necklaces of braided vines with medal medallions hanging from them, and everything around was natural—their houses, food, and tools. There was a sense of total, utter peace there, and the people seemed content—to an extent I couldn't measure, beyond my understanding, and I thought that maybe I would end my journey there. They told me, though, that if I stayed, it would be like Hell to me. "So wait," they said, "and come back later." I enjoyed seeing them at their work of grinding corn, repairing tents, and sewing clothes by hand with needles made of chiseled bones; and as they did, I talked to them, and their kind and gentle spirits were contagious.

The children were delightful, and they wanted me to join in all their games. They tried to tickle me, so I also them, and I threw them in the air, and chased and tried to find them, for they hid expertly. Kick the coconut was my favorite game—but they would always kick it before I tagged them. So I played, and kept the coconut as a souvenir.

That night, sun gone from sight, we sat at long, planked, wooden tables in a large semi-circle by the shore, under torches burning and drums that pounded. Songs were sung and children danced to music played by all the others, with hollowed gourds blown in, or crafted limbs with tightened strings they plucked, or beads they shook in pottery.

The man with the black goatee sat at my table's other end and I noticed him observing me. The eldest man that almost killed me sat next to me, and after dinner, the women spoke to tell me of their history. They told great stories of times from long ago, and the bravery, and the sadness, and the miracles ... and calamities that befell. They spoke to me of Pebbles—but I didn't know it at the time—nor to what Rule they flowed.

"Those memories are sacred," they said, "for they last forever."

"This stick," the one said, "will decay as mother sky spits, and the sun then shines, and all that again and again. But the night that brother Emgo said he slayed the Beast—and told us how—will never die. He is a true friend and we revere him."

All the children came in turn and grasped my arm and stared into my eyes with concentrated thoughts—seemingly to learn something I was giving ... but I did not know what. It seemed to me the more that looked, the weaker I got, until the last one looked and I was out of breath—left hoarse and gasping.

After that, all went to bed except the eldest man and me, and in the dark, the torches showed his mouth talking. He was perhaps of African descent. His hair was gray, but plenty to his shoulders. Like the others, contentment radiated from him and also complete peace and pleasant confidence. He wore similar clothing as the others, and a necklace with four of the medallions, each a different color of medal. But I was uneasy as it was only him and I—and before, with him, I almost died.

"This skin and teeth," he told me, and he pointed at an old wrinkled face and open mouth, "will rot away, but the teachings of my father and my mother will never leave here," and he pointed at his head and then his heart.

The man looked at the immensity of stars and slowed his speech—seemingly in reverence. We were specs in the universe. He pointed at a cloud, obscuring the stars, and it dried, clearing our view—and I wondered if I had seen correctly. "These stars," he said, "I confide in every night and their response I hear in my own thoughts. For more is there than suns and planets and space and dust. They scold me, and they praise me, and I change a little each time they leave. I wonder, am I a man of peace? Do I act with charity? The stars answer."

Then he looked at the lake and pointed, and its dancing ripples from the breeze, turned into watery glass reflecting the moons' light. "Generations past, this lake was dead. Then a quake in the earth diverted rivers so they filled it. One day again the quake may come. Then, like my teeth, this lake is dead. So the people must desert it, for its water was only fleeting—not lasting.

Not like the stars' enduring wisdom helping me. And since *time* also is a fleeting thing—most must be spent on the lasting things we can take with us."

Then he added what was a riddle to me, and I tried to ponder what he meant: "Take some Guidance: Birth is birth, and death is death—both conclusive in their happenings. From the start and to the end, time lives with untold possibilities—but only to those that use a brush! We all start with canvas clean—but some use the living thing to create their personal masterpiece . . . and some do not. Use it wisely!"

He paused, and with long, gentle, flowing movements of his hand, back and forth, he fanned the air around us, and the torches, burning low, increased their flames again. Then he looked deep into my eyes. "When you see Emgo, respect him, and thank him for his example in killing the Beast—for soon one will also come for you!"

He looked at the lake, and in more of a hushed tone, he mentioned, "The lesson from the lake is only a step on the path to the Mountain." He looked at me. "The journey you're upon is grand, but comes with great difficulty and much time. You can't do it alone, and you'll require humility to receive the help you need. The most and greatest advice you will receive will come from the Prophet, so listen with humble and attentive ears. The combined ten Rules and Maps of Ages that you seek will make you great, and give you a power only few achieve. Judge wisely what you do with it. Set your compass going east, then get the Secret from the Scholar as your first chore—it provides a second life. Keep it in your bag of tools for you will need it."

A second life? I thought. *I'm going to die? But then I can come back from it?*

He continued, "You will need it to save yourself. But even before then, in the next few days, you'll fight for your life from the unexpected."

I asked, "Do you know of the light-beam I saw in the east?"
"I do."

"What's there?"

"Ah yes! One of my favorite places! Some would say a magical place. But it's indescribable, because for some it is incredible—something never seen before—a fabulous reward for making it that far. But surprisingly, for others nothing special waits. It depends on how you look at it. Take advantage of the journey there, and then it will be as I have seen. But for all that persevere and make it there, words you've never heard before that say incredible things—and you will never be the same."

I added, "And who is Emgo? Where will I see him? And why respect him? I don't even know him?"

He didn't answer, but looked intently at me for quite some time—seemingly to discern something—to judge me for my questions. He then looked up at the stars whom he started addressing—sometimes happily, sometimes in tears—and I left him.

In the morning, the air seemed heavy and I felt sick—a slight headache, coarseness of breath, my energy depleted, my cells aging. I was pale. I staggered to the main gathering area, but the villagers didn't hail me, no breakfast was offered, and although I could tell the children wanted to play with me, they did not. The two fishermen then told me I would be going fishing with them.

Why fish? I thought. *I know they can tell I'm sick. So why aren't they taking me to the healer's hut? Or give me more of that juice? Is it something I said?* I tried to remember when I last spoke.

As we paddled away from the village, I looked back at the village and the small pillars of smoke escaping to Heaven, and though not told, I knew that I would not be going back, and the sadness almost broke my soul. *Did I do something wrong? Are the fishermen here to drown me?* Off shore a ways, the fishermen stopped but did not lay a hand on me, nor did they cast their lines. I didn't feel like fishing anyway. I suddenly felt I needed the water . . . it pulled at me and the fishermen knew it. I felt I needed to engulf myself in it (like it was life itself and currently I was without), and without thinking, I jumped. It was cool and fresh and blue, and penetrated each pore. I lived a thousand lives in its melted hands, and felt revival. When I turned back to the canoe, they were slowly paddling to their next fishing hole. I was going to shout to rescue me, but somehow I knew they would not return. Then the one in back with the black goatee looked back at me—and our eyes met. As he stared, he studied me, and I realized he was fine with letting me drown. Why such contradiction? Who were these people feeding me and teaching me and then ignoring me and letting me die? What had I done? They had seemed so good—but another side, I was discovering.

As I treaded water, I looked again at the village and saw the Elder standing on the shore—just watching my predicament like he had done before. He stood with someone else and I squinted hard to see. *Is that who I think it is? Yes,* I was sure, *It's Nikita Volkov! He's in this world? Here's my proof to MYSELF this world is real. Nikita can corroborate* ... I frowned, *But what good now?*

As my arms tired and my strength declined, and I slowly sank beneath, I looked up through the water at the faded, glowing sun, and as breath escaped me and that deathly fog enveloped my mind, the water receded with me as I sank. As it did, the village and smoke and people above, blurred like a mirage that dried and went away, and I was left lying on the parched dirt of the dry lake again—the water gone—myself coughing, and gagging, and wheezing until I breathed. *I survived!* But again my agony, as the heat baked my soul, burned my skin, chapped my lips, caused my eyes to tear!

My consciousness faded—only halfway there, but somewhere deep a sliver of thought remembered the Elder and Dry Lake (as I named it). The Elder set my mind wandering and wondering, for I had never mentioned I was on a journey to a Mountain. And how would he know a Beast would come for me? I shuddered. I thought long about his words—about their meaning, as I lay and looked up at the sun and then the stars. Then I remembered the old man by the lake in World One and his words to "Get the Guidance from the Elder," and I suddenly realized this was him! And when I did, I knew his words were not just idle chatter.

Was there a Rule in all of this? I concentrated totally. What was this experience telling me? I calmed my breathing. Thought of nothing else ... for much time. A flicker of a thought or a vision crossed my mind—and went—then another. The thoughts did start to coalesce. The Elder called it a lesson that the lake was teaching, and suddenly I had a revelation, and his words enlarged inside my mind into something other—something much bigger—a key tenet of life to remember .... They were indeed a Rule, I realized—my first, for which I searched for months and months!

He spoke about time—that it lives—and to use the living thing. He spoke about the lake's water being temporary—but to focus on lasting things. I thought about the bird nest versus the squirrel house inside a tree I saw. I smiled and thought of the Rule that I had found. THE RULE OF THE DRY LAKE: <u>Spend most time on the things that last: of knowledge, personality, and relationships</u>. And I wrote the Rule inside my mind and later in my leather-bound black book. "If I survive, I will become it!" I told myself. "Its meaning will feed my cells until I do it because that is who I am." Then I looked back at prior months and recognized the Pebbles I had found preparing me for the Rule. One Rule of ten I'd found, and with all ten, I would find the treasure and change the world (and I envisioned two of the greatest names then to be read in history books ... "Columbus and Tiz")!

But now I was just a lump of almost-dead forgotten flesh upon the dirt—exposed to whatever it was the Elder said might tear my limbs apart. Would I ever get to search for Rules again? As I thought it, my blurry eyes spied a half-buried stone in the dirt. With my last bit of energy I moved my hand to cover it, then barely pushed with my thumb against it, till it came out. I held it between my thumb and forefinger and strained to see—it was an uncut, magnificent, round, polished, perfectly clear diamond the size of a dime. It caught the sunlight and sparkled intensely. Then I passed out.

*　　*　　*

As I found out later, back at the jungle village that I no longer saw, the Elder and the man with the black goatee stood looking out over the lake. The Elder inhaled slowly while thinking, then exhaled. He reached in a pocket and pulled out a nine-inch knife of the most exquisite beauty and expert craftsmanship—golden blade—precious designs carved into it, cocobolo wooden handle inlaid with oak and cherry woods, the last fourth of it a shining ruby. He handed it to the man with the black goatee, paused, and while pointing at the lake said, "See if he survived, and if he did, and decided to continue on, envision different ways to kill him and then do what must be done. But act with stealth, for it should not be known we were involved. The knife should only be used if it's needed." The man with the black goatee took the knife and ran his finger along its shiny, sharpened edge. It cut his flesh and blood did pool, then it slowly fell as drops into the dirt.

Chapter 5

Ms. Spear / The Beast

Rule #2: OF CLEAR SKIES

Tiz took a drink of water from a glass on the lectern, then he stretched. There was a lot of conversation between neighbors in the auditorium, with many smiling and shaking their heads. "Definitely still deranged," someone said. But no one stood and all waited for him to continue.

Tiz looked at the person and then at the director and continued, "They called Columbus crazy for saying he would sail around the world. What if he also told them someday we would travel to the moon—or see and talk to people through a device held in our hand?"]

I lay on the sunbaked, cracked mud of Dry Lake, and somewhere in my subconscious mind a voice told me, *You must return.* But I was groggy—had to remember how to think. I tried. *Return where?* I thought, through the haze around my mind.

"You have two lives—the other in World One—too long here and you won't get out," the voice told me—but the voice was not within my mind this time—it was without!

My eyes popped open wide and darted around—no one was there! *I heard a voice, I'm sure!* I sat still! The voice I heard was low and hoarse. I concentrated, and remembered the voice of the old man from the park in World One! I heard it again. I froze in place. I listened carefully. "You left something behind in World One that you must have to make it to the Mountain. It will light your way, and without it, you will flounder in the dark."

"What is it?" I quickly asked, but there was no answer—he was gone. That is when I started referring to the old man simply as "Old Man," since his name I was without.

But the light-beam in the east was enticing me—so far off but so very bright. That's the way the Elder said to go—and I wanted to—but I couldn't move—too weak to. A fabulous reward was there he said—and I envisioned a metropolitan delight—parties into the night. Or riches maybe everywhere. What riches does a place so great provide, that it's advertised by such a light? I pictured myself there—an amazing city with others too—a bonanza of food and drink and beautiful things and conversation of the most magnificent subjects into the night. But I realized my deathly state. *How can I make it there?*

Then I remembered Nikita Volkov, who I saw, and wanted to talk to, and that cemented my decision, *Yes, I will return. That will prove this world's reality. Why continue if it's a dream— much of it a nightmare actually? And going back, I'll save myself from dying on this lake. And if it's true, I'll return here again— but I'll focus instead on the light-beam and transfer there, instead of to this deadly lake!*

I concentrated, and in little wisps, a faded memory started coming back to me—of reality. Another lake—but with water— me sitting by, amongst some trees—another life—World One, I then remembered. *What was the portal here and back?* I told myself, "I have to get out! I have to get back! If I see myself there, who's to say I'm not? I'll envision it, and know it's true."

I concentrated harder, trying to remember reality, but it was hard. I thought, *If I was in that, what would I see? What would I hear?* I focused my thoughts. Blurry images began to clear. I finally saw people walking 'round, joggers running by, kids flying kites, boys fishing. I saw myself in a chair, eyes closed in sleep or contemplation. I pictured myself opening my eyes—and when I did, growing from the slightest whisper, then louder, I heard the sparrow's song, and then the voices sound. I smelled sweet flowers scent and felt the sun's grand warmth.

One last glance of Dry Lake showed me a blurry image of someone walking toward me—a shiny, golden object in their hand. But through the tunnel's other end I went—returning and again rejoining my other self. He was healthy and I took on *his* state, so happy I was for that—but *my* clothes—so quite ragged.

It was now fall, but the next year, so I found that over a year I had been gone! This long I'd been away? And had just one Rule to celebrate? Thousands of miles I must have walked! *MYSELF* had been there living as normal, but *I* had been away. Now both were one again.

I made the same mistake twice when I informed a couple friends I was a great explorer and told them of the other world I visited, and the people I talked to and things I'd seen and done, like: a sparrow talking to a man, a camel with a trunk, trees with only one huge leaf on top, spitting flowers, dying and coming back from it, lakes dry as a bone then suddenly filled then dry again in seconds, how *I* wanted to go on the journey but *MYSELF* didn't. Then, on both occasions, after they said they had to make a phone call, we *just happened* to run into their friends—and guess what—they were both psychiatrists who invited me to their offices!

"Well, don't you understand?" I told one of the psychiatrists in her office. "I'm not crazy. I just talk to people others can't see, and travel to another world."

"Ohhhhhh," she said and nodded.

"I get there through my mind, but when I arrive, I think it's a real place."

She rubbed her chin, "Really . . . ."

"Maybe it's a place like Heaven, where people who have died and then come back say they have been. An Elder there disperses clouds by pointing at them. He gave me juice that let me speak his language."

Her eyebrows rose, "Oh my! I'd like to drink some of that myself! Can you speak some now?"

I spoke, "A mama llama doinda samba ay caramba."

She looked confused.

I did too, "That didn't come out right. I guess I've forgotten now."

She nodded and smiled a bit. I exclaimed, "Maybe my body is locked inside *this* world and my soul floated away there. The sky is green and there are three moons. A village is there but it disappears."

Her forehead furrowed, "Imagine that!"

"Maybe it's another dimension we can go in a perfect meditative state. Some flowers there are taller than trees and I think there might be dinosaurs. I want to find one and maybe try to ride it (her eyes got big)! I'm on a perilous journey there to find a secret map!"

When I informed her of that, I had her convinced, because she said, "Oh wow! Really? I'd love to hear about that!"

Then she mentioned, "Your story sounds like one I read, about an insane Russian man named Nikita Volkov. Have you ever heard his story?"

"Yes . . ." I warily said.

As she looked at me, she pursed her lips and raised her eyebrows. "It's a psychological order called Mirroring. You're just mirroring what you heard *him* say."

In the end, she said, "It is all pretend—a dream you are in. You need to look within yourself, and be careful, for your mentality might someday take over your life and get you fired from your job."

I couldn't let that happen, though, for the kids at the school I taught were everything to me. I so much wanted to tell them everything I'd seen, but look where it got Nikita. I respected him though, for he stuck to his beliefs—told anyone that listened, for he said what he learned could help. But I wasn't so strong or brave, so I let it go. Was I really just mirroring? I couldn't tell.

So I reeled in my thoughts and went about my mission methodically, and my students never knew about my other world. But in my lessons, some things I taught them furtively—like the importance of timeless things.

They still kept me thinking defensively, from things they said like, "Mr. Tiz, you're too boring. Why don't you get out and see the world? Put away those exciting encyclopedias of yours and go on a great adventure!"

"That's a good idea. I think I will," I said and smiled at my inside joke. "But I have to pay for it by sharing my vast knowledge with *you* knuckleheads."

"And while you're at it, find a girl!" they said. And they gave me advice on where to meet her: "There's a cashier at the store that looks in need of someone." And, "Here's my aunt's number, she hasn't been outside for a while." And, "There's a girl I always see waiting for someone outside the bar."

"I don't date girls that wait for people outside bars!" I answered.

Then with whispers, quickened by excitement, they started discussing with each other, and from the bits and pieces that I heard, I got nervous: "Here's what we can do about his looks ...." And, "...perhaps a moustache." And, "I'll talk to my dentist about his teeth." And, "You hit up the dating websites, and I'll ask my preacher." And, "His ears are kind of big. What do you suggest?" They all looked over at me, and I tried to look at my ears myself. Then, "What was his mom thinking? If I could only have been there when he was growing up." And, "If you break it, I'll reset it so it's finally straight."

Sometimes they tested me and got out of hand, but that didn't bother me. I learned that from my mom. I almost never saw her get mad.

But to make it clear, I actually did go out on dates—but I was still looking for Ms. Right. One day at my parents' house for

Sunday dinner, I told them about World Two and they were so worried. "Oh my!" my mom said looking at me sadly. Shortly after that, a pretty lady with shoulder-length light-brown hair knocked—asking for historical information about my parents house. I had seen or met her very briefly in the city twice before. I will admit, I thought her very nice, and thought, *Who knows— Ms. Right?* But I didn't get her phone number. I asked my mom to give her my phone number when she returned, but she didn't want it, my mother said. *Ms. Right—strike one.*

I tried to call Nikita Volkov to ask about his other world and how I saw him at the village by the lake at the edge of the jungle, but the mental institution would never let me through. So I wrote him a letter and waited for a reply.

One day I was called into an interview with the school superintendent (my principal's boss). She's a good lady, I'll admit, but she said the principal wanted me fired—but the superintendent was the one that had to approve it. She said the principal was complaining about me playing in a band, and that she heard I had been seeing a psychiatrist. I told the superintendent there wasn't a problem—just difficulty sleeping, so she dismissed me with a warning, "I'm sorry, but I'll have to fire you if you have psychological problems. We can't have that with the kids." Then I was sure, unlike Nikita, I would *not* tell the world and deal with the consequences.

As I waited for Nikita's reply, I kept busy and enjoyed the ease of life in World One, melting back into my comfortable, normal routine, never visiting my park or sitting by the lake or feeling a need to go adventuring.

I laughed and enjoyed myself, but most time on the lasting things, for I used the living thing—time, like the Elder and Rule One taught. I had only found one Rule, but I perfected my use of it . . . and from that, along with all the personal reflective time as I walked alone in World Two, I started seeing certain increased abilities—perhaps like monks with so much time to think—the way my thoughts coalesced. I noticed friends more often now confided in me, for the words I noticed coming out of me, "I'm sorry to hear that." "Is there anything I can do?"

I thought more clearly. Lyrics rhymed, and harmonies and melodies fit together more easily. I found that World Two was good inspiration for me to write new songs, and my friends and I booked new gigs and played them then. Thinking of what I heard in the jungle in World Two stalking me, I wrote one I called: *The Last Jaguar*. [Several people yelled from the audience, "Yes! In the year 1500!" Tiz smiled.]

Fans were increasing, and more came to hear us than before. We recorded a CD and posted our songs on YouTube so they learned our songs and then they sang along, and I was quite surprised. We were developing a little following, and as we played, the band smiled at each other.

"One, two, three, four," I would yell and we would hammer on the keys and strum the strings and beat the drums to the audience. Then I would yell the questions for *The Anthem of the People* and they would answer. "Join me now:"

> *Who are you?*
> *Who are we?*
> *How do our minds create the things we dream?*
> *Say it now ....*
> *With me ....*
> *Who are we?*
> *We are the children of the world—we sing!*

Our venues enlarged to fit the crowds, so now we were playing at parks and high school gymnasiums. [Again Tiz raised his smart phone to the microphone and half the audience sang along—then Tiz too—and it felt so good for him to sing again:] (The Last Jaguar, track 2)

Intro:
Lay on your back, and listen good

to the legend, of the last Jaguar:

Verse:
It's the year, fifteen hundred
and you are sent, on a mission
to kill the last, remaining Jaguar
in the dark, drabby, lonely wood

You think you hear, somewhere a branch snap
and look around you but see nothing
still walking-- you see a shadow
you look behind you and there it is

Chorus:
The last remaining Jaguar you've searched for
The last remaining Jaguar on earth
The last remaining Jaguar that stalks you
and soon it's either him or you
and soon it's either him or you

Verse:
You want to run, but it's too late
and you feel its paws, upon your back
you feel yourself drifting, into darkness
and see the fog, rise up over you

Crawling on, hands and knees
you emerge from the wood in the clearing
you swear that you'll never return again
to hunt what you wanted so desperately

Chorus Repeated

Music

Verse:
And from the cold, dreary wood
there emerges not one, or two, or three
for the last and lonely, only Jaguar
was a her with child on that day

And now the race, starts all over
and now the race blooms fruitfully
and now the story is told through the ages
of a hunter and the hunted
and what remained

Chorus Repeated

Although our success was improving, we needed a break-through—something else to get attention. We played at any event that would have us, but we wondered how to increase our following. Then the principal heard a couple kids playing our songs from YouTube at school and he chided me, "Now kids are wasting their time at school!"

I told him, "They only play them outside at lunch time."

"I'm going to get you fired Tiz."

The other teachers patted me on my shoulder and said, "Just ignore him, that's what *we* do. He's a tart one."

Then the principal made an announcement over the loudspeaker, "There shall be absolutely no playing of songs by *FlyTheBlue* on this campus. IT IS PROHIBITED!" But every weekend we were out there singing and playing.

I started compiling stories for a children's book about a hedgehog I read about and his valley of talking animals, for the stories inspired me—same story as mine almost, but I didn't realize it then. Chisel Hedgehog was also on a journey—and wrote songs, like me, to weather the storm—for he was on trial too! (Listen To The Breeze, track 3)

Verse:
Listen to the breeze
talk to the trees
ask Mr. Summer
what he has in store

Wave to the night
sing to the moon
wonder if tomorrow
brings a friend or two

Chorus:
Yeah, laugh with the clouds
dance with the wind
close your eyes and glide
through your mind's blue sky

Music

Chorus Repeated

I relished the summer, for our band played full-time—every night. But soon it was over, and a whole year had passed since I'd come home—over two years since I first traveled to World Two. And I was quite comfortable sleeping on a bed in my room—not on the ground under trees.

*   *   *

Then, as I was told later, an expensive-looking, long, black limousine pulled into the parking lot of Grand Park. The driver got out and came around and opened the back, passenger door. A man's legs pivoted out—feet on the ground—brown pointy shoes with buckles. His pants were blue. He got out and looked around—yellow shirt, green vest. Yes—Old Man. He smiled, and walked slowly to the lake, then all the way around it to the other side, breathing deep, enjoying the sun and clear blue sky. When he reached the other side, he looked around, then up in the trees. Again he sat by the tree—but no preaching. Soon the bird flew down and landed on his shoulder. He lifted his hand, and the bird jumped on. Old Man kissed it on its head and spoke to it, and the bird chirped back.

*   *   *

The next day, from inside my house, I noticed a finch on my outside windowsill looking in through the window at me. She had that same discolored feather in her wing—same bird from the park two years before! I opened the window but she flew off. In school the next day, again I saw the finch on a windowsill looking in at me, and then from a tree walking home, and I could feel the hair on the back of my neck stand up!

That night I had a dream. In the dream, I saw myself approaching an ancient castle with lights inside the windows. I got chills when I knew it was a vision of what might be.

Signs were beckoning me back to World Two again, and I remembered the promise of treasure maps leading to gold and riches, and my goal and quest and what could be, that would make "Tiz, the Great Discoverer," a common, household admired name. *What would I find on the Mountain? How would I be changed forever by the opened gate? I wonder if I can ride an Apatosaurus there!*

However, the psychiatrist's lack of faith in my belief had me questioning. What if she was right, and World Two *wasn't* real? The Elder said something might tear me apart, but was the *real* threat insanity? And it was pulling me into its snare?

Was Old Man an illusion—my own insane invention? I went back to the park to find him again. I could find out if he was real and if so, ask what I left behind. The only clue, he had said, was that it would light my way. I already brought a flashlight so it wasn't that. The stars? They were in both worlds. I never found Old Man at the park. I spoke out loud to him, but he didn't answer like in World Two . . . . That is where I would have to go to ask him. I realized I hadn't touched him, so I made up my mind that I needed to find him and shake his hand to see if it was firm and strong, or instead, if it went right through him—and proved he was a ghost . . . that I envisioned. And the last place I heard him was World Two . . . .

"I have to go back!" But then I remembered my principal trying to get me fired, and Nikita still stuck inside that mental institution. "I won't go back!"

Then a coconut came rolling up from behind me with two boys following it running. I reached down and lifted it and looked at it—remembering the game in World Two—then at the boys who reached me. I held it out to them.

"Thank you, mister. We were playing a game called, 'Kick the Coconut.' I found it by that tree over there." He pointed at the tree Old Man had been sitting by.

I pensively smiled and nodded and shivered again. "Yes I will return."

I mentioned it to *MYSELF*, and he was upset, "World One is reality—World Two lunacy. With concentrated mind and peaceful thoughts I was able to pull you back this time, but the more you're gone, the harder to pull you back."

I countered, "*You* didn't pull me back, *I* decided to come back. Old Man suggested it."

MYSELF answered, "Old Man isn't even real. Or if so, how do you know he isn't the Devil—pulling you into insanity?"

"For heaven's sake, Old Man is no devil! He gives advice. He had no horns!"

MYSELF countered, "But didn't he wear pointy shoes?"

"Ha! As if *that* proves something. Maybe *you're* the Devil!"

"Ha! If I am, then you are too!"

I countered, "If World Two is insanity, and he wants me there, why did he tell me to return to World One?"

"To make you think he isn't what he is—the master of deceit. The real thing to see is if he suggests that you go back!

Each time it's for a little longer—that's how he works—until the demons there take care of you and you can never return to the real world!"

"Be quiet!" I said and I turned around. But it made me think, *World Two is like a drug, enticing me. But is the drug good, and it is God—pulling me toward higher understanding? Or is the drug bad, and it's the Devil—pulling me into insanity?* I groaned, "No, I won't return."

Dusk was upon, as I pondered this, then a spotlight shone in the sky from a store in the city telling all to come—"just like in World Two!" I pulled the diamond out of my pocket and looked at it. I knew I must obey the beckoning. Surely all these things were miracles—not just coincidence. I couldn't say for sure, for there was no proof, but I thought they were.

Then at home, I received a letter . . . from Russia. In the top left corner was the name, Nikita Volkov! My hands shook as I opened it. It read, *I am so glad to receive your letter. I, too, believe in my other world, but also have a hard time proving it. But our common village by a lake seems to assure it. But you already heard me say that, so perhaps you are just mirroring what you heard me say. To know for sure, in the other world, find a monastery. Come back and tell me what looks down on it. I won't tell you what it is. If we match, we'll both know it's true.* "Yes I will return," I decided.

Then *MYSELF* buckled down, trying to convince me not to go. "Quit living in a fantasy world. You believe in miracles—in things that cannot be! You're going to bring us down. Connected by a climbing rope, when *you* fall, we all will go."

Who was he to say it wasn't real? And I wanted it to be! And I was the one with the chance to go! In World One how many get to look for dinosaurs, or see three moons and asteroids in light green skies? I loved the "looking-for," and being king of all I saw.

Our disagreement darkened my soul like stormy clouds obscure the light of the sun. I felt rage arise and surge inside at his judging me, until I felt that I might strike him. But again it caused uncertainty. *Maybe I should stay!*

That was the final straw, I guess, for the next day our town was consumed by thousands of ravens circling overhead—a storm cloud unlike anything ever seen before—at least in *this* world. The town was aghast. "Why are they here?" everyone asked. But *I* knew. The beckoning was becoming a demand!

World One was easier—funner, but it wasn't my destiny. *Something great must be at the light-beam if all of this is calling me—a reward so great—maybe it's a city made of gold!* I finally decided, "I *will* go back. I'm so close to the light-beam, I've got to go! But nine months from now I will return, for we have concerts to play all summer long."

So on the weekend I went to the park and I sat and watched, and thought—trying to get back. And I dressed appropriately, for how I was, is how I'd be. I was a blue-jeans, white T-shirt guy, but now I started wearing hiking boots instead of tennis shoes.

I envisioned the light-beam and how beautiful it is there—but the vision never caught—for I had forgot what the Elder said. I would need the journey there to see it like he did. Then I envisioned my peaceful, gentle, carefree meadow. But also there, I could never transfer. Then I found myself reflecting on lying on Dry Lake, and that is when the vision stuck and my consciousness was whisked away—and then my body, and my soul. I could feel being pulled . . . . *No! Not there!* I thought, and tried to stop. But I couldn't. I was becoming mist—sucked through an extended foggy tunnel. Then again I was lying almost dead upon the lake, still in the same dreadful condition as when I left—still as a corpse, except my eyelids sometimes slightly rising.

Through blurry eyes I saw, I think, a man with a black goatee looking at me (Goatee Man as I named him). He was holding a golden object that glistened in the sun. He bent and squinted when he felt my pulse. I discovered later, he then returned to the village and reported to the Elder, "He's almost dead on the lake. The knife may not be needed."

The Elder replied, "Keep it until we know for sure."

A lady in the same vicinity then heard a low, hoarse voice from all around, "Find a Rule out on the lake."

Sometime later, I felt cold, fresh water . . . on dry, blistered lips, filtering through teeth, over tongue, trickling down throat. Eyes opened to a lady's pretty face as my head lay upon her lap— her hair was short and blond. "Are you alive?" she asked with a voice sounding soft and sweet. I peered into her caring eyes and I couldn't talk (because of my dehydration, I'll say). More water until I sat up. With arm on shoulder—steadied—we walked off that wretched, dry, and killing lake. And although only slightly death-repaired, I could tell my arm felt good in its current position. I know I probably smelled like Hell, but my head was close to her hair and *it* smelled like Heaven.

Inside the edge of the jungle, she sat me down against a huge kapok tree in the shade, and I was thankful and told her so. In my weakness, my mind and eyes tried to process things. She was a lady about my age who wore a hat and pack, and held a spear. Standing in front of me, she smiled—and the warm way in which her lips were curved did touch me.

"Here, eat some of this," she said, and from her pack she gave me some flatbread. She ate as well and handed me her water.

As I ate, I looked at her and thought that maybe she was an angel sent to rescue me, for she looked like what I pictured one would be—and her smile convinced me further. Then I thought, *Wait. Is this the Scholar I was told to find?* Then I paused and thought . . . *or even perhaps Ms. Right?*

She finally asked with a soothing voice, "What were you doing out there?" And the way she asked made me know she was a caring soul.

(Then I thought about my students, surely disapproving of my looks in this condition, since currently I looked like death warmed over. "Mr. Tiz!" They would have frowned while shaking their heads.) I managed to talk in a raspy voice, as my throat was dry and damaged, "I just got back from a hidden village where I found a Rule."

Then she really looked and sounded interested, "How long have you been looking?"

"I'm not quite sure. I'm still quite foggy, but very long— many months."

"MONTHS?" she blurted, surprised, and pounded the end of her spear into the ground. She looked like she was about to cry. Then instead, in an instant her countenance changed, and her warm smile and soothing spirit left her in favor of a mean frown. "How 'bout something for my trouble?" she said like the neighborhood bully.

My eyebrows furrowed and I wrinkled my nose.

"Money!" she added abruptly, staring at me.

"Oh," I mumbled. I felt my pocket. Yes, there was something. I pulled out a wad of bills, opened it, and gave her one. I looked at her closer, "I think I recognize you from somewhere."

"Absolutely not," she said gruffly, and put the sharpened point of the spear on my chest and pressed. I winced and groaned a bit as it pierced my shirt and skin. She pushed a little more, and with raised eyebrows asked, "I'm sure your life was worth all of it, don't you agree?" Then she took the whole bundle. "For the rest of it, here's some advice: go around the lake next time—it's a killer!" She laughed, and seemed to try and make it sound sinister—but her laugh was cute and she couldn't disguise it. "That should make us even!" Before she left, she sneered and said, "Don't look so hurt, I'm just doing the same as done to me— I learned the trick from a man named Emgo who stole the same from me."

I tilted my head. "Emgo? If it's the same, then ... no, he wouldn't do that! He helps people."

She laughed again. "Yeah, he helps people—himself—to *my* money! And *I* helped *you* as well!" She said it sarcastically, but she looked and sounded bitter, and I got the feeling the meanness wasn't really in her.

What she said hurt me, for Emgo's people loved him so. I couldn't understand the contradiction and it hurt my head. I thought I'd like to ask him to explain himself, if this was really true.

I watched her walk away, and like her laugh, her walk was nice as well. And since I wasn't in a hurry, I continued watching. I sighed as I looked at the little spreading blood stain on my shirt where the spear had pierced. She hurt me, but I don't mean with the spear. She had seemed so nice (maybe Ms. Right)—and then to turn like that .... I frowned and a pain shot through my heart. In that fragile state I was, her compassion had tasted like pie—but then it turned, and her anger tasted like liver! "Definitely not the Scholar—nor Ms. Right." *Ms. Right—strike two.* I bowed my head and felt so alone and shut my eyes to hide them. But even though "Ms. Spear," as I named her, had stolen my money, I wished I had more time to find out where the bitterness in her came from. I would have liked to become acquainted with that nice, sweet side of her that I first met.

I looked back at Dry Lake and a thought occurred to me: *Killer that lake is, but I hadn't been looking for a nice, relaxing place. Sometimes through tears, you find a way around your fears; sometimes finding when not looking. Sometimes there are lessons only tears will teach.*

I sat back against the tree and rested for a while. But I was getting weaker. Still almost dead and getting deader, I listed. No energy to even move a finger then, just breathed—and listened, with drooping head and eyelids. I was fighting for my life. Then a mosquito buzzed around my head, and then another. I tried to wave my hand to discourage the little freaks, but couldn't move it. Then more and more came. Then landing on my face—and on my arms, and everyplace. And sticking me with needles. "Oh woe is me!" I cried.

"Is this the place I wanted to return to from World One?" I asked. "Not quite what I expected. Maybe I'll go back again." I tried to envision World One, but hard as I tried, I couldn't.

"Not time," someone said aloud. I silently gasped. Again it sounded like Old Man's voice—low and hoarse. But maybe it was really me—and I was pretending someone else was instructing me, for I was the only one there. I couldn't tell. My heart beat loud—goose bumps on my arms. I realized that life in World One had been more comfortable than I had thought—but now I was in World Two ... and couldn't get out. I heard an echo, "... *only tears will teach*."

Then a rat visited—and tasted. Gnawed at my finger and took some with him. No energy I had to deny him or to move my fragile body. But I wasn't to his liking—and he left.

Then high in the sky I saw a bird—bigger than I'd ever seen, and I remembered those giant tracks I saw—and the more I studied the bird, and the closer it got, the more sure I was: it was a Pterodactyl! Extinct in World One, but alive in World Two. As I watched, unfortunately for me, that was precisely when it happened to poop. I saw it coming down, down, down—a blob of sizable proportion. I closed my eyes and bowed my head and you know where it landed! Half on my head and the rest engulfed my chest and lap in a great KASPLASH! And the smell was not at all pleasant!

A skunk came walking next—from around a bush only three feet from me. Startled by my presence, she lifted up her tail and pointed in my direction. My eyes enlarged. *Is this really happening? Oh woe is me. Woe, woe is me! No, please don't.* She sprayed once with a direct hit, and looked behind to spray again. But then she smelled my wretched stench already from the Pterodactyl and figured she couldn't improve on that (for I saw her sniff and frown—then walk away). I closed my eyes in thanks that she resisted a final shot, and I decided things were finally getting better.

Eyes closed and mind drifted for a few minutes, and I thought about my fate and of this dismal place, and I felt my sad and lowly, empty thoughts come back. Here also lived my demons: my concerns and stress, barely enough for rent, doubts I had in myself, girlfriends that I didn't have, mean bosses that I did, family that had passed, all of my addictions, things I wished I owned, bad things I had done, fighting with myself: "I want dessert." "No, I want to lose weight." My head hurt with the thoughts. Then in my mind and all around came a shadow—and a foggy mist—thick and gray, and then the smell of a rotten, dead, decaying rat. Awful indeed it smelled. And I wondered who I was inside, for my adventurous side did not usually think these negative thoughts.

Suddenly I was awakened by a loud and vicious growl, and clenched teeth in my shoulder—shaking back and forth to pry it loose for Sunday dinner! "Ahhhhhhh!" I yelled in agony, the pain immediately exiting every pore in salty drops of sweat! The Beast was big and strong. From my poor vantage point I could see he was the size of a large bear, and looked like a mix between a wolf and bear with large bat-type ears, and a big rat-type tail, and saber tooth-type fangs (those I couldn't see, but the breaking bones inside my shoulder told me so). I could hear myself groaning and panting. My body flung back and forth, the Beast attacking from without, the demons from within, my heart ready to explode, and my head then hit a rock—with a loud and sickening thud! And within a few seconds, I felt peace—for I was floating—could see the scene from up above—looking down—slowly rising—blurry edges to the scene. Soul floating away, I guess. My blood I saw pooling under me. The Beast stopped and howled, informing others to come and feast. Then with the speed and fury of an explosion, out of a bush, an even bigger Beast fell upon the other, his hunger heightened by the howl he heard. The first one wasn't expecting this. Jaws tight on neck, constricting—the second one dragging him away, for *his* dinner!

I was lucky, I felt. At least I wasn't being eaten anymore (so I felt good about that), but now my life was over; my journey ended early—before the Rules all found, before the treasure maps discovered, before Elgobon achieved, before all historians would say, "Our greatest debt is to a man named Tiz, who discovered these things!" The skies were now quickly darkening with stormy, dreary, dungeon, hope-is-lost clouds, assembling, enveloping—themselves ready to pour and flood with wet and cold, and carry away in dark streams flowing, any last hope seeping from my corpse. All was dead. All was lost.

Oh woe is me. Why didn't I just stay in World One? Now all is lost. Now all is done. Old Man really was the Devil afterall—and he was successful! Now I'm dead. The misery!

Then I thought if I was alive, maybe all these awful things experienced were Pebbles—preparing me for a discovery. But I was not alive, and in my misery, my floating spirit noticed things. The song of birds—so sweet—still sung among the kapok tree's branches. As I floated up, the trees were so majestic from this vantage point, and still smelled so fresh and new. The grass where my dead body lay was so green and clean. I saw lightning—still flashing in the distance. A squirrel was next to me on the tree, taking a nut up to a hole. A woodpecker pecked. I was dead but life around continued. Didn't everything realize I was gone? All was done? All was lost?

It started raining—it too not understanding. Then I entered the stormy clouds. Rising—rising. Then through, and above. And guess what I saw? The sky. It was still clear and beautiful! Yes, it was dark and stormy and dead below. But here—no. Here it was clear and green and light and open and dry and gorgeous—and free! All was not lost, as it had seemed! Everything went on. I suddenly saw the world differently. I would remember this—in Heaven. Then as I gloried in this sight and this impression, I understood its significance—its grand meaning. The experiences *were* Pebbles!

And this was a Rule—come to me only after the greatest of all difficulty. I would remember THE RULE OF CLEAR SKIES: In whatever state or place you are, however bad it seems, goodness still exists—and it waits for you—like clear sky above dark clouds.

Then immediately with that thought, the cold, wet rain on dead face awakened me and I came back. Eyes opened. Death slinked and slithered away. Cold and Wet can freeze and drown, but they also can awaken, and enliven. I lay awake on the wet ground, with rain falling from dark skies. I did not move except my tongue out to get some drops, but eyes open ... and slowly— a slight smile ... that lingered; for I had conquered death a second time ... but those deaths were born of nature—and shortly it would be humanity to try and deal that deadly curse to me. But my smile stayed—for *I* had beaten the Devil.

In the grass, I saw a blue, uncut, rounded, polished sapphire, the size of a dime, and laid my hand upon it.

Chapter 6

The Deceit to Kill Me / The Holy Harp

Although it was day, the beam of light shone bright in the east, but never at night, and that I used as my heading. I envisioned a great party there—awaiting me. *Surely that's where the Scholar is.* So I was careful and sneaked along to escape from those Beasts and to find the Scholar—to save me from them . . . for I assumed this was the purpose of the Secret. I tried to envision traps I could use or make to kill the Beasts—but they seemed invincible, and I knew I would encounter more. *If I can just make it to the light, I will be okay*, I thought. My next threat didn't come from a Beast, though—it came from a conniving person—trying to kill me! And I was not aware, but the castle I dreamed of was soon to become reality.

I continued on my way, crawling on grass and dirt on a game trail through the trees and plants, shoulder limp, and eating enough bugs and ants and insects mixed with spit for a little protein shake, for I was too weak to look for other things. In this world, food was plentiful, my main sustenance coming from wild fruits and vegetables, and grains and roots, and beans and berries—also nuts. But sometimes I ran out, and something else to eat wasn't found for days or a week.

I managed onto my feet and staggered tree to tree for days. The ravens were still above and looking down and I continued to wonder why they waited, for I knew I looked like dinner. Maybe waiting till I was dead and then they'd feast on the still warm meat. Under them, in the trees, flocks of parakeets kept me company. With no nourishment, I had to look for anything to eat. I saw a frog—four feet long, and starving as I was, I thought he might be nice for dinner. But as I neared him, he vomited a wretched, massive glob of slimy, sticky snot that covered me— and made me reconsider. Then caterpillars marching by in hundreds made me salivate, but as turned out, they had piranha teeth, so they weren't the perfect french-fry-type treat (another chewed-up finger told me that)! But I did happen to find a wasp nest whose inhabitants I thought were probably filling; so after each one stung me, I popped him in my mouth, and soon I was full of black and yellow.

I continued walking, passing through a landscape filled with miles of steaming, multicolored, sulfurous pools. They were bubbling up from underneath or shooting up as geysers that whistled high with an airy "whoosh," or whistled low when falling. I traversed around and by those geysers like a cautious cat. When the sulfur bubbles burst, it sounded like a giant burp, and a nauseous light green gas spewed out like steam released from a tea kettle that I tried to duck beneath or go around. The smell was not delightful in the slightest to the nostrils (in fact I wondered if there were tons of chickens in caverns down below, laying rotten eggs)!

So bad was the stink that it made me think of things my students said—for gaseous smells make them the most animated, and their remarks the most infamous—and here it stunk like the whole class was doing them. "Oh, Mr. Tiz, how could you?" For they were always blaming me when one occurred. "Mr. Tiz, go outside next time—wait, I take it back, you might kill some plants—you're really bad today." And, "Oh, Mr. Tiz, you're really going strong! We don't need the pest control guy to come spray this month. You're doing fine." And, "Mr. Tiz, they make these diapers now for adults—to hold it in—at least think about it."

"It wasn't me!" I'd always say. "I do hold it in—without wearing *those* things." But they always ganged up on me, so you can imagine my suffering. But occasionally I would return a feeble rib, "Maybe if you guys brushed your teeth occasionally to freshen your breaths we'd be okay in here."

"Oooh, good one Mr. Tiz."

Days turned into months as my feet propelled me on and on, four months back from World One. The light-beam is what encouraged me—every day and week and month closer—the Scholar there with some unknown, eternal Secret that I needed. After the difficulty with the Beast, luckily the animals of that world had pity on me, for different animals started accompanying me. Sometimes as small as a chipmunk following that I picked up, or as big as a giraffe that walked along and I rode upon. Always with them, I'd jabber on, and we developed a special bond. The latest one a smart fox that was my friend. Animals here just aren't the same.

At night I smiled at the stars. They gave me room to contemplate: *How did this all begin? Where am I going?* I could tell that was important. As I did, the next question for *The Anthem of the People* came:

Why do we really ever start to breathe?

Often I would stand on the edge of a mountaintop or great plateau sometimes made from solid rock half broken and fallen away, so looking more like a giant fortress wall. Always then energy pulsed in me, and as its ruler I stood erect, Foxy by my side, and we looked out over the land we governed and soon would cross—the light-beam slowly growing in size as every day we got closer.

I heard howls behind me in the night, and knew that Beasts were on the prowl. One had tasted my warm, red blood and informed the others how good it was. I quickened my pace to reach the light—but I was actually surprised the Beasts hadn't found me yet—after months! And I snuggled closer to Foxy and her bushy, soft, warm tail.

On the plateau I currently stood, a herd of a million bison I watched, as it slowly moved below over grassy plains and scattered oaks. I descended to walk among, and hide me from the Beasts, and I traveled through those magnificent creatures on my way. Once, they spooked and ran, and I had to jump on the back of one and hold on tight to not be flattened out—Foxy frantically running beside until I was able to reach and lift her by the fur of her neck.

That dark night, I lay on the grass of those plains among the bison, and as I snuggled in my bedroll, baby bison as a pillow, I wished another person was with me to share the night spectacular … but I sighed, for it was quiet and I alone. But that's why I took breaks from my search and returned home. Between the bison's puffs of steam, I looked at a million shimmering stars in those skies of perfect clarity, and I envisioned myself up there exploring them in a little spaceship I had built. One constellation, very pronounced and clear, ahead and east of me, if connected dot to dot, was of a dog—and I named him Frisky. Over months, Frisky and I became quite close, for I was desperate to have more friends. I had never owned a dog before, but then I finally did; and he was a good dog—never threatening anyone.

[Eyebrows rose in the audience as they looked at the director who squinted and put his hand over his mouth.]

Lying there, I heard the echo of a distant howling—no—this one more like moaning, and I lay stiff listening, but it then abated. It sounded very sorrowful, and if it had continued, I would have tried to find and help that sorrowful thing.

*   *   *

Back at the jungle village, so far behind me and through the Dry Lake's deathly portal, Goatee Man spoke again to the Elder, "A lady was asked to help him, and saved him from the lake. And the Beast also did not kill him."

The Elder responded, "Someone is working against what we intend. Look at the stars and track Tiz closely, then pass through to where he is. Act tomorrow, but be stealthy and cunning in your deeds so we're not discovered."

*   *   *

That night, a man on a mission like mine lay at the edge of a barren wasteland waiting to start walking around it the next day. During his evening fire he heard a voice coming from the flames. It was low and hoarse, "Don't walk around. Walk across."

The next day I came to a tree limb hammered in the ground with an old, yellowed piece of paper pinned to it with writing that read: *The next Rule is found this way, only one day hence, so take no food or water.* An arrow on the paper pointed right. I had felt the path I'd chosen toward the light-beam was correct, but thought apparently someone was helping me. *Perhaps it was written long ago to help all those that followed.* But not bringing food or water made my pack much lighter—so I did appreciate the good advice, and I veered to the right.

Half a day later, I came to a barren wasteland in front of me—not a blade of grass, or cactus, or an ant, or a flea, an amoeba, or any living thing lived in that dreadful place—only the continual flocks of ravens flying high above—and following me. I was confused, for the paper said, "one day hence," yet here was this. But I figured the Rule must be on the other side, so I continued—but Foxy not accompanying farther. "Come on girl!" I said, but she sat tight and yelped a couple times. I didn't see, but someone watched from behind a tree and smiled at their successful cunning deed.

One day more I walked on hard, packed sand under an oppressive sun, passing only spires of salt, some rising as tall as me. The forest behind faded in the distance. I staggered on, fatigued and becoming weak, with nothing seen in front of me but the salt and see-through waves of heat. They didn't retreat as I approached, so I walked within—and the world around looked like a dream—like wavy glass I was looking through—an eerie place. And although the sun was not retiring, the reddish colors of a sunset rolled over, and encompassed the whole sky at noon. A day and a half without food or water, I sweat profusely, I stumbled feebly, I started feeling death come on again. But this was not Dry Lake, and death in *this* place was not something you returned from!

Then I saw a figure in the distance. After squinting, I determined it was a man trudging along, approaching me. (It was the man that was sent the opposite way.) I thought, *What would he be doing out here in this deserted wasteland?* As he came closer, we fell upon each other, and in a raspy voice, he told me, "Turn around or die, for there is no water for two more days, and I finished mine a day ago!"

I was so perplexed, for I was sure that's the way the note had said to go, and if I'd continued, I'd have been a corpse. So back we went. But I collapsed for I was too dehydrated. So we draped our arms upon each other's shoulders till the barren wasteland was behind us—Foxy waiting and yelping happily at the edge of the forest when seeing that I survived. Then in the oaks, alas, we followed Foxy who led us to water!

I wondered if the man was the Prophet, for he wore white, had facial hair, gave good advice and had performed a miracle to me. But he said, "No," he wasn't. He was on the same search as me, so we compared notes while eating dinner by a campfire. He was from Norway, blond hair like me, but his path was heading west—mine east, per the Elder's instruction. In the morning, we hugged and wished each other luck, and he went his way, and I back to where I came, with Foxy accompanying. But I wondered when I would meet the Prophet, for the Elder said I'd receive the most advice from him, yet currently nothing. He said to listen with humble and attentive ears. Maybe I just wasn't hearing—or didn't know how to look for him.

All I could figure was the sign that led me astray had been twisted by the wind—so pointing in the wrong direction. But when I came upon it once again, it was very solid where it stood. *Does someone want me dead? I've never hurt a soul!*

Then I saw someone in the shadows up ahead between two trees, amongst the many—just standing there—looking at me. Chills went down my back. When he noticed I had seen him, he quickly turned and started walking away. I yelled, "Get back here!" and ran to catch him. I ran through trees, but wind arose against me—slowing me down, then I came into a meadow where I saw him on its other side exiting the meadow, entering other trees, and although he was casually walking and I running, he was getting farther away. "Get him!" I yelled to Foxy, and she ran ahead. I tried running faster, but oh, how the wind blew against me, and then I was through, but I never saw him again. I sat and rested and thought, and eventually Foxy came trotting back. Her eyes were wide with fear and her fur in a tangled mess. I pet her and combed her hair with my fingers reassuring her. My best glance was my first. The person was far away, but it looked like a man, black hair and black goatee. It made me think of that fisherman from Dry Lake whose eyes I looked into.

I continued east, but now I had two things to guard against: the vicious villain hunting me, and more Beasts, but *I* would also be on the hunt, to stealthily find and catch the one who did the deed. I could have brought a gun for my safety, but I didn't believe in those—too much awful in World One as a result of them.

The songs of a great variety of birds thankfully accompanied me as I walked under their homes and hiding places in canopies of trees. Then something scared the birds away and while leaning on a tree to catch my breath, I realized I heard someone gently singing. I thought, *It must be Goatee Man and I can catch him.* Like a sleuth, I followed the singing, ducking and creeping to not be heard, until I thought I heard it right around some trees, but when I jumped into the opening, no one was there. I looked, confused, at Foxy, and she did too. I followed the sound, and it wasn't around the second or third set of trees, either. As I followed farther, it seemed the sound somehow carried perfectly—possibly for miles—like it was always just around another corner. Then besides the singing, I heard a harp accompanying. I followed that magical sound, for it pulled me, sounding almost holy—and no one that heard it could resist, it was so beautiful. It was like I was in a dream, being pulled. I was drifting along—feet seemingly just barely touching the ground. As I walked, the music inspired me, and I added words that flowed out of me—another song for my band to play, called: *There's a Dream,* and Foxy liked it, looking up at me: (There's A Dream, track 4)

There's a dream in my mind, that I have each night
and I can't get it out of my head

See some girls running past, on a field of grass
with their hair blown by the wind

Always in slow motion, wearing long flowing dresses
and one looks over at me

And I am caught, my sight held, by her reassuring smile
and her soft eyes that compel

Chorus:
Oh-- what does it mean, what's it trying to say
Oh-- what is the truth, that it's telling to me

Oh-- now I pray, for the dream to continue
so I'll know what it really means

there's a dream*******
there's a dream*******

Verse:

A year did pass, then two, and three went away
till a warm wind came and blew

and on a night that I tossed, and turned in my head
finally that dream went on

saw a beach at the end, of the field where they ran
and I saw her turn around

saw her beckoning forth, like an angel would from Heaven
saw her whisper "come with me"

Chorus Repeated

Don't know how, or why, but I felt my feet move
till she took hold of my hand

and we lightly walked, upon the water in the bay
till we entered in the boat

and to my surprise, it was only her and I
as the sails filled full with wind

and we held each other, with the wind in our hair
as the land behind disappeared

Chorus:
Oh-- finally I knew, what it was saying to me
Oh-- finally the truth, was revealed to me

Oh-- now I wait, for the dream to come true, yeah
and until then I live in my dream

Oh-- now I wait, but while I do, yeah
I sail with her on the golden seas

there's a dream...
there's a dream...

Yeah, if you come, to my house at midnight
you won't find me, I'll be in my dream

there's a dream...
there's a dream...

As I listened more to the other voice, I realized the singing was in a foreign language—one that I had heard before—yes, of the Elder! But I no longer recognized the words, for Dry Lake's water had washed away my understanding. Then I trembled when a thought occurred, *Was this the second trap by the deceiver—like a spider tempting me—calling me—soothingly, until too late when I was stuck inside its web?* It was like nectar pulling me, like I was a bee! I tried to resist, but I felt addicted to the sweetness of the harp's soft call—as if the words being sung were saying, "Come. Come here to me," and I had to follow as if hypnotized. Thoughts seemed forced into me, and I didn't think they were my own. They said, *I have to go that way anyway since it is east of me. I have no choice but to!* So I went—but stealthily, then if there was another trap maybe *I* would be the one to do the damage first!

Except for the music, and the beautiful sound of crickets I heard constantly in this world to keep me company, all was quiet as day had turned to moonlit night—bright enough to easily light my way. I followed through a land where no bushes grew, and trees with giant girth but slight height stood—their trunks so flexible they twisted slowly back and forth in the breeze, all creaking like swinging doors of old, abandoned shacks in ghost towns. Their branches arched like umbrellas over me, and some hung almost to the ground, so I sometimes had to part their leaves like a curtain.

I must say it scared me—and Foxy too, and I bent and pet and comforted her. Then out of the corner of my eye I saw movement and saw a Beast running past me fifty feet to my left, also going east. He stopped and looked right, then left for something. I froze, and hoped he would not see me in the shadows of the trees. Then several ravens decided he would be a tasty treat, and fell from the sky to pester him. He dodged and ducked and howled. Then I heard a distant howl ahead return and he proceeded running. Eventually I parted some leaves and saw something that stopped me in my tracks! Across a treeless open field, the bright rays of the moons shone through a hole in a cloudy sky upon an ancient castle up against a hill. It was half destroyed, with light coming through some downstairs windows—same castle from my dream! *The dream truly must have been a warning!*

I approached carefully, not knowing what I'd find and wary for my life from whatever was the trap that I was convinced awaited me. Crouching over, I crept closer and peeked inside a window, half expecting a face to pop up looking back at me—but no one was discovered. I continued looking through other windows until I made my way around the back, and in a barn behind, I saw a light. I snuck up and saw a lady seated, playing a harp and singing in that foreign language! I wondered, *Are those that speak it a band of evil? All in it together? If one doesn't kill me, the next one tries? I survived by Dry Lake, then the salt flat—now this?* I bent and pet Foxy for support.

I spied on the lady and felt my chest where the spear had pierced—this lady as well must not be trusted. A lantern lit the scene, and as she sang, two llamas stared at her in solid concentration listening ... and it seemed that they could understand, for they paid her close attention! As I listened, the song moved to the chorus, and I swear that I heard humming harmony, like from angels, but there was no one else around. I looked up, but none were coming down. Then, I swear again, I noticed those llamas' mouths were moving. And they were moving in rhythm to the music! *They* were the harmony! And they were good!

Now I had two suspects, Goatee Man, and Llama Lady, for both were in the vicinity of the failed trap, and I was cynical—trusted no one. And Llama Lady had just coaxed me there! I decided to show that I was not afraid and slowly I emerged from the dark into the light and leaned against the door frame. Llama Lady looked up, but wasn't surprised to see me. "Oh there you are," she said. She looked perhaps in her early-thirties, brown hair, and she wore a fancy hat which was most impressive—an old, wide-brimmed, faded-green, felt hat with a band of little flowers that lay around its base. She had glasses on, which looked expensive—fancy horn-rimmed ones. She wore brown leather walking shoes, an ankle-length beautiful, yellow dress, and a necklace made of braided vines with one copper-colored medallion, and beside her on a stand, an open book was there, and a pen with which to write.

When the song was done, she addressed me—in my language: "Well hello. You are quite the sight—my fellow. A little worse for wear, but happily I see, you're breathing still."

Happy? I bet! I thought with a sarcastic little smile, for I feared for my life. *She's upset I foiled her plan and still live! Why does she want me dead?* Then I remembered how I must look from frog snot, and Pterodactyl poop, and skunk pee that covered me, for I only had rain to bathe in. Also from all those mosquito bites, almost being eaten, being dead, and from so much wandering in near-starvation. "Yes," I said. "I was dead back there, but I'm alive again—so things are getting better."

Her eyebrows rose, surprised, "Oh my—well, I guess they would be better then, if back from the dead! That doesn't sound pleasant. Welcome to the castle. Us wanderers rest here from time to time. It's only me tonight, but I have some food on the stove inside—and per your looks, I think that you could use some, so come and join me."

Then poison food it is, I thought, for fear consumed me. *She doesn't know I'm onto her.*

We went inside where lanterns lit the room and we sat at the end of a long oaken table comfortable for twenty people. A fire in a large rock and mortar fireplace warmed the room. Quite the disguise she had perfected, for her apparel made her look the studious type—not a murderer. She prayed to God before we ate and thanked him for the food and delivering me. But before I ate the food, I watched her take the first bite to guard myself against the poison. Then, feeling more secure—and famished—with haste, I dished up mine from the exact same bowls, and in quick repetition started eating big mouthfuls. I asked her where she was going, and she said, "To that giant lake quite a ways west of there."

Hmm, I thought. *Is that the truth? Why would she travel to a dead, dry lake?*

"Oh no!" I said to her, with a piece of bread inside my mouth. "That's no good—it's also dead like I had been." I took a spoon of soup and then continued before I took another: "Dry as a bone—except for probably mud now from that stormy deluge."

Llama Lady tilted her head and squinted at me. "I was at the lake not long ago, and it was filled, and beautiful, with marigolds and green grass all surrounding." Then she stopped and realized something. "Oh, wait a second, I forgot when this is. You're from there and then . . . . Okay . . . yes, it would be barren then. And that storm you said there was—you rose above its clouds, I bet. Okay, I see—that storm was only yours."

I just looked at her and thought—not understanding. *This lady's words are mass confusion, she's demented, I would say. A crazy lady. But how did she know I rose above the clouds?*

Silence for a little time—and we ate our bean and noodle stew, vegetables, and bread, and drank milk from her llamas. Then with soft compassion in the sound of her voice, she asked, "What finds you here, my friend? Why have you come?"

I stared at my plate and continued chewing. After a while, I responded, "It's a long story, but I come for Pebbles, and Rules, but the most important of all is the greatest of all treasure maps."

Then I studied her, and the book on the table she brought inside. The killer had totally preoccupied my mind, but I suddenly remembered my current mission to find the Scholar—and I realized she looked like one! *But she's demented, and I figured the Scholar was at the light-beam*, I thought. I had thought she was the killer, and maybe still I did, but now I wondered. I looked into her eyes.

When I did, she also studied me—gazing in my eyes, holding my sight transfixed, seeming to study what was within. I couldn't blink. She breathed deep. It was an effort—her face strained, beads of perspiration on her forehead. I saw her age before my eyes—wrinkles forming on her face. She heavily exhaled and weakly stated, "You seek a Scholar and her Secret, don't you?"

I was shocked, and wondered how she knew, and I couldn't speak. I nodded as I thought, and then found myself mumbling, "Are you her?"

She smiled. "Well, I've read a lot, and studied much, and thankfully I've learned a bit. I guess some do call me that." She paused. "But you can call me Brinlin." She extended her hand and we shook, and I introduced myself as well. I told her in my mind I had been calling her Llama Lady, but Brinlin was good as well. She laughed and said, "I like that. I'll take it as my nickname." I looked at the open window with the llamas looking in, and they turned and smiled at each other.

I decided she probably was the Scholar, for how else would she know for what I searched, or that I rose above the clouds? I was so relieved. I found who I needed to, and now would know the Secret! With eagerness, I smiled and asked her for the Secret, but she said she hadn't yet discovered it . . . for it was inside of *me*!

"Everyone requires a different one," she said, "for everyone needs saving from something different. So I have to find it in *you*—what *you* need! Give me time." Her eyebrows rose, and she inquired, "So you were saying you were dead back there? But now you're here! Tell me your story—your death and revival, that's something I don't hear every day."

"It was a Beast—of the worst imaginable type. He clenched and thrashed, and I was back and forth like a little rag, until my head hit a rock—and crack! I was done!"

She squinted and looked at my head with a blank expression. "I'm not seeing the aftereffects. To tell you the truth, no Beasts exist—at least not in this world."

What? I asked myself with squinted eyes and wrinkled nose. *What is she talking about?* I was mad—for someone even suggesting no Beasts existed ... when I had just been ripped, and shredded, and killed by one! I saw my own limp body in his mouth—from up above! And I saw one running through the trees, and heard it howling.

I confronted her: "What do you mean there are no Beasts? You're wrong! Even an Elder said a man named Emgo defeated one not far from here. Not only that, but my shoulder still carries the ugly wounds!"

I lifted my shirt off my shoulder to show her, but no wounds were left. I sat dumbfounded and confused .... *They healed so quickly!* This time, *I* was the one with a blank expression.

She laid her hand on my shoulder and with an understanding voice said, "I'm sure the meaning of the Elder's words you just misunderstood. There are no Beasts—you need to look within yourself! You are seeing things that are not there."

That hurt me. Now someone else was telling me I was crazy. And I hadn't only seen him, I had felt his gnashing teeth! *I'm not crazy ... am I?* I thought, *This other world is filled with confusion. Who's telling the truth to me? Is it the Elder and his people, or this lady who I think is the Scholar? I must find out, for I know what I saw and felt.* I squinted. Thoughts bounced around my head .... *My healed wounds seem to support this lady. If she is right, then why would the Elder lie to me? Why try to make a fool of me? What was his motivation? Who is he? The Devil in angel's clothes?* My head was throbbing trying to understand.

Over several minutes, as my stomach filled, my mind relaxed, and we sat and talked that night in front of the fireplace while watching the fire's dancing flames, and I got to know her. The company was so appreciated, for talking only to yourself for months and months makes you sort of crazy (and demands of you friends like Frisky).

The next day we relaxed around the castle, did chores, ate and talked. She listened closely, trying to understand me, and when looking at each other, I saw her sight fall deep inside of me, staring into my eyes, studying what was within, and always then my body was paralyzed as she searched. And for her it was no easy task—straining to look, trying to find. It had affected her health, now weaker—bags under eyes, paler, much older, slower.

I found out she was also on a journey, but mainly in another world she called World Three, where she was looking for a grotto and the keys leading to it. Her voice heightened, and words quickened when she told of many things she'd seen and done, and she laughed at many mistakes she'd made. She was a compassionate, tender soul, but also full of flavor. I mentioned Old Man and she smiled and said she knew him. "He often visits a beautiful lake on the top of a mountain. There is often lightning there. And on another mountain, not far past, is where your journey ends."

I thought, *There's lightning there? Like Hell might be, where the Devil lives?* then asked, "Is it true that he's the Devil then?"

"HA! Of course not! Why would you think a thing like that?"

I felt embarrassed.

On day two she studied me further—staring harder in my eyes. Her face was now an old lady's face—tired—drooping. She bent over as she walked. She coughed a lot. I was worried for her life! I felt awful and told her to stop looking—that maybe she'd revive, but she said she would be okay.

I realized her name triggered a memory ... I had heard it once before! It was the name of a famous lady in World One, in Canada. Brinlin Tremblay had developed a website for volunteers, which branched into a think tank of medical professionals for treatments of serious illnesses. That branched into a full-service medical corporation called Tremblay Research, which became one of the largest medical companies in the world. Brinlin was still in charge, but had started spending most of her time in the charity arm of the company, where she donated tens of millions of dollars every year.

I looked at her wondering, and asked, "You're not the Brinlin from Canada, are you? Tremblay?"

She smiled. "You guessed right."

"Oh my gosh, are you kidding? Really? Why are you here? If you're so successful in World One, why submit yourself to these difficulties on these journeys?"

"Ha!" she laughed. "The same reason as you, of course. I knew there was more, and only through struggle can you find it. I felt that riches and ease are not the final goal."

"Congratulations on your firm," I said.

"It's what I was able to do with it that's most fun. But I'm not naturally an entrepreneur. It happened after the Rules and Maps, so they deserve the credit. I just followed the path they showed to take."

At dinner on the third day, as we sat across from each other and ate and talked, Brinlin was staring even longer inside of me. Besides my thoughts, she took my energy and breath away. She kept pulling harder, and I was getting weak. But her even weaker—face tense, groaning slightly, sweat pouring down her temples. She started to shake. Her hair had turned gray—decades had been added to her age. She put her hand over her heart and started panting. I asked what I could do for her, but she held up her hand and shook her head.

Finally she closed her eyes and looked down at her plate and exhaled sharply—then inhaled. And I fought to catch my breath. She looked sick, as if about to faint, but then she lifted her head slowly and thinly smiled. "I found it!" she weakly said.

I was shocked and elated. This was required for my final goal, and to be saved. "What is it?" I quickly asked.

"Listen close. This is the Secret for which you search: When one looks at anything, one sees all the matter. The molecules form touching things that seeing is so easy. But more can see than just the eyes, but only done if practiced. Look within to understand— look without and gather. If you look in *all* the ways, and differently than others, all the mysteries now untold, to you will come unraveled."

I was so disappointed! All her effort for that? I was wanting something I could hold, thinking the Secret might tell me how to kill my Beast, or how to make a good bow to practice archery on the killer.

Without me saying so, she perceived this and told me, "Exactly the reason you received the Secret that you did. You're too temporal, looking only for things you see! The Secret will save you from something worse, and more dangerous than a killer or a Beast ... for *those* you can see, but *this* you can't—and it will overtake you!"

Something I can't see? More dangerous than a killer or a Beast? I thought. *What could be so dangerous if it's not even seen—if it can't even touch me? When will it attack, and how will I defend myself from something I can't see?* I asked her but she said she didn't know, however she could feel it was close. It would attack when I was least prepared.

That night Brinlin disappeared for a while beyond the barn—she said to talk to the stars. She limped heavily away bent over. I asked how I could help and offered to go with her but she said she had to be alone. I hoped she wasn't leaving to dig her grave. I regretted, *Am I the reason she will die?*

I sat in front of the fire pondering her words for an hour. She finally returned and I sighed with relief that she was still alive. But I was absolutely shocked, for now she looked renewed like when I first met her, younger, no longer weak or sick—now energized and healthy, skin radiant, looked rested, big smile, no wrinkles, hair brown again. I was astonished and perplexed. I asked, "What happened? How can this be? Why so suddenly healthy?" But all she said was she renewed herself.

The next morning, before she awoke, I got up to enjoy the sunrise. I walked beyond the barn to see it, which I had not yet done, and—WHOA! There sitting on the dirt, leaning back against the barn four others were also watching the sunrise . . . but they were skeletons! And the last one looked like fresh, new bones! "Oh my gosh, who were these?" Then again I worried about the killer—and again if it was her! She hadn't wanted me to go with her, and once I had thought she was a crazy lady— perhaps correctly. Had I stumbled onto a serial killer? A Doctor Jekyll and Mr. Hyde? Scholar by day—killer by night? Was she working with the Devil? She, as his helper, pulls people to the castle through some magical, musical spell, claims their energy, and then extinguishes them? Was the newest skeleton a traveler that came last night whose blood she sucked, then did away with? She hadn't done *me* yet—but was she planning to? I had been sure she was a Scholar but was it all pretend—the Secret just made up? Or were the bones the work of someone else looking for me to be their next?

On tip toes I entered the castle looking around. Brinlin was up and packing and I dared not speak of what I found—then for sure she'd do me in. Had I been targeted as the next, on our last night together, narrowly escaping death in my sleep by my early waking? As I watched her pack, regardless of my questioning, it hit me that again I would be alone, and loneliness fell hard upon me. I was contradicted. Even though I wondered if I should fear her, I questioned if there could be anything between us. But for some reason, that thief Ms. Spear, that stole my money and stabbed me, crowded in my thoughts, and I didn't know why, given what she'd done. I tried to get her out, but her face, and initial smile and compassion, and the little freckles on her cheeks were implanted there. Fear or not, I didn't want the Scholar and her company to leave me. I liked her Doctor Jekyll, and the words squeezed out of me, "Are you sure I can't come with you?"

Brinlin walked closer and I became nervous. Then she reached and held both my shoulders in her hands. I stiffened a little. With a little caring smile and a soft gaze, she looked up into my eyes. "I'm sorry, but my path can only be mine alone—you'd find no Pebbles. Being told, or reading them in a book, without the experience, negates the lessons learned from them. It would be easier if we could just follow someone else, but we don't learn enough that way. In the end it's *us* that determine our fate. *We* are the ones that must DO! Following or learning doesn't *make* it happen. It's lonely, I know, but to the stars talk often, give thanks, commiserate, update, ask, and meditate. Good luck, friend. Your next task is to find the Disciple."

"Why?" I asked.

"For you I've discerned it's to ask for the Truth. I feel you'll need it to escape."

"From what?" I blurted out, concerned.

She dropped her hands and thought while looking at the ground. Then she looked at me. "Let me look." She took my hands and again I cringed. I looked at her and she stared at me— and studied what was within. "The vision is blurry, but I see you locked inside some sort of dungeon maybe—all dark inside, your arms tied up!"

She added, "I know you desire to find the Gate. If you find it, steady and brace yourself when it opens, and maintain hope while it unfolds, to make it through your agony! But before you make it that far, an impassable entrance of evil you must confront. Prepare yourself correctly or, believe me, your pain will make you wish you had. Besides the Truth, the Disciple will share, she holds the Clue to make it past that barrier. Without that knowledge, you are dead." I shortly gasped, and noted mentally.

Then she told me that rent for the night was tending to the garden. I couldn't help but hug her, for Mr. Hyde or not, I had received a Secret that might save me and I had grown to love her soul. I thanked her greatly. She kissed me on the cheek and then I watched her walk away with her llamas, and I wondered if I needed food, for I felt so empty then inside. I then heard her start to sing, moving her hand a little in the sky, and I heard two other voices start to hum. As I watched her walk, her and the llamas faded away—till she was gone. That is when I thought, and then I realized that when the Gate opened, I might also share some similar powers, and might sing and play a holy harp with llamas joining in upon the waving of my hand.

Chapter 7

Splitting My Personality in Three / "It Cleans Your Insides Out"

Rule #3: OF THE MIRROR

Tiz took another break from his speech to take a drink and he heard audience members talking to each other: "It's a demented grand illusion, for how could he evade Beasts like that?" "Or the killer," another said, "why didn't he just club Tiz when he was sleeping?" Another mentioned, "But I remember the day those ravens came, and experts couldn't explain it." And one other, "Ha! Did he have to take years and travel to a foreign place to find such simple Rules?"

Tiz continued, and first looked at them, "You're exactly right! And that's when I realized that too. The Rules *were* too simple! I could have discovered those in World One. So why did Old Man really want me in World Two? What was his ulterior motive? I began to know it wasn't really the Rules. Was I his pawn he was using for his own purpose? I had to find him and demand to know. And regarding time, it wouldn't seem it would take years, but it's very hard changing who we naturally are— and it *does* take years—a lifetime! And although the Pebbles and Rules are simple, are they really that easy to find? Have you recognized the Pebbles under *your* feet? And have you found the necessary Rules for *your* life, and have they really impacted you so much that you understand their worth and they have *changed* you? The quote is true, 'Sometimes you must travel far to see what's near.' Great accomplishments grow slowly. Greatness takes time."

Tiz paused and looked around. He frowned and thought out loud, "In World Two all I do is wander—and occasionally I come upon a Rule. This is the same in World One, for those that look. So maybe its true—I was just envisioning what I was finding in World One." The audience was confused. He had been so sure. And many wanted to believe. Tiz continued, "Like I said, *you* will have to decide." He paused again. He looked discouraged. He spoke, "Maybe we should end this now and I should go back with the director."

Many from the audience yelled, "Tiz, even if not true, it's the greatest dream I've ever heard and I want to find out who was trying to kill you—or was it really just your mind dealing with the difficulty of the principal?"

Tiz quickly responded emphatically, "No! That wasn't it! I found out later who was trying to kill me. That I know for sure. I wish it was just the stress of the principal. That would have been easy." Paused again, "Look, if everyone agrees I'm crazy, I'm not continuing. I'll admit defeat. Let's take a vote. If one of you believes, I'll continue." There were many that yelled, "We love you Tiz." "Hang in there." "It's what *you* believe. That's all that matters." "It's okay, we believe. Did you defeat the Beast?" "Did you pass the Gate?"

Tiz surveyed the audience, sighed, then closed his eyes and slowly breathed. He spoke slowly, "There's a song in my children's book. Chisel Hedgehog and his friends realized the same thing I did: it's *how* you look at things that matters:" (If You Look, track 5)

If you look, at the world

from the place, where we look at it now

You will see, differently
you will see, things aren't what you thought

Come with us, take a ride
see the world, through a whole different light
from a whole different view

Chorus:
For it's howwwwwwwwwwww, how you look, what you see
yeah, it's howwwwwwwwwwww, how you look, what you see
come with me

Verse:
If you look, at the world
through new eyes, you'll know what we mean

What was brown, now is green
and the green, changed significantly

Maybe bows, in the sky
are really just, shades of black and white
just colored with different eyes!

Chorus Repeated

    Tiz then continued.]
    I stayed a couple weeks at the castle recuperating—enjoying World Two sunrises with the skeletons unlike any sunrises in World One. When the sun first appeared, for several minutes, its rays slightly sparkled like millions of tiny, white fire crackers exploding above against the new morning light-green sky. Then they would fade away.

As I experienced life with the skeletons, I found them not that bad, and named them Sk1, 2, 3, and 4. As we talked, I could tell they liked my jokes, although they didn't laugh—except once when after my joke their teeth all chattered at the same time the wind arose. But my cooking wasn't to their liking for they never accepted my offers. At nights Foxy always showed up to share some dinner, and we sat together overlooking the grassy valley with scattered trees below, pondering as the sun moved lazily down in multi-colored shows of muted light—the fireworks seen then as well. And to the stars, and my Frisky dog, the skeletons, and Foxy too, I played a six string ukulele that I made—fashioned after those at the village. I spent good time on its construction, with a hollowed gourd as body, chiseled limb for the neck, and strings of dead leopard gut. Every day thereafter as I walked, I played, and those strings became an extension of my fingers and I spent days perfecting songs with a World Two flavor.

Then one morning, I said good bye to the skeletons. The light-beam tugged at my soul. I hopefully thought, *Maybe that's the end, and the treasure is there!* I doubted it, but the Elder said a reward so great, forever I'd be changed by it—and I had to go!

I invited the skeletons to come but they didn't budge, so I shook their hands, and continued on my journey heading east to locate the Disciple—*Maybe that is where she is,* and to reach the light-beam. I could tell the skeletons were a little sad, but they had each other so I didn't feel bad. Foxy showed up, but not to accompany! She had found a friend—a male fox to share her time—and she looked content. I looked him over, deciding he looked okay, and gave my consent and blessing—Foxy and her beau smiling. She and I had been through a lot, and I bent and kissed and hugged her, and said I was thankful, before I left.

The scary trees changed to a forest that looked like bamboo, but much more flexible, as thin as my arm—growing in a spiral motion. They were thirty feet tall, and swayed back and forth immensely in the breeze. Then I wondered ... and I pulled one down with effort, straddling its end, holding onto two others beside me. I let go, and the bamboo sprung forward and propelled me high into the air, above and past some birds (my arms and legs flailing in all directions until I got my balance, and then I looked like a speeding bullet), for that bamboo was like a spring! When coming down, I landed on another and held on until it bent the way that I was going, then I let go again—and my journey continued speedily. Once while in the air, I saw a pack of Beasts running below, just in front of me, snarling at each other as they ran, so I held on tight to the next bamboo I caught, and it bent almost to the ground, catching up to the last one of them. If I had reached out I could have scratched his back, but the bamboo and I were perfectly quiet, so the Beasts never knew that I was there. Then I watched them run ahead.

Over a month of circling moons I walked—and verified by lengthened beard, and longer hair, and nails that I chipped away—the beacon of light always bigger, and brighter, and closer—me smiling. I was never bored, for Chisel Hedgehog was always with me, telling his story—and every night I wrote it down. And my time alone gave me time to think—and wonder. My next question to the concert crowd:

Where do we travel when we go to sleep?

Finally I walked through normal trees again—now hickories, maples, and pines—all beautiful green, and through valleys they were in—lined and protected by towering walls of granite. Around or over boulders and streams, I went, making my way through elderberry and mountain laurel bushes. Rabbits and marmots I often saw, and ground squirrels' warnings I did hear. At night, those ground squirrels crowded in around me to have some different company—and nice company they were in turn— except a few skirmishes deciding who got to sleep on my stomach. The weather was mild, or rain sometimes, humidity, wind, or scorching heat. I was spooked a bit when through trees the wind arose, and clouds approached, and shadows showed, and distant animals I heard wailing.

I chose to sleep on a hill under a large and dead old tree—plenty of limbs but leaves all gone, and I hid between its trunk and a clump of large bushes, for no trap or defense against the Beasts had I invented. The sky was full of threatening clouds—black and menacing—a crack in the distance, and then thunder was heard. Before I lay, I worried about this world's obstacles, then looked down from my hill to survey where I'd come. Under the full moons shining bright, between the clouds, I squinted when I saw perhaps twenty large animals spread out in the empty valley crisscrossing the path where I had been. They had their noses to the ground, seemingly trying to find a scent. And I was suddenly, drastically worried! Then I heard one bark and howl, and the others quickly ran to where he was, and they all looked up the hill and started howling. They were a hundred yards from me, and they started sprinting up the hill.

My nerves were so much agitated, I immediately felt beads of sweat, and my breathing intensified and I felt pain inside my chest. I calmed my heart by pretending I was by that peaceful lake in World One, and I decided to climb that tree to save myself, but at that moment a great and sudden thunderous sound of fluttering wings erupted like an explosion, and every limb above me of that great tree was filled with hundreds of ravens cawing. The ravens that couldn't find a place to land, flapped their wings while looking for space, so above me was mass hysteria, then with no space left, those who couldn't land, flew away. *AHH*! I thought. *The ravens are finally ready to feast on me!* I crouched down lower inside my hiding place, hiding from the ravens above—hoping they had not seen me, and through my bushes, watched the animals approaching on a stampede—still sniffing the trail they were following. Then I recognized those animals were Beasts—the type that had killed me, and as I thought of being torn apart, my stomach retched with stress—but I tried to temper it with calming breaths—quickly in and out. When the Beasts were ten feet from my little clump of bushes around my tree, they stopped and I could hear their raspy breathing, smell their sweaty bodies, and my heart was about to explode, for I knew that I was dead! I closed my eyes and focused on tranquility, but I was surrounded! The ravens had me from above—the Beasts below, and there was going to be a bloody feast. I opened my eyes and saw the Beasts' heads rise from the trail and look up at the raven-filled tree—a dark umbrella of dreadful noise, with jagged, pointy, threatening beaks, and they suddenly didn't care about my scent, and flowed around my bush and tree and continued running faster east. When the howling finally passed me by, the ravens all departed as a blackened cloud of thunder, and I was left alone. "Oh my gosh!" A sigh of relief escaped me. "How lucky can I be the ravens happened to perch in that tree?" As I tried to relax, I noticed the howling of the Beasts went east—the ravens following, and that was my direction too, so that was disconcerting. I laughed at the words of the Scholar, though, that I remembered: "There are no Beasts .... You are seeing things that are not there."

I thought, *She obviously hasn't seen what I have seen—or heard or smelled or felt! And I didn't even tell her about the ravens!*

Luckily I had my harmonizing crickets always serenading, and that comforted me to hear them. As I listened, it seemed I heard them practicing different pieces, for their music's flow occasionally changed. But even more, looking up, I felt consoled as Frisky stood there looking down. I could tell he cared, and I appreciated it. I taught him some simple little tricks like playing dead, and told him my insecurities and secrets, and he always listened—never interrupting, always empathetic. "Thank you, Frisky."

*   *   *

At the jungle village, the Elder was speaking to Goatee Man, "Again he survived?"

"Yes. This time from the barren wasteland."

"Who saved him?"

"A man was told to cross the wasteland from the opposite direction that Tiz was headed. It was he who saved him."

"Be more vigilant next time and even more cunning to get the upper hand against the one who counters us. Tomorrow you must use your plan."

*   *   *

The clouds remained, and the next day, although I did not see, but found out later, some distance behind me hidden in a thicket of gooseberry bushes, a man's arms were moving above. The man instructed the ravens with his low, hoarse voice and flowing movement of his hands, "Move right, move left." Then the flock of a thousand ravens obeyed. "Be ready when I tell you."

The following day I found another sign pinned to a tree. Again it pointed in a different direction, away from the light-beam, and with a similar paper note saying which way to find another Rule. At first, I thought it was another trap, but I so much wanted help, and lately hadn't found a thing, and wondered if I was going right. A lynx was my co-traveler, so I asked him what *he* thought—but he was okay with whatever I decided. I still had hope in other people, so after much deliberation I decided to try it out. *Maybe the prior sign's direction was a mistake and there really is no killer,* I optimistically thought. I learned from my past mistake, though, and was more cautious this time and brought my food and water.

I walked for an hour and the forest grew thick of old-growth foliage—hard to make my way through. Then suddenly the ravens came charging—falling from the sky in hundreds, attacking me from my left in waves of diving, pointy beaks, flapping wings, and cawing, flapping anger. *Finally they're hungry,* I frantically realized, as I covered my head with my arms and fled to my right to escape—clawing and pushing through bushes to evade the ravens. Lynxy ran along, using bushes over him as his defense.

Then I came out of a thicket, and before I realized where I was stepping, I stepped off one of those granite cliffs! I yelled as I fell, and grabbed for everything! Dirt and rocks slipped under clawing hands and then my feet hit a root which slowed me down, and I grabbed it with a single hand and desperation showing in my eyes—wide and frozen. I hung there breathing in and out, my lungs expanding massively—full and empty to their full capacity. I wondered if I would die yet once again. I looked below a thousand feet, and to the right and left it was a sheer, straight cliff as far as I could see—like the edge of the world I'd just walked off. I looked above and saw Lynxy cautiously looking down at me, meowing. I was lucky I fell at this exact place, for to my right and left there were no roots to hold. I knew it now for sure—someone set me up to this. They were helping me alright—helping me into my grave!

Then Old Man's voice I heard, "Think carefully before you act."

Good advice Old Man, I thought, *but too late for any good. Why didn't he tell me that <u>before</u> I fell? What good is that now? These threats aren't in World One, and it was Old Man that compelled me to come.* I had to think again, *The Devil smiling as he plays with me?* I realized, *This world is a dangerous place. So many threats to do me in!*

I fought my way back up, squeezed against the cliff, with precarious handholds on roots and rocks protruding out, wishing my sweaty hands were dry. Finally I was up and over, and on my back, and I lay panting for quite some time. Lynxy was so happy I survived he stood there licking my face until my spirits improved and I smiled—then laughed, and said, "Okay, okay, that's all." Then I made it back through to where I'd started at. I fumed and ripped that note and looked around. My heart was heavy, knowing someone hated me. After all my trials and loneliness, it was like a spear into my heart. I had to discover who was doing this and why they wanted me dead. For a couple hours I looked for clues, widening the circle I searched, but in the end, I hadn't found any, so would look the next day too. That night, I asked Frisky if he saw who did it—but he didn't hear me—so I think that he was playing dead like I taught.

As sun faded, the light-beam too, but during the day I was thankful for it. Lynxy and I took energy from it. I was almost there! I dreamt of the party awaiting me—a great shindig happening!

Winter was half way done and night delivered a frosting of snow, a flock of sheep, keeping me warm as they squeezed around Lynxy and I—Lynxy purring loudly in my ear. The next morning, I awoke to keep looking and above the pine trees a little way off, I saw the smoke from someone's nearby morning fire. In a flurry, I threw my things into my pack and started running on an animal trail through the woods to where it was. Within a hundred yards of the fire, I saw someone exiting the camp and walking away on the trail. Surely this was my assassin! "Stop!" I demanded, and he looked back, but then continued. It was Goatee Man again. He rounded a bend and I lost sight. I followed, running, but the clouds suddenly poured down on me. Up ahead, I saw him walking, still on the path—sunny where he was, but farther away from me. "Get him Lynxy!" I yelled—hoping he would have more luck than Foxy did. But eventually as the trail wove in and out of trees, Goatee Man was gone and Lynxy came back empty handed—quite wet, disheveled, and meowing. I spit on the ground, upset. *It must be him!* So I developed a plan to catch my evil malefactor hunting me. *But he is smart and fast, so I must be cunning and pick the moment right*, and I bid my time to when I decided I would spring it. I laughed, "Soon I'll make the final move and make him pay for this!"

I tried not to complain—my dad had taught me that, in how from him I had rarely heard it. But I was not as good. All of it was getting to me—more Beasts and getting closer to me, the Elder instructing but the Scholar contradicting, fake notes posted to try and kill me, endless searching, starving, dying—and those wasp stings—ouch! I was getting little sleep and always wary, and my heart beat quicker steadily. I thought that I might lose my mind. So the decision was made to return to my first world for a break—but then I hesitated and wondered who decided that? For although life was hard, *I* didn't want to go, and *I* had left *MYSELF* at home already—so who was there to disagree? I gasped. Was my personality splitting another time? And now there would be three? Yes, I truly was going crazy! After thinking, *I* admitted: "The third is *ME* who wants to go—but it hurts my head to realize it. I can't keep the different sides of myself together! He is yet a different side of my personality. I thought and realized—he's the logical side of myself, for it did make sense I should take a break. *I* am more impetuous. *ME* takes things step by step—evaluating, before deciding what to do. It was *ME* back home who made our critical decisions—what college degree to get, where to live, what things to buy. "That new car is too expensive. We can't afford it."

I responded, "Give me a break, it's so nice. I want it!"

He is our decision-maker and I depend on him—although I often don't like it. Like *MYSELF,* he is more cautious than *I. I* would have to make them go when bungee jumping off a bridge. *I* didn't care if it made sense. "Quit thinking so much, just do it, it looks fun. Life is short."

Then I heard a voice from all around; it was Old Man's, who said, "The dead hold a clue to a Rule that is close. You'll soon pass through the dark place where they live. Live with them and learn."

After hearing that, the *ME* part of myself really wanted to go home, and he started taking steps backward! "I'm not doing that!" he said. "I'm not living with the dead! We need to go and take a break. This is exhausting *ME. MYSELF* was right, it's another trap the Devil conjured up!"

Nor did *I* want to live with the dead, and worried about the Devil, but felt I must if there was really a Rule ahead. "No, we shouldn't go back! He said the next Rule is close, and that's why we're here." I said. "*I* want the Rules that lead to that treasure map and all I'll receive from it, and I'm intent on finding it!" I looked ahead, and said, "And the light-beam is so close—and the party and reward there!" I tried to convince myself and spoke out loud, "Living with the dead is not that bad!"

ME countered, "Yes the dead are that bad. Any logical person would see. We should go back. Don't you see? The Devil is pitting us against each other—deepening the hole of insanity."

"Baah!" I opposed. "I believe in him. He answers me. He isn't the Devil."

I started breathing heavily—upset at myself for disagreeing .... No. I mean upset at *him* for disagreeing! Wait ... I shook my head confused at who I was referring to, "Ahh!" My tone was raised—again my split personality was raising its ugly head, "I already fought this battle with *MYSELF*. Who invited you? You do what you want. I'm staying!" Again, those stormy clouds darkened my soul, and I clenched my fists and raised them up to be ready to go.

ME also did the same—and breathing hard. It was a standoff. I circled, crouched and bobbing up and down, hands in fists, up and ready, waiting for him to throw a punch. Lynxy was confused, unaware who the enemy was, but circled as well—snarling and pawing in the air—claws out to defend us. Then after several seconds, *ME* yelled, "OKAY, FINE. THIS TIME, WHAT *YOU* WANT—NEXT TIME *ME!*"

[The director raised his hands and put them behind his head, pursing his lips—eyebrows raised.]

When *ME* said that, I heard thunder behind me, and felt a warm wind begin to blow and a dark energy within it. I looked behind me and saw the clouds unite as one of darkness in the sky and approaching quickly. Its front was mainly dark gray with scattered white around it, and some within, so it looked possessed—like the open mouth, and snarling teeth of a wild wolf gone crazy with rabies. It was coming to devour us. It was a devil-cloud! Thunder boomed and rolled like a vicious growl, but there was no lightning. Lynxy knew it was coming to eat him up—him a cat and the cloud a wolf, and Lynxy ran away. Fifty feet gone, he turned around and I knew what I had to do, and sadly waved goodbye—never to see my Lynxy again. It was *my* war not his. But I cried seeing him depart.

The wind was dense with humidity, but the weight didn't feel like rain. I could feel the darkened power it contained. It felt like the confusion enveloping me inside my head. It was bearing down on me! It wanted to destroy me I could tell—to smother me—suck the air out of my lungs, and I started running to escape from my insanity.

But I also knew what I was running toward—a land the dead possessed—and it hurt my head. Which way should I go? Wait for the Devil, or run to the dead? How many evil spirits were ahead, ready to swarm the trespasser of their space? *So many devils in this world!* I didn't want to go, but knew I must. I thought, *Is my sanity defeated? It's now a race to find the treasure before mentally I can't.*

I ran toward the beam of light. It was so close. *All I have to do is make it there!* But looking back, that vicious devil-cloud was following, and I know the cloud was pleased, knowing sometime before the light-beam I would tire. Then, especially, the *ME* side felt like he needed a reprieve from this place. So as we were running, *ME* reflected on his memories of World One and remembered what we had found there a few years prior.

A year before I left on my journey, I had felt a little glum about life and after several weeks of feeling such, I found myself sitting in a chair in a dark room—empty and depressed. After a while, I remembered the saying that "Life is like a mirror," and got up and decided, in the spirit of scientific research, to look at myself smiling in a mirror.

When I did, the physical action triggered something emotional. With the corners of my mouth inclined, and seeing them that way (although forced), I had a hard time feeling as bad as before, and I realized a smile breeds a feeling of happiness.

Then I started smiling at other people, which often brought the smile back, like *they* were the mirror. As I practiced over months, I could feel better by just smiling, when not even seeing myself—although I still use the mirror often as a reminder.

My students, one time after that, asked me, "Mr. Tiz, why do you smile at us when no joke was said?" I was going to answer, but before I could, they couldn't resist: "Babies sometimes do that when they're passing gas!"

Oh no, not again, I thought.

And then: "Be polite next time and warn us in advance, and we'll evacuate." And, "Let us know from now on what you're going to have for lunch—for we know that certain things affect you!" And, "Don't do the silent ones—then we can grade them A-F." And, "Darn, Mr. Tiz, how do you expect to lure the ladies in when always doing that?"

My face started feeling tomato-ish. "Oh, my word, I don't do that!"

"It's okay, Mr. Tiz. Don't feel bad. It cleans your insides out."

It was like this every day.

"I didn't do one! I smile at you because you're my mirror." Then I tried to throw a zinger back at them, "And how 'bout if you guys quit eating cafeteria food, for without you telling me, I can always tell what you're digesting!"

"Oooh, good one Mr. Tiz."

Smiling in a mirror was an epiphany of a major concept that could change my life forever. It was a key tenet to live by. But it was not until *ME* remembered that World One event that he recognized it was a Rule, and gave it a name, and told me so. It was THE RULE OF THE MIRROR: <u>Trigger an improvement in your lowly spirits by doing something physical—like seeing yourself smiling in a mirror—even when not wanting to,</u> or doing something fun.

After realizing it, as we ran, something ahead on my path glistened intensely in the sun. I stopped and found a polished emerald—same size as the other stones. Then again we practiced smiling to ourselves, as we ran, and found it helped. *If I can just reach the light-beam, I'll be okay.*

Soon after that I started hearing whispering voices in the air, and fearfully raised my arms to surrender to the dead.

Chapter 8

Spirits of the Dead

*N*ow I'll explain when I saw spirits of the dead. I'm not saying I can always see them, for I don't see any now—sitting among *you*, but I saw and lived with them then.

But I'll advise you now, it wasn't them that soon sent me fleeing World Two for home—it was another Beast that finally found me again.

I had escaped the devil-cloud but it was still following—trying to catch up, and still as menacing, so I kept walking all that night in the light of the moons ahead of me to stay ahead and not be caught. Through the pines I walked, and regretfully forwent my search for the Disciple so I could find the dead as Old Man said. But it was a scary thought, and lonely mission, and I desired some soft compassion. And you know who came into my mind? Surprisingly, Ms. Spear again. I wanted to find her to take my money back she stole. But for some reason, I also felt sorry for her when I remembered the look in her eyes—and speaking of her eyes, I still remembered how they shined (and I'll admit it now, I thought them beautiful). I wanted to see her once again—which surprised me, given the sharpness of her spear, but I doubted that I ever would.

Then at about three in the morning, as I was groggy—eyes closing involuntarily, walking in only the light of the moons, I looked to my right and there she was—Ms. Spear, walking to keep me company! "Ms. Spear?" I asked surprised. But she would only smile. I quickly looked for something to spear her with in case she tried to do it again to me. Then I thought and I was scared, *Was Ms. Spear the dead I was to meet? Had she died along the way? And this was her ghost?* My heart softened. I told her how she stuck the spear in me—had been done awkwardly—for she had seemed to cringe, and I knew that it was foreign to her ... for how could a lady that smiles so sweetly really be that mean? And I asked if she was also looking for Rules, for she sounded so excited about the one I found. I thought of my hard times on this journey and told her I knew that hers were hard as well, and I respected her for walking alone, and wished that I could someway help. Tentatively, I slowly moved my hand—a little to the right until I saw it wrap around hers as we walked. I looked at the ground, and when back up, she had excused herself and disappeared, and I was devastated, for I had shared her, but only for a while. As I walked, I envisioned myself out of this place, us sitting by a mountain lake together—pine trees surrounding, enjoying the beautiful sky and sun and birds, swimming, laughing, skimming rocks, talking and eating apples.

The morning came, and it had been days since my food had been depleted, so my belly ached. Recently all I had eaten was another bug-and-insect cocktail, some roaches I munched on like crackers, and a dead, dried-out bat I found whose wings I chewed on like jerky. I thought I'd like to find that rat that chewed on me and have a little barbeque. Or with some oil and batter, I'd like some caterpillar donuts. I thought about eating a cricket that I caught, but I opened up my hands to watch and listen to him chirp, and when I did, his music touched my soul, and I let him go, for I liked his music more than food. Him and his friends were masterful musicians, who had perfected their compositions expertly, and I thanked them daily for all their symphonies.

Many clouds ahead of me I passed beneath were very small, and low, and dense, and slowly twirled clockwise, and birds flew up and sat upon—made nests within—their young ones flying down to say hello—five or six on my shoulders at once sometimes. As I walked, I soaked up all this creativity.

When the sun did flee, I looked behind and saw the devil-cloud still chasing, lit by the moons, so I tried to continue walking to the light, for it was only days away, but after so far without stopping, I just could not, and had to stop. I sat on a log eating, a squirrel sitting with me as company, and I heard whispers around me in the air. "Who is there?" I frantically yelled with sweat developing on my brow. Yes, my night was dark, but I saw the moons reflected light and brilliance of the billion stars above and I knew their power and the worlds circling around them. So even though it was dark in my little piece of space, I felt the heaven's energy and smiled. Then I grabbed my ukulele, for over so many months I had become a master at my art and melodies. I ferociously started strumming a grand adventurous tune I invented over weeks of traveling, in hopes of scaring away the whispers and stopping the devil-cloud with my music's positivity.

When I awoke the next morning, I found the ukulele strumming hadn't worked, for the devil-cloud had caught and smothered me with choking skies of depressing gray pushing me down, pressing on my spirits in my chest, and I lost sight of my blessed pillar of light that nourished me—the devil-cloud its mortal enemy. "Oh light come back!" I pleaded. But I was swallowed up. Then thunder sounded like someone cruelly laughing like a maniac. My soul was now within the devil-cloud's clench and it wouldn't let go. Its weight was heavy upon my state of mind. It blotted out any hint of the sun's rich, optimistic energy, and I continued my journey in that state.

I entered a dark terrain—bushes mostly gone. The only sound came from the wind. Different trees I walked within. These were of a rounded state—like bowling pins—the bottoms brown, the tops a muted green, and when I knocked on them, they sounded like a drum that echoed on and on in low pitched scary thumps—a chain reaction occurring. Birds didn't like the smothering devil-cloud and flew far ahead so none were heard. Crickets hid, and stopped strumming their instruments. All animals fled so none accompanied me except a vulture who joined me, then came along—hopping and flapping beside me on the ground. Friend or foe, I didn't know, but I liked him better than neither. I could hear dry leaves crunch beneath my feet. Then in that scary place, and the whispers now increased, I started getting spooked, I started getting freaked. Animals howled in the distance. What type of ghosts and goblins would the dead present to me ahead? I wished the skeletons were there for my defense. I should have made them come.

I thought of the words of a song and sang it then—to comfort myself, for Bootle, Chisel Hedgehog's rabbit friend, sang about her home in an orchard of apple trees. She, like me, loved her home, and missed it so—for she was gone, and it comforted her to sing about it: (Apple Trees, track 6)

I look at the moon, looking down at me
and smile at the twinkling, stars I see
I feel the breeze, as it cools my cheeks
and I thank heaven, for the apple trees

Chorus 1:
And the sun shines, down on them
and they drink from the streams, that the clouds have sent
and I thank heaven, for the apple trees

Chorus 2:
And I walk, in the shade under them
and I bask in the smell, of the air therein
and I thank heaven, for the apple trees

Verse:
I look at the grass, that tickles my feet
and smile at the birds, that sing to me

I laugh when I see, what the morning brings
and I thank heaven, for the apple trees

Chorus 1 Repeated

I explore, other worlds in their limbs
and eat of the fruit, that they freely give
and I thank heaven, for the apple trees
yeah, I thank heaven, for the apple trees
I thank heaven, for the apple trees
yeah, I thank heaven, for the apple trees

Yeah, there were no wounds from the Beast, but still my shoulder hurt—so was the Beast real or not? The Elder said, "Yes," the Scholar, "No." If the Scholar really was a Scholar, and was right, why had the Elder lied? Then, *Wait, I see! It is power and position that the Elder stands to lose. And maybe he and Emgo are in on this together. I remember the Elder trying to pull me in, by telling me Emgo killed the Beast and to be thankful and respect him! They get the people to think they need protection, and to revere them in order to remain the leaders! And maybe they didn't think I believed, so they're out to get me—so I don't inform the others.*

I came across another note pinned to a tree, and this time tore it down. I wouldn't be fooled another time. But it seemed the deceiver knew that I was headed east and was placing the notes in front of me. Now that I think of it, it was the Elder that recommended going east! I looked for clues but only a few: small footprints in the sand and further off a pencil dropped. The most obvious suspects now: Goatee Man, the Elder, Emgo, or the Scholar. But I had developed my plan to catch the villain and I would soon discover! Then it was I that laughed like a maniac—many times—ever louder. I yelled with hands in fists, shaking above, "You will be mine!" And Vulture joined with frightening squawks.

Marching on, Vulture got tired of hopping along so he hitched a ride on top of my backpack. I didn't want him to, and told him "No," but he didn't listen, and we moseyed on.

Here, the trees seemed dead—had no leaves. Everything was black or gray—I think a fire had come that way. No ravens could I see—only their shadows passing in the gray mist up above. But the howls of the Beasts or other things continued in the distance. And the whispers had strengthened even more to many all-around! But I couldn't tell what they said. It panicked my heart, and I knew this was the "dark place" landscape of the dead, and my cautious steps confirmed it. I had invaded their place. When would they find me? I started passing ancient grave stones scattered here and there amongst the trees. Many of granite, some of wood, some leaning or fallen over. Many covered with spider webs—the graves with decaying leaves. *There's one to my right! Some over there on my left!* Then many I passed, but empty now—only holes in the ground! *Did an animal dig them up or what? This is where the dead live!* I was a fretful mess. *What will their decayed and rotting bodies look like, having risen from their graves, when they emerge from behind the bushes and trees?*

With anguish I pleaded, "I want to get out of this wretched place! Back on the path to find the Disciple and other Rules! I want to see my Frisky dog, green sky, three moons, heavens above, and parakeets up in the trees!" Vulture felt my anguish, and trying to help, he clamped his claws onto my pack and flapped so I lifted up—him flying quite a ways ahead—me hanging underneath him, till he tired and put me down. "Thank you, Vulture."

The devil-cloud was having its way with me, and as it pushed my spirits lower, I fought my way through bushes, then heard them breaking behind me. Some big things following—getting closer—trying to get through. *Beasts again?* I thought. *They're not pretend, like the Scholar said, because I really heard them! Or at least I think I did. Yes, I hear them now. At least I think I do. Oh my gosh, I just don't know! It's so confusing in my head! I'm going crazy here!* My head pounded, and my heart beat loud inside of me! Again I tried envisioning World One and transferring, but I could not remember a single thought of how it looked—so long I had been gone. *Oh my gosh*, I thought, *ME was right and we should have gone back. Maybe I've been gone so long, I will never be able to return*! I yelled, "Old Man, if you're not the Devil, and want to help, then save me from this hell!"

Then words I heard from all around me in the air, "I cannot save—only advise. But focus, focus on my words—think only now of charity, tranquility, and peace within your soul and all such goodly things. Close your eyes and see a place where only those exist. Then slow your heart and focus till you think of nothing else. Then breathe in deep, through your nose, and with pressed lips sigh, with the slightest of air escaping. If done right, with focused mind, and several times, the mist and smell and Beasts are gone. For the Beasts are in your mind and nowhere else."

His voice was so calm, and pleasant, and reassuring, that when I heard it, I focused on positivity until my mind was just upon it. "Oh thank you, Old Man." Then I looked back and saw ravens in volleys falling down out of the overcast into those bushes. Like spears, their beaks protruded, and howls I heard till slowly weaker—until the howling stopped completely and the ravens flew away—blood dripping from their beaks—and I envisioned what had happened. I thought, *I'm lucky those ravens and Beasts are enemies*. Then the voice came back again but in a reverent manner, "Now get yourself away from there." And I didn't care if it truly was Old Man talking, or rather my mind's invention as I feared, or if it was the Devil just prolonging my torture until the dead consumed me, for it was good advice and I was thankful. But seeing that blood made me think, *Does something that's not real bleed?* I added, *He must be talking about a different Beast.* I got clear of there but still the feeling nagged inside that something would come if I permitted, or if I put myself in threatening places.

That night Vulture and I slept with the dead. The sky was still a soupy murk and I ended up in groves of giant, ancient banyan trees with enormous, muscled limbs that reached across and intertwined, and on those mighty limbs, a village in the trees had been constructed, but now abandoned. Pieces of wood tied to those limbs created walking paths that connected limb to limb. Huts were built here and there, and in the middle a central gathering place with a thatched roof above it. That is where I slept, but I tossed and turned, for all night long I heard the whispers all around me, and felt air move past like ghosts were flying by.

The next morning, I remembered what Old Man said. I didn't want to summon them and sighed at the task ahead, but I was going for broke—hoping the dead weren't the Devil's friends—hoping Rules were really needed—hoping this all was not insanity. I thought about requesting a reprieve, but knew Old Man's command, and knew that I must follow. So, hopefully I pursed my lips and moved ahead with my dreaded chore. To see them I exhaled and held some things of theirs, and saw things in a different way as the Scholar said—so that I could *feel* them. And that made the difference—for indeed, I did start feeling something: a denser air around me, and the movement of it was like something passing by.

I thought I saw movement through the corner of my eye—a shadow moving on the path off to my left, then one to my right. *They are surrounding me!* I thought. Slowly the shadows took on a form, but they were not the goblins and ghosts and spirits that I had feared. The shadows were children laughing and running past me, mainly see-through in their form. I was there, but experiencing a former time. As I walked around, I saw women smiling, holding babies, washing dishes, making clothing, and men making sandals out of leather and cooking breakfast. I could not understand their muted voices, but through the day I saw them by their treetop fires, working, laughing, telling stories, children giggling with each other. These people were industrious—fit from work and healthy from the things they ate. But they enjoyed the simple things in life, like each night watching the sun go down together, talking and smiling as it did. I think that was the clue I was to learn.

Chapter 9

The Sky Broke Free

Rule #4: OF THE RIVER RUNNING FREE

The next morning I prepared to part from that vision, and even though they were dead, I knew I would miss the company I had shared—for I would return to my lonely state. I thought, *I know that's mean since Vulture is here, but he is not really into talking much. Should I just live with the dead?* But I wanted my Frisky back and the Disciple, and I ventured on. *I might need the Truth to escape any day.* I no longer saw the light-beam, but it had been so close.

My lonely state was furthered when I continued trudging through that dreary, darkened forest. So long I had been within, and without the sun above, now missing the dead and the skeletons, that my spirits couldn't mend and sadness filled my heart—losing hope. I did, however, remember the mirror and weakly smiled—and that propelled me on. Up ahead, I saw a curtain of moss hanging from between two trees, amongst a wall of many—with thick, mangled bushes completing the scene on either side. But my steps were slow and getting slower, "I'm so alone in this dreadful place! How much farther can I go? Maybe set up camp where I am."

But Vulture started squawking, looking ahead. "What is it boy?" I said. I came to that curtain of moss and parted it . . . AND I COULDN'T BELIEVE! The forest broke open and the sky broke free—now clear and pristine, and I could see . . . the sun— after none for so long, and a beautiful meadow under it with a river running free! Vulture squawked again, pushed off, and happily flew, and I waved as he withdrew. It was like a whole different world I came into—fresh and clean and beautiful and green. I stumbled inside, then looked behind, and the "dark place" was like a tunnel that I exited—the devil-cloud stopping at its edge. It was like *The Wizard of Oz*—first black and white, now color. Then came the Rule where the dead's clue steered—and with it I was even closer to my treasure on the blessed Mountain. Hope again was mine! Oh thank you sky!"

I hugged the banyan tree next to me as I stood and watched; I did not blink; the movie before me spellbinding. My soul was free! A great stone obelisk stood at the far, left side of the meadow, and a tremendous beam of light, from mighty mirrors inside a giant concaved disk, twenty feet wide, on top of it, reflected and focused the sun in a concentrated ray above. I yelled, "I made it!" I could see engravings all around it, and wondered what messages they shared. I walked into the movie's reality so it was all around me. Reality of bliss. Flowers up amidst. Bees humming among. Skies of the clearest green. Grassy meadow under feet. The river gently flowing, casually meandering! So wonderful, it was like a fantasy created just for me.

I had seen grass before—but . . . it now smelled sweet like blades of spearmint candy, flowers so colorful, the different colors radiated from them, bees buzzing like a finger down piano keys, the river with a scent of lime. I stopped and enjoyed my principality. Bites of apples I ate, so crisp, and mangos so sweet, their tangy, flowing juices energized my feet with a spontaneous quick-step dance. *How much does the movie cost?* Nothing—it was gratis. Then I liked it even more. *Oh what a reward indeed!*

I lay down and smiled, enjoying as the plot thickened with a few white ambling clouds pedaling slowly over on invisible bikes. Now the birds, for this is where they all had flown—their songs like sweet, high-pitched chimes and bells and xylophones. Then the music I had never really heard of wind hitting leaves like a choir singing a whispered song, and the leaves gently hitting each other—and creaking, tapping branches. An art design of filtered light danced on grass beside leaf shadows—perfect for a gallery. Like an orchestra—the wind, and leaves and branches together—and birds, and crickets, and river over rocks, all cascading in my perception. I finally saw the beauty of the world I lived in! It isn't the moon with only gray rocks and dust. Enjoyed sun's warmth and river's coolness on my feet. Miraculous simplicity perfected. No one's to own. For all to enjoy—just stand outside and experience the feeling. *Thank you!* I closed my eyes and listened to the melody. We all have it around us.

I sat on grass on the river's edge, my feet within, still—like a sponge and put away my snack of dead and dried-out ants, instead to feast on wild raspberries by the handful. I looked at my reflection in the river where its ripples calmed. Then I looked around and thought. A feeling overcame me. I perceived greatness in this incident. The Elder said it depends on how you look at it. What I experienced (or needed) was not grand or magnificent. I hadn't seen a massive snow-capped mountain range, or the most gorgeous colored sunset filling the entire sky. What I saw was the most basic simplicity. But because of the trials, because of the difficult, because of the depressing, murky sky, because of the dark and dreary for so long, because what I learned from the dead, I just saw it differently than before. I realized it was not fantasy as I had thought. THE RULE OF THE RIVER RUNNING FREE I'd found: The FREE and SIMPLE things in life produce the greatest pleasure, like nature all around us in its beauty, and so much else—and how we look at it, determines how wonderful it is. So I knew from then, even when life hurts, to look around, and the simple things will bring a smile to my face—and the words, "It's okay," to my lips. When I'm down, I'll remind myself to, "Enjoy the world!" And in the river a pink object shined—a tourmaline gemstone I realized, as I pulled it out.

I looked over at the obelisk and noticed it was at the entrance of a magnificent city—this meadow its front yard. It was somewhat overgrown with vines, and giant roots of trees, and bushes and grass—a great, ancient temple complex—reminding me of Angkor Wat.

Then I saw animals looking down at me from its ruins and I realized my original vision of this place was right—a metropolitan delight. I entered inside—an expansive grassy courtyard—fruit trees to feast from all throughout, waterfall of the purest water to drink from to the right.

Then the animals came down and the shindig did indeed begin, for they could also hear the music I had heard. I smiled at bees playing their piano keys, hundreds of birds of different types singing in the trees, monkeys swinging and shrieking from the limbs, deer and antelope kicking in the air, hyenas laughing on the grass. More and more animals came until the meadow was a tremendous dancing festival with everyone yipping and hollering! Even Vulture reappeared—jumping and flapping— moving his feet—doing a jig with others around him. I had prophesied! "Ha!" I laughed, "Just not exactly what I saw. But riches? Yes!" And it cemented in my mind how special this second world was.

Then the sun went down, the beam of light went out, but the moons lit up our scene, and it was time for some ukulele. My fingers played with quickened pace and emphatic strumming energy that in World One would have caused the concert crowd to clap and shout and rise on their feet. And I sang my next song my band would play. I called it: *All of Us*: (All Of Us, track 7)

Well look at the people who came today

came to hear us and watch us play
Yeah look at the people all gathered around
one big family enjoying the sound
we're not much different not you or me
all feel deeply-- the music

Chorus 1:
Yeah all of us, all of you
we all feel the sorrow of a few
and just like that, we all know
when we sing together, something grows
deep within-side ourselves
there's a bond yearning to extend itself

Cause we all feel what it's telling us
the man in Iran and the African
we all have something common inside
that tells us
what is wrong and right
and just the same we all share as one
a spirit that is touched by song

Verse:
Well look at the faces up in the stands
singing together and with the band
yeah look at the people from near and far
we're all family if we think that we are
we share with each other our love for the sound
that softens the hearts of most everyone

Chorus 2:
Yeah all of us, all of you
we all fear when the worst is on the news
and just the same, we all feel
when we share notes of songs, we somewhat heal

so feel free, to join on in
sing the songs of peace that are within

Cause we all know that we do need it
the lady in France and the Jamaican
and we all smile when someone smiles at us
it's natural to feel and react like that
and from when we were born and young
we all need the words in the songs that are sung

Yeah all of us, all of you

Well look at the friends that are with us today
came to escape and to get away
yeah look at the people in every seat
sharing the music that feeds our needs
we're in this together and we can't deny
the common emotion that music provides

Chorus 1 Repeated

Cause we all hail what it does give us
the children in Chad and the Australian
and we all sway and feel it down inside
when words and the music do fit just right
and we all pray for just one more song
that brings us together to be written

Chorus 2 Repeated

I slept with birds and monkeys around me in the trees, and bobcats, foxes, deer, and quail on the ground. The next morning we awoke, half-drunk from dance fatigue, lack of sleep, bellies full of fruit, and crystal water that we drank. Then I studied the obelisk. Its great disk had holes in the bottom for rain to flow, and on it those before had chiseled notes in lines around. I read the advice passed down through time from hundreds who had written—the greatest collected thoughts of the ages. The school of life written on an obelisk. It took me a day to study them for I knew this was a reward for making it this far, and I would learn from the greatest.

All day long I read—many things explaining mysteries that up till then I wondered of, other things brand new I'd never heard, and many things not grand or great and at another place—another time, I wouldn't have thought twice of them—but here I understood them differently—and they changed my soul and how I looked at things and understood them. My mind was opened up to possibilities never known before. One especially caught my eye—signed Emgo! Simple, but true it read: *The bird living free, flying tree to tree, sleeping somewhere different every night, learns a special lesson, also good for us: Don't chain yourself to ruts. Fly free and learn.*

I felt like maybe those who reached this place were supposed to write—expected to. So I decided I should write my own. The stone was sixty feet high—a chisel and hammer and ladder laying at its base, so I chiseled mine at fifteen feet: *Keep a special bowl of gold—coins saved for just one purpose. Pass one out when need is seen, for those, whom to you are strangers. They'll buy food—and you will buy contentment.*

As I chiseled the last letter and looked at my message to those who came forth after me, a peace came over me like maybe this journey was worth it, and actually meant to be. Having read the words, I was a different man. I had learned enough to leave a part of myself, and maybe help another. And once again, I had "met" Emgo. So, whether he was a fake, or not, I strongly desired to meet him and find out more. When would I meet him as the Elder said? When would I meet the Prophet?

I stayed for a week enjoying this, and each night I played and sang new songs to my concert crowd. In the far-away distance, I started to see the sky light up with lightning storms and wondered if Old Man was there as the Scholar said. It was east of me and beckoning. Soon the light at day would fade away behind me, but would be brighter and brighter at night, and I was ready to venture to it. What awaited at the mountaintop if this was only the halfway point? If this was only a *reward*—and at the top it was a *treasure*?

Finally it was time for me to go. In the morning I placed my things into my pack to continue on my mission and said good-bye to the party crowd. But my journey was postponed when by the river I saw some sticks stuck together lying on the ground poking out from underneath a dried-out tumble weed ... but the sticks didn't really look like sticks! I shuddered, s*urely not again!* I walked to the tumble weed and yanked it to the side—AND THEN I YELLED! There before me was another skeleton sitting on the ground and leaning back against a rock overlooking the river and meadow! It took my breath away, and I jumped back, but after a minute I recovered. The skeleton held a piece of leather, and I pulled it from its boney hand. Scratched on the bottom side was writing. It said: *My time as Disciple has come to an end. Good luck to all. Farewell.*

My heart sank! I couldn't believe it! My head dropped and my eyebrows rose. I thought, *The Disciple is dead? How did she die?* Then I feared. *Or was she murdered by the serial killer, just like he or she was trying to do to me, and I was next!* I quickly looked around. *How will I know how to pass the evil entrance? How will I escape the dungeon? She was the one to tell me! This is catastrophic!* I was so happy before, now so depressed. I needed help on this mission, and she was my next contact. I couldn't succeed without her! *And how is the killer doing the deeds? I see no broken bones. Poison perhaps, in a drink she was given?*

I then agreed with *ME*. I couldn't take this anymore! I had to get out! I had to get back—before I was killed like the Disciple, and was the second skeleton overlooking the meadow, or found myself attacked by some vague, invisible force, or locked inside those dungeon walls, or torn apart by Beasts! I was stressed! I thought of Ms. Spear's caring face when I first saw her, and her arm around my waist, walking off the lake, and I wished I could embrace her now and feel that comfort once again. But she was not there—no comfort shared. I needed to go home—if I still could! Old Man had said I couldn't tarry too long, and now I saw why. With all this stress I'd go insane—lost in the dark. I wanted to teach my students again—play in the band.

Then a thought occurred, *Does Brinlin know the Truth? Maybe I can get it from her, instead of the Disciple. She completed World Two already. Can I find her in World One and ask?* Then I thought of Nikita too, *Two I've met who say that they have also come this way ... hmm, are there others in World One that have also come? Is there some sort of secret society?*

So I sat on a rock and closed my eyes and tried to imagine World One to transfer there. "Please," I said. As I did, I started remembering people's faces, and then places where we'd been together. But still I couldn't make myself transfer. "Ahh!" I groaned. Then as I thought about *MYSELF* with utmost concentration, I saw him in World One at a restaurant eating, and again I tried to get through, but I couldn't and I thought, *Maybe it's the place.* So I whispered into his mind and told him, "Go sit by the lake." I was frantic to get through—away from this, and I looked around—scared and nervous of someone watching me. And since *MYSELF* hated my part of himself being in the other world, he smiled and immediately started walking there.

My imagination, though, was disturbed by familiar sounds of a Beast howling in the distance and then bushes breaking, and I knew the Beasts were not in favor of me leaving. They only wanted me inside World Two which others called Insanity. My eyes shot open, but then I squeezed them shut again and focused harder on a vision of World One's lake—but the howling was getting louder, so it was hard to concentrate! And *MYSELF* was not there yet!

So, harder and with a frantic pace, I closed my eyes and focused on other things around the lake: people walking, fishing, kids playing, I envisioned! But I forgot tranquility. Then I called upon the ravens and informed them there was prey in the bushes, but they did not assist this time and I frantically wondered why? Still more desperate crashing trying to get through all the bushes in time, until I heard it exit the bushes and the "dark place" tunnel across the river and meadow!

I opened my eyes and saw a Beast barreling toward me. My breathing accelerated, almost to hyperventilation, and I turned around, and squeezed my eyes to concentrate! But *MYSELF* was still not there yet, and I yelled to him, "Hurry, my life's at stake!" and he ran. Then, besides the visions, I tried to hear the sounds of World One: dogs barking, people laughing, geese by the lake honking! But I also heard the running sound of the Beast's feet rushing toward me. Then a splash, and him frantically charging across the shallow river. But as I concentrated harder and my visions became more vivid, finally I saw *MYSELF*, out of breath, arrive and seat himself upon the ground, and I felt my mind begin to go, and then my body following. On my way, I felt claws come down upon my side and scratch their bloody anger into me. "Ahhh!" I yelled with deadly pain, the gory scratches deep—the full length of my side . . . but I was gone—like through the tunnel some people have described when dying. But I did not end up in Heaven.

Chapter 10

Insanity Expanding

I awoke with a start—drenched in sweat—and looked around. I was sitting on the ground inside the trees by the lake in World One and safe. I groaned from my wounds, but I had escaped! I had reunited with *MYSELF,* and my emotions took control of both of us. I jumped up and threw my arms up in the air, relieved. I yelled, "Hallelujah glory! I survived!" My psychiatrist had told me World Two was all in my mind—an escape from reality, but no. No! That Beast had bloodied my side with vengeful claws, but I luckily, barely escaped and now was safe, and I remembered other things explicitly that I had seen and heard and felt and smelled: the stone obelisk, all kinds of different landscapes, the music of the Scholar, the sharpness of a spear in me, a Pterodactyl in the sky— and the smell of what he gave to me. My heart beat fast and I started crying. I thankfully yelled out loud excitedly: "It's really real! I'm not crazy! I saw and heard and felt and smelled it!"

I dashed outside the pocket of trees, so happy and relieved, grabbed a man's arm that passed me, and looked straight into his eyes, "I was in another world!" I quickly said, with an excited smile, our faces close together. "A Beast almost killed me, but I escaped, and came back through a portal. I lived with dead people up in some trees, and they still have Pterodactyls there and four-foot frogs, and piranha caterpillars, and the sky is green! It's fantastic! Maybe next time you can come with me!" But the man jerked his arm away and continued walking—only faster while looking back.

Several picnic tables I visited and exclaimed the same, so thankful that I made it back, running to them smiling, yelling, arms flailing, out of breath, but with the same effect. I added, "and bird songs sound like xylophones and crickets like an orchestra. Look, this mud on my shoes—it's from the other world! I'm a great explorer—just like Christopher Columbus— our autographs will be sold for millions!"

Some thought I was joking, for they laughed out loud hysterically, until the police officer that had talked to me before, grabbed my elbow. "You again? You can't be doing that," and he looked into my eyes. "You need to see someone!" So after a trip to the station, I had a little mandatory time with my psychiatrist. (*Oh boy,* I thought, *not this again.*)

"But I found a portal," I kept telling her in her office the next day. "I go from here to there. Ghosts are there, but they're not the goblin type—they are nice."

She tapped her upper lip with her finger, "Hmmmm."

"Maybe it's a place that we can't see that's all around us! Or a place above the clouds—another world. Rivers there smell like lime, and birds make nests in clouds."

She pursed her lips, "I see."

"A Beast that is part wolf and bear and bat and rat clawed my side as I was leaving. You must believe me."

"We've talked about this before," she said in the sweetest tone. "It's a place to go and find peace, and be secure, or to live a wild fantasy. But it's not real; it's a place inside your mind."

"How do you know it isn't real? Maybe it's a place only a few visit because it's just so hard to understand. Bees there sound like piano keys."

She looked surprised, "I've never heard a bee like that!"

"I flew over trees from a vulture holding me."

"Oh, that sounds fun."

"I danced at a party with deer and antelope."

"Even funner."

"Got drunk from pristine water, and played my ukulele with crickets accompanying."

"My last party was really boring compared to that!"

I nodded my head. "Maybe it's a place you have to go to be perfected! *Heaven* is another world, and we don't know where *that* is. Maybe I found another way to get there! Maybe most don't go until they're dead, but some like me go early. Llamas there sing."

She actually laughed out loud but in a second controlled herself. "I'm sorry," she said, "but it's not real, and it's not Heaven, and llamas don't sing—it's in your mind."

"It's different there," I said. I lifted my shirt to show her the bloody claw marks down my side, but she said that none were there! "I guess I was already mist by then," I said.

She shook her head. "It's not reality. You're the one that told me that—you envision another place inside your mind and go to escape from all your troubles. Look within yourself."

When she said those last words, they rang a bell and I said, "I've heard those words before in World Two—a Scholar also told me them—Brinlin Tremblay from Canada. She's the Scholar in the other world."

She answered, "The famous Brinlin Tremblay? She's in the other world? I just saw her on the news last night."

"Well . . . yeah, I know. She's in this world *and* in that one."

"No," she shook her head. "It was me—last time you were here. 'Look within yourself,' I said. The Scholar is someone your mind invented to help confront your worries, and support your fantasy. You probably fell asleep in front of the television last night and dreamt of her."

Actually, that was true. I *had* fallen asleep in front of the television. But then I said, "We could call her."

She looked sorrowful, "If she said she was the Scholar, I would have to ask her if she had also heard Nikita Volkov's demented story. I would expect that she is mirroring as well."

Oh! My head went dizzy and I thought, *What is real and what is not? I cannot tell.* I told her, "I have a pet dog there in the stars named Frisky."

"No," she shook her head again, and squeezed her lips together. And I had to admit it sounded weird.

I added, "There's someone else that can corroborate my story." Then *I* introduced *ME* and *MYSELF*.

"No, no, no. That's not right!" she said with added emphasis.

And I admit that did me in—and them too—for it caused confusion in knowing who I really was. And unfortunately, the psychiatrist witnessed it. So she gave me some pills that calmed me down and I rested at my home. And I avoided going to the lake, for not knowing true reality started giving me headaches, and I sometimes started jabbering senselessly during times of mass confusion.

But *MYSELF* calmed me with his gentle thoughts and *ME* reminded what could help.

Half a year I'd been away since my last World One visit—another couple thousand miles walked, so I relaxed my heart and mind, and over time, I eventually came back around to my old laughing, playful self. April Fools were always good, and barbeques, and holidays enjoyed with family and friends. And I entertained them with ukulele solos and they were amazed by my skill and crafted instrument. "Where did you get that, and when did you learn to play that good? You're amazing!"

"I had plenty of time to practice."

Word had gotten out that I might have a mental disease, and once again my principal reported it to the district. The superintendent asked me about the incident at the park and I tried to temper it, "Oh that ... yeah, that *was* a little weird I must admit. I was ... creating—a song for my band to play about a crazy man and his journey, and I needed inspiration at the park. I guess I took it a little too far."

"Hmm," she said. "Okay Tiz. I like you ... in fact I've heard your songs and like them as well, so I'm on your side. But don't be doing stuff like that. Don't give your principal ammunition. He's a bitter one, we've found. If he proves you are mentally unfit, we will have to fire you."

But that was not enough for my principal. He hated me and my band even worse, for after his edict to the students to never play my band's songs, *all* the students played them! So he was irate, and convinced the city to evaluate me. I told them the same story I told the superintendent, and they let me go. "But watch yourself," they said, "for he's an acidic one." Passing him in the halls he started coughing, and under his breath I thought I heard him say, "Barfbag." Then other times, "Toedirt," "Warthog," "Pigsnot," and "B.O. Joe." But the other teachers told me to not let him get to me, "Just do your job and enjoy the students."

My students were always understanding, and I noticed more now ate lunch with me, and asked me how I was doing, and gave me little poems, and practiced the concept of THE MIRROR that *MYSELF* had taught them, for they smiled at me for no apparent reason. This was a different class than I last taught, but *MYSELF* had been teaching them, and they were very close, so now with him, I knew them all and was close as well. Some told me to call them anytime when I needed to talk. Others made me cookies, or gave me gifts like hand-made pottery, and from their charity, I felt my heart was melting. And they went easy on me with the gaseous accusations, and only once a day did they make an allegation.

They still made me laugh, though: "Mr. Tiz, I'm thinking of playing in a band."

"Great. What instrument do you play?" I asked.

"The radio."

"Mr. Tiz, I won't be at school tomorrow—there's a sale at the mall."

"That's a bad excuse," I said.

"Blame yourself. You taught us to save money, and I'm going to save a lot!"

"Mr. Tiz, how do you like my new dress?"

"Very pretty," I responded.

"Why don't you like it?" she asked.

"I do."

"Then you're supposed to say, 'That's sick!'"

"Oh. Well then, that's so sick I'm going to throw up on it."

"Oh gee, Mr. Tiz, that's sick!"

With my closest friends, we joked about what I had gone through often, and I laughed out loud with them, for hearing it in World One, it *did* sound crazy!

"Hey, Tiz, let's go get some of that Pterodactyl poop of yours—I heard it's good fertilizer for my garden."

"Hey, Tiz, bring me one of those twenty-foot-tall flowers—it's my anniversary next week and it's much better than some roses!"

I replied, "It's too big to bring."

"Then bring me some seeds."

"Hey, Tiz, it's the fair next week—bring along your four-foot frog . . . he'd surely win the frog jumping contest!"

[Tiz stopped his lecture and smiled and pointed at his friends seated in the front row of the auditorium.]

I did go out on some dates, and although the girls were all nice, they didn't seem to be my type. Some talked, talked, talked too much, so I didn't get a word in. Others laughed hysterically at every single thing I said. And others demanded such pricey restaurants I practically had to leave a leg for payment. And as we ate and I listened to them talk, I must admit it was often Ms. Spear that I saw.

Time flew by as I settled into my World One routine, enjoying its ease and simplicity—without World Two's stress. I flawlessly lived the Rules I found, for they changed the way I looked at things, and when the principal would yell at me, I would look ahead to better times. I found myself spending more time with my parents, and smiling more at others. Air was fresher. My mind was more open. Notes and words were easy. Music's simplicity made me happy. I taught my band, *There's a Dream*, and *All of Us*, and we added them to our performances.

Success was coming more easily. When summer came, on most weekends we traveled to big cities and played at universities. While I was gone, the band had developed quite the following, and I was surprised by the packed concert halls we played in, myself enjoying our fans and their excitement. I found out our break-through came with my principal's edict for the students not to play our songs! Then not only did they all play them, but they shared them on social media! We became known as "The Band the Principal Hates." Then my principal was *really* enraged! His eagle eyes were upon me like never before. It was a tug of war between him and I for my job—him trying to gather enough evidence to get me fired. Who would win?

My stress-relief came from what he hated most, and I and the band wrote more songs, creating our second album, and we posted them on YouTube, and our audiences quickly sang them word for word with us when we played. As usual we started each concert with all of us jamming on our instruments, then I yelled the questions (with the new ones added) and the audience yelled back and we all joined in *The Anthem of the People*.

Then, "Here's a new one for you:"

There's a dream in my mind, that I have each night
and I can't get it out of my head ...

I reveled in the fun that people had when listening—all of us immersed in a common energy, and my band let me play some solos with crazy ukulele tracks, and the audience loved them. All summer long I enjoyed our success, everyday a different venue, everyday a different concert crowd cheering us on and singing along, and I chose not to think about treasures and gates and amazing things.

By the end of summer I was pretty tired, but also healed from World Two stress, and I looked forward to a break just teaching again. And I continued writing too. Chisel Hedgehog was experiencing the hard, but often great, sometimes he was sad, or sometimes laughed. It was a Crazy Great Summer.

*   *   *

Then, as I was told later, one day a private business jet touched down at our small, local airport. Everyone there stared to see who it was, and a well-dressed lady got out—but well disguised with hat and sunglasses on. It was Brinlin Tremblay.

In the dusk of the evening, when most were gone, a limousine pulled into the park, and Brinlin walked to the tree, and waited. The bird flew down and Brinlin kissed it and laughed. Then she spoke, and the bird chirped.

*   *   *

The next day was Saturday. School would start again in a week, and I went fishing. While moving down river from hole to hole, I realized a chirping sound was following me. I looked around to find it, and on a branch, I saw a finch looking down at me. We held our stare for quite some time and then she flew away. As she flew I noticed one discolored feather in her wing. Then I remembered the finch that led me to World Two so long before. I hadn't thought much of that place for half a year, but the finch brought back my memories.

That night I looked into a mirror and I figured my vision was worsening, for my reflection was a little blurred. *Must be a faulty mirror,* I thought, for otherwise my sight was fine. But then the reflection changed to ripples of water and my reflection in a river—as I remembered that time I saw myself in World Two; and I thought about that other world and all its differences and possibilities, for the Beast no longer seemed so threatening, and I yearned to reach the Mountain to find the treasure, and open the Gate. They would change the poem, I thought:

In 1492

Columbus sailed
the ocean blue

In century twenty-one
Tiz found more
And went to explore ...

Through the Gate I would be changed forever. What did that mean? Would I be immortal? What powers would I attain? I already knew my mind was clearer—songs came easier. In World Two especially, my creative juices flowed—songs were created I never would have otherwise. But the Disciple now was dead, so the path to the mountain would be impossible.

Then I remembered my thought to talk to Brinlin Tremblay who made it through World One. Maybe she learned the Truth before the Disciple died! With that, I could continue on. I tried calling her company but they wouldn't put me through and neither could I find her cell number.

Then I made a bold decision. I studied Tremblay Research, maxed out my credit card, and flew to Canada. I made it to the headquarters of Tremblay Research, but the front desk told me they couldn't relay a message. "I came all the way from America!"

They escorted me out of the building and I sat on the wide front steps—depressed. Fifteen minutes later a limousine pulled up and a lady with two body guards walked up the many steps. I walked toward her—along with many others and a newspaper reporter.

The first body guard said, "Sorry folks, no interviews today," and they kept walking—her in between.

"Brinlin," I yelled, along with all the others. She smiled as she walked and held up her hand to everyone. She passed me— almost to the top step. I was desperate. Without thinking, I yelled, "WORLD TWO."

She stopped, paused, and turned back toward the crowd. She took some steps toward us. "Who said that?" I raised my hand. "Come with me."

Her large office was on the top floor of the high-rise. Floor to ceiling windows provided a view of the whole city. Leather upholstered furniture adorned the space. She asked me to sit and closed the door. She sat as well, close to me. "How do you know?"

"I'm on the journey too—in fact it was you who tutored me as a scholar—or probably your other self."

"Where are you from?"

I told her my city in the United States.

She immediately smiled. "Okay, okay. Yes, I believe you. I know your town quite well."

I thought that was strange since it was so small.

"Why have you come?" She asked.

"I hit a road block. The Disciple died. I found her skeleton, and I need the Truth from her to continue."

She answered, "We found the same thing—almost ten years ago. My other self found her skeleton on a mountain overlooking a valley and was distraught."

I was confused. "No. In a meadow overlooking a river."

We looked at each other confused.

Brinlin noted, "My other self did go back and she told me she *did* find the Disciple after all, and that the skeleton wasn't really dead!"

I laughed hard out loud. "What? They're skeletons! Just bones! Yes, they are dead!"

Brinlin shrugged her shoulders. "I don't know all the details. My other self hasn't left a journal for me to read, and of course I wasn't there. But she said that skeletons are a key to passing through the Gate."

I laughed again, "Oh man! Well, can you tell me the Truth?"

"We didn't need the Truth—we needed something else from her."

AAAHHH! It hurt my head. I was so upset. And how could she have found the Disciple if she was dead? (Yes, skeletons *are* dead!)

Brinlin said, "I wish I could have helped. I'm sorry."

We talked for an hour, then went to lunch, and then as I was about to leave I said, "Hey, by the way, have you ever heard about a man named Nikita Volkov?"

"Yes. I know his story well. In fact he talked at a meeting I went to recently. His journey he described was amazing. He's a good man—trying to help others—so charitable. He was judged not to be a threat and released from the mental institution. He entered the oil exploration business and is now actively improving mental institutions."

Hmmm, I contemplated as I thought of my psychiatrist, *are Brinlin and I both just mirroring?*

"Are there others too? And have you met—a secret society?"

"Yes, there are many others, and yes we meet. I wouldn't call it secret—it's just that others can't relate, so you need a necklace to attend."

Then I left for home.

More concerts we played on weekends:

Well look at the people who came today
Came to hear us and watch us play ...

Then, walking down a street one day I passed a costume shop, and outside, to advertise, stood a plastic skeleton, but they put eye balls in its sockets, and he had a little grin. I stopped and looked, and those eye balls stared straight at me like he was alive! It freaked me out—my heart beat loud. It was a sign. I envisioned his mouth open up and heard him talk, and his voice's low and gravelly tone made him sound upset, "I'm not dead." I shivered and squeezed my eyes shut—when open again, his mouth was shut with that grin again. Then I was really freaked. It seemed that he was beckoning me, and it made me think. *I need to go back to see if the skeleton is still there by the river. Maybe I don't understand something. World Two is so complex. How could the skeleton have moved from the mountain to the meadow as Brinlin seemed to say? The Secret provides a second life—is that why skeletons aren't really dead? Maybe there is some way to find the Disciple. Maybe World Two has me imagining things and the Disciple isn't dead.*

In the morning, I sat in a chair and thought. I loved my World One life, but the bird, and skeleton started me thinking. I pulled out the gemstones from my pocket and looked at them. Was it time to leave? I remembered all the way I'd gone. My friends told me it wasn't real, but I wanted that treasure.

"There is no treasure!" they told me.

But I knew there was. "I'm not living a fantasy."

"Stay and play in the band."

"Hmm," I pondered.

I hadn't found what I left behind that would light my way. Maybe that would quicken my pace to the treasure and then I'd return in a flash. So in this world, I did everything I could to find it—looking everywhere, wondering what it could be. I remembered instruction received to look within, and I thought of looking in a different way: within myself, sitting, contemplating, thinking it out. And I spent much time in learning traits that made me kinder, gentler, and more patient, and on weaknesses and correcting my mistakes. But I felt something was missing, like on a teeter-totter with no one on the other side. Or like roadblocks stopping my way and the other side only accessible through some other place—and we all know where that was ... but even though I wanted to go, it scared me when I thought of the increased difficulties without the Disciple, and of the doubts from my psychiatrist. So I just didn't know. *Should I go?*

In my apartment, I remembered the psychiatrist's words: "Your other world is not real," and memories of several people telling me the Beast that had attacked me was not real! I thought,

Have I gone mad? But I have proof: I saw him and felt his ripping teeth! I brought back World Two's mud upon my feet.

Then I countered myself: *But how can llamas sing? How can Pterodactyls live? How can caterpillars have piranha teeth? Maybe she's right and it isn't real. Why submit myself to such a torturous adventure if my journeys are only within my mind? Is Old Man fiction? Is Old Man the Devil? Yes or No? I have to know!*

Oh, I was so conflicted. Life was a blur. I could no longer decipher what was reality. *How did my wounds from the Beast heal so quickly and perfectly?* I felt a stab inside my head. "Ahhh," I groaned, and woke up sometime later on my floor. I was debilitated, short of breath, on the verge of a major stress attack ... an aneurism of the brain! My heart was thumping—my head a fuzzy mess. Lying there, again the psychiatrist's words floated through my mind: "Look within yourself." Then somewhere deep a hazy thought emerged—those words again from someone else ... *who? A Scholar!* Then a vague memory arose of what she gave me—a Secret that would save me. And that is when I needed saving most of all—not from something physical that I could see or touch, but from my troubled mind! Psychedelic lights were pulsing through my head! Again I started getting dizzy. I had to heal myself or I might die. I tried to focus on what the Scholar said, "If you look ... in *all* the ways ... and differently than others ... all the mysteries now untold, to you will come unraveled." Wow! It hit me then! I needed to look in a different way than all these other people! *People's hearts often hold the answer that their eyes and minds do not. Looking like that I will know reality—and knowing that is what will save me!*

So instead of looking with my mind to clear my thickening confusion, I instead *felt* with my heart, for the mind is often overrated, for being too sure of one's intelligence can kill one's sense of feeling. But it was hard to do, and while lying there, it took hours of reflection and introspection to clear my leaden mind and calm the psychedelic lights. I prayed to God and meditated ... contemplated, to find the answers that my heart did hold. I remembered how to breathe and see and over time I let myself relax and *feel*.

My heart asked, "What do you *feel* you should do?" I thought, and felt it answering, "You have done well in World One and learned a lot. Now it's time to once again make a visit to the other." Then I remembered my mission and it heightened my focus and mental clarity, and my mind began to lighten—began to clear. Many said World Two was just a myth, but my heart said, "No, it isn't" ... and I believed my heart. The storm clouds in my mind withdrew; my heart felt peace; I exhaled and I was calm. The Secret saved me—gave me second life.

When I told *MYSELF* and *ME* I would return, they told me not to go. And it infuriated me that they couldn't see. "Leave me alone!" I said.

But even as I said it, I worried they might be right, for they had their strengths as well as me, and *ME* was the best of us at reasoning, "I pulled you back to reality again. I meditated—contemplated—calmed my mind till you returned, but it's getting harder as you get further in."

I spit back, "Quit saying that! It wasn't you. *I* brought myself back."

MYSELF spoke again, "Those times you said the Beast attacked you ... those were the days the principal was hounding us worst of all. We're convinced Old Man is a deceiving one. He created an awful plot you're the main character in. He keeps fooling you—telling you the Beasts are not real so you'll return and die for good by one. If you ask for his help, but he won't, then what does it mean? He's fooling you with a devilish scheme! Come back to World One again like you did *this* time, and they'll lock you up in a mental institution! Stay and perform with us! Our band is finally getting big. People know our songs!"

It was a temptation, for I loved the shows so much. Maybe World Two was insanity, but it was also adventure, and exploration, and great discoveries. And I loved the time to contemplate, to meditate, the newness of each day and every place, sparkling sunrises, accompanying animals, and powers building in my bones. I salivated thinking if I found a dinosaur, I might ride him! I smiled and realized, *The first in history!* I frowned, *Unless a caveman did—hmm, yeah I bet one already did. Maybe they had dinosaur rodeos back then.* And was a Welcome-back shindig awaiting me at the light-beam? And I wanted more—the reward to a quest—that only World Two offered. Would *you* go if you found the map to a treasure of gold? But what I might find was even greater. Most don't know the intense focus required to do great things.

In my mind I could see a distant sky light up with lightning flashes. And that's where I was told Old Man was! I would finally see if he was real—and if so, was the Devil—horns hiding under his hair. I could finally see where the treasure was buried—and I wanted it! I couldn't leave it in the ground, and that finally convinced me. "You guys continue on. I have to find a skeleton and other things. There's something about skeletons that I don't understand. But I'll be back before the summer with a whole new album of songs to sing, and we'll play some more. I'll speed through the race, get to the lightning source, find the treasure, and return. It's best for all of us—as a whole."

I reminded them of our meeting with Ms. Tremblay. "She is crazy like you. Skeletons are not alive!" They laughed in my face. I was at war with my other selves, and my neighbors heard me yelling at myself, and I left and slammed the door—turned off the light—to my soul. But of course, they had to accompany to the park—for this side of me was a little stronger.

So by the lake I found myself. I still hadn't found World One's hidden light that I left behind, but it would have to wait. I was out of practice transferring, and time went by till I relaxed more than before, pictured where I'd been, closed my eyes and visualized and FELT that other world.

Chapter 11

Third Trap to Kill Me

I transferred there, and there I was—sitting, overlooking that beautiful meadow, and its river, and the light-beam obelisk. I jerked my head to my left and looked for the skeleton. *AHHH! Yep, still there—and just as dead!* I got up and poked it with a stick. *Dead alright.* I knocked on its head a couple times with my knuckles, but there was no reprisal. *I'm not imagining anything! The Disciple is definitely dead!* I smirked, *I guess the Disciple's skeleton that Brinlin found was more alive than mine! Ha!* I stood in front of it—no key was by its feet to open the Gate, and I saw nothing else it could help me with! "HA!" I smirked again.

I looked at my reflection in the river and I looked younger than when I looked into the mirror at home, and I couldn't understand it, but this reflection was also blurry, like the mirror in World One. *Perhaps the movement of the water,* I thought.

I looked at the light-beam and temple ruins, and at the animals that assembled, and told them it was time for me to go. An iguana partially climbed up on my leg, and I knew he wanted to accompany, so I put him on my shoulders and had someone to talk to.

I walked a ways and then turned back to cement the memory of the meadow in my mind to help me later … and I smiled and continued, now trying to find my way without the Disciple's help.

My next stop would be a lightning source. But I felt free, for I had left *MYSELF* and *ME* behind. I felt those two were just weights that hung around my neck and inch by inch they were pulling me—down, down, down.

The journey would now be harder without the Disciple's knowledge, so I had to find some other way, some other method, some technique I hadn't yet used to save me from the forthcoming deathly obstacles. While thinking and looking for anything, I followed my only instruction to go east. Each day I watched that beautiful sunrise—so many, day after day as I walked that way, six months went by—nearing four years from the start, and a savanna biome I did enter.

I looked back to see my progress, and miles away, from where I'd come, I saw smoke from fires—three distinct pillars of smoke rising from the hills in back of me. *That's an SOS,* I knew. Someone was in trouble and needed help. My heart ached to backtrack and cancel out my forward progress, but I knew I should, and so I did.

An hour I walked then twice again, until following a path through a grove of baobab trees, leading toward the fires. When I got close, the path stopped at thickly growing vines surrounding the burning flames, fifty yards ahead.

I raised my foot to step into the vines, and fight my way on through, when Iguana started hissing, and coughing and sneezing. Then a hand clasped my shoulder and pulled me back— or I thought it did. I spun around, but there was no one there. Eyes wide, I looked around—everything was quiet. I looked back at the vines. Then I had a flashback of advice from Old Man, "Think carefully before you act." I looked closer at the leaves. Then I noticed three together. These weren't just vines—they were poison oak! If I had waded through all that until I made it to the fires, I would have been a mess—unable to continue on my trek, or worse! Then I knew this was another deliberate, intended disaster!

I fumed and looked around, wondering if the felon was watching me at that very moment. Iguana was upset too and made a threatening wheezing sound. I looked for Goatee Man but didn't see him. Again, though, I was interested in some footprints I found behind a tree. I studied them leading away from the tree—small steps, light weight and it seemed he used a walking stick for I saw the indentations in the dirt.

I started back to where I'd turned around. Whoever it was had outsmarted me again, but as I walked, I finalized my plan to finally snare the criminal, and I would set it in motion and snap the trap three weeks from then when the light of the moons would be their lowest. I would snare him and laugh when rejoicing, for I would finally know who the culprit was—and I started counting the days.

That night I watched the energized sky from lightning in the east—so much closer than before. As I watched, I started to worry. The light-beam emitted energy, but nothing like a place where lightning lived! A beam of light is obviously good. But who can say of a lightning force? Who would live at such a place? I thought what Heaven was like: peace and serenity—right? Then Hell: fire and tempests, and danger there—a place where lightning would be—the Devil living in a dirty cave! Was I really on Old Man's death march then—his final trick? I didn't know—so all I could do was hope Old Man was good. And I wouldn't quit for the possible reward.

I slept under trees, but with no bushes around to hide within, to douse my scent from nearby Beasts, I piled mounds of fresh, soft bison manure around me, sticks across the top, and more manure on that. Then I lay inside my scented tomb. Iguana too, but not happy about it. But it was a good idea, for again the Beasts ran by—thirty or forty this time. Looking out a small opening, I noticed the Beasts were growing in number. The Rules and Gate would have to be found in a timely manner.

My walk continued for several days, and through the savanna I passed meerkats watching me—forty joining me for a mile on my walk. Then another group approached, a skirmish ensued, and the second set accompanied me. "Wo! Take it easy guys!" I walked by an ocean to my right, enjoyed time lying in the sand, took a dip and rode its waves, fire on the beach at night, and then continued on. But going east I never ran out of land.

Each day, more and more eager I became, knowing the villain would soon be mine and I laughed, thinking of when I caught him—two and a half weeks left by then.

Then up and up, in rocky terrain, and on a mountain cliff between great walls of granite, overlooking the land below, I found an old abandoned monastery that monks had built of chiseled stones now weathered and old, but solid and strong as when they were forged. I rejoiced for I found what Nikita said to, and I looked up to see what looked down upon it. There to its side, carved in the granite of a massive mountain wall towering above me, were two huge eyes looking down at me.

Evening had come—the sun just down—only its glow left, and I hit the gong outside to announce my presence and went inside. All was in order, nothing astray, so I knew that all had lived and died there peacefully. I found an orchard, garden, and small cemetery in the back, and "AAAAHH! There they are again—the skeletons—but they're not in their place!" Twenty were *above* the ground—enjoying the place—sitting, relaxing against their grave stones.

The closest one had a chisel in his hand. "So many skeletons in this world!" I said. I pulled the skeleton forward a bit to see the words that he had carved . . . AND I GASPED! It said, *Here lies Nikita Volkov, he learned much on a great journey.* I just stood there, eyes wide. I thought, *Nikita Volkov really was here! That means he wasn't insane like the doctors said! He was just telling his journey like me . . . or me like him—we are the same. I wasn't just mirroring. But he didn't make it!* Oh my heart sank, so sad for him. Did he already know in World One? I would be the one to have to tell him.

And as this is proclaimed to you, fear falls over me, for *I* is still gone, in the other world, and I can't be sure he too has not befallen a similar fate—and now also, is just a skeleton ....

But I continue in his words. I sat there depressed and cried for Nikita that his World Two self had died. We were brothers, and I respected him for what he did. But now my brother was dead! His journey ended fruitlessly. I thought, *This second world is too intense—the obstacles too difficult. Nikita and the Disciple now are watching from above.*

The seriousness of the difficulty was now explicit. *How can I succeed?* I walked back inside the monastery and lit candles on the walls.

Everything was just the same as when the monks had lived. I discovered an ancient, massive book they wrote, listing written chants that they would say, and pictures showing their meditation methods. They drew instead of write, so all could understand, and I was interested in how they showed to breathe, and what to see. I thought of Nikita outside, and read some of the listed chants out loud. I thought and realized Nikita had probably also sat and held the same book I was holding and pronounced those chants as well.

I thought some more, and sat on the ground, legs crossed, and started chanting, Iguana curiously looking up at me. I focused forcefully. I created my own chant which I practiced faithfully, "Ali, Ali, Ali, Ali, Oh-Oh-Oh." Over and over I chanted it, then I chanted more, "Give me peace, give me strength, let my wounded spirit heal. Show me how I can succeed, tell me words I need to heed." I recited it over and over.

Then besides *my* chanting, I heard another—and I froze! Mantras I heard echoing off stone walls and through the rooms and halls. I stood and wandered through a hall, lighting candles on the way, until I came to a large hall—and I stopped. There sitting cross-legged on the flat stone floor, in the middle of the room, facing away from me, was the form of a man chanting.

I stood watching, then carefully walked inside, lighting more candles, then to where he was—and around him. It was Nikita Volkov! He was see-through like the dead with whom I lived, but I could hear him chant—from sometime past. Iguana and I sat down beside him. I listened to his chant: "Grasp the power this world has, not found in any other. Believe you have the strength. Know you have the power. That is when you do." The chant repeated over and over and I memorized it.

That night, before I slept, I sat, and breathed, and saw, and chanted. The killer hadn't broken *me*, but he *had* my heart, and along with seeing Nikita dead, my heart was so heavy now … and I realized that Chisel Hedgehog's was heavy as well. I felt sorry for him. In candle-light, I continued writing the story and wrote of a difficult time for him and the song around it. He and I were so alike. He needed someone to give him comfort. And as someone sang to him, I pictured Ms. Spear having a change of heart and singing to me: (Thinking Of The Memories, track 8)

I'm thinking of the memories, we've shared throughout our lives
and I would not return one, I have them wrapped up tight

So if you ever feel, all alone inside
know that someone's, thinking of you, all the time

Yeah, know that you, are not alone, and feel it inside
know that someone's, thinking of you, all the time

Chorus 1:
I'm thinking of you-u-u-u-u, I'm thinking of the times
I'm thinking of you-u-u-u-u, the times of our lives

Chorus 2:
I'm thinking of the silly, serious, profound
the funny and sublime
the times that you did this, and that, and the other thing

now frozen in my mind

Verse:
So if you think that no one cares, and no one understands
picture me within your mind, and maybe then you can

And if you ever feel, all dragged down inside
know that someone's, thinking of you, all the time

Yeah, if you think, you can't go on, and feel it inside,
know that someone's, thinking of you, all the time

Chorus 1 Repeated
Chorus 2 Repeated

The next morning, when I awoke, I found the monastery was full of activity! Like Nikita's ghost, now I saw the others too—performing their daily activities they once had done—and I joined them and rejoiced in the feeling of it all! "Oh thank you for the company!" Each evening I joined the end of their line and followed them out to the cemetery to watch the sun go down. They sat where their skeletons are now—and where their bones would finally rest—enjoying many *more* sunsets. I said good night to them each night, for when the sun would set, the monks would melt into those bones.

For a week I watched the sun arise, and through the pictures in the book, I read of life philosophies, ate noodles and fresh fruit, breathed the fresh mountain air, and had a wonderful reprieve with the monks inside the monastery walls. As I lived with them, and watched, I learned. Meditation became a favored trait, and all they taught I soaked up like a sponge. I hated to leave, but I finally did—but I left with more than when I came.

From the mountains, I looked down on the savanna plains; and as the mountains watched me walk away, they watched a lone soul traveling across the land—a week and a half left when I would catch my evil conniver.

That night, I thought of Nikita's chant, "Grasp the power this world has," and the next question for *The Anthem of the People* came:

What powers do we gain?

Besides Nikita's chant, I thought of the Elder's and Scholar's powers and thought, *Four rules I've found and maybe they contain some powers in this other world that now I have and didn't know.* The crickets were performing majestically ... and I squinted as I thought of them. I concentrated profusely on my ability—summoning a hidden power I hoped I earned, and this world would now present me. I wanted to hear it so bad, and knew I could, and that's how I did. I yelled, "Crickets, follow me, and sing!" And they did—when I conducted them! They responded splendidly—loud and triumphant and forceful when my arms flung wide open, and quickly up and down, and soft and serene and tranquil when instead I slowed my hands in gentle, flowing movements. And so my evenings were filled with me conducting symphonies—a cappella performances that rivaled the best in World One; for choirs there don't have ten thousand members in the round, singing under open skies of moonlit wonder. And I would often add accompaniment, when ukulele chords enhanced the sound.

[Tiz paused and thought of the magnificence—and of the impossibility of what he remembered and just said. He continued, "That world has possibilities unknown here."]

The grass decayed, dirt to sand, becoming a desert with giant twelve-foot-tall saguaro cacti that dwarfed me. All together, they looked like an army, marching together, arms up, ready for battle; but they let me pass beneath them undeterred; and in the heat, and my fatigue, when I passed them and looked back, I swear it looked like they were slowly moving away from me to my left.

By then, I had walked so far around this world that Frisky was halfway to the horizon in back of me, and I missed him so, for harder there he was to talk to. But as I looked above, I met a smiling alligator, and named him Thorny-Tooth. I started to get to know him—but nothing would ever replace my Frisky dog.

While lying looking at the stars one night, with someone hating me so much (wanting me dead), and Frisky leaving, and the monks too, I was overcome; and I'll admit I cried, and my soul retched with pain. All I had was Iguana with me, Thorny-Tooth above, and quite a ways behind, my Frisky dog—but day by day he was leaving me ... as everyone in this world eventually did—for I was often alone. Those moons above heard and looked down at me, past asteroids, clouds, and open country filled with cactus plants and Joshua trees. Their bright light scattered shadows in the night, and they *also* cried with me—through the clouds. But hearing my pain, Iguana coughed and sneezed to call some animal friends who came on in to comfort me: a kangaroo, and lizards, and snakes, and a couple donkeys who cried as well, "Hee-haw, hee-haw, hee-haw."

To give me peace, I thought of my plan—now only a week away—that would catch my murderous traitor if he still was tracking me. And I tried again to remember Ms. Spear's caring face, but like my Frisky, the memory of her face was also leaving me. So again, with new-world powers, I focused entirely on my desire, and with the help of the stars and both my hands and all my fingers moving simultaneously, I rearranged those stars so again I saw her face and gentle smile in the sky. I wanted to see it so bad, and knew I could, and that's how I did. I knew that moving the stars could not be—but they *could* be moved in my perception—and that was the power I had gained. Perception sometimes even greater than reality. The mind can do amazing things! As I looked at her face, the next song came, and this time *I* sang it to *her* with the animals listening. I called it: *She Smiles Bright,* and all night, as I looked above, I was comforted and wished the sun would not arise again. (She Smiles Bright, track 9)

Hey Girl, you're everything
your walk is always new
I'm stuck, I can't get off
of this stellar path, around you

Hey Girl, you're precious
I love the way you talk
think of you when the moon is high
and then again when the sun comes up

Hey girl, you're crazy
I love the way you laugh
I'm like an asteroid
falling towards you, ready to crash

Chorus:
She smiles bright on life like light
shining on morning dew
and gentle words of sweet advise
like summer winds in June
and like the clouds floating overhead
on a sunny day
eyes of peace like the twilight hue
of painted canvas shades
and if you captured every sparkle
put them in a glass
her spirit shines just like that

Verse:
Hey Girl, look in my eyes
your soul is sparkling white
my moon revolves around

the pull from your heavens heights

Hey girl, you hypnotize
with the motion of your hands
I'm a comet out in space
being pulled by your orbits' grasp.

Hey girl, you're energy
comes from a heart thats free
I'm a falling star that glows
and is shooting cross your planets' sea

Chorus Repeated

Chapter 12

The Magic Cloud

Rule #5: OF THE RIVER ROCKS

Iz paused, "You'll consider this next part craziest of all, for it deals with a magic cloud. HA! I know. But I have to say it, for it's what I saw.]

Iguana left with his friends and I scratched his back as a thank you card. My journey continued over sand dunes, then desert plants again, seeing dozens of jack-rabbits and road-runner birds racing past to some unseen finish line ahead. I watched as a spectator and then I raced as well. I made a cap from a Prickly-Pear cactus pad, the spines on the bottom plucked out and the rest protruding all around, and by a muddy watering hole, I noticed more of those animal tracks again—of the giant reptile variety. I had seen none yet, but I was interested (at least in the non-meat eaters)!

That night, storm clouds approached and then enveloped me. I dug a little cave in the side of a hill and sat chanting to clear my mind. I looked out over the desert, and the clouds poured and spawned a lightning storm, and I sought a sign from it. I yelled beyond the booming noise, "Old Man, I want to believe! Show me a sign which path to take, for 'east' is pretty wide, and on the

Disciple's guidance I no longer can rely. Is all of this an endless maze?"

Then I jumped when a voice came down in spiderweb-bolts of thunderous electrified energy in front of me: "Signs are not what's needed. Your path is yours alone, and the longer it is, the better. Shortcuts only slow you down, for you have to start again, to accumulate the things that you must learn—from experience— to reach the place you want to end."

My mind repeated words *MYSELF* had stated, "If you ask for his help, but he won't, then what does it mean?" But I said to myself, "No. He's like a father-figure to me here. He didn't help, but that was good advice." But still it made me wonder.

The rain abated, sun and heat returned, and I ventured inside the heated atmosphere, the heat intensifying till I panted like a dog, and sweat like a hog. Sometimes I looked around and laughed like a maniac and wrung my hands together when I thought of my plan to catch my killer, for only three days were left when my trap could be employed. I passed manzanita, desert brush, and dry river beds, snakes, lizards, and horny toads—that I played with. My elevation increased a bit, and I found myself on a great plateau and at its edge, looking down at a vast expanse of desert terrain where my path would lead me. Standing there, I pumped my arms into the air and yelled to everything below to let them know that I was coming.

In the far distance I saw one small cloud, alone in the sky, and I could tell by its shape that it was raining. But this cloud looked different. All by itself how could it rain like that? It seemed too strange. Something was odd. I descended, and the next morning I noticed neither the cloud nor its rain had abated, and oh how much I wanted to feel its refreshing water shower down on me. But then I started to worry. How could this cloud still be raining? Was it real or just a mirage like Dry Lake's water? I suddenly caught fear as I thought about the skeletons and their serial killer, and then about the fires that had beckoned me— and now this cloud was doing the same. Was it another trick the serial killer had devised? Had I run out of time to spring my trap? I wanted the rain so much, so I decided, "People can make fires, but not clouds." Then I thought, *Right?*

I increased my pace to reach the magic cloud and, while walking, was plagued with difficult memories. I asked *ME,* with his good reasoning, why, but then I remembered he wasn't there, and it saddened me. I was free to do as I wanted, but I lacked the others' strengths. I remembered hardships I had passed, thought of my sweat in all endeavors. I sighed, thinking of my foolishness in different situations. I wondered, *Why are these memories tormenting me?*

I tried to jog to attain the cloud before it sputtered out, but I was so tired I would jog a step and then walk a few and jog another. When I got there, at noon, there was a woman I'd never seen—standing, enjoying the coolness of the gentle rain. She looked fatigued, but healthy, slightly slouched, perhaps early-thirties, like many others I had seen. Long black hair she wore straight down, and a long, pink flowing dress, and a necklace of braided vines with two medallions—one copper-colored in the back the size of a nickel, and one silver in front, the size of a penny. And with her she had two goats.

She stood outside a large circle of great monoliths—and the rain fell very lightly in a twenty-foot circle around her. I stood outside the rain and wondered, *Is this woman a black widow spider that tried to snare and do me in? Is it really her that did the deeds and not Goatee Man, the Elder, or Emgo? Maybe this is really acid rain that falls!* She was also standing in the rain, so I assumed it was okay, and anyway, I had to feel its cool wetness. I entered and the rain felt soothingly delicious, my pores slurping up its moisture. She smiled, and suggested I join her inside the circle of stones. *Does she think I'm dumb? What trap does she have in there?*

She walked inside, and the cloud and rain drifted there as well, so again I was in the heat. I walked to a monolith and peeked around so just my eyes were showing. She was sitting on a rock with another by it in the middle of the circle. "Come," she said.

I pulled away and leaned my back against the monolith—looking out where I had come. *Should I go?* I remembered Nikita's words, "Believe you have the strength. Know you have the power." I inhaled deeply, "I'll go inside."

I closed my eyes and walked around the monolith into the circle and the rain. I smiled when I felt it and opened my eyes. "AAAAHHH!" I yelled. Indeed it was a trap! I was surrounded by twenty others—skeletons sitting on the ground—two leaning back against each stone. A great conference they seemed to be having and I was the intruder! The monks were quite nice, but these guys looked older and quite serious. Was this my trial and sentencing?

The lady spoke, "Don't worry. They're friendly," and she smiled. "Come sit," she said, and motioned to the other rock.

I was frozen—but my confidence increased, for in this circle I felt energy. I took a step forward and stopped. They didn't move so that was good. I wanted to sit. I looked over the rock carefully and then I walked to it and it felt so good to rest!

I paused, then quickly spun my head around to check the skeletons behind—they hadn't moved—weren't sneaking up. I spoke, "I see you also found the cloud to come and cool yourself under. It's amazing it's so little, and yet it's been raining for so long."

"Yes, it keeps me cool upon my journey, but I've only had it raining lightly," she said—as if she thought it followed her, and shaded her, and she controlled it, and its moisture! I couldn't control a burst of laughter, but managed to disguise it as a cough. "Oh," I said as I patted my chest.

I measured Black Widow-Woman. She didn't appear to be the killer, but she might be wearing pink to fool me. I glanced behind again then looked around for a trap to spring and snap, but didn't see one, so I asked her some questions to test her.

"I'm Tiz—good to meet you." I shook her hand and sat back down.

She said hello, and that her name was Cyla. I hadn't done this for a while—no words in months since always by myself. Was rusty what words to use and how to say them. I was apprehensive.

I thought, *Hmm ... what question should I ask, and how to ask it?* So I asked, "Are the goats for eating (for I'd been salivating)?"

Instantly, her eyes widened, and she gasped. "Of course not!" she blurted. "They're part of my family! That one's Tom, and that one's Becky."

The goats turned toward me, and I swear they glared and frowned!

I was so embarrassed. "Oh my, I'm so sorry. That just popped into my head—a World One type question—I'd never do that here! I haven't done this for a while! Now I see the resemblance."

"WHAT?" she exclaimed.

"Oh my gosh! No. Not with you—I meant with each other!" I felt my face start reddening. "*You* don't look like a goat! You're very pretty."

Then those goats looked even angrier—thinking I was saying they were ugly, and they started snorting.

"Umm ..." I tried another question: "Uh, is the cloud real or just a mirage?" *AH DANG!* I immediately thought. *That wasn't a good one, either.*

The goats started neighing like horses, sounding like they were laughing at me, looking at me and then at each other.

Black Widow-Woman got a confused look on her face. "You can feel the rain, can't you?"

"Of course, of course," I answered, embarrassed. *Oh my gosh I'm making a mess of this!*

She waved her hand above her head and the rain lessened to a drizzle.

I was amazed, and thought that maybe she really could control the cloud. Then fear abruptly struck. Maybe she really *had* pulled me in! Now I was right where Black Widow-Woman wanted me. The rain was suddenly not so soothingly delicious. I looked around, perturbed. *Can she also control the skeletons?* I stared at her hand, ready for it to wave and the skeletons to obey, and rise and run and jump on me. *Their teeth are still sharp!* I thought. But she didn't wave her hand again, and the skeletons didn't move, and didn't say a word.

The four people I was looking for were Old Man, whom she didn't resemble and neither was she Emgo. So the two remaining were a killer and Disciple—but the Disciple was dead, so only the killer remained! *I better not let her know I suspect she's possibly the killer.* So I asked the last, pretending that is what I sought. "Are you the Disciple?"

"What is this? The Three Questions game?" She smiled. "Really I'm just a person with a long, pink flowing dress. But . . . yes, some do call me that."

WHAT? I thought. Now I knew she was the killer, for I caught her in a lie, for the Disciple was dead! I played along to try to find out more about her, "Why do they call you the Disciple?"

Black Widow-Woman paused before answering, "Because I follow. As a Disciple, I follow mentors—but only their examples, for their paths I cannot walk upon. They can't share Pebbles, for to each they are their own. But far more Pebbles than me they have, and insights they have shared."

Again she paused. She stared at me and then inhaled deeply, through lips pressed close together. When she did, I was paralyzed, like when the Scholar looked inside of me. But this lady did not look inside. Something else—when she breathed! I could tell that she was also searching for something.

She finally spoke: "Why have you come?"

I was surprised how genuine she was, and that reassured me a little; but still I was timid in my reply, "Before I answer, I have a question of my own." I paused. "I know you lie—why? I know you're not the Disciple. I found her skeleton a while back."

The goats snorted and pawed the dirt, upset. She said, "It's okay guys." She pursed her lips and squinted, then inhaled again, before smiling. "I understand your concern. But wouldn't it be arrogant of us to think there is only one? There are many Disciples—but only one will have the thing *you* need."

It took several seconds for the thought to register. I squinted and thought some more. "Oh my gosh!" I blurted, "You mean you're not dead?" (*Oh dang, another bad one*! I groaned, embarrassed.)

The goats laughed again, jumping up and down.

She squinted, "Uh . . . no!"

As I looked at her, and her countenance, I felt it could be true! It hadn't even occurred to me there could be many! She really might be the Disciple with the information that I needed! I put my hands on my head, "I can't believe it! Really? I worried so long, for nothing?" I couldn't believe my luck. I excitedly started thinking what the answer was to her earlier question, *I'm here on a journey to find Rules, and Maps, and a secret Mountain where there are amazing things! But lately I haven't found a single thing!*

As I was thinking, she slightly opened up her mouth and breathed, and it seemed that when she did, she could taste the air—and the thoughts and feelings in it exuding from my pores and they were bare to her. She took pressure from the air—had some sort of spell on me—till I was hypnotized. But much of her strength it took as well, until she finally sighed and bowed her head with her shoulders slouched. She aged before my eyes—like the Scholar, paler, weaker. She looked at me and loudly whispered, "Are you really sure that lately you haven't found a single thing?" She spoke, "Have you forgotten how to look? Your thoughts confirm it." She paused and then continued, "You're searching for the Truth, aren't you? I saw and heard you on the ridge last night and felt that I should wait. So I sat in meditation to discover why. All night long and then today—all I did was contemplate. The answer was very deep and all my strength was used to uncover it. Of the many things I've learned, the Truth kept coming to my mind. The Truth is the same for everyone ... but used for different things. For you, I can tell, it's to escape. Is that for what you've come?"

My eyes widened. I softly spoke, "It is."

She continued, "I testify of Truth. Truth from all the ages past, handed down from old to young. It's found in books, and scrolls, and scribbled in caves, in stories told and notes saved, in people's journals and their traditions, when people talk and their opinions. All have added to the whole."

I was listening and, now I'm ashamed to say, confidence greatly renewed in me, so utterly relieved that I might again succeed—soon to know the Truth, I thought was lost. With fervor and pride I breathed deep, and smiled, and like a rooster, with my feathers puffed up, I interrupted her, "You asked me why I came? Well. Let me tell you! I came to find all of that! And then for a marvelous treasure and a Gate that opens to incredible things! Then I'll share it with the world, and in great halls, with their announcement echoing, they will formally pronounce, 'Introducing, The Noble Sir Tiz ... the Great Discoverer of Other Worlds!'" When I said it, I swear those goats laughed again, and then rolled on their backs kicking their legs. I realized what I had done, and felt embarrassed when the Disciple shook her head and frowned—first at them and then at me.

She spoke, "What you want is so profound. Remember this, for it's the Truth: Instead of always looking for something grandiose or faraway, remember to look down. Keep looking for the Pebbles on the ground. No one looks for pieces of sand, but those make up the beach. Trees make the forest. Birds make the flock. Rocks make the mountain. Look for the pieces and put them together and then you'll see the whole. Is it the few people who invent the great thing that makes the most difference? Or are they just most visible? And the real difference comes from the many tiny deeds the rest of us do that number in the billions! What really changes the world? Stop looking for the great and grand—and focus on the small. That is the Truth of which I speak. We all are the sand that makes the beach." She looked at me trying to gauge the impact, and then smiled. "That's why I needed to wait, isn't it?"

I nodded. There was no doubt she really was the Disciple. Now I had the Truth to escape from the dungeon.

Then a loud sound behind! "AAAH!" I yelled, and again spun around—but one of the skeletons had just fallen over—asleep I guess. Cyla stood up and helped her sit again.

That night, we camped together enjoying a fire and dinner together. I gave her some of my sundried snails, and she gave me some of her beans, potatoes, wild strawberries, and goat milk (I think I traded well). She prayed to God before we ate, and then she thanked the earth for what it grew. The cloud was gone when I looked up in the dark, and we enjoyed an immensity of stars in skies of endless, boundless, all-encompassing eternity. Once she went a ways and talked to them, and I admit I tried to listen, but the words were in that other tongue—and it, I had forgotten. I introduced her to Thorny-Tooth, and she introduced me to Hairy-Cat (whom I hadn't noticed before—but then I clearly did).

We talked for most the night. She was only in World Two on a diversion from a journey in World Four, she said when asked. She told me of the difficulties and challenges in searching for an island there and the passage leading to it, but her description of World Four was far beyond incredible.

Then a memory came to me of an article I read about a businesswoman in China named Yang Cyla. At the start of large manufacturing there, she contacted businesses about shipping their products. From a few initial clients, she eventually developed the largest shipping line in the country, becoming one of the wealthiest people there—worth hundreds of millions. Then she started focusing on her charity.

I asked if she was her, and she smiled and admitted it. She took no credit, though, and gave it to the Maps. "They showed the path and steps. In World One, all us wanderers are successful, but many want something else than worldly victory. And we all feel compelled to follow the path to charity. Making money becomes easy. Sometimes it's correctly giving that's hard. But more than anything, I want to visit Elgobon. Each world is more incredible, and I can't imagine what it's like."

I asked her why no one mentions these other-world journeys back home—only Nikita Volkov. She said many try, but they are considered fanatical. "It's too out of the ordinary for most to understand or believe." (And I could relate to that—and I thought of Nikita in the asylum for so long, and frowned.)

The next morning, we woke up late—for the sun was high in the sky, but not upon us shining, since again the cloud was there, and shading. Its rain is what awoke us, until the Disciple waved her hand to stop it, and said it must be ten, for that is when she told it. I felt renewed and the skeletons too—them sleeping even sounder than me. I smiled knowing only one day was left to set my trap to catch my killer. I looked around—wondering if he was out there somewhere—watching. The Disciple still used a stick to walk around and lean upon. I was surprised, for inside the circle seemed to heal *me*. I didn't need a week of recovery like at the castle. After a night of sleeping there, I was renewed and energetic and healthy.

We talked over breakfast and she said, "A man named Emgo told me long ago I carried something special, and I would find out what it was if I journeyed to a place called the Glowing Rock. I journeyed—for months . . . so difficult. But in the end, I found from others, there is no Glowing Rock. It was a trick he also played on them. But I am thankful."

Thankful? I thought. *Why so many thankful to someone who does those things like that?* This Emgo man intrigued but enraged me. Everyone called him good—but his deeds were atrocious—but some way he got people actually liking him for doing them!

He had tricked and lied and stolen, but so many thankful. For myself, I made a note to never let him do those things to me; and on my journeys, I would look for him—I would find him—and discover if he was good or bad.

"Do you know where Emgo is?" I asked.

"Sometimes he visits a village called Po," she said.

"What can you tell me about the lightning lake?"

"Oh yes," she said. "Continue east. As incredible as the light-beam, but far different—majestic you might say. Powerful indeed."

A thought arose. I spoke, "Hey if I come with you, we'd both have someone to talk to! You could ride Becky, and I, Tom."

"RIDE THEM?" she exclaimed. "I don't do that! Poor things."

This time besides the glares and frowns, the goats stomped their right front hooves as if threatening me!

"Oh my gosh, I'm sorry!" I said, and thinking, *Dang! I did it again.*

She mentioned, "If you make it to the Gate, take caution when it opens! Shield yourself if possible. Passing gates to higher worlds requires all that we have. The body must be renewed—leaving behind the old—attaining the new. So the agony is sometimes the worst torture possible. And the obstacle at the evil entrance at the base of the Mountain will rip you apart limb by limb, eat your flesh and drink your blood, and then enjoy your bones .... But here's a Clue to help you survive (and I listened close, for I had been waiting for this): You will surely die ... unless you see yourself as water, as an ancient Chinese leader said to do. So focus entirely and unwaveringly through the duration of the ordeal."

My eyes widened and I groaned, but I told her I was thankful for everything and hugged her, then finally let go to walk past her. Before she let go, she whispered in my ear, "Look in your pockets for something special you are carrying." Then as final instruction, "Emgo can tell you where the Mountain is. Without his guidance, the mountains will all look similar. But with his guidance, the special Mountain will look profound—and you will know your destiny. And ask the Prophet what opens the Gate—for it is sealed without that knowledge, and all is lost without it. Now get yourself to the lightning source."

I listened intently and then kissed her on the cheek. "Thank you so much! And good luck on *your* journey." I walked past her, and as I was passing her goats I said, "Sorry goats," but they turned around and kicked dirt on me with their back hooves! I shrugged my shoulders and walked away, waving good bye to the skeletons, then between the monoliths, and I looked back at Cyla. When I did, I saw her reach into her backpack and pull out a piece of leather and sit down on the ground between two skeletons.

I was happy to leave those skeletons, for the whole time there, they just stared at me! And when I left, I was no longer surrounded. I walked for fifty yards checking all my pockets, but only found the gemstones and pulled them out. Those weren't the Pebbles she was talking of and I placed them in my pack. I stopped and focused my thoughts. I closed my eyes, and when I opened them I saw a sign that I hadn't seen before. Carved into wood shaped like an arrow, pointing one direction, the engraving said, *The Glowing Rock.*

"Oh! I'll not follow Emgo's folly!" I thought how sad it'd been—the Disciple's trip to the Glowing Rock ... for months and months ... so difficult ... so very long and lonely. I squinted. That reminded me of the months of hardships that I had during *my* walk and throughout my life, and my memories that I had of all *my* struggles. Then a vision came to mind of all the rivers on my walk that I had crossed. I thought, *All of us are like rough and jagged rocks, and that is what this life is for—to fall from the mountain into the river of life and be pushed and pounded, ground and sanded, smoothed and finally polished like rocks in a river for a thousand years.* That's the special thing we carry: all our memories of struggles and what we learn from them—and if we don't learn and change, we waste them. I realized this was a key concept I must remember, that for me might open up a Gate.

This was a Rule! THE RULE OF THE RIVER ROCKS: <u>There is value and lessons in life's hardest times, so be happy for your struggles, for their lessons teach you and perfect you—if you let them</u>. This, I realized, was what I earlier heard the river rocks whispering.

Her words on Truth hit me harder with that in mind. *The little make the big. All those little Pebbles can't forget, for those make who I am.* I checked my pockets again—and they were filled with Pebbles that I had found and learned while on my journey, but had not recognized. Then I fully understood the Truth—to never look beyond the small and insignificant, whether they be Pebbles or they be people, for they make up the world. I removed the Pebbles and smiled, then let them fall between my fingers—watching them, for now I had secured them in my mind. As they fell, and collected on the ground, I noticed a sparkle beneath them. I parted them and picked up a stone—a ruby to go with the other ones.

I looked back and saw the Disciple walking away—no more walking stick. Walked lively, looked energetic again. Her arms were celebrating in the air. She was veering to my right, and I realized that cloud was moving with her—casting shade down on her as she walked, and as I watched, she moved one hand in a circle in the air, and the cloud again began to lightly rain (and I thought I would like to get one of those). As I watched, she and her goats and cloud faded away.

I thought of the Disciple's powers to read my mind, and hypnotize, and control the elements, and I knew when through the Gate that something similar I might receive. It was exciting—but also scary. Worldly success? Yes, that would be easy with the Maps, I could tell, but much, much more than that. Up ahead, though, according to many, trials awaited that would test my very core—and I would have to pass through hell to make it to the Gate!

I sighed as I walked on. Yes, I had found the Truth, and the fifth Rule, but again someone had left, and it felt horrible .... Then I thought of her last advice, "Get yourself to the lightning source." Why would she suggest that? I was getting fearful of the place. *Will it be the final blow?* But I would go—for I had to see Old Man again! I had to prove it to myself that he was real and he was good. I had heard such good advice from him, I was thankful and wanted to believe.

But the worst was soon to come—when I sprung my trap and discovered who the criminal was who hated me worst of all.

Chapter 13

The Deceiving, Note-Leaver, Perpetrator

Tiz stretched and another drink. He could hear someone tell their neighbor, "I learned that Rule myself—in *this* world."

Tiz continued, but first to her, "*That* you learned it is the key—not where. It sounds like you are on the journey too—but in World One. Maybe you didn't realize it."]

Three weeks had come and gone, and I wondered if my killer still was planning traps ahead. That night, the moons would be their slightest, and I wouldn't be discovered, so as I walked that day, I decided that would be the night . . . to finally find out who he was.

Pleading for the sun to quicken its pace, while I was walking, I watched it inch across the sky as I started passing scattered desert willow trees, bushes and shrubs. Again with fear, I passed those reptile tracks, and some plants shaped like a bell, which made a humming sound when jostled. Other plants were woody—long and hollow—and when the wind arose, they whistled. It was there I came around some trees and in an opening stood a Tyrannosaurus Rex eating those humming and whistling bushes one by one! His were the tracks that I had seen. He had so many plants in his mouth that when he chewed while opening and closing his mouth and breathing, he sounded like a choir singing on and off again—and even more when he yawned for the finale.

I stood transfixed and almost ran, not wanting myself to be the protein for his lunch. But the music was so amusing, and I noticed he ate plants! Maybe he wouldn't eat me after all! He saw me, but indeed he did not eat me—in this world not a meat eater (so that was reassuring). He also spit no snot at me, so that was nice as well—for he was ten times bigger than the frog. But I'll admit it was fun to see, something that in my world was long since dead and gone.

Then around some bushes came his family: the female and three youngsters (who were a foot taller than me). The young ones were running—bumping each other in play, and when they saw me, they filled with wonder. They came and smelled, and licked, and one sucked on my whole head like a lolly-pop— lifting me a couple inches off the ground, until I pushed my head out of his mouth. His thick saliva was abundant and intense, and when back down, I shook my soaking, dripping, gooey head and wiped it off with my hands, and I'll admit I got upset and scolded him. Then they nudged me until I also played their game. I realized my dinosaur-ride was finally ready to be fulfilled—*Oh how wonderful to complete my fantasy!* So I climbed on one's back, but before I could encourage him with a, "Giddyup!" I got down fast—faster than I wanted when the mother jaunted over and opened her mouth to show her teeth as a warning with an extended growl so forceful, it was like sticking my head out the window of a moving car. It blew me off my dinosaur, but before it did, it dried up all the spit, and then my wind-blown hairdo looked more like spines on a porcupine. My dinosaur-ride was so close, but would have to wait.

I moseyed on, and finally came the night, and I ate my dinner around a fire. Then in the blackness of the night, when only slivers of the moons were up, instead of sleep, I continued on. But I made a great detour around the path I would have strode, and by morning light I had again rejoined my path, but ten miles farther on. Now *I* was ahead of *him*, and *he* would be coming to *me*.

I settled down in a hiding spot and dozed off during the day. Twice I saw packs of Beasts run by a ways away. I could tell the time was close at hand when they were going to find me and there was going to be a mighty battle. But without a trap or means to fight, the battle would be between themselves who got which parts of me.

Around dinnertime as the sun was signing off and shadows started their day, I saw movement quite a ways away through the bushes and the Joshua trees. The sun went down and it was dark. In the distant sky to the east I saw my usual clouds of exploding light, but now close enough to also see the lightning flashes coming down—closer and closer every day until soon I would be at my journey's end. But that did not preoccupy my mind that night. My plan was in motion to catch the evil offender, and I felt energy replace my tiredness for what I'd catch ahead, but also sorrow in my heart because it had to come to this.

As I expected, soon the glow of a small fire was projected, and carefully I crouched over and snuck toward it. As I crept closer, I could hear someone crying—but painfully ... so it sounded more like the moaning or sobbing I had heard on nights before. I stealthily tip-toed through the brush, but I guess my "stealthiness" was not quite stealthy enough, for when I got there, the person was gone—escaped into the dark of the night. It looked like their departure was in haste, for not enough dirt thrown on fire to negate, water they had been boiling was spilled upon the ground, and a couple items left behind they had forgot— the most interesting ones a paper that said, "Go this way to the next Rule," and ... a spear!

"NOOOOO!" I cried with my hands in fists and shaking. Oh my heart saddened, and started to hurt, believing it was Ms. Spear, for it was her who I so often dreamed about, but I still remembered her jabbing me with a spear in my chest! And she was the only one I had ever seen with one. Yeah, it might be somebody else's, but it looked like I remembered it ... and the tip was red—with *my* blood probably!

I sat upon the earth and sighed—double hard this time, and felt the sigh then settle in my heart like it was tearing.

At the same time, Chisel Hedgehog also felt the pain: (All Alone In A Cave, track 10)

All alone, in a cave like this
and I can feel, the loneliness ...

Where's that sun, and where's that sky
that make me smile, as the day goes by

Where's my friends, in the cold dark night
when the stars don't shine, and there is no light

Chorus:
Yeah, where am I, and where have I been
and where am I going, and where's the end

Where's there a hand, that I can hold
that lights the fire, down inside my soul ...

Verse:
All alone, in a cave like this...
Does anyone care ... and am I missed?

The memory of Ms. Spear laughing, even though done sarcastically, filled my mind. For some reason when I pictured her face, I pictured what had been and could be again, and not what it became. *Maybe she was alone and lonely—just like me*, I thought. Maybe that was why her crying! I could picture her face with tears on it and my heart felt heavy for her. If she would have only let me help. But lonely or not, she hated me—that much was for certain—and I no longer wanted her or her meanness, or deceitfulness. Now that I think of it, it should have been obvious she was the evil one—but I was blind, I guess ... for I didn't want that answer.

As I thought of that, and of my breaking heart, I didn't think I could go on. It now seems silly, for I'd only met her once, but like a little kid, it was a crush I guess that I never had like that. Or it was her initial reassuring smile and her comfort that I wanted. Or maybe I had an intuition that it could have been true love—and that is why it hit so hard ... harder than I would have thought. Now to find out she was the one that did the deeds—tears welled up—and not only in the same vicinity I didn't want to be, but not even in this same World Two. And all the other difficulties there compounded it. And not even knowing if this world was reality. This was the final straw. I had to get out. I had to get back.

I would miss Frisky, and Thorny-Tooth, and my cricket symphonies, and the ravens always up above, and the light green sky, and multiple moons, and ever-changing creative landscapes. Five Rules I'd found (five precious gemstones too), and I was so close to finding Old Man by the lightning flashes, confronting Emgo, reaching the Mountain and the Maps, and discovering what is unimaginable with the opening of the Gate. But the air was now out of my lungs. I no longer cared about having the treasure, or being changed forever, or controlling clouds, or reading minds, or speaking foreign languages, or making llamas sing, or following Maps to becoming rich, or even being Columbus's chum (with our bronzed busts displayed prominently at adventurers' clubs).

I would be relieved of evading Beasts. Their numbers were growing—so many recruits. It would have been soon again when we would meet, and I would have been their dinner's treat! Neither would I have to wonder why they were going east, or endure the agony at the Gate, or the hellish entrance to the Mountain that might shred me, and neither would I be tied up and locked in a dungeon and have to use the Truth to escape. I wouldn't have to find Old Man to see if he was really an illusion and this was just a dream—a phony journey just in my mind. For remembering everything, it was inconceivable. Goats don't laugh, and clouds are not controlled. How ridiculous to think so. Things are only true if they are normal, and understood, and proven, and everyone agrees—right? I was tired of wondering. This wasn't how I wanted to return. I was even earlier than I had said—April had come.

I was also tired of my inner war with *ME*, *MYSELF*, and *I*. I wanted all my sides to agree and no longer play that game of tug of war upon my heart and mind and soul. Maybe if I had found what I left behind that would light my way I could have continued. But now I was lost in the dark. I was going back.

Then the lightning flashes in the east increased till it was like a war—thrashing down like never before, one after the other, and many at once. I felt their anger—upset at me, at my abandoning, and they were beckoning for me to stay and go to them. It was night, but the sky in the east was lit like day. I watched for quite some time, but then I turned around so I wouldn't see.

With a low and labored voice, I asked *MYSELF* to meet me at the lake, and then I focused and transferred there—back to World One. *MYSELF* wanted to talk about it, but I didn't say a word, and just ignored him—I was too depressed .... I wanted no one's help. Now I was done. I would never go back.

I went home and sat in my room, turned off the light, never coming out, and let *ME* and *MYSELF* carry on ... in World One. But World Two was done—for part of me died ... and it was *I*.

*   *   *

[Tiz was depressed remembering, and exhausted from his speech to the audience so he took his leave, but they begged him to finish his story the next day. One in the back yelled, "Did you make it back, and to the Gate?" Tiz told them he would return the next day and tell them the most treacherous part and end of his journey.

With honor, they all stood up, transfixed—perfectly silent, and waited for him to pass as he walked down the aisle to the door, like he was a foreign dignitary. Now, no one shook their heads, but as he passed he could hear soft-voiced debates begin, "The story can't be real, can it?" "But there's so much detail and he tells it so precisely."

Tiz stopped and spoke to them, "Maybe this story isn't even about me. Maybe it's about *us*! Maybe it's about life itself, that all of us are living, and we're all on the journey but only a few recognize it! Maybe it doesn't even matter if there is a real other world, or if it is in my or *our* minds. Maybe it's only what happens there that matters."]

— End Part One —

— Part Two —

Chapter 14

The Dreaded Days / A Thousand Roses / I Was Twelve

Rule #6: OF THE NEXT TREE

As Tiz left the university auditorium, again the news reporters crowded in to film and question him and the crowd of people had grown to a thousand souls. They were in a throng on the grass outside and listened to his discourse over loud speakers, and policemen tried to keep the peace. He gave interviews and then people wanted autographs or to simply pat him on the back or shake his hand. "You inspire us," so many said.

"I'm confused," he replied. "Why do I inspire you? I've been in a mental institution. How did you all learn of this?" But there was too much noise and so many people pushing and crowding in for pictures.

One from the back yelled, "Marry me Tiz!" And Tiz laughed, surprised.

"We're behind you Tiz. Get out and play for us again!" Tiz waved.

Another yelled, "Did you get back and find the Maps Tiz?"

"I'll tell you tomorrow," Tiz said, and he waved goodbye, and the event coordinator led him to a hotel across the street.

The director and superintendent exited the auditorium and received a resounding, "BOOOO!" "Get him out of there. He's perfectly fine!" "Let him think what he wants to!" "It's a free world! We can say what we want."

The director responded, "We're behind him as much as you. We're hoping for the best. Let's see what he says tomorrow."

In the morning, Tiz returned and continued his speech and told the most treacherous part and what happened at the end of his trip.]

Now back home, *MYSELF* and *ME* discovered a tiny flicker of adventurous spirit alive in them and knew that it was *I*—and felt they could revive him, so they kept our body fed and talked to *I* each day to keep the tiny light alive—even though *I* didn't want them to. But they knew if not successful, a part of them would die—the adventurous side—so they continued every day, for although adventure scared them, it was a fear they liked—but only *I* would force it on them.

In those dreaded days in my dark room, I prayed for night to let me sleep, for being awake was like hell to me. Once during the day, when *MYSELF* and *ME* were away, it was quiet and dark and I heard a whispering. I gasped and listened. It was a low, hoarse voice, "Come back to us. It's okay. Don't let others deter you. And don't fret the Beasts—they're not real."

"Yes they are! I know they're real. Why do you tell me such dirty lies? They're hunting me." I yelled, "Why do you tempt me so? You're upset I evaded them! Get out of here—out of my head," and I groaned with pain in my chest.

My head was a wreck, but I was nurtured by my other sides. *MYSELF* would talk to me about the students, and *ME* would stand in front of a mirror and try to get me to look at him smiling, but I refused. And being awake was not really so, for consciousness was a foggy mist, and only slightly could I tell I was awake, and when people spoke to me, I only heard faded sounds around me. I killed all memories I could of World Two, and as time progressed, World Two totally faded. But after a month of compassionate care by my other sides, I started to see a light like at the end of a tunnel.

Then when people spoke, a word was occasionally understood subconsciously. One day, I heard the word "students," and one day I heard "Rules," and then my mind reflected on those things. Another day I heard laughter from a group, and I remembered: "Mr. Tiz." Then I saw some polished rocks inside a river when I had to accompany *MYSELF* fishing, and I surprised myself by wondering what it meant. That night when *ME* and *MYSELF* talked, it started sinking in—of what they were reminding me, and the next day, I had an intense desire to go and see those students.

So I went and watched through the eyes of *MYSELF* and joined in what he did. As I watched as a spectator, I saw the master teacher that *MYSELF* was, and how well he related to the class, and I was so impressed. This was his strength. It was him the students loved the most—that caring side of me, and he taught so well. As always, my students were magical—still so kind, and my job was not in jeopardy for the psychiatrist didn't know that *I* still existed. *MYSELF* had been having to see her once a month because my principal insisted so. "He's a vinegary one," she said. He disparaged me to the district every chance he got, but all the other teachers stood up for me. As my band got bigger, when I was away, he knew it was he that partly started it, and he got more upset and told everyone, "He should spend his weekends at the school, not playing silly songs in that band!" But artists know that greatness comes from endless hours working on their dreams. There are always disbelievers—those who consider their work on them a waste of time. They can't see the passion and the love an artist has for them. He was out to get me and wanted to prove I wasn't mentally fit so that he could fire me. But *MYSELF* always hid *ME* and *I* and convinced the psychiatrist that everything was fine.

I wasn't great at basketball, but I played with the boys, for height I had, and you can't teach that; and the girls included me in their pottery-making class during my free period, and although not the best, they smiled and said, "Mr. Tiz, your mug is good (but I noticed crossed fingers behind their backs)." After that, *I'm* the one who smiled.

I thought about dating again, but my heart was not much into it, for there was someone who had broken it. But of course my students kept me going: "Mr. Tiz," the girls said, "let's dress you up correctly so the ladies can't resist." Then, walking around, I looked fourteen again! And the boys would say, "Don't listen to them! What ladies like are muscles in their men," so they brought me pads to go under my shirts, and 1 looked buff. One boy brought me glasses to look sophisticated; one taught me to walk with my arms out a ways and sway a little. Some boys taught me lines to say, and how, like with an upraised chin: "Hey, girl— how *you* doin?" like I was from New Jersey. Or, "Try one of these, Mr. Tiz: 'Fancy meeting you here. I just saw you in my dreams last night!' Or, 'How many Tizzes does it take to screw in a light bulb? None when you're around, because you light up my life already.' Or, 'When I see you, I'm light on my feet, for my heart is fluttering.'"

But the girls said, "Don't listen to that garbage! Sweep her off her feet. Light like a thousand candles and have her over to your house." Then I thought, *Ah ... fire hazard!* Or they mentioned, "Buy like a thousand roses and have them delivered all at once." Then several of them swooned, saying, "Oh my gosh can you imagine!" And I thought, *Do these girls know what money is?* But I think they read my mind, for they said, "Don't be cheap, Mr. Tiz! You can't put a price on love." And I thought, *My banker can—and he did last time I wrote a check and he bounced it. Now that I think of it, that was for flowers too ... and only twelve of them.*

From my interaction with them, I felt like I could breathe again, and as weeks went by while teaching them, I started telling jokes again, and being the accuser first when I smelled an odor percolating. Again, I started making them laugh, and helping them, and I realized when someone makes another happy, they are happier themselves. This pleased *MYSELF* and *ME* immensely. Then I started opening my eyes when *ME* would smile in the mirror. *ME* rationalized with me, "You can get through this and here are the steps to do it." And *MYSELF* showed love, "I won't give up. I'll stay with you."

Every day my heart raced as I got to school, and I looked around corners for the principal, waiting for him to find and denigrate me over my ... songs, or ... hair, or ... shirt, or ... fingernails not looking right .... Then one day we were informed that he had been reassigned ... to Alaska! "Too many complaints, and too much attitude!" the superintendent said. "A cold, frozen place for a cold-hearted soul." The other teachers happily yelled and threw a huge party, and I breathed a sigh of relief. That eased my stress and helped me heal further. But I was surprised, for I felt sorry for him, and wished he would learn and change.

I started writing songs again, for music calms my soul. I felt like I was freed from a prison, so I wrote one I called, *Living for the Weekend,* and with my band, we practiced it, and *She Smiles Bright* as well. I hadn't played with them in nine months, but in that time they continued, and our fame had grown. We were now on the radio! We had an agent now, and during summer, we set out on our *The Band the Principal Hates Tour*. Forty cities we played in all, and as we sang to moving, singing audiences in the thousands, I gloried in the energy.

Lights shone on us in concert halls, speakers echoed in stadiums, I saw us on the television and the news, and heard us in my car. I did interviews, and it totally healed me from my funk. Always started the same: the lights are out and then us jamming on our instruments and then *The Anthem of the People*. Then the lights come on and we sing: (Living For The Weekend, track 11)

The lights of the city, turn on at six o'clock
and people shuffle home, at the end of the day

and all Friday night, people kicking to the music
and they yell and shout, and they rock and shake

Chorus 1:
and everywhere you go, people living for the weekend
spending all the money, that they made that week

and everywhere you look, people enjoying their freedom
finally have escaped, and their ready to play

Chorus 2:
and couples use the night, as a means to escape
and they wine and dine, till the sun does shine

Drums

Verse:
they listen to the tick, and the tock of the clock
till they hear the whistle yell, and they run to escape

and bars and pubs, and restaurants and dancing spots
welcome in the masses, with a smiling face

Chorus 1 Repeated

and filtered through the lights, of the night people letting loose
peeling off their jackets, and their vests and their ties

Drums

Verse:
The keys for the locks, on the chains of the people
are released on a Friday, when the clock strikes five

and no one can hold them, and no more can scold them
and when they're out the gate, they holler that they're free

Chorus 1 Repeated

and as the clock ticks on, and people soak up all the energy
they revel in the synergy, and they are finally free.

But when September came, I was back at school and we only
played on weekends again, flying somewhere new, for I loved my
students and our interplay. That's how I started, and where my
inspiration grew.

I exhaled with relief at being free from my depressed state,
and I relished everything exciting. I started skydiving again, like
when in college, fishing, hiking, movies with my friends. With
MYSELF I wrote more songs, for he wrote as good as I—just with
a different flavor. My bandmates added more, and we recorded
them all, and our third album was released. One year came and
went, and I only focused on World One events.

*   *   *

Then, as I was told later, a ship arrived in a major port in a
big city several hours away from my town. A lady walked out
and stood at the top of the gang plank. She yelled some

instructions to workers securing the ship and to those starting the process to unload its cargo. Then she took off her sunglasses and looked out on the city. It was Yang Cyla. She walked down the ramp and entered an awaiting limousine . . . .

*   *   *

The next day, I was walking on my street and a bird was chirping loudly in a tree ahead of me. I noticed a discolored feather in her wing. As I approached, she flew away to another tree ahead on my path that I could see. After several such encounters I started following, and eventually she flew to a tree inside a park with a lake in the middle of it. I entered and felt a comfortable warmth inside of me. She flew inside a little grove of trees. I entered and looked around, then through them at the lake, and when I did, my heart pounded and my breathing quickened. I looked at the grove again with heightened tension and mental clearness, and when I did I started remembering something. I remembered planning my trip to another world so long before. Then BOOM—everything came back to me like a thousand memories dumped into my brain. My whole journey came back and what I learned and all my thoughts; and when they did, it was all too much. I remembered I had a goal, and purpose, and was almost to the end of it, and I contemplated continuing; but I feared the trials in World Two would end my journey tragically.

That reminded me of a time when I was only twelve years old, and so the twenty-pound pack on my back seemed like a ton of bricks after having hiked for ten miles and being out of shape and hiking in the thin air of high altitude in the mountains. We were a group of Scouts and we had all lost hope; we were so tired; we would not be able to make it to our base camp. After that, one of my leaders told us, "Don't focus on getting to the base camp. See that next tree up ahead? Get there. Then look for the next tree."

Hmm ... I looked at the next tree. *Yes, I can make it there (but it would have been nice if someone had put them a little closer together)!*

The lesson had been many years prior, and I had not identified its worth. But now I knew what I had found: the sixth Rule! THE RULE OF THE NEXT TREE: <u>Maintain hope by making little goals and taking little steps to get there</u>. I looked around—sure enough. This time an amethyst.

Then I thought of Nikita again, and I researched and found his phone number in Russia and called him. I told him of the giant eyes looking down upon the monastery and he confirmed the same. Surely this should propel me on. Then sorrowfully I told him about his skeleton I found. "I'm so sorry, but you didn't make it to the Gate," I said. "That's where you died."

That night in a dream, I saw myself on a mountaintop, looking at the most beautiful scene in the universe—sunshine flowing down in all the rainbow colors, slightly sparkling on the earth, myself with arms outstretched receiving it. This, I knew, awaited me if I could conquer the distress—and my quest was a success! But how could I get to a place like this?

I knew again I was being beckoned. But no, I wouldn't go. Summer had come again and we were starting our second tour: The *Seeds to Sequoias Tour*. And it was great! So fun! A concert every other night across the country. Sometimes unannounced we'd set up in a huge park and play and watch the crowds roll in (although the police were not enthused).

Anthem of the People:

Who are you?
Who are we? ...

Then:

Hey girl, you're everything
Your walk is always new ...

So much fun, but again I taught when September came.

Then one night a storm arrived. I awoke and looked out my second-story window. It started to rain and lightning flashed in the eastern sky. It flashed again and again, and became a storm, and I suddenly felt I had seen the exact same sequence of flashes before—a great feeling of Déjà vu filled my heart—chills down my back. It seemed to be the same storm I saw when leaving World Two!

World Two was calling again. Should I go? I wanted the discovery, the enlightening, the changes to my soul. I inhaled deeply. No I wouldn't. I would miss our concerts too much, playing to the frenzied crowds, recording different songs. I couldn't convince myself to go. But I felt I must. I wanted the treasure! I was conflicted. Again I was the rope being pulled. What would call me next?

After the rain, a terrible wind blew and a tornado opened up above the lake in Grand Park. It stayed in that one place until all the water it sucked away and then it dried the dirt below. In the morning, lots of people were on its shore observing it. Again the chills went down my back as I approached and looked. It was totally dry and parched—mud cracked just like on Dry Lake where I had died. I stood awhile—then felt I had to walk onto. I sat cross-legged in the middle—just as I had done—everyone watching—rain clouds threatening from above. Then those clouds opened up and water poured as never before—like out of a faucet. In an instant the lake was filled and over my head. It was trying to drown me! I was trying to keep my head above, but it was pouring down in sheets! I yelled, "Okay, okay!" And when I did, the rain immediately stopped. I swam out of, and looked back to. Déjà vu, and I knew—what it meant—I must go back, and to the lake and village I would return.

[Someone in the audience yelled, "I can vouch. I was there. I saw it all—just like he said. I even heard him yell and then it stopped and he swam out." There was a collected gasp from the audience.]

For sure, I had to go back. The signs were everywhere, and clear—to finish my quest—but the difficulty of the test!

I looked at the trees in the park around me—and my forehead furrowed as I remembered my boyhood hike and Sixth Rule. Then an overwhelming feeling came over me that I could conquer any obstacle in World Two by looking for trees—and walking to the next one! And if I couldn't see another up ahead, I would envision one and then walk there. Another Rule I had discovered—and only four of them remained. Pieced together, I would have the map to ultimate success—or anything I wanted.

But I still hadn't found what Old Man said I left behind, and I was near the end so I couldn't go—I would get lost in the dark. It humbled my heart and I thought of *MYSELF* and *ME*—how they had saved me from my death. At first, I had not wanted it, but once recovered, so thankful I was for all their tireless, daily effort. In that *dark* room, they had been the *light*. My forehead furrowed, thinking what I said: *Dark and light.* I thought, *Oh my! I know what I left behind! It's MYSELF and ME. What lights our way is a rounded state with all our sides working together toward a common purpose! When they oppose each other, we are doomed to flounder in the dark—some all the way to insanity.* Now we were all in agreement. I exhaled, relieved. Peace enveloped me. Old Man's instruction was fulfilled—I would not flounder in the dark.

I thought back over the year in World One and I saw the greatness of their different attributes and finally recognized their value. I realized that I was a little over the top, a little too intense, always in a race, only focused on results. They rounded me out into the person that I am, and I realized my life's job was to nurture and to elevate *all* of us—build up the strength of each, reduce their weaknesses. I realized that I was blessed—and told them so, and apologized for my hurtful thoughts.

Many of you might think of a split personality as insanity, but are you sure that you are not the same? Different sides of yourself disagreeing with each other: "I should help that person." "No. I'm too embarrassed to." "I want revenge." "No. I should forgive."

[Tiz paused. Silence—as people reflected on the different sides of *themselves*.]

I told *MYSELF* and *ME* that signs were calling me back. I felt I must obey, but I also felt that maybe I didn't want to go and leave my other sides—and my rounded nature. It was such a pleasure to finally feel that way. But they told me that over all the time when I'd been back, they had come to realize how the Rules had *indeed* improved us. They saw the difference in me—calmer, more patient, softer, and the greatness of my task, and knew how much I wanted it, and they respected my tenacity. We had grown together in this time of need, and I told them all that I had found in World Two and we agreed it changed *all* of us.

They told me, "Maybe World Two is real—maybe not—but it's improving us. But who sent you there? It was you before Old Man. So just be careful who he might be. Make sure you're led to miracles—not to the final depths of insanity. You have the chance to go to different worlds, discover things never seen, receive powers never known. But everything has its opposite: light-dark, sweet-sour, nice-mean. So be careful what paths you take."

I smiled and adventure whispered in my ear, "Come back to me."

But I told *MYSELF*, "I'm not even sure it's the Rules I must locate. I have another purpose there I think. And what about the band?"

"We're closer now. Close enough for you to feel us, to view life through our eyes, to talk so we can hear. You're practically here with us. And so you'll join us when we play. You don't have far to go. Finish and return for next summer's tour."

It was true. I *was* close. I looked at my polished stones. I would go and finish and then return. The majesty of World Two awaited me. I would fulfill my destiny. Five years from the start, and now is when I'd finish.

So with the blessing of *MYSELF* and *ME*, we planned for my departure—and I thanked them from the bottom of my heart for all their nurturing. And I told them if the tables were ever turned, that I'd be there for them.

Yes. I was ready once again to wander (Columbus and I would soon be brothers—our mothers bragging of what their sons discovered)! But first, I wrote the Rule I found and rehearsed the others, so they became my nature.

Then I had second thoughts for I remembered what had sent me to my darkened room. Someone that I loved had rejected me to the ultimate degree—in the ultimate way—trying to kill me! It almost killed part of me and now air escaped my lungs—my heart it filled with sorrow. Another debacle like that and *I* really *would* die for real. I thought of it and pondered quite some time . . . . *Then* sorrow left, and it was *revenge* that filled my heart!

Pebbles and *Rules* said, "No. Don't think like that." Then *Revenge* said, "Yes. Don't listen to them. Remember what she did." And I thought of collapsing by the salt pillars, hanging on the cliff, and almost walking through the poison oak. As I thought of it, *Revenge's* echo spoke louder in my ears and heart. I smiled. *Yes. I will return, and it will be me to lay some traps for her—not because I have to, but want to.* I laughed. Yes, now I really wanted to return. But as I laughed some more, a feeling said the Gate would never open up like that. But I couldn't feel then.

My psychiatrist stopped by and asked me if I was mirroring anymore, but I said, "No," to protect my job.

I knew when in World Two, the Beasts would look to slaughter me—and even more this time before I made it through the Gate. So before I went, I decided to finally educate myself on traps to snare and kill them. So at the local library I read many books about mythical beasts and many pictures I saw of all sorts of different ones. I then believed I could defeat them.

Through the Dark Ages especially, it seemed they existed, and people adorned their buildings with the gargoyle-looking creatures, and all sorts of ways they suggested to extinguish them: a silver spear into the heart, the bark of an oak soaked with blood as a shield, water with onion, ash, and ground-up liver of mouse, thrown on to dissolve—and so on. As I read, I envisioned myself in medieval times dressed in light armor in search of them. Then in the middle square of a little village, with sword in hand, I found and battled them, and did them in with the town all watching through their windows, and coming out in grand applause and celebration to the great knight that conquered them.

One of the mythical beasts listed that I laughed at was the Boogie Man. "Ha!" I snorted. "The Boogie Man! Why would that be in a book about real beasts?" He was very, very real when I was young, for the dark was a scary thing, and I feared tremendously as I felt him watching me from my closet's opening, and heard his careful breathing, and saw his shadow moving underneath my bed! But as I aged, I found he was not the monster that I first thought. I found I had felt and heard and seen something not really there, and I grew up, and I grew out—of the fear that once so heavily consumed me.

My Beast, though, in World Two, was of a different sort, and he really *was* real. And although the scars I'd lost, and the wounds had healed (surprisingly almost instantly), and everyone told me otherwise, they were wrong and I was right, for the fear I had, and what I felt and heard and saw, told me he was different. He was not just in my mind like it turned out the Boogie Man had been.

I found what I left behind, discovered traps to kill the Beast, and relished in the decision to avenge myself from my killer, so now I was ready to return and face my final challenges. So again by the lake I sat, but now I was getting better at transferring as I prayed and used my techniques to breathe and see, and the monk's meditation methods. My only guide would be to travel east. But this time, it would guide me to the worst place in that world that I had been.

Chapter 15

Skunk for Lunch / I Cried on the Way to Po

Rule #7: OF THE STARS

Back in World Two, I claimed the left-behind spear and continued on; my current goal to find the village of Po—and Emgo in it as the Disciple said. I wanted to find out which mountain, and ask Emgo of his deceitfulness and verbally thrash if it was so. I also needed to find the Prophet. Five years before, the Elder said from him I would receive the most and greatest advice, but still I hadn't seen him, and I was told the obstacles ahead were the worst on the journey. I needed his instruction. And lastly, I would look for Ms. Spear for I wanted my revenge.

The lightning in the east was getting so close, if I didn't find the others, at least I would find Old Man. If he was good, then he would help. If bad, and this was the final trap, then, "Oh well—good by to all."

The sun was my friend, and as I walked and searched, I watched it glide from east to west. I traveled for days through a swampy place, under the giant cypress trees that grew out of the water—moss hanging from them. Birds I readily saw and heard that I never had before—their strange and different calls filling the day and night with sounds of wonder—or to get spooked from. On two logs I tied together I stood and pushed myself along with a branch as oar, and watched a world of reptiles I had never seen before: turtles jumping from floating logs into the water, strange ripples and movement on the water and fins of fish that rose then dove, and a twelve-foot alligator that I whacked on the head when he swam in thinking I looked like dinner. At nights, I camped on small islands with water all around as far as I could see—with the trees rising from—and while asleep I felt snakes slither over me.

I walked and rose for a couple months—no sign yet of those for whom I searched, till I came to a blessed forest—the crisp smell of the trees gorgeous, and a beautiful clear sky above. I walked and walked, seeing different forest animals and hearing blue jays calling to each other. These were all sequoias, thousands of years old I thought, so I felt amidst giants looking down on me. And while walking thereunder, I thought I heard above me muted singing of low voices. I guess it was the wind through their branches, but it sounded more like the serenading of giants to each other:

Hey, my brother, how are you today?
Good, my brother. Tell me what you see.
There's a two-legged bug walking under me.
Save him for dinner and we'll eat him then.

Then they both chimed in together,

And we'll eat him then.
Save him for dinner and we'll eat him then.
With some salt and pepper we'll spice him up,
so he goes down good.
Pull him apart so we can split him up.
One will eat the bottom and the other the top.

And we'll eat him then,
And we'll eat him then.
Ummmmmm!

But they were just playing with me.

I laughed and asked, "Chisel, are the trees singing to you too?" As I walked, then wrote at night, Chisel had become much less character—and much more friend. More than anyone, he could relate to me.

I got used to, and even started enjoying the diversity of World Two's menu. One day for breakfast, I ate spiders, and termites, and a dried-out lizard skin. Lunch's menu better: centipede for appetizer, deer hoof soup, and dead skunk for main course. But it gave me indigestion, and you can't imagine the odorous aftereffects ... (but I knew my students could, and what they would say, "Mr. Tiz! Mr. Tiiiiiz!" "I'm going to call the Principal." "I have some formaldehyde you can drink. Maybe that will help." "Bottle that and sell it as natural tear gas." "Enter a contest and you'll win first place!"). Then on dinner's tab: a banana slug found by a stream, some gopher meat I saw a vulture regurgitate, for it was spoiled (but I boiled it, which I figured made it good again), and for dessert, rabbit droppings that looked like little round chocolate candy pieces. I popped a couple in my mouth ... but after those, I decided against.

Sunset sparkling lights lit the sky, but only for a minute or two on the sun's final wave goodnight, so I was always prepared and waited. One night, I camped on a ledge overlooking a valley, and looking down, I saw packs of Beasts running east in the light of the moons. I told Thorny-Tooth, and Hairy-Cat of my fear of the Beasts, and although they didn't say much—it was enough— to console me. I realized they might not have met each other and I introduced them—and then immediately worried when Thorny looked hungry, and I said, "Now, Thorny, don't get any ideas— Hairy's my friend." Then I added another friend, when looking in my pack—my coconut souvenir; for it had three black circles on its end, in a triangle, looking like a surprised face on a shrunken head with coarse brown hair, and I named him Bill. No animal came to accompany, so I strapped him on the outside of my pack and we enjoyed our time together journeying.

Snow descended on me so the world in which I hiked was only white and chilled. I kept warm with a grizzly bearskin wrapped around myself, claws still hanging from its paws, and head as a hat upon my hair—Bill looking scared to see it. A blizzard came and postponed my progress for a week as I bunkered down beneath a rocky ledge, waiting for the storm to pass. Then over the icy waters of a giant frozen lake I crossed with homemade skis. For another couple months I traveled as such—each night the sky getting brighter as I approached the lightning strikes, until the snow all melted and winter was almost spring.

Sitting by my fire one night, a feeling came over me. I could faintly hear singing and felt my fingers forming guitar chords and the others strumming .... In my mind I saw *MYSELF* at a concert singing—and so I joined as well. I knew there were animals down in the valley below me, so when the Beasts had all passed by, I decided the animals needed music to calm their lives. So on my uke I joined my band in the songs they played, and asked the crickets to join me. Then I conducted what might be recorded as "The Concert for Eternity," for we played in perfection to the audience down below, and to Bill who looked surprised how good we were, me providing my instrument, and a hundred thousand choir members strong, spreading out on the ledge for a mile to my right and to my left, with the moons providing moving spotlights to the masses. All the animals came out from under trees and bushes and holes and into meadows that spotted the valley. After two hours, my band finished, and the crickets and I did too, and the adulation was extreme, with the audience all standing, and instead of clapping, the valley was filled with howling, chirping, squealing, squeaking, growling, grunting, and barking. We were pleased, and as my band did bow, the crickets and I did too (except of course for those that curtsied).

Now in the night, the distant lightning was close enough I could faintly hear its thunder. But as I watched it, I wondered, *What creates the lightning there? If not Hell, then unlike the Disciple, have I found the Glowing Rock? And it attracts the lightning like an energized orb attracts electricity? The sign I saw was leading there?* I started feeling a slight charge of static electricity in the air—some hairs on my arms pointing out. I knew the end of my journey was close as well. But would I survive what was prophesied?

As I continued walking, the sky turned dark, and in the trees I found old abandoned villages from medieval times, and houses of rocks and wood and heavy, wavy glass that made the windows. I stopped in each village and looked and listened, and it hurt my heart and soul what I experienced. But it provided the Pebbles for the seventh Rule.

In one village, I heard pounding horse hoofs all around me; and as I heard, I saw the faint shape of a horse charging almost down upon me, and I jumped away to safety. Orders then I heard like echoes from the past, as if from men around me, also swords unsheathed, and semi-transparent arrows I saw flying by from crossbows. Then I felt heat, and like in a dream, I saw flames on the current houses, and homes no longer there I saw burning as a vision. Then the sound of running feet on dirt around me, and cries and screams echoing—the feeling of despair—and then just silence. With sorrow inside, I ran ahead to get away.

Another village up ahead I found, and in that one the smell of sickness from a plague, and I covered my mouth and nose with a handkerchief. When I looked in windows in the homes around me, I saw ghost-people with drawn eyes, shallow cheeks, gray faces, beds filled. Then from down the main road came marching ghosts in black—passing me, going to a funeral—carrying a coffin to a cemetery up on the hill. One by one, people overcome, and finally I saw the rest fleeing. Then silence. And I ran ahead to get away.

I came to another. Storms this time, and I saw and really felt their past occurrences, and the people they affected: Wind as a monster—not caring—slashing like a giant whip at any being or structure before it, myself cowering behind, and holding a tree to not be blown away—my feet blowing up off the ground—legs parallel to the dirt; rumbling of earth and swallowing and bending and falling—many buried, myself thrown to the ground and rolling to avoid a giant bouncing boulder; water as the avenger— so tranquil and cool, smooth and bending, pliable and gentle when young, and so ominously strong and pounding, overrunning and churning, uncaring and big and brutal, when grown. It swept me away on a wave of a sudden see-through river that appeared down Main Street till I was almost drowned by its semi-transparent current—until I caught a tree and held. Many people were throughout and all around. I heard screaming. Then silence.

I did not like this place—felt sick inside, and all used up . . . all depleted. Felt evil all around me. Only the energy in the air I felt was saving me. I looked up at the sky with arms opened up and cried, "Please, oh please, remove me!" And *MYSELF* and *ME* could feel my misery.

Then Old Man's voice spoke out to me: "Don't worry, brother, carry on. Move forward. Move past. I know it's hard, but just keep focus. Find the next tree. Clear your mind of all that's evil. Move your feet and then just follow." I listened and obeyed, for many other times the voice had given good advice. *He's not the Devil! He is helping me ... or so good at what he does the lightning source is the ultimate temptation.*

My emotions were spent. I needed help to carry on. I looked at the sky that night as I lay in the dark. Intense nostalgia floated over me, and I desired to see my home on the movie screen above. I wanted to see it so bad, and knew I could, and that's how I did. Memories of World One passed in the sky before my eyes— illuminated in slow-flowing, phosphorescent, colored streams of mist like the Northern Lights. I remembered and saw myself fly-fishing on those Saturday mornings. I pictured my friends and I playing music to a concert crowd, and at home playing computer games against each other and the howling and celebration by whomever it was that won (this memory of a friend prancing around like a haughty chicken). I pictured my city streets, and the bakery I often visited, and the front of the school where I taught, and my students laughing. And as I thought all this, I sighed a little and squeezed the moistness from my eyes, and after a little time, I fell asleep.

Finally I found the village of Po. The people were nice, by a river in a valley surrounded by trees, a range of mountains in the distance. All were farming a large patch, talking as they worked, singing a happy song, animosity gone, giving to each other, one providing food, another beverage. I stood by the edge of the field and watched with harmony and was offered dinner.

Thanks was given from the head of the table, for the seeds that sprouted and the plants that grew, as all ate in one great lodge with doors on the sides to housing. Sixty in all were there. The simplest clothes they wore. The simplest meals. No extras of any kind. No movies, no phones, no jewels—no. But smiling—yes—and everyone happy; having little—enjoying much. I looked around the table and asked the person seated next to me if Emgo was one of these, but she said, "No." Emgo had visited a while back but then he left.

I stayed and lent my hand and replenished my soul for several days. Working in this place was easy—never out of breath—never any sweat. "There is energy here—in the air," I said.

"Yes, this area is a special place. Energy flows down to this valley from the mountains."

I loved these folks. "How did this come about?" I queried.

"Quite simply actually," they told me. "We were all living in a little town, in our own pretty homes, with the best of things around—the best furniture, and fancy clothes, and golden jewelry. Then Emgo burned it down—the whole town clear to the ground. Then when all was lost, so poor we did become, roots and herbs kept us alive, the simplest clothes we made ourselves, humbled to the lowest point—all living in one house which had not burnt."

"What? Emgo did it?" I spit with anger. "Now I'm sick of this, and hearing what he's done! This is preposterous. That's the final straw. This Emgo truly is so evil! I know it now!"

"No, no. Don't say that so," they said to me, and started to explain, but I would not let them.

"I'll hear no more; he's also brainwashed you!" I said to them. "I'm too disgusted. But tell me where to find him so I can confront him." I thought, *The Disciple told me he holds the clue to finding out which mountain, but I don't need his help. I'll find it on my own*! But as I thought it, I was saddened, for everything was so hard in this world and without that clue I doubted I would succeed.

They didn't know where he was, for they said he came and went, but he did sometimes visit a certain lake up in the mountains. So I bid them all good-bye and continued on, with anger filling every cell. I thought, *Now for sure I'm going back. Back to Dry and Deadly Lake to find the team of traitors*—the *Elder and Emgo once again and confront them on their filthy lying, for now it seems more evident they are deceiving everyone about the Beast. For the man the Elder said to respect and thank is filled with evil. I can't continue on an inspired journey if my first contact was a tramp—only interested in maintaining his position of leader and fooling people to do it. It might mean my struggle is in vain—there is no treasure at the end. It's all a lie! My effort all a waste! And I will be the one who finally ends their grand charade!*

But I knew Dry Lake was halfway around that world, and years it would take to get there! *I can't do that! And I'm feeling energy from the air flowing into me, and wonder if it's from the lightning strikes. If this much here, how much there? I'll be invincible up at the lake ...! Hmm, or it will be the end of me. But I will think the best. So I don't want to backtrack to the lake— I want the lightning!* Then I thought of a plan—full of danger and peril, but it was the only way to get to the village and settle the score between us! But first I had to find something to make it happen—and off I went to find it. Now this was my goal.

I had been sure it was Ms. Spear trying to kill me, but now I hopefully thought again, with this new revelation. *Maybe Ms. Spear is innocent!* Oh it warmed my heart to think it. *Maybe indeed it was the Elder and Emgo! Or Goatee Man, for he was always there—and maybe he's at the village now. I'll find out if they are lying, and also trying to kill me to protect their stations, and if Emgo isn't there, I'll make the Elder tell me where he is. I've been looking for him so long. I think he's hiding from me. I'll make Emgo answer for his deeds, and tell him what I think of him—for someone must stop his treacherous conniving. Too many friends of mine have been hurt by him. And maybe the next is myself—with the worst result!*

I continued on, but a day later I fell gravely ill, with a fever and chills, stomach wrenching, head pounding, body aching. Weak and weary, lying on the ground—as the sun rose and stars appeared and again and then again.

Once in a dream, or through blurry eyes, I thought I saw a face looking down at me—hair seemed black, and black on his chin, and I dreamed I felt him touch my head. But all was out of focus while my head was spinning. I heard mumbling. In blurry scenes in and out of consciousness I thought I saw him sitting on a rock, a fire burning he had made, and water I was given.

On the fourth day, the sickness left. I woke up with two guinea pigs on my chest looking at me and I said, "Hello." I bathed in a stream and cleaned my weakened body, and for breakfast ate apples and figs and nuts that were sitting on a rock— the Piggies, as I called them (for I didn't know if they were married, friends, engaged, or what) liking the figs the best. I regained my strength during the day, and as I sat by my fire at night and looked at the stars, I was so thankful to be alive and again have energy, that energized music filled my mind, and the song that came from it, I sang around the campfire and called, *Somethin Bout Her Jeans:* (Somethin Bout Her Jeans, track 12)

Something is happening, inside her attic
for I see a light, every midnight

and I saw a glimpse of her, one morning at three or four
up on her roof, as something fell from the sky

and I can't say for sure, I think she's making something
for I hear a buzzing sound, late in the night

Chorus 1:
and something is strange, everyday I look at her
and I find I'm more attracted, and my eyes do linger

Chorus 2:
It's somethin bout her jeans, how she's wearing them
somethin bout her jeans, and they don't tell no lies

somethin bout her jeans, that's a mystery
somethin bout her jeans, and they are killing me

somethin bout her jeans, and the way they fit
got a special look, that is flooring me

Verse:
One day I thought I'd search, so I went up and took a look
and I found something, that you'd never guess

some kind of instrument, that looked mighty mysterious
with thousands of needles, hooked to spools of thread

*and it sort of looked like, you'd open it and get inside
and turn it on and wait for, somethin to happen*

Chorus 1:
*and I can't explain, but that night when she came home
and she smiled as I waved, there was major chemistry*

Chorus 2:
*It's somethin bout her jeans, and the way they fit
got a special look, that is flooring me*

*Next day I looked at her, and saw her jeans had no seams
they had no hems, no zipper, and no latch*

*that night I stole up to her ledge, and stealthily I peered within
I saw her standing in that thing, and it was on*

*I saw her walk on out of there, and wearing a nice brand new
pair
and when I gazed upon them, I was love struck*

Chorus 1:
*and my heart skipped a beat, and the world turned blurry
my legs started trembleling, she had swept me off my feet*

Chorus 2 Repeated:

Chorus 1:
*Its that magical, mystical, jean thing
and it sews and it spins, while you're within*

*and when girls wear them, It's the truth, I'm not lyin
takes the breath from all the guys, and they can't resist*

Its the magical, mystical, jean thing ...

In the morning, I looked at the sun and remembered the weeks of overcast, and of the sun, thought, *What if it never was? Never the light dispensed. Never the warmth released. Never the glow of positivity.* I started feeling my thoughts coalesce—wheels in my brain were turning—inspiration coming. I lay down to sleep that night by the side of a river and looked at the endless sky that engulfed me. I saw the stars—a million ... no more! They were filling the sky—sparkling ... twinkling ... falling through space and time. They shone brighter and bigger and clearer and blinking. "Do you realize?" they asked. I looked again and then I did—after all those years. They'd always been, but I finally saw and thought: *What if they never were?* My heart tore at the thought. And it was then that I knew my gift: of awareness of the beauty of the stars and the heavens they are within.

I searched for more and thought of the war horses I had heard, of the arrows and swords and flames and cries, and thought of my house far away. Hadn't thought before, but then I did. And I knew my gift: of the safety and comfort and peace I had at home from evilness.

I thought of the sicknesses through the ages that I saw, taking loved ones, hurting limbs, crippling and fatigue setting in. My sorrow for them. And my own sickness, and when finally healthy once again—oh, the feeling I had won—and I knew my gift: of health and those that help us.

I remembered the storms in those villages that I felt and the havoc they brought to the people—and the terror they played on their hearts. The wind and the earth, and the water came through, but none had I witnessed myself—not in my town, not in my house—and it was then that I knew my gift: of safety from the elements.

And finally ... peace in the village of Po. Life without this and life without that, but happiness plentiful.

Because of that, I looked around and I thought differently. All the Pebbles were found and seven Rules I had. It was THE

RULE OF THE STARS: <u>Recognize and be happy for what you have, and don't take things for granted</u>. And in my book, I wrote it down. In the dark I searched for something else, and a beam of moonlight, through some leaves, framed its glow—an orange, polished citrine stone.

Happy I was to find the seventh of ten, but sad at the task ahead—for again I would have to submit myself to death to see the Elder.

Chapter 16

Back to the Elder

No, I didn't want to, but the anger was flowing over to yell with fury at the Elder for his villainy, and I had to understand. Was my purpose true? Or was the reason for my mission fake? I had come to feel that this other world was special. I couldn't let Emgo's and the Elder's evil contaminate it—like a plague that spreads. I felt obliged to be the one to set it right—to finally get revenge for my friends and stop it all for those that followed. So I felt I must someway get back to the Elder's village. Then I came to a lake—this one dry as well. I had found for what I searched—and knew what I must try . . . .

I said goodbye to the Piggies, and said I hoped I would return, then not at its core I lay, but this time at the far edge of the lake. I died on the first dry lake because I had to, but this time I chose to; for I hoped that was the method to also fill *this* lake, and see the village and grass around, hear the bird sounds; for how else to attain the Elder's village? I knew it was a risk, for this lake might hold no portal to the village, as the last one did, and I might die for nothing, just like Nikita; but I had to try. First, though, I must die from scorching rays, driest heat, nothing to eat, chapped lips, burned skin. I lay—and decayed—and slipped away—in agony—till death did its part—to let me through—the last thing seen, a lightning strike somewhere far away and I felt an earthquake. Then, after those vultures flew away with chunks of me, I felt cool; I felt wet seeping up below me—and knew what

I was getting in. When it surrounded and engulfed me, it soaked within my cells to revive me—and heal my skin, and I finally stood and rose out of the water. Dripping, I looked around ... I was there.

I looked for Goatee Man in his fishing boat, but he wasn't there. I was a sight to see for all those villagers, for no one had returned like that, and they viewed me with even more surprise than the first time. I was a dead corpse walking—all ragged and beat and skinny throughout, red and chapped and tongue hanging out (and I hadn't done my hair in a week), but with determination I stood as straight and tall as I could, and with purpose and anger more developing, I staggered to the right, down the shore, and to the back of the camp—straight to the hut of the Elder, for which I needed no directions—I just knew which one it was. A log was laying to its side—and six skeletons sat back against it. I gasped. *Oh no! Why did I come? I see what happens to those who come and question him—who discover his charade!* I suddenly stopped and looked around and thought again. *I can't do this now!* But I had fought too hard to get there, and I thought of Nikita's ghost telling me of extra powers in this world. So I wouldn't turn around. I stood in front of the hut and caught my breath.

"May I come in?" I asked from without.

"Yes, you are welcome, my friend," came the answer from within, in my own tongue.

I parted the hanging mats and entered. It was a round thatched hut covered by palm leaves intertwined, nice size inside, with a little fire burning in the middle. The floor was dirt, with mats and colored rugs that covered it. It was very clean—everything was in its place. He sat cross-legged on the far side of the fire, and peace did glow around him, as in the way he sat, the warm smile on his face, the caring in his eyes. Tranquility was evident in his manner, and I sat down on the fire's opposite.

I intended to yell as soon as I found myself inside, but the feeling there took me off-guard. So instead, I said something nice to cut the ice, and give the anger time to flow—but I said it flat, "Very nice hut you've made for yourself."

Taken off guard, he responded in like manner: "I had someone design it."

At that, I didn't know what to say for I had no idea they did that sort of thing!

"No one has returned so quickly," he said. "And so I'll let you ask me what you will."

"How did you know I came to ask?" I queried.

"I saw you on the lake the past few days and asked the stars why you returned."

When I had lain upon the lake, I wanted to yell at my possible killer, and deceiver, and to address the sins of Emgo. But within this hut, and in the presence of the Elder, I just could not. I wanted to let him know—of my anger and distrust, and that his beloved brother Emgo was a fraud, and that I knew it, and I knew he was also in on it—living against what I had journeyed so long for and worked so awfully hard for ... against my ideals and lessons I'd found and been taught. So instead, I simply told him.

"I know!" I said. "I know it is you that's been trying to kill me, isn't it?"

He didn't look shocked—and didn't refute. But he responded, "In looking at me, what does your heart say?"

Well ... it didn't surprise me, him saying a response like that—really no answer at all; but on this journey, I had learned to feel from within a bit—and I'll admit, I tried but couldn't feel guilt disseminating from him, and he distracted me. So then I addressed the Emgo matter: "In my journeys, I have found that brother Emgo isn't what you said. He's no example! He's a liar and a thief, he misleads, and he destroys. He has evil in his bones."

The Elder winced when I said that last part. "Please don't talk out loud. Please don't bring that word into this place."

I felt what he was saying, for something about this hut felt almost holy. And I could feel in myself that even the mention of the word "evil" was not appropriate.

I was mad, but felt I must apologize. "I'm sorry," I said to him. "But what about the Beast you said he killed? Everyone is saying he's not real—there is no Beast. So that would mean he never killed him like you said he did, and he also lied to your people telling them how. And you've been in on it! Not only that, he stole from the less fortunate, tricked the weary into life-threatening journeys, and he burned a village to the ground, and other things I'm sure I haven't found."

The Elder looked sad; he frowned and looked at the fire. He threw some spices in the tiny flames and watched them sparkle and lightly crackle as they lit and floated and danced in the heat then fall upon the coals. Then he looked at me.

"You're right in what you claim. I know the Beast is not real. But look at all these villagers who revere Emgo, thankful for what he did—and having something to hold onto and learn from. Most everything has a reason. And yes, he did the other things you speak of, but don't let it churn you that he stole, and tricked, and burned the village down. Let it go. Let them all revere him."

I was aghast! *Did I just hear him right?* I was speechless—for a second couldn't breathe. I had actually been starting to hope and even expecting I'd find I was mistaken. I thought to myself, *What? The Elder really is a liar and admits it? He was my first contact I was told to find. Emgo and him really are cheats? Before, he tried to convince me Emgo killed the Beast and to thank and revere him for it—and now the Elder admits the Beast isn't real, and that Emgo did the other things? The peace I feel here, and his posture, seemed to convince me otherwise. I encountered death to get here only to discover this? This whole journey's been a lie? I spent all this time and effort on a purpose that's not real? How dare this second world for having called me! How dare the voices that I've heard. I'm such a fool. My friends and doctor all were right—even the principal—all along.*

I was wrong. There is no other world or other time or any portal here to there. I'm on a false, misleading journey—a fake reality only inside my mind. It really is just a dream I'm in I fashioned for myself. I must get out of here—no longer play the fool the Elder and the others made of me!

Those spices on the coals were lightly smoking—a haze filling up the tent. I coughed a couple times. They exuded an awful smell—it came thick over me: a rat and his decaying body, like I had smelled before, but many more this time. The smell so bad in this confined hut that even with hand over mouth, and fingers squeezing nose, the smell was still most dreadful. But looking at the Elder, it seemed to not affect *him*. I was getting dizzy—almost fainting. As I smelled, in my hazy mind I wondered what it meant. I thought I didn't want to smell, so I thought of other things—things I'd seen and learned—people met—weaknesses overcome—Pebbles, Secrets, Rules, and Truths discovered. While thinking of those, I remembered the energy where I had been—and a feeling overcame me—a feeling of determination .... *Why let others determine my fate? I can do anything!*

I decided that despite these dishonest, fake, and disgusting ones, I would continue on—by myself—without their help. For dream or not, I had learned so much and I was so close! So then finally I knew for sure after all that time, this was proof—Old Man *wasn't* the Devil—it was the Elder! And Emgo his helper! *So Old Man must be the opposite—the counter balance—an angel!* Knowing this I smiled. Oh how sweet it finally smelled. *My father-figure who I love isn't the Devil! And since he's not, I'll assume the lightning source comes from the Glowing Rock— not from a hellish storm!*

Now all I had to worry about was whether Old Man was real—not actually *me*—a figment of my own imagination. I would *hope* that he was real and that the purpose for this journey indeed was true even though the Elder and Emgo were not; and with that in mind, I would continue. When I decided that, a great thing happened. That sordid smell immediately dispersed—and was replaced by another! The smell of crisp, cool morning, after fresh, clean rain, with a slight scent of watermelon. Oh, the majesty! I breathed it in, in spades . . . I would continue on!

I realized the Elder had tried to kill me with poison smoke, but I had foiled his attempt! *I have to quickly flee this place before he springs another trap and I join the skeletons. Now he knows for sure I'm onto him.* I no longer cared about asking for help in finding Emgo. I jumped up from my sitting position and out the door. I started running away as best I could. I feared for a spear into my back and looked behind. Yes, he also was exiting . . . but he didn't have a spear. Instead, he sat down next to the skeletons.

I feared then the villagers would be the ones—running to grab me! I ran to the lake and dove into—to find the passage back to my other place—where I was safe from all of these. I bobbed up to the surface and looked at the shore. No one was following, but they were standing as a crowd, looking at me, and I was sad in my heart for those poor, misguided souls. I wanted to tell them of the Elder's evilness, but I decided it merciful not to. *Ha!* I thought and sneered. *Most everything has a reason! There's no reason for awful—no reason for bad—no reason for being stolen from. And you don't learn from lies!* Then I saw a man walk out of the crowd. I was exhausted and starting to dip beneath, but I squinted at what I saw. *Wait a second!* I fought to stay above and get a better look at who it was. Then I knew . . . it was Nikita Volkov! *How can this be?* Now I knew for sure that was a deathly place, for Nikita was dead—a skeleton. And all those others must also be! But then I thought again, for I had seen Goatee Man there, but other places too. So how could that be?

I was told that skeletons are not dead. *Could it be? Nikita's alive? And if so, what does it mean? Why is he here—with the Elder? Is he also in on it? Was the skeleton on his tomb a ploy? I told him of the granite eyes. He didn't tell me! He just agreed. Are he and the Elder working together against me? The Devil and his helpers pulling me to a dark abyss? Never to escape the foggy realm of senselessness? Myself a captive spirit in my grave without a mind to think? All this in a village appearing angelic? Maybe this is really Hell—this whole other world just make believe—a temptation sending people to insanity, so they'll never reach heavenly higher understanding!*

Then the water went over my head, and struggling for air, I blacked out. When I awoke, the sun was hotter than ever—shining on me; and sweating and weak, I advised *MYSELF* and *ME,* through my mind, of the matter and what had happened since I left.

Chapter 17

Heaven's Valley of Chimes / When All the Animals Came

Rule #8: OF THE FIRE

The Piggies had wandered off, but a snow-white leopard joined me as I walked through trees and then approached an enormous lake so big I built a raft to float across—Snowy sailing with me. Giant ten-foot-long sturgeon fish accompanied me—eyeing me from the corner of their eyes, and they made me row a little harder—Snowy snarling and pawing at them—protecting me! With my attention on them, I didn't notice a mighty thunder, and realized quite late the water exited over mighty cliffs! I rowed and splashed with all my might to avoid the stronger flow of water leading to and over them, until I came to land between great waterfalls. I walked down into an enormous, grassy valley and saw where their water flowed: falling on both sides of me down tremendous granite cliffs. Forty-three waterfalls in all I would count after reaching the end. I walked in between some, and behind others, and sometimes wading through their runoff—the most gorgeous thing I'd ever seen. For days, I walked among them, and the mist above the valley from their crashing, when mixed with rays of sun, created rainbows everywhere. Each drop from every waterfall hit pools below—and when they did, a chime was heard, the ring high or low depending on the size of drop—so a million at once I heard in harmony all around me ... it was the music of God! Imagine it! Then I couldn't resist, and standing on a giant rock and looking out over all of it, I asked the crickets to assist, "Crickets, follow me in glorious chorus and let your voices sing!" With the heavenly chimes in the background, I lifted my arms, then flung them down, and when I did, the crickets flooded the valley with music with me accompanying, and Snowy meowing and howling in tune. The valley had perfect acoustics, and the music was far beyond anything the world had heard—stopping the breaths of listeners.

I eventually, regretfully, left my friends, the waterfalls, and just kept going. I started up into the range of mountains and saw the lightning coming down ahead inside of them. The mountain range was tall and rough, so it would be awhile, but now I could actually see the mountain, beyond a few others, where the lightning landed, and every day energy increased from it as I got closer. *What powers does the Glowing Rock contain that I'll receive?* The Elder and Emgo now might try to spoil my trek—or do me in, so Old Man was crucial to find. I needed help, and I finally knew, and could see, where to go to find him.

Chisel was fighting a battle too. Each night I wrote as he neared the end. Would he win—or be defeated? I felt for him. But with resolve he would carry on to the end! We were in this thing together! He sang: (I've Made Mistakes, track 13)

Well, I've made mistakes in life
but this I can say, I always try
to do what is right, when I stumble along my way

And, I'm sorry for my faults
and I'm sorry for, the things I've done
but I'm thankful for, all of the way I've come

Chorus:
And I've fought the battles, and I've fought the war
and I'll keep trying, just one time more
and when I fall down, well, I will always get up
until I am told, well, you're forgiven son

And I'm looking for, the hidden sun
'cause after the rain, I know the sunshine comes
you just gotta wait, and stand up straight
and then pretty soon, all the clouds have gone

Verse:
Yeah, I've made mistakes in life
but this I can say, I always try
to do what is right, every step along my own way.

The mountains were filled with birch, and aspen, then redwoods, pines, and sequoias, and with even more dogged determination than before I marched on, intent on finishing this myself without help from Emgo or the Elder (the evil ones). The Elder said from the Prophet I'd receive the most instruction, and yet still I hadn't even seen him. *Oh my!* I suddenly realized, *Just another lie—after all these years looking! A wild goose-chase to throw me off my course!* But I would continue. By myself I would soon summit the Mountain and receive the secret, cherished Maps (with those, Columbus would not have gotten lost).

I made a little hidden fire in the night. The dancing of the flames I could tell was saying something I needed to know, but I could not tell what. I laughed at myself for thinking so. Then animals started coming and surrounding me and my fire—no Beasts, but a wolf and bear and cougar and wolverine. They came so stealthily that I didn't notice they were there the first time, until

I looked up from my fire and saw them all. I shook and feared for my life and pleaded, "Leave me alone. What do you want?" For they were the dangerous breeds. But I was safe, for they quietly stayed until the fire was out and then they left. They had never come like that before, so why now? I worried they would come again.

I summited one and then another as that mountain approached and summer too—each day the morning fog heavier, and energy stronger in the air. I had no friends, so I looked to Bill and Snowy and to the moons and stars above for comfort. And as I walked, the sun looked down, past asteroids, past one of the moons above my world, and past that wonderful green sky. It watched me walking somewhat concealed under trees, then crossing rivers, traversing sides of mountains as I rose.

How much farther must I go? Of which of these was I told? "Find the Mountain," he had said, and "Go east." *But where, and how much farther?* I was so exhausted from my trip, so out of breath from scaling mountains, and without the final help and guidance I needed. Maybe stop this trip and rest—forever. I could just return to World One and hang out with *MYSELF* and *ME*. It was a relief to think about finally stopping and turning around— no more hills—no more sweat and pain. It had been so long since Pebbles found. Then a fantastic thought occurred to me, and I said out loud, "Wait a second. Can I sit down and wait? Maybe the Pebbles will come to *me*!" It was a revelation to my mind after all that suffering of every kind! Then I heard the trees start laughing at me, and I looked, then frowned—embarrassed, and bent and looked down at my feet. In a high-pitched voice, I heard a tree say, "Maybe the Pebbles will come to me," and she followed that with laughter. Then another with a low-pitched voice, "Maybe the Pebbles will come to me!" And after, he laughed like Santa Claus, "Ho, ho, ho, ho, ho!" When I heard that, I looked up and also had to laugh—and I admitted, "How foolish of me to think a thing like that." They would not come to me. It was up to me to work and find them.

Another night enjoying the lightning show—but too, another fright—as the animals came in. *Why here? Why now? What is happening?* I talked to Thorny and Hairy, "Guys, I'd like to introduce you both to Snowy and Bill." I held Bill up for them to meet, and Bill was quite surprised that they were there. "Thorny-Tooth," I said, "what is the meaning of this great life? You seem to have all the answers;" for he appeared to be some type of guru looking down on me, for he would ponder my questions quite meticulously and quietly for hours (but I usually forgot what I had asked by then). And not to leave out Hairy-Cat, I'd tell him what I did that day. Then to all three, and all the animals, I played some little ukulele jingles to leave them smiling (except Bill who always looked surprised how good I was). I had become so expert that I could play any piece that they suggested, so for hours I played their preferences. And I wrote a song that was just for them and asked them to sing it with me. I called it: *Go Go Zulo:* (Go Go Zulo, track 14)

News reporter:
There's just been a sighting... of a U.F.O.
Crowd noise--
wait! there's-- something!... here it comes again!!....
Get down!!...(big whoosh sound).
Dang! -- just buzzed us!-- and it's gone!
Crowd noise--
Most incredible thing I've ever seen--
totally amazing -- astonishing!--
so close, must have been --
surveying the land --
for minerals -- or future colonies --
or -- intelligence gathering --

Verse:

There's a boy on Mars, whose parents named him Zulo
Drives a rocket ship that, we call a U.F.O.

and he speeds across the skies, chasing the lightning
and the folks back home, just shake their heads and frown

Chorus 1:
and when you and I, see a flash in the sky
we gasp at the sight, of the falling star
but then you and I, have erred in ignorance

For it's only Zulo, in the night
as he speeds from one, to another star
as he traverses each, galaxy in sight

Chorus 2:
Go Go Zulo Go Go. Go Go Zulo Go
Go Go Zulo Go Go. He's the guy that flies those U.F.O.'s

Verse:
And his folks tell him, these things weren't made to play in
and they say "You shouldn't, buzz the other worlds."

but he says "he'll watch out, for planes and be careful
and he'll only race when, the MIGS after burners swirl

Chorus 2 Repeated

And he's only been, seen once or twice by earthlings
but his speed made the picture, look like it wasn't real

and his leaders say, that's not what Martians act like
and to leave no more, designs in old wheat fields

Chorus 1 Repeated

Chorus 2 Repeated

and he's the fastest thing, on air in this whole universe
and when he kicks into hyper space, he gets a thrill

and there aint no one, who can catch him or can touch him
when he kicks it in high gear, and leaves a trail

Chorus 2 Repeated and fade

I came into a spacious valley—green grass, beautiful skies with scattered cumulus clouds, thick trees around, and I heard a mighty rumbling. *What in the world is this?* It felt bigger than any earthquake! I hid behind a tree and watched a herd of elephants run by. I was about to walk out from behind my tree, when not to be outdone, a herd of Apatosaurus's also ran by (making the elephants look like babies in front of them)! I was looking at a herd of Apatosaurus's! *Mom, look what I found!* I thought of yelling. They stopped in the meadow in front of me and I ventured out among those beautiful things (but I watched my step for they had eaten and were now again . . . and they are enormous—think cow times twenty). I thought I'd like to touch one, and so I did. That went well, and I salivated thinking of my fantasy—one thing I wanted before I died—to ride a dinosaur! So, *Hey,* I started climbing up his tail to get onto his back— Snowy coming with, but . . . he didn't like that, and we got down fast—faster than I wanted—when flung across the meadow. Later I tried another, and suggested to Snowy she walk beside, and the dinosaur let me on! "Woohoo!" I yelled and twirled my arm up in the air like at a rodeo! After awhile, I yelled down to Snowy, "Try it again Snowy—come on up." She did—running fast, and we rode in bliss and luxury. I was so proud, riding her bare-back as I did! Oh! My goal was finally fulfilled. What a thrill! Better than any bucking bronco, that's for sure. I got to ride a dinosaur! We rode her all that day till we got to my final mountain where the lightning was. [Tiz looked at his parents in the front row, "Mom, you would have been so proud!" All the audience smiled, then a person started to clap and all joined in—standing—Tiz waving.]

Another night around my fire, the animals came—but every time more ferocious-looking ones, and I couldn't explain their presence. "Why are you here? I demand you tell me!"

It seemed that powers were increasing in my soul. When I moved my hand that special way, the weather seemed to maybe change a little, and I wondered if it was me. The journey had taught me something, I could tell. I was starting to look at things differently. My mind enlightened when I talked to the stars of the Rules I found and Pebbles leading to them. My mind was focusing more succinctly, intuition more attuned. Ideas flowed easily. My goal was solid and wouldn't break.

Now, I saw the lightning so nearby that I also felt the rumbling of the thunder from it—the energy in the air making me stronger—no longer tired as I climbed. I would finally find Old Man by it if the Scholar was right. I knew that he could help, so I continued toward it. The end of my journey, successful or not, was very near—the Glowing Rock, some sort of energy orb, I visualized was coming close.

The mountain fortress at the top was strong—surrounded and protected by an army of rivers and rocks and trees as the elevation increased. Under sequoias quietly I went amongst their shadows—for deer I spied, unknown to them, walking in small meadows, or watering at streams, but also Beasts—and they looked not interested in deer or water, and more intent on finding something ... and I knew what that something was. Their numbers now were even more and getting closer—and if a whole pack of them found me, I was dead. So I kept a heightened attention, and as I did, I was not seen.

Each night, after hiking farther up, I camped and I worked (as the book I read in the World One library had said to do): Silver I found, and melted, and dipped my spear into, then sharpened; a large piece of bark I gathered and bathed in the blood of a possum; water was boiled and saved with just the right mixture of other ingredients to dissolve my dreaded Beast. And I practiced my technique in using them. And even though by everyone the Beasts had been denied, my eyes saw them and didn't lie. *I* was right and would prove it to *them*. I then was ready, and hiked with my blood-soaked bark, and silver spear, and dissolving water recipe, always ready to shield, and stab, and dissolve the Beasts.

Snake I ate, and the mouse inside, and other contents. Fish bones I found and stewed for their marrow—its head quite crunchy like a potato chip. Huge worms plump with larvae I boiled, tasted, and consumed. The severed twelve-inch tail of a rat I found and held like a cigarette while sucking and chomping on it. The carcass of a beaver, four days after a falling tree had finished him, I roasted, along with its maggots. Then I ate some other things (but those ones might disgust you). They disgusted Snowy too, so she found her own dinners.

That night, Bill and I and Snowy sat in the dark, for I didn't want to start my fire—not wanting those animals coming in. I didn't know why they were coming, or what they intended, and it frightened me. I looked at Bill who was staring at me, surprised I wouldn't light it. He wouldn't turn away, and I knew what he was saying. "No!" I answered emphatically. But he just kept staring and wouldn't take "no" for an answer. I looked at Snowy and she agreed—meowing. But anyway, I felt I needed the fire. So again the fire, and again the animals came and stared. "What?" I asked them.

The next morning, I saw the lightning was only half a day away. Old Man could help me, but would I survive the lightning's anger? My journey had been so long to get there—my feet proceeded with reverence and caution.

Then finally that day the Pebbles came. On my way, I met a horse carrying someone's heavy belongings. So much weight and so many hills, but no one was around—no answer to my yell.

When I looked deep into the horse's eyes, what I expected was not there—they had no quit in them. It would be easy to—with all that weight and hills, but I knew that horse would just keep going. Something happened to her master, I was sure. "I'm sorry ole girl." I thought of riding her on the rest of my journey, but no. I felt she earned something else, and I untied her pack and let it fall, then watched her rise and buck, and whinny and run.

I saw a hawk fluttering—waiting. Same the day before—his steady routine to find his dinner.

A fish in the stream I watched—against the water swam. Against the current always moved its tail.

I climbed a large rock to get from here to there, and in the middle growing from a crack—a pine. In almost no ground to grow, little water it received. Yet day to day, it tried.

That afternoon as I got closer and closer to the top, I anticipated what I'd find. Finally I came around some trees and there I was—finally I had made it! I inhaled and held my breath and quickly looked around ... but saw nothing unusual! I was sure this was the mountain where the lightning was! There was just a beautiful small lake on the edge of a little plateau and I set up camp in some pines at the far end of it. I saw no Glowing Rock, Old Man, or Emgo either. I had looked so forward to the Glowing Rock. From it, I was going to take energy—but nothing. But I *did* feel more alive. Energy was greater there. I ate berries, and swam as dusk approached. I usually didn't swim on nights like that, but the water tingled on my toes and their soreness went away. They felt renewed, and so I swam, and my body too. I never before had a bath like *that*! I was energized—to where I thought that I could tame the world!

I warmed up by a fire and waited, for again I knew they'd come. And then they did. First two bears. Walked up and stood and stared at me, me sitting on the fire's other side, across from them. "I don't have any food," I said (and felt a poor host I was, sitting there upon my log). But they wanted none. Then a pack of wolves came and did the same. Then the cougar, and wolverine, and also a fox, weasel, beaver, deer, and more—a whole crowd coming in! What was I to think (other than, I'm embarrassed to admit, *Man, that's a lot of meat*)? Did they expect a sermon? Well, I had not prepared one! So I thought their expectation kind of rude. We all just stared. Bill and I and Snowy at them—them at us—Bill surprised how many of them there were. Then, in time, I finally saw. In them, I saw the horse, the hawk, the fish, the pine. They were just the same. I should also credit them. No house to cover, no bed to sleep, no stores to buy their food, no clothes to keep them warm. And yet each day they continued on—one foot forward and then the next. There's no back. There's only ahead. Just keep trying. The Rule was forming in my mind.

That's when I noticed the animals did not stare at me, "They are staring at the flames! For *it* they came (so then I was embarrassed for my "rude" comment)!" So I watched the fire as well—flames dancing, glowing, speaking silent words. I asked it for its message. *Why do they come for you?* Then I realized that as long as there was wood and air, that fire would not stop burning. It didn't question whether it should, or ask itself if it wanted to, or decide if it was feeling too lazy that day. It just continued no matter what the difficulties, and would, as long as there was air and fuel. It was for this the animals came, this motivation—inspiration—they received, to pull them through another day. And then I thought of me, and my difficulties. I had to do the same.

With that realization, I got up and walked around the ring of animals, patting, hugging, petting them on their backs. "You've done well," I told each one. "I congratulate you. Good job and thank you." Then they walked away—and Snowy too. First she rubbed against my leg, but another snow leopard awaited and she couldn't resist. "It's okay. I love you," I said as I knelt and looked at her with her head in my hands—then scratching her back and hugging her.

Easily I recognized, as I continued watching the fire and this pressed upon my heart and mind; it was THE RULE OF THE

FIRE: <u>Never quit trying. Always keep going—one step at a time, and then one more</u>. Life is hard, so focus on one day at a time, and carry on. *Eight of ten,* I thought. *So close now.* And in the fire an object shone. I got two sticks and rescued it—an iridescent opal stone.

Then I heard a voice say, "But what if?" And then noises in the bushes I thought I heard. This was not Old Man's voice. I gasped and looked around.

I spoke out loud, "The fire taught me to carry on. There is no '*what if?*' I'm going to carry on."

"What if you already passed the final Mountain? Feel how tired your legs are! How can you go on? It's so hard."

"No, that's not what I am now about." I tried to concentrate, and I wondered from where the voice had come; for I had thought the negativity came from *ME*, but he was gone—and I was sorry I had misjudged him.

"But remember that time you didn't do so well? And mistakes you've made? Are you really good enough? You want to take a break and quit this exercise."

The voice was desperate after the Rule I found, and so few left to go—and so it tempted me.

That sounded so true. I *was* very tired—no longer had Emgo's help to know which mountain. The question was so valid— "Can I really find the mountain? How can I go on?" I thought about it—and that was my mistake: permitting my mind to ponder on the temptation—on the negative! For as I did, I opened the door a little crack, and my demons gratefully accepted that and then came flowing in.

I felt like the final Mountain was getting closer ... "But what if ...?" I was sure I'd find Old Man here to help me—and yet he's not—and no Glowing Rock-energy orb. It's been so long, and I haven't found the Mountain yet. What if I'm not strong enough? If I'm not smart enough? If I get too tired? If I'm not worthy? I don't forgive enough? I don't help? I am not humble? Weaknesses I have not overcome?" On and on, I asked myself. And my demons took firm hold of me. I forgot to replace the bad with good and think of other things, without a single thought of peace, tranquility, or charity—as I'd been told to think. My headache returned worse than ever, then the smell of the rat and the foggy mist. Then the sound was loud! Crashing through the bushes. One of the Beasts had found me (I didn't know it then, but like the smell of blood attracting sharks, the smell of decaying rat attracted Beasts)! *Oh I wish all the animals had stayed!* I thought. *They would have ripped this thing apart!*

I stood and threw my grizzly bear robe and headgear on and grabbed my pack. Surely this would scare him off. I looked behind toward the bushes and there he was, bigger now than ever—bigger than a male grizzly bear! He had crashed through the final bush, and paused, looking around, till he saw me—and his dinner! And this time, no, he wouldn't be attacked by another bigger, or by ravens with beaks protruding, for my mind on goodness was not focused, and I worried, *would I be welcomed into Heaven?* The costume in no way phased him, and the Beast did growl with fangs now seen, spit flowing out, and eyes of bloodshot resin. AND I ... DID ... RUN!

Chapter 18

The "Retreat for Those Mentally Recovering"

Rule #9: OF PAVLOV'S DOG

I guessed the Elder lied again, this time saying the Beast was *not* real, for there he was! I guessed he tried to convince me of that, so I wouldn't try to run from him and I would be killed by him. Within twenty feet, the Beast caught up and I turned and first I held out the bloody bark in front of my face as a shield, as the library book had said to do, and that I prepared for. I waited—for a force field to establish .... I peeked around to see if he was gone ... but, I saw him there and his eyes widen and redden. The bark just intrigued him, and the smell of the blood attracted him. He sniffed the air, and his sharp two-inch-long claws came crashing down upon the bark and shredded it and we were left face to face staring in each other's eyes. I staggered back ten feet, fumbling for my water bucket, and as he lunged, I threw off the lid and threw the water on him—and waited for him to fizzle—but ... it was cool and refreshing, and like a bath, it just invigorated him. He landed three feet from me and shook the water off his body, then smiled and opened his mouth and growled so loud that it hurt my ears, splattering me with spit from his forceful breath. I was face to face with the

Devil! Then with the spear I had dipped into the silver, I lunged, and sunk it straight and deep into his heart, and waited for him to die. I smiled, relieved, having hit my target perfectly. But ... he just looked at it ... then pulled it out with his teeth, dropped it, and frowning, looked back at me—annoyed by it. His eyebrows sunk. My eyebrows rose—higher than they ever had.

Then ... I decided it best to run again. I turned and ran, and he jumped and sank his teeth into my side—blood immediately gushing out, I saw. I screamed out loud in agony. Oh yes, I felt the pain. Oh yes, this thing was real (I wanted to introduce him to my psychiatrist and let him have a turn at *her*—and *then* see what she thought. *Old Man and the Scholar would have to alter their opinions if they were here.*). With his teeth clenched in my side, and his legs pushing against the ground trying to stop my stride, I continued trying to run—feeling teeth grinding on my bones—sweat pouring off my face.

Then an amazing thought occurred to me. *I will die soon from this thing, but maybe if I'm back in World One, that officer by the lake can shoot him with his gun!* I was sure Old Man was around there somewhere—and the final Mountain and treasure too, so it broke my soul to try and leave. I yelled, "I don't want to go!" *Is there no other way for me to stay? I have my goal— don't want to quit!* But I was panting, trying to endure the pain and not black out. I beat on the Beast's head, but it was no use, and it didn't take long to choose leaving over dying. So, desperately I yelled, "Are you there?" And so thankfully I heard *MYSELF* yell back, "Yes, I am." And he could feel my pain. I had to get out! I had to get back!

So I thought of that lake and grove and people, and smelled the smells, heard the sounds, and saw the different sky of blue. As I continued trying to run, I yelled in pain as he ravishingly kept gnawing on my side through the grizzly bear hide—tearing at my flesh, my whole left side a mess. I concentrated profusely, sweating to focus forcefully, mind squeezing its thoughts to one thing only. Then a great bolt of lightning flashed nearby—everything white.

When the blindness cleared, the scene had changed. I had transferred there—back in my grove of trees by the lake. The sun was also setting there, with people ending their day by the lake. I screamed in pain, "AHHHH!" and ran out from among the trees yelling and running to the lake—arms gesticulating above my head as if attacked by bees, grizzly bear head on top, hide wrapped around and paws with claws hanging down! "Help, anybody!" I screamed. "Get him off me. The Beast is killing me!"

I joyfully saw the officer I talked to twice before standing there, and I approached him in neurotic frenzy. Running toward him, I yelled, "Get your gun and shoot the Beast attached to me!" I reached him and grabbed for his gun, but he sidestepped, lunged, and took me down ... for I hadn't seen, but the Beast had not come through with me.

Next thing I knew, I was waking up—strapped to a bed in what looked to me like a mental hospital with perhaps forty beds lined up in four long rows in a large room on the second floor. People had white, restraining straitjackets on. It was old. The walls were made of large rocks with mortar holding them together. I asked an older, compassionate looking nurse, named Betty, assigned to me, and she said, "Oh no! Definitely not! It's not a mental hospital, it's a 'retreat for those mentally recovering.'" Didn't look like much of a "retreat" to me.

Why would this be? I thought. *People attacked by Beasts should not be coming here.* I also wore a straitjacket with my arms crossed—sleeves tied like that. I wanted to see the horrible damage done to my side but couldn't lift my shirt. A mirror by my bed revealed nothing. I'll admit, though, I was mentally exhausted—and I drifted in and out of sleep. *MYSELF* and *ME* were there with *I*, for the mental difficulty had its effect on them as well, and even worse, for I had kept them well apprised of all my tribulations, and they weren't as strong as I was and hadn't practiced how to breathe and see: my breathing methods to relax, the sight of my peaceful meadow, the meditative chants to focus. And only hearing of the challenges in World Two, and not being there, made it even worse for them, for their minds enlarged what I was going through—and they could feel it; like the fear a parent has for their child. And I told them I heard voices telling me negative things, and I knew it wasn't them, for they were in World One; and it hurt us all to contemplate.

So that is when my teaching and the band did stop and fans were left to wonder what went wrong. We had been ready to start our next summer tour, but it was postponed.

When next awake, my psychiatrist was by my side. With compassion in her gaze, she smiled and asked me how I was. I was woozy—had to think about her words. I replied, "Not good. But at least I have Bill here to keep me company," and I nodded at the coconut tied to my pack looking at her. She looked, and her eyebrows rose, and mouth opened—her looking just like him— them both looking surprised to see each other. Then I tried to explain my situation and their mistake: "I ... should be at a regular hospital for my wounds!"

"There are no wounds," she said.

"On my side." I showed her with my eyes and tilting head. "Fang and teeth punctures, flesh torn away and blood gushing out, crushed bones, and organs perforated!"

"No, I'm sorry, none of that."

I tried to think, but it didn't make sense. My eyebrows fell. "I was in a different world."

"No. You were always in this town teaching school and playing in your band."

I felt my demon taking hold, and my head again ached, and my confusion worsened.

"A great journey?"

"No."

"Dinosaurs?"

"No. I'm sorry. They don't exist—long since dead!"

"I thought I rode one!"

Her eyebrows rose, "Sounds . . . fun, but no."

I thought . . . . I spoke out loud to myself, "A Pterodactyl pooped all over me."

Her eyes still wide—and wider. She quickly covered her mouth with her hand as if hiding a laugh. She cleared her throat. After a bit, "How likely is that?"

I frowned and weakly said, "One in a million?"

She nodded.

"I drowned in a lake and came back from the dead when the water disappeared in a second—twice I did!"

"Definitely not. Water doesn't disappear like that."

It did sound inconceivable.

"I was friends with a wolf and bear and cougar and wolverine."

"They wouldn't be friends with *you*, would they?"

I squinted and mumbled . . . "No."

A pain shot through my head.

". . . ate spiders, termites, and dried out lizard skins. Deer hoof soup, roasted dead skunk, rat tails, maggots, and rabbit droppings for dessert."

"Ooooh! You wouldn't really eat all that would you?"

I looked at her, "It doesn't sound good—now. But I had gotten use to it—and started liking it."

She frowned and shook her head, "It doesn't sound good to me."

I thought and had to agree.

My eyesight blurred. My headache heightened.

"I didn't really go?"

"No."

"Ahhh!"

I heard myself start talking faster but the words were jumbled up. I started jabbering—something about, "Little white-clothed fellows, with fluffy pink hair, on green and red horses in puffy white clouds . . ." and then I started babbling incoherently,

"La babba a kama hama ...." I was going fast ... and then again I drifted.

I received medication, and for a month I slept long each night and then awoke, and every time I did, Nurse Betty was delivering more and more flowers to me, placing them, and a hundred cards on a nightstand next to me. Of course, many cards were from my family and friends, but most from fans and students with well-wishes.

[As Tiz said this, two teenagers from the second row of the audience yelled, "We delivered those Mr. Tiz."

Tiz smiled. "Thank you. Your thoughts and kind words broke my heart to know how much you cared."]

"You have quite the fan club," Nurse Betty said smiling. "I can tell you're very loved."

Some students tried to cheer me up with little jokes in their cards: "Mr. Tiz, I finally found a girl for you, and it's okay where you are—she lives there too—permanently!" And, "Mr. Tiz, go easy on the other patients. Their noses aren't as strong as ours—and they must endure you all day long, and then the whole night too—and we get recesses to get a break from it." And, "Mr. Tiz, hurry back, our last substitute teacher only lasted a day!" *I'm surprised that long*, I thought.

That day a finch flew in from an open window and perched on a high shelf looking down at me. For several days, the staff tried shooing her out with brooms and throwing little things like towels at her, but she would only fly to another shelf. She gave all us patients a great entertaining diversion—us all laughing and rooting for the bird.

Some night later, something awoke me in the dark. Moonlight sifted in through open, barred windows, and the sound of crickets was unusually loud. All others slept in their beds in rows. I heard the clock ticking, a man lightly snoring, the lady next to me turning over. I thought why I was there, and wondered what year it was, and a calendar on the wall surprised me with what it said. I remembered my psychiatrist sitting by me, and me seeing some little white men floating by on puffy clouds, and I remembered a terrible Beast. Then I heard a voice, and it was not just in my head, for the lady next to me sat up and looked around. I gasped. "Tiz, this is Old Man. I'm sorry you are there, but listen to me here. Come back to us—out of your troubled mental state. Relax; let the confusion pass; set your troubles free—floating down a stream. You are okay; you're not crazy. Don't fear the Beast, he's not real ... but even so, he will kill you if you let him—but only *if* you let him! Come back to us and finish this trek. You're very, very close."

My neighbor had a fearful look and I feared too. But I told her maybe it was just someone on the intercom. Then I tried to remember what the voice just said, for he knew my name, and I thought it best to try and follow his instruction. I thought of good. Troubles I set free down a stream. I inhaled through my nose, and then slowly exhaled through pursed lips—and out of my mind and through my mouth I visualized dark clouds exiting. Carefully I did the same for so much time, but I was so far gone, it wasn't easy, and eventually I gave up—too confused with what the voice had wanted.

The next day I took a stroll and looked out the window, and there were crowds of people outside, but I didn't know why. They saw me looking down and yelled to me, "Tiz come back to us!" They knew my name! *How is that? Who are they?* It scared me and I walked away.

The following day I had a visitor. He sat on my bed and said, "Hello," in a Russian accent. He was a nice-looking man in his early-thirties possibly. I seemed to remember his face from somewhere. "My name is Nikita Volkov," he said. "Do you know who I am?"

"The name sounds familiar, but I'm quite groggy. Remind me."

"I was in a mental hospital just like you—in Russia. I know what you're going through. Everyone told me I was crazy, and for a while I believed it, but I wasn't. I was taking trips to another world—and I would get there through my mind—just like you."

I squinted and said, "That's what I thought I remembered, and told my psychiatrist."

Nikita added, "I finally convinced the doctors I wasn't a threat and they released me. You're not crazy. Don't believe them. You can get out too. You have to relax your mind like you've been told."

A vague picture came to my mind . . . a gravestone with the name Nikita Volkov—and a skeleton on top of it. I shivered, "I . . . saw your gravestone—and your skeleton. You were . . . are . . . dead!"

He smiled, "I'm fine, as you can see. You must have seen that in the *other* world. But understand that skeletons aren't really dead."

What? I scrunched my nose—even more confused. I tried to reach over to hold his hand to verify that he was real, not just my imagination, but I couldn't with the straitjacket on. I asked him to touch my leg—his grasp was firm. I felt a connection to this man. I studied my feelings—a close connection, like we were brothers.

We talked for quite a while and then he wished me luck and stood to leave, and Nurse Betty came over and spoke, "Excuse me, but I heard you were here. Mr. Volkov from Russia, right? The oil baron?"

He nodded, "Yes," and smiled.

"Oh my, I've seen and read about you in the newspaper. It's such an honor to meet you. I've read about all your mental hospitals in Russia—all your charity—how much good you've done. Thank you!"

"It's my pleasure," he said, and hugged her. They spoke awhile, and he left.

He was a stranger to me for I was still confused—but he was a good stranger, I felt. I didn't like being in there, so I liked his advice. He gave me hope that I wasn't really crazy like they told me, and I could regain my sanity.

Then I remembered something. I spoke out loud excitedly, "Nikita Volkov. He's the one I saw on the television show so long ago. Indeed, he was like me in a straitjacket—and he got out!"

It was a relief to think it, and it calmed my heart. With greater clarity I again practiced all the relaxation methods he and the voice in the night had told me. Lying there on my bed, for much time, until the night, I blew dark clouds of confusion out of my mouth. Then eventually crystallized white clouds started replacing the dark clouds I was envisioning blowing out. Then to compliment, as I envisioned those white clouds float up to a beautiful blue sky and enlarge, myself lying on my back on a grassy hill enjoying it, I rehearsed a slow and steady mantra, "Ha—La—Kaloowa-Oh," again and again and again. Then when so relaxed and so at peace, eventually I saw my body, with arms and legs dangling, float up from that hill into those clouds. And when it did, I inhaled those fine crystals and a clean energy—slightly electrified, and felt it filter through my brain and every cell—again like it was smelling salts—cleaning it from every worry . . . . I slept hard—and good, and restarted my relaxation the next day too. Again that night I slept like a log—no stress in my heart.

The next morning I opened my eyes wide and looked around. I realized that *I* was free! My mind was no longer foggy. I was okay. I sighed, relieved. I remembered everything. I thought of things before my last encounter with the Beast: the fire and animals, the RULE OF THE FIRE, the wonderful village of Po, the RULE OF THE STARS and NEXT TREE, and all my journeys. I remembered Old Man so long ago and all that he had told me, and I realized I had done almost all that he had said before attaining the Mountain. *I'm so close.*

I thought again of Nikita and his skeleton, *He was dead in World Two and yet he is rich in this World.* My forehead furrowed. *Had he someway passed the Gate and seen the Maps of Ages? Was what he said true? Skeletons aren't really dead?* I knew someway he had succeeded and I rejoiced for him.

Then I thought of the Beast attacking me and my fear of him. (And, yes, I know—he is not real! Yeah, right. *You* feel his fangs crushing in your bones, and see the blood gushing out, and then say that.) And I thought of headaches caused by the other world, eating dried out bat wings, falling off cliffs, drowning in "imaginary" water, the Elder's awful lying, the putrid smell of rat, that skunk I ate—and the aftereffects. Then I thought about my lovely town and great family and band and students I had in this world. So I thought, *Why would I return to World Two?*

I remembered the first day of my journey so long before .... One minute before 6:00 a.m., I woke up. It was the day to leave World One and venture to World Two. The alarm was set, but I didn't need it. I had been getting up at that time for so long that my body just did it. My mind's clock just knew it. And I was hungry for breakfast ... or was I?

As I sat down at my kitchen table, I thought of Pavlov, the researcher who rang a bell and would always then feed his dog. Finally his dog started salivating whenever he heard the bell— mealtime or not; and I realized I was the human version of Pavlov's dog. Hungry or not, 6:00 a.m. and I felt ready for breakfast. And many other habits made me think the same.

I thought of going deep-sea fishing as a kid, and the seagulls all following the boat—habitually knowing we would be catching fish and then throwing the scraps overboard.

Also the thickening winter coat of rabbits, the salmons known path up streams where they were born, or the arc of the arrow to hit a distant target—learned through hours of practice but then just instinct and habit.

I once went parachuting in college. But before I solo jumped, I had to pass a four-hour class that taught, over and over again, how. We reviewed it so many times, that on the jump, it was just habit. Standing on the wing, I let go. I counted one to five. I looked up. Parachute open. Through thin air floated down.

I remembered my instruction: "Look at the horizon, legs together, bend your knees, hit and roll."

Like the drug addict, we all have habits—those so hard to change and to correct. And too, like the runner, we all desire those that invigorate and improve. People are a collection of habits, that tell us what to do—controls our thoughts and moves. Once developed—good or bad—so hard they are to destroy. Quite possibly the life or death of us. As I thought this, my mind instructed to memorize, "Never ever start the bad—refuse to think of it—replace the thought with something other—stay away from it—go and do another thing—stamp the habit REJECTED, and say, 'I WON'T!' See your weaknesses as a mold growing on you and attack them—spraying bleach on them. Work to overcome the bad habit *before* it tempts and consumes you! When tempted worst, remember how bad you want to change—the negative effects. Motivate yourself by thinking of all the times you've already overcome." And for the good, the opposite, "Start them NOW, no matter what, don't wait or they won't happen—like the tiger, pounce! Think of the resulting positive outcome. Then remember with a note to yourself inside your book—that you read daily."

If this journey, which I now embraced, was a crossroads, these habits I had formed—and would continue to—would lead me either to my grave or to a Mountaintop.

It was clear to me. This I knew was another Rule. It was THE RULE OF PAVLOV'S DOG: Habits make you who you are—the good and the bad!

On her way out, going home, Nurse Betty gave me a little wrapped present. "To boost your spirits," she said. I had her open it: a round, light-green, polished peridot stone the size of a dime. I smiled and thanked her, "Can you put it in my pocket?" She put it there and was surprised to find eight others.

Lying in my hospital bed, I had found the ninth Rule—now I only had one more to find, and as the sun went down, it worked upon my mind. Should I stay, or should I go? They were perfectly even arguments and it hurt my head again. Maybe this was the final trap constructed by the Devil—the final abyss I was ready to fall into. Look where it took me last time—here to a mental hospital! Each time back, I was returning worse than the last. Or was this the storm before the sunrise? I could stay here and carefully work to get out and then sing and play in the band again to all our fans. Or I could risk it all for the final reward.

Then on the wall—guess who I saw a painting of: Columbus on a wooden dock, standing by his sailing ship. *Hmmm,* I thought, *would he have stayed behind?* Then I saw myself in ancient dress, walking into the picture and standing next to him—very dignified in our stature, serious while posing for the painting—two great explorers finally side by side. We then entered his ship and sailed away, him asking me which direction was correct, and me pointing the way.

Then a person, slightly illuminated, I saw approach. At first I didn't recognize her in the dark, but closer in the moonlight through the open windows, I did. It was an apparition of Ms. Spear—looking like a hologram. She reached me and leaned over me again, sweetly asking, "Are you okay?"—just like the first time, but now her voice somewhat distant and echoing a bit, but that lovely smile just the same. But unlike the first time, asking about me physically, she seemed to be worried about my mental state—her eyes concerned. I looked at her amazed—my eyes wide. I closed my eyes, hoping she'd go away. But she didn't. *I'm just remembering another time*, I told myself. *I hate her. She tried to kill me probably! Unless it was possibly Emgo, the Elder, or Goatee Man. I want revenge, not reconciliation. Forget her!* But I could not. I wanted at least to confront her—but why? To release my anger? Or was it really something else—just to see her once again. I hoped not! As I thought, I regretfully knew that's why it was. It made me mad, but once was not enough ... I needed her. But there was no indication she thought the same— in fact the opposite ... she tried to kill me! She continued looking at me with those thoughtful, caring eyes and smile. For some reason, I had built up an affection for her—even though it was absurd, for only once I'd met her! She seemed so nice at first, and that's the part that I remembered—before she suddenly turned mean. Maybe there was an explanation for the deeds—yes, maybe there was! She spoke, "Come back to me."

And whether it was my wish or really her thoughts, I couldn't resist the plea, and it convinced me. I softly said, "Just one more time I'd like to hear your laugh, and in this world I never will." I tried to reach up and touch her face, but my hands were tied. Then her apparition turned and walked away—past beds, through pine trees lit by the moonlight—and then the picture faded away.

Chapter 19

Old Man / The Sleeping Giant

I had recovered, but *MYSELF* and *ME* were babbling worse than ever with the confusion and the stress, and so I would not leave them in that state. They managed to convey to me that I should go and finish the journey for all of us. "You must kill the Beast," They said, "That's the only way. He's the one that sent us here—the main affliction of our mental state. With him alive, we'll never get out." I shivered and almost cried. I had just failed with a silver-tipped spear! That was not the needed trap. How could I accomplish this?

Up to now I had *avoided* the Beasts, but to save the sanity of my different selves, I would have to return to World Two and *hunt* them—not because I *wanted* to, but *had* to (while they also hunted me)! I had no choice. *I must find a way! Some secret I haven't yet thought of.* A battle was coming. One of us would die and one would live—and I shivered at the thought. I lay and thought, *My greatest test in life!*

I told *MYSELF* and *ME* that I would go, and I would double my pace and soon return to help them get out. I told them I worried, though, for I had come to realize that the only way for me to finish my journey would be for all of us to go together, for I would need *all* our strengths to overcome the final obstacles— for they were reported to be almost insurmountable. We had to be one. I needed their light. I thought, *Slowly breathe in and out and let my spirits mend and mold together to make me the person that I really am—strong as stone with all my strengths combined in a common purpose.* They hesitated. Their fear of the Beast was so intense. Then they conveyed to me that they would accompany ... but by seeing through my eyes, hearing with my ears, and feeling with my heart, and as a unified force we would prevail!

I was still in that stupid straitjacket, so I asked Nurse Betty to take my journal out of my pack and put it on my nightstand. As she did, I spoke out loud to *MYSELF* and *ME*, "Take my journal and read it if you can, for it will help." But Nurse Betty thought I was talking to *her*. I asked her if she would buy me a new journal. I thought, *I will take that and fill it once again, from the start, and continue to the end.*

She bought the new journal and put it in my pack, and said she would read the one on my nightstand to me—thinking that is what I asked (but of course *I* would not be the one read to, for *I* would be gone. It would be *MYSELF* and *ME*).

"Thanks," I replied. "I have no money here for the new journal, so for payment please take the seeds in my pack. I think you'll find their flowers are rather nice."

[Tiz lifted his hand a bit and smiled at Nurse Betty sitting by his friends and family in the front row. She sat up taller and proudly smiled, looking to her right, then left.]

During the day, while managing to hold my backpack, I slipped my boots on, and tried to leave the mental hospital. ["Oh, excuse me," Tiz said sheepishly to Nurse Betty looking up at him, "the retreat for those mentally recovering." Nurse Betty pursed her lips and nodded.] But I found it not easy, for insanity had taken a toll on me, and my thoughts were not as clear; and I was not at the peaceful park this time to help focus my mind, so I didn't even know if transferring was possible. I would not be able to do it like before. I tried to think of where I'd been and all the Rules I'd found, but that didn't help. I tried squeezing my mind in concentration. I tried repeating the words "World Two" over and over—but nothing. All that day I forcefully tried with all the different methods I had learned, until it was night and dark, and I was exhausted. I thought, *I'm a prisoner in this place—all tied up, inside a cell. No pleading words will get me out. No posse of mine to blow the gate. No way to escape from this retreat!* I lay down on my bed and rested—perfectly dejected.

The next day some exterminators came with nets to finally catch the bird. All of us watched as they prepared their traps. I looked up at the finch—who was looking down at me. I noticed a discolored feather in her wing. My eyebrows rose as I remembered. Then I felt compelled to stand, and I walked to the middle of the large room still with my straitjacket on. Everyone looked over at me. I loudly spoke, "Bird ... come down to me." When I did, the bird flew to my shoulder. I looked at her and she at me. Peace radiated from her and I smiled. I walked toward an open window with careful, thoughtful steps, and as I did, she chirped. I thought, *What do I feel she is telling me?* As everyone watched, I stood at the window for a moment looking out, and the bird and I looked at each other feeling it would be the last time we saw each other—at least for a while. She chirped, and then with great feeling filling my heart, and a tear from my eye down my cheek, I said, "Thank you bird," for she had pushed me on so many times. "Goodbye." At that, she jumped over to my neck and rubbed it with her head. She then looked out the window and I watched her fly away, but not to a tree—higher. I continued watching her fly farther away, but always higher, and higher, and higher—till she was out of sight.

["That's true," a man yelled out. "I saw it. I was the exterminator."]

Outside, there were throngs of people, for the band was now huge—our songs around the world, and the media had heard of my location, but the "retreat" staff kept them outside. There was constant speculation in the news that I had overdosed from drugs, but I'm glad to finally clear my name. It wasn't drugs, it's what most of you call insanity. I know that doesn't sound much better, but don't believe it's so. I'm not crazy. Do I sound like it?

Someone saw me looking down from the window, and they all started cheering. "Come back to us Tiz!" I smiled and waved with my shoulder as best I could. I continued standing, soaking up the roars. The applause is a mighty boost to buoy up the soul. I smiled again and words forcefully flowed out of me without me thinking, "Who are we?"

They yelled back, "We are the children of the world—we sing!"

I laughed. It felt so good to hear that. Then I yelled, "It's the year ...."

And the audience yelled back, "1500!"

I yelled again, "All of us ...."

Them back, "All of you."

I laughed and yelled, "How about your own personal concert right here? Here's a couple you're the first to hear:"

Something is happening
Inside her attic
For I see a light
Every midnight ....

Then:

There's a boy on Mars
Whose parents named him Zulo
Drives a rocket ship that
We call a U.F.O. ....

I laughed, and yelled, "I'll be out shortly and sing again." Then I turned around and returned to my bed—all eyes upon me, and everyone silent.

That night as I rested, my mind reflected on the chirping of the bird. I listened to it in my mind, for every chirp was recorded there and the tune in which she delivered it. My mind replayed it over and over. I knew there was a message. As I focused, a word started forming in my mind. *What is the word?* I thought. The word I realized was TRUTH. I then thought of the words that I had heard, "I see you locked inside some sort of dungeon, maybe—all dark inside, your arms tied up!" I looked around, and although it wasn't, this place *looked* like a dungeon, with rock walls, and it was dark, and I was tied—in a straitjacket! Then I remembered words that I just thought: "No way to escape." Then some other words arose that I had heard: "Truth—you'll need it to escape." And I remembered, "The little make the big." *That's right. I had been told the Truth, and for me she said it would be used to escape!*

I thought about climbing a mountain. The top comes not all at once, but by little increments, step after little step, steadfast, with patience. So with that in mind, I tried a different tactic to escape. I slowed my desire, relaxed my heart and mind—had patience. "*Don't think so hard,*" I told myself. "*Breathe deep, imagine peace, enjoy the experience.*" I smiled and tried to remember all the *little* things and happenings from where I'd been—a horse, hawk, fish, deer, and other animals by a fire. I thought of how the sky looked there, and how the air smelled, how the water tasted, and the dirt felt. I only thought of little things. And as I thought of all the little details, the memory became more realistic and molded itself into a bigger vision. Over an hour, my mind reflected, and it ejected any clouds that obscured my revelation, so the vision became pristine ... and that helped me escape. I had no ingenious plans with escape routes or tools made out of spoons, or maps I'd figured out, or bed sheets tied together—I did it through the little memories in my mind! "The little make the big," I had remembered. The Truth let me escape!

I awoke by my smoldering fire the next morning in World Two. I felt invigorated to have made it back—out of the "dungeon." All was quiet except my cricket choir singing—and I was proud of them. I looked around—no sign of the Beast— which relieved me, and my blood was all dried up and gone. Only the spear on the ground was left and five of the fiercest animals awaiting my return: the bear, wolf, cougar, fox, and wolverine— my little army wanting to escort me.

Nine Rules I had found and one more I needed before the Beast took care of me for good. But now *I* had to take care of *him*. I think my little army felt tension in the air—knew I was going to need their help, and were coming along to assist. Finally I had something to help me kill the Beast! I smelled the air so crisp and clean. The sky so green. One to nine, the Rules were etched into my mind and soul, from years repeated and always practiced, so that is who I was and always I'd be ready, for the opening of the Gate.

I still had that straitjacket on, but managed to cut the ties on a rock. I looked down toward the small lake twenty yards away, and in the middle, I saw something floating on top of the water. I squinted to recognize it. It appeared to be someone floating on their back. I squinted harder when he seemed to rise a little just over the water and, with his hands in the water, push his body over to the shore toward the end of the lake, and then rise onto his feet on the ground. He faced away from me, but I noticed he wore a white outfit of pants and a long flowing shirt—and the clothing did not look wet!

It was a man … and my mind went back to people's suggestions where to find Old Man and Emgo, and I thought this must be one of them!

I started walking toward him—the animals waiting in the trees. The man was facing the other direction and saying something to the sky and deep valley below beyond the lake, with his head tilted backward and arms extended outward to his sides, palms up. As I reached the lake and was twenty yards away from the man, without notice, lightning flashed, and before I was knocked onto my back, I thought I saw the lightning land upon him! When I awoke some seconds later, I presume, I squinted at the brightness and saw the outline of him still standing there— lightning bolts hitting each of his extended palms. This continued for five more seconds, and as the lightning stopped, his arms and head sagged.

I lay, catching my breath for a full minute and watching. *Had I just witnessed that for real? And he was still alive?* I had to know who this was! I was about to get up, then BAM! Another one hit—this time in the lake. I squinted, and as the lightning stayed for another sixty seconds, the lake glowed and boiled and steamed, and that steam flowed heavily from the lake—but close to the ground, like fog flowing off dry ice through the trees and down the mountain as morning fog. Much flowed to me. It was cool, and when I breathed it in, it was like smelling salts again, and I was awake like never before. I was invincible, it felt. I could do incredible things!

Eventually it dissipated and I got up very slow and approached the man—but crouching over, waiting for another strike, nearing him inch by inch. When I got there, his head rose and he turned around toward me.

"AHH!" I yelled.

It wasn't Old Man (my angel) *or* Emgo. It was Goatee Man! I put my hands up to protect myself. I was still not positive my intended murderer really *was* Ms. Spear, for Goatee Man was always there. Or maybe it was both of them together.

"Oh good, you're awake." He smiled, not affected by my fright. His voice was that same low, hoarse tone that I had heard so many times before. It was so pleasant, and peaceful. He smiled. "I decided to take a dip while waiting." He paused and then continued, "I'm proud of you. You've made it so far. I saw you and the animals enjoying the fire. It's quite a message that it sends, isn't it? Most just see the dancing flames and miss the message it's conveying. Congratulations. How long has it been since we first met?"

He seemed so friendly that fear somewhat abated. He wore a necklace of braided vines with three medallions, the front most the size of a dime and gold. He smiled. I paused before answering, "You are the fisherman from Dry Lake, right?"

He smiled. "I am."

"I've been calling you Goatee Man."

"Ha!" he laughed, stroking his goatee. "I guess that fits."

"What do you have to say for yourself? I question your motives," I said—still on guard and wary he might be the murderous one. "It was always you I saw when I was almost killed." I interrogated, "Why were you there? And why did you walk away from me those times?"

"Your job here isn't to follow. I didn't mean for you to see me, so I left. I was looking out for you, to see if I needed to assist. I had become aware of someone laying traps, so I helped you. But only a little. For help is often more a hinderance in the long run. Strength is built by struggle. Weakness built by ease. So ease is often the enemy. You mainly survived by yourself . . . and that is most important."

I was not necessarily convinced and looked down at the lake, thinking. I saw my reflection—and there I stood again . . . a youngster—only a couple years older than when I started—even though my journey had been much longer! I looked older in World One. I was confused and looked again at Goatee Man.

He was holding his palms up toward me, fingers slightly bent, and I could tell he knew what I was thinking, like he could feel my thoughts coming from me as energy. He smiled. "Time moves different in this world."

I also smiled and said, "I like it." But this time, I did not think my reflection's blur was from the water, for in any mirror or water that I looked, it was the same, and I tried to think why it would be. I thought and said, "But the Elder . . . he is old."

He smiled. "That's just something that he wears. His age helps newcomers believe his words, and his teeth provide a lesson. Inside he's young, and when you left, he then renewed himself again—with help from smoke from spices thrown in a fire."

I agreed, "He's a tricky one—for sure—easily fools everyone," and I thought, *That's what the Devil does.*

I thought about this. *Time moves different in this place.* Then I thought about Goatee Man's voice, how similar it was to Old Man's, and how similar his features were! But Goatee Man looked in his early thirties. Old Man in his eighties. *Oh my gosh!* I thought. People had said Old Man and Emgo visit a lake. I looked at him. Slowly I asked, "Are you ... Old Man?"

Again that friendly smile and he paused while looking at the trees before replying. I inhaled and held my breath—myself on pins and needles, for I had searched for him so long. He looked at me and finally answered, "Hello again, Tiz. Yes. It's me."

Oh my gosh, I had to smile. "Yes!" I shouted and clinched my fists. Although looking for, I was relieved it wasn't Emgo, and that messy situation it would have caused. But instead, my beloved Old Man. I thrust out my hand to shake his, like I had been wanting to for oh so long. He held out his as well and I gasped in anticipation as our hands were coming together after all those years. Would the touch be firm and strong? Or would our hands pass through each other, proving he was an apparition inside a dream I made? As they came together ... I could feel his, like flesh and blood, and firm and strong and warm—for he was real!

Oh the glory! I thought. *He is not an illusion! I was not talking to myself all those times! I think this means I am not crazy! I think it means this world is real!* The relief I felt was magical!

With elation, I asked, "It was you then, right? You who guided me so many times? Yours has been the most and greatest advice."

"Yes, it was me. I tried to help. But more importantly, you listened! And then you DID. Without that, my words would have been defeated—of no purpose and no worth. You gave life to them. Thank you so much for that. It's almost a small death when my words only fall on deafened ears."

I smiled. "I was worried you were not real, for before you told me to look for Rules, I had thought of looking for them myself."

"And that is what brought me to you! You desired and then I came—for the journey is so hard, no one can be convinced to go, before first wanting to."

I felt so good again to meet him, and to see him so different. And I was so thankful. I felt like it was Christmas morning and I a kid again. I couldn't stop my smile. "So you're my angel right?"

He laughed loud, "HA! No, no. I'm just like you. You felt me right?"

I was surprised and then remembered his question and I thought of the calendar in the "retreat," and then replied, "My gosh! It's been six years since we first met!"

He smiled. "Six years ago, we met. Oh my! It seems like yesterday. But then, time flies when on a journey like you're on. You sleep somewhere different every night, like a bird living free, flying from tree to tree."

What he said hit me subtly, and I almost asked him to repeat himself. I had heard the words before ... but where? I remembered: the obelisk. Emgo had written them! I looked at him and squinted. I wondered. Had he also read them and remembered? Something stirred inside me. I had a funny feeling in my gut. My smile faded. They had told me Emgo also visits a lake in the mountains.

I looked at the ground and then at him, "I read those same words on a stone obelisk, written by a man named Emgo." I got a chill and almost shook. I paused and licked my lips and after a moment, garnered my courage and asked, "So ... I never actually learned your name. What is it?"

He laughed. "Well, some like yourself just call me 'Old Man'—or I guess 'Goatee Man'." Then he laughed again. "But my mother called me 'Hungry,' for as a kid, it always fit!"

I smiled, but I didn't laugh, for somewhere deep, a feeling tugged inside of me and I noticed my heart beating rapidly. *Was the saying he just quoted, what he read—or was it he that wrote it?* It no longer seemed like Christmas morning. I asked again, but in a pensive tone, "But now ... what do people call you?"

He paused and looked out over the lake and then slowly back again at me. He looked into my eyes. "You've found for whom you searched. It is I ... I ... am Emgo."

My eyes popped open wider. I yelled, "You ... are Emgo—the thief, and liar, and arson? The conniver? Oh my gosh! You really *are* the Devil then! You and the Elder co-conspirators. *MYSELF* was right! Oh no!" I looked around for the lightning to strike again—on him—for energy, and on me as my final end.

So happy I had been just moments before, and now to hear and learn this! I felt my world compress. I loved Old Man so much; he was my example, my friend, my mentor. And to hear that he was really Emgo—that dirty cheat? It almost killed me—a double personality—one I loved and one I hated, and I was in the middle! A real Doctor Jekyll and Mr. Hyde this time. Maybe he really was the serial killer! Maybe he said he was aware of someone laying traps, because it was him! He sucks people in with good, then chews and spits them out.

"You traitor!" I yelled. And then with hatred, I fumed while almost out of breath, "Why'd you do it? You stole my trust away from me—for at first I revered you, but then discovered truth! You conned me into a six-year journey based on lies—pretending you're a gentle old man with great advice, but really a dirty cheat with cowardly deeds. You are masterful, I'll give you that. I also fell within your trap—like all the others—that I swore I wouldn't do. But unlike them, I am not thankful! You lied to your people about the Beast and that you killed him. You stole money from people in their time of need. You misled others on false journeys. AND ... worst of all, you burned a village down! You coward! How could you?" I paused. "And maybe it really was you that tried to kill me, huh? With those lying notes and fires—maybe working with the Elder!"

He prepared to respond, but then I said, "No, wait. Don't tell me—you don't deserve to explain yourself. Wait, yes, go ahead—Wait! No, you don't deserve to ...." I struggled back and forth, "Wait ... Go ... Wait ... Go," and finally decided, "Just go ahead, although you don't deserve to—I want to know."

"First, I didn't try to kill you. I left no notes or fires. But I did have to think up cunning ways to counter all the threats." He laughed. "And it was definitely not the Elder. That was another. I did slay the Beast, however. Not only that, but I taught others how. And that is why they're thankful."

"No, that isn't true," I countered. "The Elder told me personally that the Beast is not real."

"It isn't," Emgo replied.

I just looked at him, unbelieving. Just like I caught the Elder, I caught him in his lies. "How can you say you slew something that isn't real?"

He sighed and smiled. "I can't tell you. You wouldn't understand. You will have to find the answer. To kill him, look within yourself."

"What about the money you stole, and those misled?"

He answered, "You think life should be easy? Just a piece of cake to make and eat? Is there no purpose for our struggles? Nothing learned from them? You've learned nothing from all of yours on this great journey? Based on lies or not, didn't you learn something? Think a little differently. Think of when Ms. Spear stole your money and I stole hers ... did it start the path of humility, so you could learn a Rule? And didn't those misled learn something from their journey? There really is a Glowing Rock—just not in *this* world; but getting to it teaches triumph over struggle. And the burning village you're so upset about? Did you ask the people how they felt with what they ended up? Didn't you see the results? There was a reason. And when times got worst of all, did I not come? Did I not help? It was I who sent the extra Beast before the first one fully killed you. I who sent the man the other way on the barren wasteland to rescue you. I who sent the ravens by the cliff. I who helped when you were sick. I who sent others with wise words and gracious hearts that helped you. I was your *mentor* on this trip. I who was responsible. I who spoke so clearly—guiding you through many troubles. Many never hear for they're not in-tune. But you were. Don't you remember? Think a little differently—with humility and a different perspective and be thankful."

I stood perplexed and thought out loud, "You let me almost die on Dry Lake."

"No. I felt your pulse and then informed Ms. Spear you needed help. We try to work through others when possible—let them expand."

I thought again, and said, "The ravens almost killed me, forcing me off the cliff."

"They didn't force you *off* the cliff," Emgo replied. "They forced you toward the only place on it with handholds to survive!"

"Why not just tell me there was a cliff?"

"I try to limit my interaction. Life's difficulties have to be lived to be learned from, and to fully appreciate Elgobon."

I pondered—and exhaled. A vision opened up to me and I saw myself through time—days walking, Rules finding, advice from voices hearing, Pebbles picking up, years advancing, lessons learned, myself improved. I was so mad, and although still so hard to comprehend, I started thinking there was a chance that what he said was true. I thought of the Secret: to look at things differently—and as I thought and pondered, I realized my heart no longer held the grudge . . . it was only in my mind.

I exhaled again and hung my head. I said out loud, "This world is all so complicated." I paused, and it was my turn to look out on the lake and at its ripples from the breeze. I took a breath and then looked back. "Perhaps I judged too quickly, but what was I to think? What you say makes sense—when heard *that* way." I looked at my feet and while I did, my heart whispered to my mind, and my mind cleared of my vengeful thoughts, and I could feel he indeed was right. I had misjudged. I looked back and paused before I spoke: "I'm sorry. Now I can feel you are right. Thank you for all you've given me—and for your example." I realized that like the others, now also *I* was thankful.

Emgo laughed. "With most, it is the same. You're no different from others—so don't let it trouble."

I thought and said, "If you're not the Devil's helper, is the Elder then not the Devil?"

"Ha! No. He's *my* mentor."

"Then who's been pushing me toward insanity? Only the Beasts?"

He responded, "No. You, yourself."

I rebutted, "No. The Beasts stress me out. They, with their demons, are pushing me down."

"No. Remember? I said you must learn how to see. You haven't yet mastered it."

Then I had to ask: "Did you also mentor others? The Scholar, and Disciple?"

"Yes, the Scholar and Disciple and even a lady I believe you call Ms. Spear! But not everyone. There are plenty of other mentors."

I gasped. "Ms. Spear? She's on the journey too?"

"Yes," he said. "But she has struggled, and I doubt she will make it. Longer than you she's looked and still no Rules completed."

I looked at the lake and thought, *Oh my word, longer than me and no Rules found? She must be devastated. More tenacity than me she has—without even learning the fire's Rule!* My heart went out to her. But then I realized, it wasn't the Elder or Emgo who did the deeds, so that left only one other—and I frowned.

Then I asked, "You said to find the Mountain before, and I have summited so many and sat and waited, but find nothing. How will I know which one? I was told you could tell me."

"Yes, I can. Every day, you are getting closer. Look for a Sleeping Giant on top of a mountain, and when you see it, you will have found the Mountain. I know it's hard, but just keep moving forward—if you had been ready, you would have already seen and found it. But it takes much time to work in preparing oneself." He looked out over the end of the lake, and beyond it over the cliff and valley to a range of mountains and pointed across at them. "See there in the far away distance—the Sleeping Giant, now lying on the tallest mountain?"

I jerked my head to look beyond him, searching—but there was no such thing I saw.

He turned and smiled at me and put his hand on my shoulder. "I'm sorry, but it will come. Carry on. Like I said six years ago, 'For everyone, it is somewhere different.' I will tell you this, though, the Mountain that you search is not what you must find."

"What? But you told me to find it! Your instructions are confusing. You told me to find the Mountain, and now you say not to. You said the Beast isn't real and yet it will kill me if I let it. You told me my destiny was Elgobon, but it should never be my goal. You told me to find Rules. Was I really ever supposed to?"

He answered, "I never told you to find Rules. Think again of what I said. And regarding the Mountain, find it, yes, but here's some advice: In times of greatest glory, ponder where you came from. The end is not the end; from it see the beginning. Look beyond the finish to find the hidden message. Else all you've gained is lost and buried."

All I could think was, *More riddles I must discern? This whole journey has been a riddle.*

I thought about the name Emgo, for I remembered a television special I had seen chronicling the life of a man named Emgo Delgado from Ecuador.

When thirty years old, he gathered money from many friends, and in a partnership, he got a loan and bought a small piece of land and cattle. This was successful and so he did the same over and over again, the partnerships and ranches becoming larger. He kept buying other real estate through bigger partnerships until one day he was the largest real estate holder in

South America and worth billions. Then he focused his time on charity.

I smiled and slowly asked, "Is your last name Delgado?"

He smiled back, "It is."

I told him I had learned the Scholar's and Disciple's stories, so asked him his.

"The Maps led me to success, and with that success, I was able to help others, and that was fun. I am very close to Elgobon; in fact, mentoring you is my final mission."

I asked him why he was at Dry Lake and the other places that I saw him. He laughed. "Protecting my investment. But of course, it was just *I* there, for *MYSELF* was still fulfilling our life and doing good in South America. But I'm getting old there, and soon I'll pass away. Then *I* and *MYSELF* will finally reunite for good, and *I* will show him Elgobon."

We spoke for quite a while of my other World Two events where he and others had been involved, and I tried to ask other things and most he answered, but many he said were best unanswered. He said to wait and see and find out for myself, for experience is the best advisor. He advised that energy from the lake was needed for my final journey. So it's good I swam in it.

Then from a pocket underneath his shirt he withdrew a most exquisite nine-inch knife and sheath and gave me it. "I was told to give this to you, but I've been waiting quite a while. You can use it against the Beast—but only if it's needed!" He shook my hand, "Carry on my friend." He then walked back into the lake and waved his hand a certain way at the water, and it seemed to stiffen a bit. He lay down on it, floating on his back, drifting to the middle, smiling at the sky.

I left him there, and that night I wrote—and laughed. The same type thing was happening to Chisel—our courses on parallel paths. What happened to me was happening to him. (Luck's Been With Me, track 15)

Well, luck's been with me today

and from what I see, life's going my way
uh huh, oh yeah, uh huh, oh yeah
no matter what! No, no, no, no. No matter if—

Chorus:
And when the rain clouds are stormin' and the sun is a scorchin'
when somebody says, they don't like my face

I look at all the grass around, I hear the birds making sounds
I look at trees, that seem to smile at me

I grab the corners of my mouth, and pull them up toward my ears
until they finally stay there, all by themselves

And then the world's not so bad, and I feel luck comin' back
and life is wonderful, all over again

Verse:
Yeah, yeah, yeah, luck's been with me today
and from what I see, life's going my way
uh huh, oh yeah, uh huh, oh yeah
no matter what! No, no, no, no. No matter if—
No, no. No matter what! No matter if—

Chapter 20

Killing Something That's Not Real

I thought about his powers and of the necklace he wore like the Elder, Scholar, and Disciple—but his necklace had three medallions, I noticed. *So if I pass the Gate, like Emgo, will I also swim and not get wet, and hear and talk to people in other places, and take energy from lightning bolts?* I looked at the knife resting in my hands and felt the weight of it—perfectly balanced, and admired its extreme beauty. It looked magical— like the stake you can use to kill a vampire. I smiled, "This is what they lacked in medieval times. And this is what I've been looking for. I finally have what I need to kill the Beast. With my army of animals fighting below, and ravens diving from above, *and* now also with the knife, I cannot fail!"

With my little army, myself and the wolverine riding on the bear, I looked at every mountain to find the Beast and the Sleeping Giant, each night filling in my journal with what had happened to me before. I journeyed up one mountain, through nature's pristine beauty of meadows, rocks, pines, and streams, through air so crisp I savored its scent and feel. Then up the second, then third—each higher than the last—myself king of each, with my walking stick/spear/scepter in my hand—raised to rule the summit and the valleys below. I gloried when on top of each, knowing that I made it, and it came to mind, that every so often everyone needs to get on top of mountains and look down to know the glory of it, and know what they can do. On top of each mountain, I pondered where I came. I tried to see the start. I tried to find the message. But I couldn't, and I questioned if I ever would. And still I hadn't seen the Prophet, and I worried that all was lost and buried. The ravens still flew above, but surprisingly now in a great circling motion directly above me unlike they had ever done before. They filled the sky like a great black, turning cloud obscuring the sun—thousands and thousands, like vultures waiting for a Beast to leave, and then to finish off what it attacked.

[Tiz stopped and closed his eyes and raised his head, breathing deep a couple times.]

On top of that third mountain, as I worried, I started feeling ... something—something following; that old familiar feeling of being watched. *The Beast is near*, I thought. *The time is now to finish him and set ME and MYSELF free! Emgo said to kill the Beast I would have to look within myself.* I thought and decided to kill the Beast I must know he wasn't really there! I told myself, *It's my imagination, the Beast is not real*, as I'd been told. But when you've seen the bloodshot eyes, and heard the growling, drooling mouth, and felt the sharpness of the teeth, it's so hard to understand. I was wearied of walking and that enhanced the worry. "No!" I yelled. "I'll not let it come back!"

"What if?" that voice of negativity then asked, as his initial question of examination.

"No! I will not ask it once again!" I yelled. "Who are you that's asking this of me, feeding me negativity? Tell me who you are!" I wanted to know who was tempting me.

I felt pessimism in my heart, it beating faster steadily, with stress that I now felt. "No! I will not feel it," I said. It was my debilitating habit, that I hadn't beat—still forcefully tempting me. "AHHH!" I yelled and put my hands around my head, which hurt from all these thoughts. My army gathered around me rubbing my legs with their bodies, then formed a protective circle three feet out and around me.

"You can't do it," that negative voice said out loud, adding to his arsenal.

My head throbbed and I started to cry, and softly through my sobs, I told him, "Yes, I can—you're a liar."

"Let it go," my own voice said to me. "Don't let the negativity, and doubts, and worries drag you down. Set them floating on the stream. Let them go and be at peace."

That other voice then responded, doubling his intensity as if in his final cross-examination, for he knew this was the point of no return—for both of us, "You failed before, you've sinned and are not forgiven, continue your feelings of sorrow, remember things gone bad, when you've been sad, jobs lost, not smart enough. Think of all your worries, about your pettiness and greed, your anger over something, doubts you have in yourself, someone done you wrong, love not reciprocated, spears thrown at you, your addictions not overcome. The Beast *is* real—don't believe them! You've seen and felt his ragged teeth. He's too strong to overcome! You don't have courage to resist. You're too weak to oppose him."

Then the skies darkened even more with blackened clouds enveloping the ravens. And lightning came in nearby skies— encircling me, and thunder. Then the smell—from everywhere in all directions—decaying there upon the ground—and now I could actually see those dead rats—thousands of them all around me— covering the mountaintop—and faint, gray mist flowing in. My army was confused—looking around—not knowing what was bothering me.

I fell to my knees upon those rats, extended my arms, and looked up toward the storm-filled sky above. "AHHH!" I yelled, "*MYSELF* and *ME* give me your power that I need! The Beast is tempting me!" That is when the Beast burst out from behind a boulder, ten feet to my side. "ATTACK!" I yelled to my little army . . . but unbelievably they seemed not to notice the Beast— only my fatigue, and they didn't move—not knowing what to attack. I realized, *This is <u>my</u> fight*. They were only there for moral support, and they howled at haunting decibels to buoy me.

I rose on my feet and saw it charging down on me—in between my army, but ... I did not run—and I felt the fangs sink deep inside again, heard the growling parasite tearing at his dinner, and saw my blood in torrents. I threw my arms out and head back as I groaned in awful pain. And Chisel also felt the pain. I yelled, "Sorry Chisel for the agony!" I realized the only times the Beast had attacked was when my mind was filled with disharmony.

SO ....

I did not listen to that voice this time that told me negativity. I did not open the door, not even a little crack. I realized this time, it was either the Beast or me—and one must die! I would not run away this time. I grabbed Emgo's golden knife from the sheath on my belt and held it up to stab the Beast between his shoulder blades and finally be done with him. The blade glistened in the sun—like it was licking its lips—ready to finally accomplish its mission—what it was made for—to pierce the hide and flesh of a mighty Beast—to watch it bleed and finally kill the thing—as Emgo did. So thankful I was that Emgo had delivered it to save me from this thing ....

The knife hung there in the air .... "Look within yourself," I heard. I paused—and breathed. After thinking, I said out loud, "No," and dropped the blade. The knife would have killed it, but I decided I didn't want it after all. I also could have called those ravens down to spear him with a hundred bloody beaks, for my mind had erased any negativity, which now I knew repulsed the ravens, and my positivity attracted them. But even though they waited to help from up above, I also decided against *their* help. I had to do this on my own this time. "I choose to do this with my mind. I choose to not let my negative thoughts destroy me. I choose to be happy. I will always keep fighting the Beast." I let the Beast tear flesh from me, seeing his bloody muzzle feeding, and felt life slip away—BUT ....

I would not listen to that negative voice. I looked within and realized the rats were my negative thoughts and worries and weaknesses and addictions—and the smell of those attracted the Beasts—the smell being the warning from within that something is wrong. I remembered the Elder's Guidance and used time wisely, this time not rushing, but permitting myself time to contemplate. Knowing how to breathe and see, I breathed correctly and pictured myself in a beautiful place where I would like to be where all is right and void of stress. I remembered the Scholar's Secret and thought about the Beast differently—not just what I saw. I remembered the Disciple's Truth. One grand thing would not deliver me, but all those little memories of things I'd learned that would give me the combined power that I needed. I convinced myself to never quit trying and just keep going—one step at a time, and then one more, to smile in the mirror even when not wanting, to remember goodness still exists when all seems lost and dreary, like clear sky above dark clouds, to remember there is value and lessons in life's hardest times, so to be happy for my struggles—for their lessons perfect me. After six and a half years of work and practice, I replaced bad thoughts with good by thinking of other things to fill my mind, and still I let him work on me—grimacing and groaning in pain with sweat pouring from me. But as he did, I thought of charity, tranquility, and peace within my soul. I gave thanks for what I'd been given—listing them, and remembered all my weaknesses I'd overcome, mistakes I was correcting. I remembered to ask for help and do my very best, and knowing so, to be at peace. Of my current worry, I asked, "Does it really, truly matter?" I didn't worry about the past. I smiled about the future. And then ... I just let go, and saw myself standing in the rain with arms outstretched, head back a bit, and I let my worries wash off me then watched them floating down a stream. And that is how I stood, eyes closed. "I will not let my worries kill me!" I said out loud.

Then I opened my eyes and looked up at the sky, and those storm clouds looked alive, for they were filled with darting madness. The clouds started quickly dissipating, but as they did, they were replaced by another more violent—for those ravens were now a mass of dark confusion darting in and out of one another, wings now flapping in a quick and agitated manner, and their shrieking cries sounding like high-pitched thunder. But amidst the noise, I could suddenly hear sweet bird sounds from the lone tree on the mountaintop. I looked at the tree, and I saw sparrows chirping and squirrels in its piney branches running 'round. Then I smelled the smell—but not of rats now—now of morning air, after rain, fresh and clean, crisp and clear, with that slight watermelon scent, and perhaps a little lime as well ... and then I thought and realized—*Nothing felt! No fangs in me, no gushing blood*—and I looked down.

The Beast was dead and lying there upon the ground—and a shadow came over me and confusion reigned in blackened skies of flapping wings descending like a hail storm, and everywhere engulfing me in the sound of cawing, slapping, hysteric pandemonium. I crouched and covered my head with my hands being hit by diving birds and flapping wings. The ravens each landed hard with a thud, and sunk their claws into a rat and flew away (and with them my thousands of negative thoughts I once had had, which now were dead)—and filling the skies with blackness once again till they were far away and looked and sounded like a giant, screaming storm cloud moving west, revealing a giant rainbow up above them.

I stood upright as I watched them fade, then when I looked down at my side, I saw no skin was torn, no flesh was gone, no blood was spilt, no bones were broken ... the Beast had *not* been real! And yet—I had killed him! Emgo and the Elder had *not* lied. The villagers were *not* deceived. It was not a Beast at all, it never was—it was an "InBeast:" a Beast not real *outside* of me, but real *inside* my mind!

I thought, *What the Scholar said was true. There are no Beasts in this world ... but now I know there are InBeasts ... in all worlds—and in all of us.* InBeasts are the manifestations of all our negativity and worry—and the actual stress we envision and feel from that, when the stress becomes so great that it affects a person mentally or physically. It is then that an InBeast has power over us—controlling us. He doesn't want us to succeed. Our difficulties and struggles in the form of rats *are* real, but the Beast is not ... unless we *let* him be, and *worship* him, by ingesting his smoky stress into our chest—creating an InBeast devouring us inside.

Now I understood. And as I looked at him on the ground, his body decayed in rapid motion. First eyes dried and withered away in their sockets, then fur aged and fell away, and then the skin, then meat from the bones, until just a skeleton. I realized *that* would not decay, for even though dead, he would live again if I let him. My next question came to ask the audience:

What Beasts do we tame?

So many of us still have baby blankets that we pull around but do not really need: eating when bored, smoking when stressed, drugs to escape—but it's hard to recognize and retire them. But finally I had retired mine.

It was then I realized who the voice of negativity was. The voice of negativity had come from me! I was my own worst enemy! I was not alone as I had thought, and I was not fighting a Beast—I was fighting myself! *ME* and *MYSELF* were gone, but now I knew there was yet another one of me. And all along *HE* had been accompanying me. It was *HE* who brought the demons and the InBeast. *HE* who let them in. *I* was more in tune with positivity and goodness, but *HE* was my negative side, for *HE* let evil persuade him and convince him. *HE* was the InBeast! But after all this time, I had found a way to help him change. I closed my eyes and contemplated—and let it all sink in. I had finally won. *Finally now I am not at war.*

Chapter 21

Throwing Spears Away

iz got a drink from his water cup and looked at the audience. They no longer talked among themselves, instead you could see their foreheads furrowed in reflective thought. Tiz could imagine them wondering what the Beast in their own lives was.]

My little army came to me and rubbed against to congratulate and we celebrated with pets and hugs. Then they left and I was thankful they had come. I staggered on, my mind fatigued, and found a cave of bones to rest within. There I took refuge for the night, and from the rain, and I healed from my mental fight. Inside, I played some gentle ukulele tracks, and finished filling in my journal from the start of my journey. I read stories in pictures on the wall—of men fighting men, of journeys overseas and back again, of men and women wed, and one of an obelisk. So I added my own of a person on a journey and a Beast that he defeated, hoping someone would learn from it.

Then by the firepit, in my weariness I sat, relaxed my heart and mind, and pleaded, "Please come in and keep me company." Then after a couple minutes they entered. First a somewhat transparent woman and two children—cave people long since dead—for I saw them in their realm. They had just come in from picking berries and pine nuts. They placed wood in the fire pit, lit it, and sat beside me around it. I talked to them, but they didn't hear or see me. It seemed they sensed me, though, for they looked in my direction. Later, the father with a butchered deer came in, and oh so glad the family was to see it. The children did a caveman happy dance that I admit was very good. They cooked it on a spit over the fire and I salivated—like Pavlov's dog, for I swear that I could smell its smoky, savory scent. I thought that I might steal a bite—and tried—and although it was semi-transparent, I pulled some off, and in my mouth I relished it. Then, also *I* did the caveman happy dance! And when the deer was done and eaten, they placed the bones on that pile in the corner and prayed over them awhile, giving thanks.

With them, I felt I had the family that in World Two I didn't have. So much I loved it, I stayed for days accompanying them to their work, and then again enjoying the nightly fire. I sensed they somehow knew that I was there, for day by day they looked and smiled more often in my direction—sometimes extending their arms and hands through my invisible figure. By the end, they were leaving a seat open between them at the fire, and I accommodated them.

Each night after dinner, I wrote in my journal and then read out loud to *MYSELF* and *ME*, so they would know the continuing story. But I knew that *MYSELF* and *ME* could also see, for I felt their power when I fought the InBeast.

Finally one morning, to the cave people I said good-bye and patted them on their shoulders. When I did, I saw a little sadness in their eyes. But they pursed their lips and slightly smiled and nodded as if to say good-bye, the father also patting me where *my* shoulder would be.

I traveled on—a great meadow entered—miles wide and miles across, with jagged mountains behind. I crossed the grass, and waded its river, to approach those mountains I soon would climb. I entered the mountains and three bighorn sheep accompanied—a ram and two ewes. I told them I was okay, they didn't have to, but they wanted to—insisted on. They knew the paths to take and waited patiently, but I could see they were surprised sometimes how much I had to rest. Then after months, when on a morning going up ... who knows which mountain, for I quit counting, I came around a corner and approached a woman coming down. She was seated on a log and resting there, and I surprised her. I spit on the ground, for you can guess who I had found—finally after all those years—Ms. Spear! She wore no hat this time, and her blond hair was longer, and after five years she looked slightly different, but still I recognized her for sure. I hadn't needed any trap—she just fell into my lap. Revenge could finally be mine, and this time it was *I* that had the spear! This time *I* was the one with energy and power and *she* sat below *me*. I would be the judge and executioner. She saw my boots and didn't look up as I walked up to her, for I think she recognized the brand and knew who they belonged to. I planted my walking stick between her feet and said, "I think you forgot this," for my walking stick was sharpened on the end like a spear (only now it was silver-tipped)—and one time it had punctured me!

It took a while, and then she looked up and looked remorseful and embarrassed.

I was hoping the answer was somehow, "No," but as the judge and jury in this place, I had to solemnly ask it and then determine her fate. "Was it you, then?"

She looked back down at the ground and knew this was her time of reckoning. Her judgement and sentencing were finally at hand. Slightly I heard her reply: "Yes, it was me. I'm truly sorry."

I heavily sighed, then frowned. Revenge was on my mind. Should I stab her now like she had done to me? It crossed my mind and I breathed in deep ... but then I exhaled, for now I was just sad it was really her. "Why would you do a thing like that? And why rescue me from Dry Lake just to later try and kill me?" I was so angry with her, but more than that, sorry for her that she had let meanness overtake her.

She slowly looked up and to the right down the trail. "Anger and jealousy," she answered, then looked at me. "You never called me back after we saw each other at your parents' house, and it really hurt, and then, here, I heard what you had done that I could not—after two years of trying, and for it, hatred took control of me. But I couldn't let you die when I found you on the lake—for you still had a pulse, and during our meeting at your parent's house I felt a special bond, and the jealousy came later. I didn't try to kill you. I was trying to dissuade you from continuing by setting my little traps, hoping they would make you want to quit, but you wouldn't have it. But ... I guess my traps were almost a little *too* effective!"

I was confused. "What are you talking about—meeting at my parent's house?" It was five years before so we both looked different—especially here, journeying as we were, so I didn't recognize her, but I studied her and then I did. "Wait, of course. Now I recognize your accent. Then you had brown hair, but now I see. It was you that knocked on our door for some information about our house, and my mom said you returned, but didn't want my phone number I left her to give to you."

Then it was Ms. Spear who looked confused. "I never said that. She never offered your phone number, and I gave your mom *my* phone number, hoping *you* would call *me*. But you never did. And yes, you're right, my hair was dyed and long back then, then I cut it short and now it's long again."

"Oh my gosh," we both said together. I mentioned, "She was trying to protect us both from my insanity."

[Tiz looked at his mom in the front row who was softly crying. "It's okay mom."]

We both sat and pondered this revelation. Then she sighed and paused, looking at the ground, then back at me. "I tried to follow you and find the Rules that way, but it didn't work, and it made me even more jealous. But when I saw all your progress, you inspired me, and I decided to again start trying myself."

Again she paused. "I don't think I'll ever make it, but as I followed you, and watched you for so long, I finally realized you deserve it. You just kept going—no matter what. I saw how hard you work, and your tenacity, and your love for others, and I admired you for it. And I realized the awful extent of what I'd done. And I saw you talking to the stars, and crying, and my heart softened, and I quit my deceiving practices."

Another pause and she looked deep into my eyes, as hers were tearing up. "I'm truly so, so sorry! Maybe . . ." she looked down and blinked a couple times as a couple tears fell out. "Maybe someday, you can forgive me."

I looked down the trail myself, and after a time, I sat down beside her on her left.

She looked at her feet and spoke softly, "I guess I wasn't cut out for this. I guess this isn't me. The valley down below us now is so inviting. I've decided to turn and walk that way instead—and then keep going—back that way from where I came: to my city, my house, my friends, and in my precious bed I'll lie. I just won't dream like I did before of reaching Mountaintops, and reading Maps that Rules unfold."

In silence we sat, and I pondered her words as I looked through the trees of the forest, and in the far distance above them to the next mountain I would gain, and I thought of the ones already. I, like her, had thought the same, but that was not me anymore. Not in my heart, not in my thoughts, not in my bones, so never in my actions anymore. I had become the horse, the hawk, the fish, the tree of pine. I had become the fire. So many years I jumped and then I counted. Over and over made habit and now just instinct. And now just DO.

I gave her my water and moved a rock on the trail with my boot. "Down is not an option," I informed. "There is no scepter waiting there. No clouds below, no view to see, no valleys to rule, no glorious destiny reached. Down is not the way. I can understand your pain and jealousy, for from experience I know how hard you've worked and wanted it. I'm proud of you. You're getting close. Stay on the path and do not sway and you will get there."

I paused, and we sat quietly. Eventually I put my right hand on her left shoulder. "I forgive you," I said. She had her head down and she rubbed her forehead and I heard her breathe heavily a couple times. Silence again, and then I reached into my pack and lifted out a book. It was my journal. "I want you to have this. With your desire, you are one that it can help. I've been writing it for almost seven years. In it are all my journeys and what happened, and the Pebbles and Rules I found. You'll have to journey on your own paths to make it there, and your Pebbles and Rules will be individualized to you, but this can teach you how to look, to go with your experience and make your trip much faster. You've probably found most of your Pebbles, but just not recognized the Rules—they can't be seen with frustration, anger, or jealousy, so now for you it will go very quickly." I handed it to her.

She was dumbstruck. "I can't take this," she said. "It's like gold you're handing over, and even more—because you created it."

I laughed. "Don't worry. I know what's in it—I've memorized it—so I always have it with me." I laughed again. "Not only that, I've written it twice, and left a copy in World One." I tilted the spear toward her. "And you can have your spear back too."

She smiled. "Thanks ... but I don't want it. I found another walking stick—*without* a point."

We both laughed, and I said, "And I no longer need its silver point." And I stood and threw it like a javelin over the trees.

"I guess now I'll have to call you by your real name— Francine if I recall from back then. I was calling you 'Ms. Spear.'"

She laughed. "Oh no! But I deserve it of course," she said with a cute Irish accent. "My father is Irish, mother French—my full name Francine Elizabeth. I recently moved from Ireland to America for a job."

I noticed she wore no ring, and I told her I was Tiz. "You know me as Jeremy, for at home they call me by my middle name."

We sat in silence, and then she sighed and said, "I should tell you a secret, but it's quite embarrassing."

I replied, "Well ... after you left me that first time, a Pterodactyl pooped on me—and I doubt you can better that .... Now that I think of it, a frog also 'snotted' me, and an Apatosaurus I thought was nice, because he wagged his tail, wagged me clear across a meadow."

"Oh my gosh!" she said, and started laughing. "I'm so sorry."

"Now your turn," I said.

"Well ... after the Dry Lake incident isn't when I started following you—it was before. I wouldn't say I'm vain, but I saw you earlier and ... I was intrigued, let's say." Her face flushed a bit. "I recognized you from your parents house and although hurt, I wanted to forgive you and followed you until I saw you walk out on that lake. You turned around and almost saw me after I stepped on a stick, but I hid behind a tree. I left you then, and sometime later heard a voice that said to pass that way again, and I saw you lying on that lake and figured you were dead. I thought I'd go and bury you, but found you slightly had a pulse, and for a night I sat there hoping you'd come back. Then with my water, you revived. But ... sitting there looking at your face that night upon my lap ... well ... you know—I didn't think you're ugly, let's say that! But more than that, your face looked calm and nice and I could tell your soul was good. And I started falling ...." She cleared her throat. "Well, you really scared me lying there! And then my intense jealousy, which brought the hurt back from your rejection ... and then I started setting the traps. I felt so conflicted in my heart and so guilty that I cried and cried at nights, for when I followed, I saw how good you are. And a couple times, I heard someone offer help to me and knew that it was you."

"HA-HA, YES!" I yelled and laughed and threw my fist into the air. "I was right! I knew the meanness wasn't in you! And I'll admit to you, over all this time, the picture of your face kept resurrecting in my mind ... and—well, you know—I didn't think that it was ugly either ... it was beautiful! In fact, it brought me back to this world from World One to see it once again—to see *you* once again!"

She blushed again.

I was intent on finding my Mountain ... but decided it could wait. We spent the rest of that day together by a nearby lake, pine trees surrounding, beautiful sky and sun and birds. We swam, and laughed, and skimmed rocks, talked about our childhoods, and ate apples (I offered her some dried lizard tails from my pack, but she was full, she said). Then we caught some fish and roasted them over our fire that night with wild onions, and for dessert, bowls of raspberries we picked together.

We lay by each other and gazed at the stars, and talked about our families and friends, and hobbies and homes, and jobs and wishes, and exchanged addresses in World One. We were one in spirit and respected each other's tenacity in climbing mountains and looking for clues to achieve a goal. I told her about *MYSELF* and *ME* in the mental hospital. "I have to get back and tell them in person that I killed the Beast. They are free." Then I introduced her to Thorny-Tooth, and Hairy-Cat, and told her of my Frisky dog beyond the horizon. She laughed and laughed.

"Well, I was lonely!" I said, defending myself. "And besides ... I respect their opinions. And although Hairy doesn't look rough, you can see he has long claws and he is quite protective. So ... I had that going for me." I sat up and held up Bill, who was hanging from my pack, to look at her. "And Bill here, although he is always surprised about different things, is actually calm and reassuring."

She sat up as well—and looking at Bill, her eyebrows rose. Then she looked at me and back at Bill. She hesitantly said, "Helloooo, Bill," and patted him on the head.

Then I added a little music to the night by playing my ukulele and conducting a cricket symphony—and she was so impressed. Then I asked, "How 'bout a personal concert? I actually wrote this first song for you!" And I started out:

Hey Girl, you're everything
your walk is always new
I'm stuck, I can't get off
of this stellar path, around you ...

She applauded. "Ha! Very nice. But I know you didn't write it. That's my favorite song by *FlyTheBlue*. I have all their albums. But you do sound just like the lead singer!" Then her eyebrows furrowed. "Wait. You said your name is Tiz? I knew you as Jeremy. Oh my gosh!" She stared at me. "Now I recognize you. You are Tiz from *FlyTheBlue!*"

I acknowledged.

"It was really written for me then?"

"Yes. One lonely night when I was looking at the stars."

"Oh my gosh. I love it even more!" She asked, "If you're so successful in World One, why submit yourself to these difficulties?"

"Ha!" I laughed; and then repeated an answer *I* had heard, "The same reason as you, of course. I knew there was more, and only through struggle can you find it. I felt that riches and ease are not the final goal."

Sometime in the night, when sleep had reached us, I guess she reached and held my hand (or maybe it was me), for in the morning, that's how we awoke.

"I'd call that a pretty good first date," I told her.

She playfully gasped. "That was no date, you scoundrel! You never even asked me out!"

We were each packing to leave and go our own ways, but then decided maybe one more day would be okay—more berries, and fish, talking, laughing, another concert in the night—and then another day came and went. But the next morning, as we ate, we both dreaded what was coming—and packing went unusually slow. Then we unpacked a couple times to do it better—and then we were packed and there were no more excuses.

"Can I give you a hug?" she asked as she walked toward me. But she didn't sound excited.

I smiled and tried to make it lighter, "If you don't mind the smell—I've been walking for a while!"

She laughed. "Me too!" Then she looked down and softly asked, "You sure I can't come with you?"

Oh, it broke my heart, for I had asked the same, and this was twenty times as hard. I lifted her chin and looked into her eyes. "I want you to come with me *all* the way—through all the Gates—and there's only one way that can happen .... You're going to see a lot of me, though—I assure you!"

I looked at the bighorn sheep, "Guys, can you now accompany Francine? She could use your company, and I think what's left for me I have to do alone. Besides ... she smells better than me!" The ewes came and rubbed against her bleating, and the ram ran and forcefully rammed his head against a pine tree to show he could protect her. "Ooh, good job Rammy—you're tough alright," I said. He stood up straight, looking back and forth at all of us. Then I looked again at Francine, "And next time I see you, I'll bring a couple llamas too (I didn't think to offer goats—for some of them have attitudes). But they're not for eating or riding on!"

She laughed.

"No, I'm serious," I advised.

"Ha! Of course! Who would ever think of doing that?"

I reddened. "Or maybe I'll bring an Apatosaurus—for you *could* ride her!" Then I added, "And if we find a restaurant, I'll take you to dinner and we'll officially call it a date."

She laughed even harder. "Well, you would have to ask me first!"

"Will you?"

She looked surprised, then squinted, then smiled. She tilted her head down a little and looked up with just her eyes, "I do." Then she realized what she said and gasped, and her face flushed red, and she corrected herself: "I mean, I *will* . . . date you—that is!" And she blushed again.

"HA-HA, YES!" I yelled.

We hugged for quite some time, and I didn't relish letting go, then I looked into her eyes. "I'm going to make sure you make this! I'm almost done with this world, so would you mind if I return to check on you?"

She brightened and smiled and reached up and held my face in her hands. "I'd mind it if you didn't!" And she laughed and added, "If you don't mind the smell!"

We stood there staring at each other waiting for the other to walk away. But neither could be the one to do it. Then finally we hugged once more even longer, and I put my cheek on hers and held it there my hand behind her head. Then I sighed and paused and backed away—a little farther still—then I turned my feet and followed them sluggishly. Up the trail, I stopped and looked back and she and the sheep were waiting, and we waved; and I concentrated very hard to imprint upon my mind the looks of that sweet face, and the sound of that soft voice and cute accent—for it would be a while until I heard it once again.

Chapter 22

The Evil Impasse

As I continued, a voice came to me—all around, and through the trees, "You are now ready to see."

From here to there was difficult, but I had a smile on my face for who I found, and as I walked, I sang a song to commemorate the occasion. I called it, *Fantasy Wishes:* (Fantasy Wishes, track 16)

Fantasy Wishes can come true
I have been waiting all my life
patiently knew that if I did
all my dreams they would come due
everything I'd do for you

When I was young and growing up
pictured a girl inside my mind
knew that the chance of meeting her
were one in a million times
she was a fantasy in my mind

Chorus 1:
worth the sighs upon my pillow, worth the years that I did wait
worth the evenings by myself, worth the loneliness inside

Chorus 2:
inside her spirit spoke to me, inside I knew my destiny

inside I knew that I should wait, inside I knew it was my fate

Verse:
Were they illusions in my head
coming from something that I read
simply mirages that I saw
never to materialize
only dreams that were all lies

But then I walked out of the fog
and saw the girl I'd been dreaming of
had to look twice to just make sure
it was'nt fantasy anymore
all the waiting was over

Chorus 2 Repeated

Music-----

Now I'm complete since I have her
had always felt something missing
knew there was someone waiting
who was there just for me
it was always meant to be

travel the country, see the world
always be looking for that girl
know that she's waiting there too
keeping her eye out for you
waiting till her dream comes true

    Down and over and under and across I walked. I came across
a stream and got a drink, then peered into its mirror in some water
that was still. As I looked at my reflection, I studied hard, for my
vision was now corrected! My reflection was no longer blurred!

I laughed. How glorious to finally once again see myself in clarity. I thought hard, and then I smiled and knew why it had been. My different sides had been at odds so long. So I always saw myself and another one as well, or even two or three .... Now my reflection showed what I felt—all myselves were one again. And it showed peace of mind as well. And that was good, for soon I needed it.

From a forested ridge, I looked down at the base of a mountain and what I saw took my breath away. A great valley lay all around that mountain, and filling that valley were thousands of InBeasts—and they were waiting! And I knew who they were waiting for—for it was me! One last time they would try. But this time many more—and all at once. All together they would see if they could make me break. They were biting, and growling, and gnawing on each other while waiting, but they all stood facing away from the mountain, surrounding it. This is where they all were running to—in case their brothers failed. This was the impassable entrance of evil! I had killed their brother, but I knew my positivity alone would not kill these—there were too many. But now I recognized them for what they were. Yes, they were just inside my mind, I knew, but their combined power caused enough stress to become real, by making me physically and mentally sick from it—and I couldn't just discard it. I would have to find another way.

Then I thought, *Why here?* And I lost my breath as I remembered Emgo's words, and I slowly looked up, up, up, at that great Mountain. The range was like the Himalayas and that one like Mount Everest. Miles away I saw the top ... and when I did, I clearly saw, without mistake, a giant, that was lying there sleeping. His head was made up of boulders and dirt and ridges, and the same for his shoulder and his arm that lay down at his side, then bent up on top, which was his hand resting on his stomach. And the sun on top was a little brighter than its surroundings. "Oh my word!" I sighed. "I know which one to climb! The treasure and Gate are up there waiting."

Almost seven years (in World One time) I'd worked to get there but the InBeasts were between me and my sought-out summit, and the Sleeping Giant now seemed untouchable! I looked at the sky in hope of seeing ravens, but none were there—the skies were clear.

Then an old familiar sound I heard, of crickets chirping separately, then those chirps combined in harmony to form a gentle choral arrangement made to calm the soul. As I listened, my quickened heart found peace, and my shortened breath found length, and I knew what I must do—but it would take everything I had inside. Then, one of the InBeasts must have seen me, because I heard one louder than the rest barking and howling frantically, and I looked down and all of them started looking up and yelping and growling and snarling, showing their teeth—staying where they were, but excitedly jumping in place, some turning in circles, like a dog so hungry for its dinner.

I swallowed hard a couple times and started making my way down to them. Down the mountain I was on, around rocks and trees. They followed my progress, and the closer *I* got, the louder *they* got, and the more excited.

Right before I made it down, I knelt behind some trees and said a prayer and meditated to clear my mind and slow my heart, and I rehearsed my defenses. Over several minutes, I set my focus on my peaceful meadow and feeding the squirrels, and I made sure my mind was free of any stress and negativity and full of goodness and tranquility and I continued meditating on this. I breathed as had been taught, and saw any worries disperse—as darkened clouds, as they were leaving me. *Peace* engulfed my soul. That would be my first defense. Then I asked *MYSELF* and *ME* to assist and I smiled ... and walked around the trees—armed with light and strength.

I entered the meadow and walked toward those InBeasts fifty feet away. The Sleeping Giant was the backdrop so far away, so it was he I focused on. The InBeasts didn't charge, but held their place, and their excitement heightened twofold, then more, as I approached. Their barrier was a tightly packed, massive wall, six InBeasts deep, and I smiled bigger as I reached them. They were standing on all four legs, but almost as tall as me. Their eyes were all trained on me, their teeth were gnashing, and they were salivating—drooling, growling, snarling, some howling, wanting to attack and feast, but they did not strike. I paused before their frenzy, surveying their concentrated hate. I knew they were just inside my mind, but even though I had cleansed it of negativity, there is always the slightest doubt, and even when we don't succumb, temptations always come, so I could still see, and hear, and feel them. The key was to not let that doubt or worry grow into something bigger that could harm me. I told myself, *All worries are uncomfortable, but are they unbearable? Of your current one, ask yourself, "Does it really matter?" If not, then let it go. Life is short, with challenges every day. That is normal. Don't think of the bad. Hail the good. Don't worry about the past. Smile about the future.*

Then I chose a spot and slowly started trying to push through them—grabbing fur on their backs and pulling with my hands and might—smiling as I did. But they were big and strong, so it wasn't easy. They were biting the air an inch from my face, and jumping and snarling with slobber spilling out, and spit showering on me from their foaming mouths (like they had rabies), in a desperate last attempt to have me, wanting to feast so desperately. But it didn't matter, for all inside my mind was peace and love—and I knew that was the key—for it provided me a power that without I lacked.

The InBeasts not affected by the action left their stations and ran and crowded behind me to watch, barking and howling in support of their brothers.

I inched my way through. But I focused totally, and I sweat from my strained mentality. When I had made it to the middle of their barrier, the sound increased intensely, and the energy was frantic. I had three InBeasts left to go.

Then before me, InBeasts crowded in more tightly and many from the outskirts ran to help their brothers out. They climbed on top of the others as their hearts were almost bursting with desire to kill and tear and rip and taste and enjoy me. So a more difficult wall was formed, three InBeasts thick and three InBeasts high, and I could feel my mental concentration start to waver—and death I felt accompany it, for I felt my power start to fail with the stress.

I realized now was the time for my second defense. The Disciple had said to pass the evil at the entrance I would have to picture myself as water. But why? I had studied and come to understand the Clue she gave me: Picture yourself as water— humble to the point where evil cannot hurt you, where its arrows will pass right through you, and you just flow around them. I realized, *Rocks are strong and hard, but they eventually all break and decay into dust. Water is humble and weak, but it lasts forever! All my troubles are like arrows shot at me. And I'm okay with them, and pity them, and choose not to feel them. And as I flow around them, they disappear behind me as they lose power, and fall, and fade, and decay.* I said out loud, "I forgive those who hate—and feel sorrow for your misguided souls."

Greater Peace engulfed my soul. If I was perfect, the InBeasts would have totally died. But it is hard to kill every shadow of lingering stress. However, now, I had the power to beat them. Sweat was pouring off me, but I pictured myself as humble liquid. Again I smiled, and bent over, and inch by inch I progressed—pushing and pulling myself—sliding on the backs of the bottom row of them, and under those on top, squeezing in between—feeling their muscled, constricting bodies and continuing to hear their teeth gnashing and InBeasts not close to me barking and howling in agony. But I continued to claw and dig and inch my way through, and they all whined for they could see their feast escaping right through them—and them not understanding why, and they hated it.

Then ... yes! I got my head through, and slowly I squeezed and pulled and wriggled my shoulders, and my torso, and finally my right leg through! Then I got my foot on the ground and then the other—and unsteadily I stood and stepped onto that Mountain—and maybe it was holy, for they did not follow. I staggered ten feet farther and turned around in sheer exhaustion—face red, panting like one of them, slouched over with my hands resting on my knees—sweat dripping off my face. Then the frantic barking largely stopped except a few remaining howls—for their energy was consumed, and there was nothing they could do.

The InBeasts all turned around looking at me, and I looked at them. I had beat them, and the feeling of self-confidence pounded in my heart! I smiled. I had fully conquered my distress. I had overcome myself. *I* was in control! Not *Peace*, or *Greater Peace*, but now *Total Peace* engulfed my soul. I slowly stood—erect, strong, and proud. I felt the power Nikita said that I would hold. I knew I had it now. I inhaled while extending my arms out, with palms up, fingers apart. My arms shook with the power that now pulsed in them. I addressed my audience of InBeasts—now as their master, them my subjects, in a commanding voice of thunder, "Let your stress depart from here, back to your shadows and your caves ....." I then turned my hands over and around to face them, pulled back my arms and forcefully flung them out. "BE GONE!" I yelled. A wave of power hit the InBeasts, sending them all falling back onto each other and the ground! And when they did, in an instant they turned to skeletons.

As I looked at the bones, I knew we all have different InBeasts that stalk us—all for different reasons based on each of our fears, or worries, or weaknesses, or any challenge confronting us ... but they're only in our minds. They're the influence to make us fail, but we can defeat them if we follow the principles that tell us how!

I had conquered the evil entrance.

Chapter 23

The Mountain / Journeys to Elgobon

Rule #10: OF THE MOUNTAINTOP

I lay down and gloried in the overcoming and concentrated to remember this feeling—to use it later when needed. I looked at the path that I would take to reach the Mountaintop, and eventually my eyes reached the Sleeping Giant up above. Now I knew which mountain, so all I had to do was climb. After all I'd done, that was easy.

I rose up the Mountain and rested in a clearing by a river under pine trees for the night. I smiled knowing no more Beasts were on the prowl and lit a fire. Animals came in and sat around the fire with me and now I knew why, and welcomed them, and we all enjoyed its warmth and message, and they stayed with me all night.

In the morning I continued rising. Air got thin; on snowy patches then I climbed; one breath in and one step forward; against wind that blew against me, against sun that beat me down; over rocky ridges of that Mountain, around boulders tentatively tilted, up precarious slopes of shale; always slowly up—but moving. Evening came and I camped again. This time on a ledge overlooking the scattered clouds below, and land and trees and carpets of green in the valleys, with the Sleeping Giant looking down on me, a day away.

I sat looking out over all of it with the sun about to set and a feeling overtook me knowing I was almost there. I could see the destination up ahead! Oh what a feeling! My arms flung wide and with power inside, I yelled, "My paths' end made, glorious feeling I can't explain, the finish I've won and now is done!"

As I reflected on those words, Emgo's advice came to my mind: "The end is not the end; from it see the beginning." And, "In times of greatest glory, ponder where you came." And, "Look beyond the finish to find the hidden message."

Then I stood with quite a different thought—and tried to see the start. Far to the west, I looked below, and even though this world was round, and the start was on the other side—I saw the edges of the world curl up and flatten out for me to see! Almost seven years past where I had been—Dry and Deadly Lake. I remembered the time and the Elder's words and the Rule he taught me. And flying in the sky I saw that stupid Pterodactyl. And I remembered what I learned everywhere else I saw: the castle, and skeletons, and sulfur pools (and again could hear my students, "Oh, Mr. Tiz!"). Then the spires of salt, the beautiful meadow with river and obelisk and beam of light, the herd of Apatosaurus's—one nice, and one that sent me on a flight. Sadly next, I spied the villages in the oaks, but happily after, the village of Po, and lightning strikes into the lake. These, and all the other places been, I spied. And the ravens I thanked, with a thoughtful wave, who were flying in the sky.

I stood looking and wondering and thinking. What if the past I had forgotten? The Pebbles, the Rules, the Secret, the Truth. I realized all the lessons that I learned had got me there ... those were what's important—not the end. Without them, this Mountaintop would not have significance, and all I gained would be lost and buried. Who we are, is largely based on what we've done and what we've learned to help us change, and because of that we must remember. And then I understood, *It's not learning the Rules, it's experiencing the journey that makes us appreciate and teaches how to use them.*

My heart beat strong as I realized it was the final Rule I sought. It was THE RULE OF THE MOUNTAINTOP: <u>The end is of no consequence—it's the journey that counts! Fulfill the journey faithfully, and learn and change along the way, and the end takes care of itself</u>. It wasn't so much the ten Rules I found, it was the *search* for them—wondering about and analyzing every pebble. Who knows how many thousands of *those* I found!

I realized and said out loud, "Indeed there *was* an ulterior motive why Old Man sent me here. Before attaining the Gate, there were obstacles I had to endure and overcome, and that required the journey. Each of us has certain obstacles that we can only overcome with the journey of life, but also with contemplation in the deepest reaches of our minds. *This* was where I killed the Beast. This was where I resolved the conflicts with my other selves. But it's the Rules that propelled me on."

I fell on my knees, weak—and wept. After almost seven years wandering, I'd found the Rules—all the glorious ten! And when the moons arrived they did congratulate.

[A yell from the back of the auditorium was heard, "Yes!" and Tiz smiled.]

And wouldn't you know it, Chisel also accomplished his goal. "We made it Chisel!" I yelled. I was so proud of him, having tried so hard, and fought so far, with so many against him—not believing in. But he didn't let the doubters win. Some hated him for his extended effort, but he believed in himself—and his purpose's end, and that was enough to propel him on, in spite of them. I cried for the relief I felt for him when he did succeed! And it was sung about him (and also me, I guess): (Steer High, track 17)

This is to all the people, who never thought they could
This is to all the people, who never thought they would
This is to all the people, who don't have faith enough
they don't trust, just quite enough, they don't know

This is to all the people, who have a pounding dream
This is to all the people, with never-dying needs
This is to all the people, who work like rabid dogs
Through sweat and pain, goals to attain, they never stop

Chorus:
Keep right, don't change your course now
Set your sights, aim in at your goal
Hold tight, don't ever let go

Steer high, Don't look at the ground
Always try, Never say I can't
By and by, you'll make it somehow

Verse:
The peaks of mountains, are never reached by easy steps
The valleys down below, require no test
And those with hope, do know that they can never rest
They just fight on, till the battle's won, victorious

In olden days, the deathly seas, were hard to cross
But people sailed in boats for weeks, willing to risk the loss
They knew that if they doubted, then they would never start
So look ahead, into the wind, follow your heart

Chorus Repeated

This is to all the people, who have a burning want
Who swim against the tide, and never think to quit
This is to all the people, who've written songs unsung
Don't look back, Don't think if, Just think when

One final night I lit a fire and I camped, and a great swooshing, flapping sound fell down beside me. I shook and yelled with fright, "AAH!" It was the Pterodactyl, on this last night, come to keep me company! We watched the fire together awhile and I told him of the Rule I found. Then he squawked and coughed—choking—something in his throat, until he threw up a gooey blob onto the ground. "Oooh," I said with a scrunched up nose. Something sparkled inside the mess. I squinted, looking at it, "Of course!" I laughed. I walked around the fire, "You have to be kidding me! So this is how it ends?" I bent and picked up an object out of the slime and wiped it off on my pants. "My last— a beautiful, aquamarine gemstone." I pulled the others out, and looked at them all in the fire's glow—a rainbow of color in my hand.

I was almost there; one final night I looked up at the stars. There as always were my Thorny Tooth and Hairy Cat, and with the flattened world, I also saw my Frisky dog! "Oh Frisky! How are you?" Then I said to all, "I'll say my Good-byes my friends for tonight could be my last. Tomorrow I'll either be dead by the opening of the Gate or through it to a different world." They looked a little sad, but I said we'd always have our memories, and I'd come back to see them. Then I heard the crickets chorus heighten. I smiled, "No, I didn't forget about you! You've been fabulous. My band back home is good—but you're the best ... thank you so much for helping me!" And we played our music one last time together—the Pterodactyl enjoying it—squawking and bobbing, moving his wings up and down, and feet around.

The next day when I awoke, the world was round again, and I started early for I was eager to finally make it! Half the day I climbed. Up dirt and shale, then to rocks I had to climb, hours up and over. From where I was, just dirt and boulders on top of one another in a prominent posture, but from below—the Sleeping Giant's body! Then I saw it once again—the top majestic in its stature. It was a sentinel for all who could finally see—the Sleeping Giant's nose. From down below, so small, but here, fifty yards wide! My destiny I knew.

Two hours later, the final steps, and finally then on top, and my new walking stick/scepter I did raise—high in the air I forced it up, for this was now my kingdom! All those years of work, and sweat, and pain. I looked below and saw it all. I'd made it all the way! I breathed deep! With exhilaration I yelled, "VICTORY!" and listened to my echo.

I had conquered the Mountain.

I lay down and rested, and finally sat up and got a drink and a snack from my pack, and admired the view. I knew what the mountaintop afforded me—a journey through Gate One, and the treasured Maps of Ages. But I never met the Prophet who I was told would tell me the method to open the Gate. I sat there thinking. I waited for inspiration . . . nothing came.

I wasn't sure what I should do. I stood and looked out over the valleys far below me. I scratched my head, *What could the method be to get there?* I squinted. I thought I'd try. I held my arms out wide, then while yelling louder and louder, "AAAAAHHH," I excitedly brought my hands together in a *mighty* clap, gasping in anticipation of an incredible scene that opened up! . . . nothing.

I waited and thought. I crossed my hands over each other and waited while clinching my arm muscles stronger and stronger, then quickly rotated each hand up while snapping my fingers forcefully . . . nothing.

I waited and thought. I raised my hands by the side of my face, fingers spread, palms forward and yelled, "GATE OOOOOOONE—OPEN UP!" And I pushed my hands forward . . . nothing.

I contemplated my situation. With exhilaration I thought of all I had accomplished and having attained this mountaintop. I looked at my scepter on the ground. I squinted. I thought. *Hmm. Maybe I'm now invincible! Hmm, yes, maybe so! And maybe the Gate is all around me and I have to jump off the mountain and fly right through it!"* My eyebrows rose. I smiled.

I looked at the valleys below me and at the edge of the thousand-foot cliff. I would run and jump—through the Gate, then extend my arms, catch the wind, and I'd fly free—and glide to my destiny! I raised my arms, inhaled, and took a step ... toward infinity.

[Tiz took a long drink of water and looked at the audience. All were still and deathly quiet.]

I was startled by a voice behind me, "My friend. Hold on there. What are you doing? I wish it was that easy!"

I stopped one inch from the edge of the cliff and thousand-foot drop and twisted around. It was Old Man ... Goatee Man ... it was Emgo.

"I see you made it to the Mountaintop and found the Mountain's Rule. Congratulations! You now have the knowledge to change yourself forever, and having lived and experienced the Rules and not just having learned them, you became them. The secret, cherished Maps of Ages that lead to ultimate success will soon be yours to see. But the Gate is not yet open with the final things you'll see and feel, so wait awhile to take the jump; your wings are not yet large enough to catch the windy breeze, and it's quite a ways down to fall!"

I looked back over my shoulder down the thousand-foot cliff and slowly moved my feet closer to him—suddenly scared of heights. I smiled, still exhilarated, and mentioned, "I finally made it! And I did what you said: I wrote in a book what I found and how to get there, for I felt inspired. I'm not saying necessarily from a godly sense or something spiritual, or maybe so, but like something I was meant to do, something I was good at. All the words went down so easily—like they were meant to be. Something you wake up at 2:00 a.m. for! It feels great, like a purpose in my life fulfilled—and I can finally be at peace—and breathe ... it feels so good! 'Columbus and Tiz,' finally will be said! We'll be neighbors in 'The Great Discoverer's Hall of Fame'! The Nina, Pinta, and Santa Maria will now be joined in fame by The Park, The Meadow, and The Mountain." Emgo laughed and laughed—but it didn't deter me, "My book will ROCK the world! Will change the way they think, the way they act, the way they breathe! I named it, *Journeys to Elgobon*."

Emgo laughed again. "Ha! So you slayed the Beast, which wasn't real, and now you will tell others, and tell them how? Sounds like someone else I know!"

I smiled, for then I understood. I was just like him. "And I hope you don't mind," I said, "but I gave the book to Ms. Spear—also known as Francine."

He laughed again and continued, "You finally learned her name, huh? No, I don't mind at all, and I think for her it will really help. I like your enthusiasm, but unfortunately your book will *NOT* ROCK the world! How many have believed your story so far? YOU can tell, but THEY must believe and listen and learn and work. And that is not easy. And people easily forget. How long did it take *you* to believe *us* that the Beast wasn't real? Attaining the Mountain and changing oneself requires knowledge and experience and desire. For everyone, the tests are different based upon their needs. Everyone must slay their own InBeast and find their own Pebbles and Rules, but what you say can help them learn how."

He walked to my side and looked over the cliff at the scenery below. Then he looked at me and compassionately smiled. "Take this as my gift. You deserve it." He showed me a necklace of some sort of thin vines and silk, intricately woven, of exquisite looks and strength. It was shiny—some sort of lacquer covering it. On the bottom hung a small, flat, round, copper-colored, metal disk, the size of a nickel, with a creatively carved "S" character. "You've earned the Scholar's necklace, for after almost seven years of study and work, many Pebbles you have found, and the Guidance, and the Secret and the Truth, and the Rules. You had a goal and you stuck with it. One doesn't *accomplish* much without *doing* much. Great achievements come from great effort and much time. To do great things, you have to give up some too. You wrote the book, and persevered. You discovered how to conquer many traits, and through your mind, you killed the InBeast. Open Gate One to continue on."

He then put the necklace over my head, and I looked down at it and smiled. It was a prized possession—only worn by those who have earned it—by years of effort and struggle.

"And after the Gate, you must go on. Find the Keys to open the Lock that opens the Tunnel and leads you to the Message and then the Grotto. Gate Two will then be opened up to you. But it will be harder than Gate One for the endeavors there are far different than you've ever experienced."

I said, "I don't know how to open the Gate. I was told to ask that of a Prophet. But still I've never met him."

Emgo smiled. "Hmm, maybe I can help. I told you I have many names, didn't I?"

My eyes enlarged. I was shocked. "You mean you're the Prophet? For all these years I've known you and didn't know it?"

"Maybe knowing would have changed your attitude. Maybe you revered the words of others differently because you didn't know if it was them. For whether they're called Prophets or not, don't many have great advice and a stellar example to offer? And shouldn't we search for that in everyone, and not discount the person less who owns no title?"

I pondered and thought of the man who saved me on the barren wasteland, and I nodded. Then I thought of "Old Man's" words and help over my whole trip. He was the Prophet, and indeed the words had been the most and greatest as the Elder said.

"So can you see the future?" I asked.

"I've lived long enough to have seen the consequences of good and bad decisions—so now I'm pretty good at seeing what will happen before it does. So in that respect, yes, I do. But in World Two and beyond is where my powers show themselves. But I also share another title with some others, of—the Gate Keeper."

My eyes widened. I nodded again, before I asked the biggest question: "So, can you tell me how to open the Gate?"

"Yes. It is time. So, remember this: In seven years' time, so much you've done, and steps you took, and what you heard, and tried to learn, and very focused, always been. Always on the goal, always on the end. Like that, it's hard to take the time to feel. But some you did and much you learned and quite a ways you came. So now it is your final test. Sit down and contemplate, and FEEL the Gate—what and where it is. When you know that, it will open up for you."

He smiled and held out his hand and we shook. Then I hugged him. He was like a second father to me now. "I'm eternally grateful. Thank you so much." I suddenly felt empty with the thought of no longer feeling his presence or hearing his advice. I pulled away and paused and looked at him. "But will you still help me? Please, I can't go on alone. I'll miss you too much and need your advice."

He smiled, "Don't fret, we will all see and enjoy each other in the end. And I can come and check on you—but you don't need me anymore. In fact, it's best without my continued guidance. Learning by yourself is the greatest teacher—even if sometimes harder—and you've graduated. Talk to the stars and ask and heed their good advice. Carry on. We will all be cheering your success! And in the next world, other help you will receive."

He put his hand on my shoulder and I felt energy coming into me. "That is for the opening," he said. "You'll need it."

He looked deep into my eyes, we hugged again, he smiled, and then walked to the edge of the cliff and it was him that extended his arms, moving his hands a bit, saying something foreign, and he walked off it. But he did not fall. The breeze gently lifted him, and he floated away with his long white shirt flowing behind, his legs bent up at the knees, arms wide, head high.

Chapter 24

The Gate and the Agony

The memory and emotions were too much—remembering the agony and enormity of what came next, remembered by *MYSELF* through the eyes and heart of *I*. Tiz collapsed in the chair behind him—spent. He was breathing hard as he looked out at the audience. He needed a drink. "Water please," he said.

The event coordinator got him more water and addressed the audience. "Perhaps we should continue tomorrow." But the audience roared, and many voices could be heard above the rest: "No." "Please Tiz." "Just try to finish." "Did you make it?" "What was the Gate?" No longer did he hear the doubters questioning. Instead, neighbors asked each other, "What powers did he receive?" "How did he open the gate?" "What did he have to feel?"

Tiz took another drink and then stood with effort and trudged slowly back to the podium. The coordinator told him he could wait, but he told her he would be okay. He closed his eyes and thought. He paused and then breathed deep—and saw a peaceful place that *I* had taught him how to. He opened his eyes and continued.]

I watched the Prophet floating slowly toward the almost setting sun. Then some ravens approached, flying in from under him, and landed in front of me, and the Pterodactyl too. They looked at me, then rubbed against my legs, seemingly to give me comfort they felt I needed. I pet them all and then they backed away and turned and jumped off the cliff and flew away.

Then I turned around and, "WHOA!" I realized my previous excitement in reaching the Mountain peak had obscured my vision! All behind me, now clearly seen lying on the ground, were sunbaked skeletons—dozens of them strewn all around! "Skeletons are the key," I remembered. I paused and thought—and realized. *They are my army to assist me through the Gate!* I yelled, "Arise and help me now!" It was time for them to live again like Brinlin said.

I waited for their bones to creak and rattle and slowly assemble vertically—first a little wobbly, then attain their balance . . . but nothing!

I frowned and knew ... that was too easy. I thought, *These ones aren't alive. These must be those who didn't make it through the Gate!* I remembered the Scholar's and Disciple's words to: "brace yourself, maintain hope ... through your agony, take caution," and, "shield yourself if possible." Then I shook with fear for events that were to come. But I felt horrible for those who had succumbed after so much work . . . and perhaps for myself as well!

I sat down and started to contemplate so that I could feel the Gate. As the monk's recommended, I crossed my legs, fingers touching, eyes closed: the perfect form to feel! Find the gate, I must, I would, for that is why I came this far.

My meditation took me on a ride through space, but all was fuzzy. I lost track of everything, and time seemed like a wave I rode. I sat focused, trying to feel. I tried so hard, and wanted so bad, and my waiting-time went on and on—seemed infinite. Every second seemed like hours. I felt the sun come up, then down again, many times—but still I sat—eyes closed in meditation. Then I felt the seasons' change: myself sitting through shortened days and snow, then new leaves on the trees below, then sweating in the heat of lengthened days, then the leaves on the trees did fall. And still I sat in my cross-legged position—not yet having felt. I felt like so much time went by, that time itself was getting old! My body aging more. *Perhaps this is how the skeletons behind me died,* I thought. *Just too much time—got old and passed away—and never felt the gate.*

No food I ate, but none I felt I needed. No water I drank for I felt perfectly hydrated. Oh I tried to feel that gate but all I felt was agony in my heart—for what I could not feel! I tried to cry— maybe to convince myself that I was feeling (like the Prophet said), for I had been so long just sitting there—getting nowhere— feeling nothing. I could not feel the Gate—had no idea what or where it was! Then eventually I really did cry—because of all the time gone by—with no results! I just couldn't make it right. I couldn't make it happen. This far and I couldn't get through.

When my body was thus shaken—spent, I fell on my side, breathed hard and sighed; I ached inside, and this time I didn't think—no longer could. I rolled on my back. The Prophet said not to think but contemplate—and feel. I was in too much of a rush. I realized I wanted it too much. And after realizing that, and because I was so spent, lying there upon that special Mountain, indeed I finally *did* start to feel. I didn't try—just let life filter through my mind and heart. Time slowed down it seemed, and my mind opened up to everything. Things became more clear— and clearer over time. I felt electricity build in the air around me like lightning might explode. Things were changing on the Mountaintop. I sat up and exhaled ... my skin felt different ... it seemed to tingle a bit. I looked at it—my forehead furrowed, and I realized I could feel my hairs growing out of it. My sensitivity increased. Movement was slow-motion to me now. I heard something flying in the sky. I looked ... a butterfly. Heard the clouds floating by. Heard grass growing under feet. Heard my eyelashes when I blinked, and eyes when they swiveled left to right. Felt the earth rotating. Felt my nails lengthening, cells dying and new ones growing. I felt my blood moving through my veins, felt dust particles landing on my head, felt my brain thinking and heart feeling. I didn't try. I just felt. After all that time just sitting there, I was finally able . . . .

I asked myself, "What do I feel?" And I realized what I did: Hardship makes you humble—and humbleness makes you thankful. And thankfulness lets you appreciate others. Then love filled my heart for all those I had known. All my family, all my friends, all my students caring. So much love I had been given—and all the help. Help from the Scholar, and Disciple, and all the others, and Francine, too, for her memory many times propelled me. And on this journey so thankful for the Prophet. Was kindness when all seemed lost, words of wisdom in the dark, advice not known before, guiding from afar. My heart was slow—full, the magical smell was back—love filled every part. I felt the Gate—and that is what it was! And where it was—was everywhere. "The Gate is love," I said out loud. "Can't pass through without it. All people need it—no matter how tough they appear to be or feel that they are. It's a universal need of the heart. We must accept it when we're too mad to. We must give it when we're too proud to. We must let its warmth melt away our pride and warm our souls."

When I said those words, suddenly there was a loud sound beneath me like massive gears that started turning, or tectonic plates moving, and I could feel a vibration in the earth. I stood up and looked around, whatever later time this was, and I breathed deep with fear. I staggered back amidst the skeletons—their encouraging expressions nurturing me—for they had done this too, and knew what I was going through—one for all and all for one, like an army team together, I stood amongst their protecting bones.

It was then I saw the Gate opening. The clouds above grew, and darkened, and covered the sky and started turning clockwise. Lightning started spilling and thrashing, thunder growling, earth shaking. I steadied myself to not fall off my Mountaintop. Wind arose like a hurricane—twisting and churning wildly. The noise from all, sounded like a freight train bearing down on me.

Meteors started falling from the sky in all directions. The valleys down below took their impact and caught fire. Birds in large flocks flew away below me. Deer in large numbers ran through the valleys. Ice as hail, the size of golf balls, pelted me and started breaking bones—my hands upon my head to shield it. The earth cracked open and lava shot up around me. The wind turned hot, drying all rivers and lakes below me, plastering me with their sand and grating my skin, pulling sweat from me in torrents. The heat intensified, engulfing me. My clothes it scorched which started falling off me till almost gone. My hair it burnt till most fell out. My skin turned red while burning, then blistering, and finally starting to peel off—my skeletal bones starting to show from different patches of my body. I held my damaged arms out and up, one hand totally skeletal, and yelled as I shook, but no sound was heard above the massive noise of everything, "AHHHHHH," a half-skinned skeleton was seen to yell.

Far away on another mountaintop, Francine was rejoicing at a Rule just found, but then was thrown to the ground by the shaking earth. And to the east she saw the Mountain in the direction that I walked. It looked like the end of the world on top of it, the elements battling each other, and she raised and extended her arm and open hand, knowing the agony I faced and praying I was safe.

My mind was dizzy and I realized, *I just can't do this*. But I heard other words, "Yes you *can* do this Tiz. I've done similar and you can too!" It was Chisel talking.

AND THEN, STOP. All the elements in reverse did go. Wind started spinning counter clockwise, changing the clouds rotation. Thunder: first the echo and then the boom. Lightning from the opposite direction. Rain descended in torrents, stopping the fires, filling the rivers and lakes, and perfectly renewing the forests—myself almost drowning in its deluge, and it peeling more of my remaining skin so I was mainly skeletal. And then it stopped. The earth sucked back down its lava, closed its crevices, and then the air stopped spinning and retreated from the earth to the sky in a great extended whoosh, pulling whatever hail was left back to their clouds, and then the meteors back up. It pulled my remaining hair on end, hard to get a breath, began to suffocate, mind was throbbing, getting dizzy, blacking out from lack of oxygen, started pulling my limp body into the air—three feet . . . six feet . . . .

AND THEN, STOP—FREEZE. The wind stopped in an instant. I fell back to earth with a thud, sitting hunched over on the dirt—a lump of used-up skin and bones. Barely a rag hung from my waist. The clouds evaporated, all noise stopped, all birds fell, grass stopped growing under feet, dust stopped floating, rivers stopped flowing, waves stopped breaking, the planet stopped its rotation, heart stopped beating, blood stopped pumping, the planet was still but snow did fall from empty places. But this snow was different. It was not cold, and it sparkled intensely. But life for me was at its end—without my pumping blood, or beating heart, and with lungs now stopped and bones exposed. Like so many others, I sadly had not made it past the Gate. Death was now upon my shattered soul. With my final bit of energy, I laid myself back, upon the ground, looking up, and watched the snow fall down from the empty sky—letting it create my grave and slowly bury me entirely—the rest of my skin falling off. I would be the latest skeleton upon the Mountaintop.

Then I thought . . . and tried to smile. *Maybe I was not like the others, and I had made it through the Gate. But the Gate was something different than I thought!* I realized then, the Gate was death! And I was sad that death was it, for never again would I see Francine, or my family, friends, or students. Never again would I play in the band. I realized that all my mentors on this trip were ghosts—already having passed through the Gates of Death. *But Emgo's shake was firm!* I thought, confused.

On the other mountain, Francine had seen everything in reverse and a great WHOOSH of air in the end being sucked up through a giant hole to Heaven, and everything with it pulled back to the sky. And then WHAP! The hole in space closed, it was so quiet, and it started to snow on the Mountain. When the snow stopped, nothing was different than before—as if it never happened. The sun set as normal and the moons did rise. She lay down on her side, her pack as pillow, and covered herself with her blanket. She lay looking at the moonlit Mountaintop and slightly smiled.

As I lay inside that snowy tomb—totally consumed by two feet of it, every cell was touched by snow. And as the flakes' soft liquid residue touched every cell, I could feel skin regrow—every part of my body renew. And as it did, I was changed forever—into something different. I could feel it. My body was now ready to enter Heaven (and this was the process and the Gate)! Then motion started once again, and my heart again beat, which started my blood, and I gasped for air and started coughing until I caught my breath. The snow had stopped, and I started digging myself out of my grave. First, space for air around my mouth, and more I dug till my hand shot out. This was the tunnel up to Heaven, and once out of the snow, I would gaze upon it.

I emerged from my grave, raised myself up, and wearily stood. I looked around to see what Heaven was like. There are also sunsets in Heaven, I saw, but the most beautiful you've ever seen, as evidenced by the one before me. Then something remarkable happened. The sun that was almost ready to dip below, started to come back up, and with it, it pulled the reds and oranges, yellows and greens, and blues and purples of the sunset, until the sun perched at the top of the sky, and lit the world with multi, muted, sunset-colored streams of light coming down from the sunset that accompanied it—the brightest colored light falling down in rays beyond the distant ocean.

The Gate had opened up for me.

Chapter 25

The Secret Maps of Ages

iz reached for his water and took another long drink.]
I felt inclined to lift my hand and move it in that certain secret way that I had seen the Elder do. And when I did ... I SAW THE WORLD! It flattened out again before me, but this time it was like a real-life map before and below me, looking like a giant board game, a quarter mile in each direction, that had unfolded before my eyes with the earth's places shown, and inhabitants living out history like little ants, and everything that had ever been I saw transpire in fast motion, like with time-lapse photography. A little sun shone above, and a moon and stars, and sometimes clouds and rain and lightning materialized inside a light blue sky.

First I saw a large island, and then I saw it breaking up, and jungles sprouting up and dinosaurs everywhere, and the pieces moving until looking like Africa and South America. A great meteor hit, then came clouds, and it was very cold, and I watched it snow and snow. Snow then melted along the equator, and people I saw coming out of forests, and they multiplied. Then ancient history I saw, too old to teach in classes. Next, I started seeing things I'd read and heard about like the pyramids erected, ships discovering new lands, wars, and other history. Eventually I saw myself in youth, then older, sitting by my lake, and eventually, even older, in a grave they put me, and thousands paid their respects, but I didn't know why so many.

Sometime later, I saw it getting hot and ice at the poles did melt, hotter still, and so much so that almost all expired, but many animals survived. Then stars sometimes fell, replaced by different ones, and a couple extra moons arrived. Volcanic eruptions along tectonic plates intensified, and continents continued their migration rapidly, so all land again touched, but in a different configuration. Smog receded, ozone renewed, and the sky, I noticed, slowly turning light green with increased clarity. Temperate weather once again; seeds sprouted and grew easily, and nature replenished beautifully. Then rain came, and vegetation thickly grew, covering almost all that man had made. Many years later—perhaps millions, animals once extinct I saw come forth and multiply again. Eventually I saw myself appear on a path and walking to a peaceful meadow with trees and birds and squirrels.

I swept my hand across my view in front of me, and as that map folded up and to the right, a different 3-D map unfolded right behind it—with a path lit up—leading to a place far on the horizon with the word RICHES above it. Points were marked along the way with a title above each one, which were Pebbles and Rules if combined and used as shown, would lead to the final destination. Again my hand swept, and a different map and path was seen to ADVENTURE, and then to FAME, and then to FULFILLMENT ... and anywhere I'd want to go if I just thought it. I then realized the Maps are personalized—needing our fingerprints to reach a destination. The Pebbles rearrange based on each of our weaknesses and strengths and needs. And for anyone it can be the same. Then a map unfolded which I realized is what I wanted most of all—PEACE OF MIND; for I no longer had an InBeast that was stalking me. And I had already found all the Pebbles and Rules to *that* map. The edges of the map then curved down creating the circular world again. Then I wondered, *Why need all this now? Are there also paths in Heaven?*

I looked again at the horizon, and far, far that way I noticed the Prophet—still floating away! *What? Why can I see him?* Was this the same day? Had time not come and gone? I realized the seasons hadn't changed. But wasn't this Heaven? Hadn't I just risen through the tunnel to it? I happily thought, *I guess the Gate isn't death, and I was luckily wrong!*

I looked behind me down at the hole in the snow, AND I YELLED! There before me was my skeleton—looking up at me—with his empty holes—the pure white bones now petrified! "Oh my gosh! Death *is* the Gate after all, and I *am* a ghost!" But I felt my head ... it was hard! "Ghosts are not tangible," I said. I realized I was not a ghost ... just like Emgo wasn't one! I thought, and looked around. I looked at the Mountaintop, and the valleys down below. The landscape was all the same—or at least similar—just prettier—even more vegetation, and colors more vibrant. The river below had now carved a great extended canyon, and different trees were growing in various places. I studied it all and realized, I was indeed in the same place—but I, and the prophet, were there at a different time .... Passing through the Gate only took minutes, but on the other side it was eons later. I was not dead, nor in Heaven! "YES!" I yelled, with my fingers in fists. I saw the lumps in the snow and I knew they were the skeletons of those who *did* make it through the Gate! The skeletons technically *had not* died. Nikita had not passed away—*his* Gate was at the monastery! And his mountaintop was above it! He had just moved on! The skeletons' changed selves had continued on. They were all alive—just as I—more than ever. Indeed, I was changed forever—so much so, I was leaving my old skeleton behind! And that permitted me to attain the next world. *Skeletons are the key!* I had made it to World Three!

It was all so incredible, and almost unbelievable, and I had to remind myself it wasn't *The Wizard of Oz* and I wasn't Dorothy waking up from a dream.

I don't know, maybe we are all a little insane—to different degrees, struggling with the different sides of our personalities, pushing our bodies and minds and hearts and souls in different directions; one saying, "Do this," and the other "Do that," and our mission in life is to take the journey of self-discovery that teaches how to balance them, and guide them toward a common course ... and maybe it's when we don't, *that* is what can truly drive us crazy. Maybe we're all on the journey, but some recognize the journey they are on and most do not, and the Pebbles and Rules that are passed, and Gate to achieve, are only there for those that try to see and learn from them.

I no longer needed to be hailed by the masses as Columbus's equal and have fifty-foot statues of us unveiled outside the capitals of every country of the world (*hmm ... although it would be nice*); for the peace I gained inside more than sufficed. And I knew the final question for *The Anthem of the People*.

What fame do we attain?

I saw a shimmer on the horizon on the faraway blue of the sea. *What is beyond where the rays of the brightest light shine?* I wondered. *What has the Gate opened up to? Is this where I can fly? The Keys will open the Lock and then the Tunnel will open up, and there is found the Message.*

Then I heard a voice from the sky and all around, and Old Man's words from almost seven years past, by World One's lake, came back to me to, "Find the Grotto."

*   *   *

So that's the end of the story. Seven years went since it all began.

And I'll say it straight—I *do* believe in other worlds. I'm thankful for all of it—how I changed. A real world or only in our minds it doesn't matter—the journey is the same.

I also no longer believe in Beasts! I defeated mine! I conquered it! I used to believe—for it was my anxiety and other things—but *that* I overcame—and it no longer affects my actions.

And that's why now I'm free—I'm at peace. You can lock me up, but it won't matter. I can see the good in everything. Every adversity I'll take in stride—and enjoy my life. Yes, I do have my opinions which others do not own, but like Nikita, it doesn't make me a threat.

So I'll ask the question, am I crazy? I say, "No." I found out a split personality is normal (at least my type of split personality), and the Beast that seemed so real, really isn't, and the world that seemed it couldn't be—really is. There's no real proof it isn't real, so just because it doesn't seem to be, doesn't make it so. It's up to each of us to decide for ourselves. Belief doesn't prove insanity.

[The audience was silent—as if they didn't breathe. Many now thought they were the same, and reflected on *their* Beasts, *their* different personalities, *their* journey. Then someone yelled out, "I'm the same. But in *this* world." And another yelled also, and then many. Then one yelled, "Director, are you going to intern all of us?"

Silence again filled the hall. Finally Tiz spoke, "So what do you say? Should I be released?"

There was loud unanimous applause and yells. Then all looked over at the director and superintendent. They sighed and looked at each other, then walked to the stage. The director joined Tiz at the microphone. "Thank you Tiz for your honesty. You didn't try to hide what you believe .... But imagine what the mental health profession would say if I release a patient with a split personality, that believes he's been traveling to other worlds. Per one of the definitions of insanity, this proves you are insane. Don't you see Tiz? What you described are the struggles of life itself that we all face. You are just coping with them in a fantasy world. Perhaps we should discuss this more at the mental hospital."

Tiz thought and frowned and nodded his head. "I guess you're right."

All the audience groaned, "No. No Tiz, don't believe it!"

Tiz noticed the audience all look up and behind him at the screen and a collected, "Aaahhh" was heard. Tiz and the director looked around and saw that the outside live feed camera had been redirected to the sky. There, flew a massive flock of ravens circling above the auditorium like a great black tornado churning in the sky.

Then Nurse Betty stood and walked to the stage and to the microphone, and spoke to the director. "The band and I brought something that might change your mind. It grew in my garden from the seeds I received and planted, and I had it inspected by the Botanical Society. They brought in many experts for they couldn't explain it. They said it's a flower species never known before." She smiled extra big, "They named it the 'Beautiful Betty.'"

The band then lifted a five foot round flower supported by a fifteen foot stem and walked it to the stage, standing it up. There was a hushed, "Ahhh!" from the audience, and the director's eyebrows rose. Then there was a mighty roar, "YES!"

The director looked at the floor and shook his head and grinned, then looked at the outside live feed picture again, then turned to the superintendent behind him saying something. He turned back around, and shook his head while smiling. He looked at Tiz while speaking in the microphone, "What can I say? ... Tiz, you've proven one thing for sure, although you have different beliefs, with your organized words, immaculate speech, and tempered manner, it's clear you're not a threat .... Tiz, you're free—you are released."

"RAAAAAGGGHHHH!"

Tiz smiled. He held up his hand and spoke, "Ha! That's it then. My band's hiatus is over. How 'bout a concert outside right now to celebrate?" Again the roar, and his bandmates smiled.

"And first we'll play the three new songs I wrote since our last concert."

Standing at the back of the audience was an old man with shoulder-length, white-gray hair and goatee, pointy, leather shoes, corduroy pants of royal blue, yellow shirt, and green vest. He smiled, then he turned and walked away. (Later that night, though, during the party after the concert, he was seen approaching Tiz and them embracing).

Tiz continued speaking to the audience.]

And like I said before, *MYSELF* and *ME* are surprised by all the hype. So finally tell us how do so many already know the story? We haven't been told that yet, but we're glad to have shared the end.

And we are truly grateful for our Irish date today for bringing us, for after ten months in our confusion, she came and told us what we had to hear to heal us, and that is why they let us out to give this speech. And now we just hope that *I* can make it back again—for he hasn't yet been able to transfer like before. He's tried often, but hasn't found the way, for World Three is different. As soon as he can, he will come back. But we can say that many things we have seen and *I* has been able to relay, and what is beyond the ocean where those brightest rays shine has thoroughly intrigued us, and sent our minds to unbelievable places, but fear has also caught our souls for what he is enduring. And we are praying for him mightily, and ask for you to do the same. Luckily the added powers he attained and the changes he experienced so far, have saved him. But our hearts go out to him, and he can feel it, and that is all that we can do.

... And finally, to end, we reiterate. Is the Boogie Man real or pretend? You will say pretend. But to children he is all too real—for when all alone, shadows are filled with fear, and the fear is very real. So does the fear itself not make it real? But adults are not scared of shadows, so there is no Boogie Man. But is there something else, for different reasons? And so we pray—those of you that also feel a Beast stalking and bearing down on you, or hiding in your shadows, find out if it's real—and what defeats it—before it drives you to insanity!

[Suddenly Tiz winced in pain and held his heart, groaning. He stumbled backward to his chair, falling into it. He doubled over in pain. Those on the stage rushed to him, but he held up his hands to hold them away. He breathed heavily—hands falling to his sides. People blinked and looked again, for his blue jeans and white T-shirt looked more disheveled than they remembered before. His groaning receded, he coughed a couple times, then took some deep cleansing breaths. He leaned back in his chair, eyes still closed. Breathed deep again, released the tension so his shoulders fell. He opened his eyes and looked around—his eyelids rose, "YES!" he yelled and threw his arms in the air, jumping up—his left hand holding his pack with a coconut and ukulele hanging from it. The director thought, *I don't remember that ukulele hanging from his pack when he came today*. Tiz slowly looked around, and when his eyes fell on Francine standing on the stage to his right, they widened. Loudly, he said, "Francine?" She gazed at him and knew what it meant. She smiled and he ran to her. He threw his arms around her. "I made it back!" They melted in each others arms, smiling.

Tiz let go and surveyed the whole audience. He walked to the podium, "You look remarkable! And this place is amazing! But you know what I want, more than anything?" He yelled, "I want to play some muuusiiiiiiiiiic! I'm back just in time for a summer tour. This one I'm calling, *The Back Home Tour*." He threw both arms in the air and yelled, "YEAHHH!" and the crowd erupted. Tiz added, "Join me:"

Who are you?
Who are we?

How do our minds create the things we dream?
Why do we really ever start to breathe?
Where do we travel when we go to sleep?

What powers do we gain?
What Beasts do we tame?
What fame do we attain?
When we release and fly free to another-world dream-state.

Say it now ...
With me ...
Who are we?
We are the children of the world—we sing!

"Let's go outside and sing some songs!"

When they went outside, Tiz smiled and waved at the ravens up above. Then he yelled, "EEKS, LOX, PIROX!" and when he did, they flew away.]

*   *   *

[In his room, at his desk, Tiz wrote the final lines for his children's book story compilation. Chisel Hedgehog's Crazy Great Summer had come to an end. He had helped Tiz cope with his adversities and Tiz was sad to see it end. With Francine he wrote and sang this song:] (Good Friend, Good Bye, track 18)

Never is easy, to do
ain't somethin' I, look forward to
often brings a tear, to a good man's eye
always is hard, when the time comes by

Remember all the things, that we have done
always have them, to ponder on
funny how the time, is finally gone
hard to say the words, but the time has come

Chorus:

Well, gotta say good-bye now, 'cause I know you have to run
gotta think of the times, that we did have
Gotta fight back, when the tears almost come
gotta hold my head, up in the air
Yeah, gotta smile, and think of things you've said
gotta say, good friend, Good-bye to you

Verse:
Never lived a year, when I didn't see
the flowers not bloom, or the seasons change
only one thing, that I know for sure
everything will change, a little more

So take a final picture, here with me
remember this place, and the final scene
never thought it would, but time ran out
hard to put in words, what I'm thinking about

Chorus Repeated

Can't stop the smoke, rising in the air
can't stop the snow, falling everywhere
the world keeps turning, have to turn with it
and we should always, remember this

At least the memories, we have are great
at least the days were filled, with loving grace
but now the time is over, and the hour's done
don't wanna say the words, so they must be sung

Chorus Repeated

—THE END—

Summary of Rules

Rule 1: OF THE DRY LAKE: Spend most time on the things that last—of knowledge, personality, and relationships.

Rule 2: OF CLEAR SKIES: In whatever state or place you are, however bad it seems, goodness still exists—and it waits for you—like clear, blue sky above dark clouds.

Rule 3: OF THE MIRROR: Trigger an improvement in your lowly spirits by doing something physical—like seeing yourself smiling in a mirror—even when not wanting to.

Rule 4: OF THE RIVER RUNNING FREE: The FREE and SIMPLE things in life produce the greatest pleasure.

Rule 5: OF THE RIVER ROCKS: There is value and lessons in life's hardest times, so be happy for your struggles, for their lessons perfect you—if you let them.

Rule 6: OF THE NEXT TREE: Maintain hope by making little goals and taking little steps to get there.

Rule 7: OF THE STARS: Recognize and be happy for what you have, and don't take things for granted.

Rule 8: OF THE FIRE: Never quit trying. Always keep going—one step at a time, and then one more. Life is hard, so focus on one day at a time, and carry on.

Rule 9: OF PAVLOV'S DOG: Habits make you who you are—the good and the bad!

Rule 10: OF THE MOUNTAINTOP: The end is of no consequence—it's the journey that counts! Fulfill the journey faithfully, and learn and change along the way, and the end takes care of itself.

THE SECRET: More can see than just the eyes, but only done if practiced. Look within to understand—look without and gather. If you look in *all* the ways, and differently than others, all the mysteries now untold, to you will come unraveled.

THE TRUTH: Never look beyond the small and insignificant, whether they be Pebbles or they be people.

THE CLUE: Picture yourself as water—humble to the point where evil cannot hurt you, where its arrows pass right through you, and you just flow around them. Rocks are strong and hard, but they also break and decay into dust. Water is humble and weak, but it lasts forever! All worries are uncomfortable, but are they unbearable? Of your current worry ask, "Does it really matter?"

InBeast: Our worries, stress, fears, weaknesses, or any challenge confronting us, accepted to the point of being an actual physical or mental ailment.

GATE ONE: is love! All people need it—no matter how tough they appear to be. It's a universal need of the heart. We must accept it when we're too mad to. We must give it when we're too proud to. We must let its warmth melt away our pride and warm our souls.

BEAST-KILLER PRINCIPLES: 1. Choose to not let your negative thoughts destroy you. Choose to be happy. Always keep fighting the InBeast. 2. Remember how to breathe and see: Breathe in through your nose and out through your mouth, seeing dark clouds of stress exiting. See yourself in a peaceful place where all is good. 3. Use the Secret and think of things differently—not just what you see but also feel. 4. Use the Truth and realize one grand thing will not deliver you, but all those little memories of things you've learned that will give you the combined power needed. 5. Use the Clue and picture yourself as water: humble to the point where arrows pass right through you. 6. Use the Rules of the Fire, Mirror, Clear Skies, and River Rocks. 7. Replace bad thoughts with good by thinking of other things to fill your mind, thinking only now of charity, tranquility, and peace within your soul and all such goodly things. 8. Give thanks for what you've been given—listing them, and remember all your weaknesses overcome, mistakes you are correcting. 9. Ask for help and do your very best, and knowing so, be at peace. 10. Remember when you help another and make them happy, you also help yourself. 11. All worries are uncomfortable, but are they unbearable? Of your current one, ask yourself, "Does it really matter?" Life is short. Don't worry about the past. Smile about the future. 12. Stand in the rain with arms outstretched, head back a bit, and let your worries wash off of you, then watch them floating down a stream.

About the Author

Perry Crompton is also author of the children's picture books, *We Were the Parade*, and *Aisley's New Best Friend*, as well as the children's book series, "*Chisel Hedgehog: Crazy Great Summer*," with seven books, three hundred color illustrations, a thirty-six-song musical soundtrack CD, and master map, all guaranteeing a "hootbalootin" fun time of adventure, mystery, and optimism.

Chisel Hedgehog finds himself on a perilous adventure, which will teach him many lifelong lessons, but also push him into danger's open grasp. It was early one morning when he made the awful mistake for which he was now hunted—but which also started him, and his best friend Bootle, on their own hunt ... for answers to a hundred-year-old mystery.

They must travel to distant places like the jungles of Volcano Island, the Haunted Woods, and the Cave of the Tooth. They develop plans of escape, including disguises #1, 2, and 3; use their flying skateboard plane; and create the worst stink bomb recipe in the world. Read (or listen to) Book One, view the illustrations, follow where he's at on the master map, and listen to the songs he sings, at *ChiselHedgehog.com*. Then see all the books at *Amazon.com*, and envision Chisel saying, "Hope is free, and hope is mine. Today I grab it, and will not let go! And if anyone has lost it, come see me. I have plenty you can borrow."

Author's Note

This book suggests a PMA (Positive Mental Attitude) approach to improve a person's mental outlook, but it does not suppose this is a cure-all. For many, other approaches are required—but I hope that this at least can help.

www.ingramcontent.com/pod-product-compliance
Lightning Source LLC
Chambersburg PA
CBHW020301200626
46814CB00006BA/2027